A PERFECT CHRISTMAS

When Glen Trainer is framed for a crime he didn't commit he is powerless to stop his scheming wife from taking his home, his business and, worst of all, his beautiful daughter away from him. Years later, living rough on the streets of Leicester, Glen meets Jan Clayton. She, too, has a heartbreaking story to tell but she is determined to put the past behind her and together they find the courage to start afresh. As Christmas approaches, Glen gets ever closer to finding his daughter but will his wish come true or does more heartache lie ahead?

A PERFECT CHRISTMAS

A PERFECT CHRISTMAS

by

Lynda Page

Magna Large Print Books
Long Preston, North Yorkshire,
BD23 4ND, England.

British Library Cataloguing in Publication Data.

Page, Lynda
    A perfect christmas.

    A catalogue record of this book is
    available from the British Library

    ISBN   978-0-7505-3755-1

First published in Great Britain in 2012 by
Headline Publishing Group Ltd.

Copyright © 2012 Lynda Page

Cover illustration © Elizabeth Ansley by arrangement with
Arcangel Images

The right of Lynda Page to be identified as the author of this work has
been asserted by her in accordance with the Copyright, Designs and
Patents Act, 1988

Published in Large Print 2013 by arrangement with
Headline Publishing Group Ltd.

Magna Large Print is an imprint of Library Magna Books Ltd.

Printed and bound in Great Britain by
T.J. (International) Ltd., Cornwall, PL28 8RW

For
Dawn Archer –
an extraordinary woman.

You are the stuff that heroines in books are made of – strong-minded, feisty, dependable, belly-achingly funny, an exceptional mother, a devoted wife ... the list is endless. And not only that, but you are beautiful too. My life has been enriched beyond measure by having you in it.

With love
Your friend
Lynda x

CHAPTER ONE

The ragged man woke with a sudden jolt, sitting bolt upright, all his senses screaming danger at him. Urgently shaking off sleep, he fought to accustom his eyes to the dark as he looked around, trying to see what had woken him.

It might have been the drunken ravings of the group of tattered winos several yards away who huddled around a rusting brazier, kept going with anything they had been able to lay hands on. From the eye-watering stench and flares of black smoke spouting upward it was currently old lino and rubber tyres, the flames casting eerie shadows all around. It might have been the snoring or crying out in their sleep of those sheltering close by in their makeshift beds, or the religious maniac continuously reciting passages from the Bible in a fog-horn of a voice, completely ignoring the angry objections from those round about: *'Shut the fuck up, for God's sake, we're trying to sleep.'* It might have been the scurrying and scratching of rats, some the size of cats, or flea-ridden stray dogs scavenging for scraps; the howl of the icy wind or the steady drips of water running down the crumbling brick walls to splash into puddles on the uneven ground below. But having joined the rest of the city's unfortunates who had been reduced to seeking shelter inside the dank, gloomy railway arches,

Glen Trainer was used to all these distractions.

His eyes came to rest on a shadowy figure lurking in a recess several feet away from him. Despite the murkiness of the dark winter's night he knew it was a man – a tall one, apparently heavily built, but Glen was of the opinion it was the layers of threadbare clothes he was wearing that produced that impression – and that his eyes were fixed on Glen, weighing him up, planning to relieve him of anything of worth.

Under the holed brown blanket covering him, Glen flicked open the penknife he always carried close to hand. Since he'd arrived here not a single night had gone by without some sort of confrontation taking place, mostly over trivial matters. On his first night, in fact, he'd been powerless to prevent a pack of drink-crazed men from beating another virtually to a pulp, leaving him for dead, for the sake of the half-empty bottle of methylated spirits he was in the process of downing. The man would be dead now had not Glen carried him to the hospital for urgent treatment. Glen hadn't seen him since and hoped the other man had more sense than to return here. He himself had been robbed several times in the past, and what possessions he'd managed to accumulate since could be contained in a small sack. No doubt most people would consider them worthless, but to Glen they were priceless and he wasn't about to let this stranger steal them from him.

Taking a deep breath, he addressed the menacing shadow in a firm tone. 'Look, I don't drink, don't smoke, and have nothing on me worth risking your life for. I do have a knife, though,

12

which I will use if you give me no other choice.' To prove his threat was no bluff, Glen withdrew his hand from under the blanket and held out the knife in such a way that light from the brazier glinted on the blade.

Despite this warning the other man moved not a muscle. Glen began to feel afraid. Had the man a weapon that would make his own penknife seem puny? There was no point in hoping any of the other inhabitants would come to his aid, he knew. Fear escalated as a terrible thought occurred to him. Would these breaths he was taking prove to be his last? His current way of life might be considered pretty worthless, but regardless he didn't wish for death as the way out of it, and especially not in this hellhole of a place at the hands of a stranger. It was the coward's way out but he knew that the only sensible thing for him to do would be to throw over his sack of belongings to the aggressor then make a run for it, hoping he didn't give chase. As he made to pick up the sack and throw it over, however, to Glen's shock the other man turned and strode off, disappearing into the depths of the arches, his tattered clothing billowing out behind him.

After a few moments had passed Glen exhaled in relief. His words seemed to have done the trick and this sinister meeting had passed without incident. But if he stayed here amongst such desperate men he knew there would inevitably be a next time and then he might not get off so lightly. For all he knew the other man was still lurking somewhere, waiting for him to slump back into sleep before he made another attempt to relieve Glen of his precious belongings. It was time he found somewhere else to lay down his head.

Sack of belongings secured to the worn belt of his frayed trousers and concealed underneath a shabby army greatcoat, holey woollen hat pulled right down over his bush of matted hair, equally holey scarf wrapped around his neck, he began to make his way out of the arches, hoping to depart without attracting any attention to himself.

He'd taken no more than half a dozen steps when he stopped dead, hearing someone crying nearby. It was unmistakably the sound of a woman in great distress. He frowned. The women he had encountered in the underworld he now inhabited were definitely not the sort to display any shred of vulnerability, not in a place like this where they would without doubt be taken advantage of by those who perceived themselves as stronger. But as desperate as he was to be away from here Glen couldn't bring himself to leave a woman at the mercy of the rabble who sheltered in the arches.

Following the sound of the crying, he manoeuvred his way around several sleeping bodies, all clutching their pitiful belongings, and towards a recess in the wall. As he neared it, the outline of a huddled figure, knees bent, arms wrapped around its head, materialised in the gloom. From what he could see it didn't appear that this woman was the sort who belonged in a place like this. Although rumpled, her clothes looked to him far too clean and in too good a condition for someone who lived rough. Glen decided that the woman must have lost her way, found herself in this den of iniquity by accident and needed help finding her way out.

He leaned over and placed one hand gently on her knee. He was just about to offer his help in whatever way he could, when a loud scream of terror rent the air. Following that, he felt a tremendous thud against the side of his head. As he crumpled to the floor and before everything blacked out, Glen realised that his life probably was going to end in this hellhole of a place, not while attempting to fend off an assailant but because he'd tried to be a Good Samaritan.

CHAPTER TWO

The searing pain in his head brought Glen back to consciousness. If someone had told him a piston was inside his skull, thumping away rhythmically at full speed, he wouldn't have questioned it. But the pounding in his head wasn't the only thing he was having to contend with. Someone was shrieking ... hysterically. In his befuddled state he couldn't tell whether it was a man or a woman or decipher what they were yelling. But the racket they were making was preventing him from gathering his jumbled thoughts together, to work out just what had happened to him.

He managed to groan, 'Please will you stop that yelling or my head will explode?'

Mercifully the shouting ceased and a woman's voice cried, 'Oh, thank God you're not dead!

Thank God. Thank God.' Then her tone of relief became defensive. 'But if I had killed you, I was only acting in self-defence.'

Glen was tentatively examining the side of his head with one hand, fully expecting to find half of it gone considering the pain he felt. His fingers touched a lump under his hat. It felt as big as an ostrich egg and he let out a small cry of: 'Ouch!' How on earth did he come to be lying here on the ground with an injury like this to his head? Then memory flooded back and he accused her, 'You attacked me!'

Her tone of voice was still defensive. 'Well, what did you expect me to do? Just sit back and allow you to do whatever you were about to?'

He managed to force open his eyes but couldn't lift his head to look at his assailant as he was feeling disorientated, still seeing stars, though not so many as when he'd first come round. Scowling down at the hard ground, he queried: 'What was I about to do?'

'Rob me or...'

'Or what?' he snapped. 'Listen, lady, the only thing I was attempting was to offer my help. You were upset ... crying. I was concerned for you.'

There was silence for a moment before she uttered, 'Oh! Oh, I see.' Then defiance returned to her voice. 'Well, how was I to know?'

'You could have asked before you whacked me! Just what did you hit me with, by the way?'

'My handbag.'

'A handbag! What do you carry in it ... a ton of bricks?'

'No, just one. A woman has to protect herself

16

from the likes of you in this Godforsaken place.'

He managed to lift his head then and look at her. The light was poor and it was difficult to tell her age or what she looked like, her face being cast into shadow, but he guessed she was in her early-forties and, from the coat and headscarf she was wearing, appeared just like an ordinary housewife, albeit with her clothes rumpled and a little dishevelled. What the likes of her was doing in this place he couldn't begin to guess. He wanted to be angry with her for inflicting such unprovoked injury on him, but he also appreciated the reason why she'd lashed out. The characters who frequented this place were about as unsavoury as they came and she would have no reason to believe he was any different. 'Look, I know I might not look exactly my best,' he said, 'but we're not all thieves, winos, drug addicts or murderers, you know. Many of us haven't chosen to live this life, but circumstances have given us no choice in the matter.'

Janet Clayton narrowed her eyes and looked him over. What she saw was a shambles of an individual, wearing clothes that should have been cremated a long time ago. It was hard to determine his age and whether he was good-looking or ugly as his face was hidden under a mass of facial hair, and it was her guess that under his holey woollen hat the hair on his head was equally as bushy and matted. The smell coming off him was vile. She doubted his body or clothes had seen soap and water for a very long time. She shuddered as it struck her that he was probably riddled with body and head lice and that she was in close

17

enough proximity to catch them from him. There was one thing that confused her about this man, though. He didn't blaspheme or have a coarse tone of voice, as she had always expected from low-bred people of his ilk.

Her look of utter revulsion made Glen inwardly cringe. He had lost count of the number of times he'd been viewed in this way by the general public. The humiliation and shame he experienced never diminished. As always he felt a desire to crawl into a hole and hide himself away from critical eyes. Despite still feeling woozy from the blow to his head, he struggled up, muttering, 'I need to get off.'

Jan watched him stumble away unsteadily, keeping as close to the wall as possible, skirting around the rowdy drunken group gathered around the brazier. The fright and disgust she felt were making her nauseous.

Under normal circumstances she would never have placed herself within a dozen yards of such lowlifes, let alone actually be close enough to breathe the same air as them, but then her circumstances were far from normal at present and she was acutely aware that if she didn't do something to change them, and quickly, very soon she would look and smell like the dirty creatures she found herself amongst now, being perceived as the dregs of the earth by the rest of society.

But how she'd get herself out of this situation was anyone's guess.

Thinking of her circumstances brought a fresh swell of miserable tears to her eyes. She felt so alone and vulnerable. She was ravenously hungry but all she wanted to do was sleep for a while, to find some relief from the nightmare she was living. She pulled her coat around her and turned up her collar. Clutching her handbag to her, she slumped back against the hard wall and tried to make herself comfortable on the uneven ground, but just as she was about to close her eyes she realised with horror that several of the inebriated men around the brazier had noticed her and were taking more than a passing interest. Sheer panic overwhelmed her. When she had believed she was being accosted a few minutes ago she had screamed blue murder yet not one of the other inhabitants in this place had even looked in her direction to see what she was howling about, nor had they when she thought she had killed her suspected attacker, so if these men were taking an interest in her now it was for no good reason and she couldn't expect anyone else to come to her aid, no matter how loud she screamed.

Her heart was pounding. She needed to get out of here … fast.

The only exit she was aware of was the way by which she around had come: past the men closely watching her now, standing around the blazing brazier; the same way that the tramp she was sure had been about to attack her had made his departure. Holding her handbag like a weapon, a determined look on her face, she took a deep breath before weaving her way towards the entrance. On nearing the men by the brazier, she skirted around them as far as was possible and in a meaningful tone addressed the ones taking an interest in her.

'I'm warning you, don't any of you make a move

towards me or you'll be on the receiving end of this.' She waved the bag at them. 'It's got a ... boulder in it. A huge one. Big enough to knock any of you into next Wednesday. If you think I'm bluffing then go and ask the man who's just left. He tried it on with me, and he's lucky to be alive.'

She was almost past them now, daring to think that her threat had worked. The men's interest, in her had waned and they seemed to have returned to carrying on with their drinking and rowdy gambling games. Then she noticed that one of them was still staring at her intently, a nasty glint in his beady eyes as he drained the dregs of his bottle of meths. If she had been able to see his mouth under his matted beard she would have seen a malicious smirk. There was no question what was on his mind.

Horror filled her. Without looking away from him, giving her handbag a threatening thrust in his direction, she hastened towards the entrance. It was only a few yards away but to Jan it seemed like miles. Then, to her absolute terror, she saw the leering man chuck away the empty bottle. It crashed against the wall behind him, smashing into smithereens, as with surprising agility he wormed round the back of the brazier and stood between her and the entrance, blocking her way.

Despite being aware that it would do her no good, Jan let out a terrified scream, which echoed around the cavernous walls. The light from the brazier flashed in the man's eyes and she could see he was laughing at her, knowing he had her cornered. The next thing she knew he had lunged across and grabbed her wrist, holding her handbag to prevent her from attacking him with it while yanking her hard towards the back of the pitch-dark arches, where it was apparent he planned to have his way with her.

Screaming hysterically, she tried to dig her heels into the ground to counteract his fierce grip, but to no avail as the earth was too hard. She tried to kick out at him but her foot only contacted air. Then she tried to bite his wrist but the pair of filthy gloves and coat he had on left no bare patches for her to dig her teeth into. She was powerless to put a stop to his evil intentions. Her mind froze, her subconscious dreading to visualise what lay ahead.

He had dragged her almost as far as the light from the brazier reached. Ahead lay darkness where only the most fearless vagrants chose to sleep. Then, to her astonishment, he suddenly stopped dead and she heard a low voice say: 'Let her go unless you want a taste of this.' In the feeble light she could just make out the shape of a man standing in front of her assailant, pressing something into his side.

Jan held her breath, her heart thumping wildly, as the two men stared at each other for what seemed an age but was in truth a matter of a few seconds. Then her aggressor gave a grunt, released his grip on her and spun on his heel, giving her a rough shove out of his way. She watched, hardly daring to breathe, as he returned to the brazier, swearing and cursing en route, and snatched a bottle out of a crony's hand, much to his displeasure, glugging back the contents.

She jumped as she felt a prod in her own side

and a voice said, 'I'd make a run for it, if I were you, before he changes his mind. And if you have any sense, you'll give this place a wide berth in future.'

She realised from his voice that this was the vagrant she had clobbered with the brick inside her handbag only minutes ago. Before she could say anything to him he had turned away and was heading towards the entrance.

Jan was so befuddled by this sudden turn of events that she stared after him without saying anything for several long moments. Then her perilous situation occurred to her and she acted on her rescuer's advice. She hurried after him, careful not to fall over any sleeping bodies, speeding up as she ran past the brazier and the men gathered around it, not daring to look in the direction of the vile creature who'd been about to rape her. Outside she did not pause to draw breath, desperate only to put some distance between herself and that awful place.

Suddenly she crashed into an unexpected obstacle and let out a cry of shock as the force of the impact sent her careering backwards. She landed heavily on her backside, handbag flying out of her hand and landing with a thud some feet away. She sat there feeling confused for a moment, wondering what she had collided with, then stiffened with alarm when she heard a groan of pain. She flashed a look around but it was too dark for her to see much as the street lights around here had been deliberately broken. Finally she saw the dim outline of a shape prostrate on the ground several feet away from her. She stared as it struggled to sit up, groaning painfully all the while. It was obviously a man.

It seemed he was better at seeing in the dark than she was. Rubbing his head where it had made contact with the pavement, he grumbled, 'You seem hell-bent on finishing me off. Have you got some sort of vendetta against me?'

She recognised his voice. The man she had collided with was her saviour from the arches. 'I'm sorry,' she blurted, 'I didn't see you. I was trying to put some distance between me and that awful place. I was terrified that dreadful man might follow me.'

Glen had managed to get himself sitting upright now, one hand cradling another lump on his head, which he'd sustained at the hands of this woman. She was on her feet by now and stepped over to him, holding out her hand. 'Let me help you up.'

He didn't need to look at her face to tell that the thought of touching him was repellent to her. Ignoring her hand, he said gruffly, 'I can manage, thank you.' Once he'd managed to stand up, he checked that his sack of belongings was still attached to his frayed trouser belt, straightened his tattered clothes, then offered her a piece of advice before he turned and made his departure. 'What you're doing in these parts is your business, but as you've found out these are dangerous streets. If you've any sense, you'll give the likes of the Grand Union arches a wide berth in future.'

She watched as he shambled off, shoulders hunched against the biting winter wind. The darkness soon swallowed him up, and then it seemed to descend on her, immobilising her with pure panic. Jan's imagination ran riot. She envisaged eyes watching her, the people to whom they belonged ready to pounce. Maybe it was the man from the arches she was sensing; maybe he'd decided to come after her. If that were the case then she could forget her rescuer coming to her aid again as he had gone. She gave a violent shudder. She needed to get out of here and into the better-lit streets where she'd feel safer. She urgently needed to find some sort of shelter for the night, believing she had done so in the arches until she realised she had chosen just about the most dangerous place there was for the likes of her. It was barely past eight o'clock but bitterly cold already. There was no telling how much colder it was going to get as the night wore on. People froze to death in weather like this. But where could she find somewhere safe to rest her head, with no money in her purse? A vision of her saviour flooded back to mind. He was obviously a veteran of the streets so it was likely he would know. He was probably heading for it now, a safe haven for the night. She would follow him and see where he went.

Glen knew he was being followed. Whoever it was wasn't trying to hide the fact. If they were after robbing him then they were wasting their time. He thrust his hand in his pocket and grabbed hold of his penknife, flicking open the blade. He stepped swiftly sideways into the shadows of an entry. As soon as the footsteps drew level with his hiding place, he jumped out, brandishing the

24

knife at his suspected assailant. Before he could say anything his pursuer let out a scream. He recognised that sound. 'You again!' he snapped accusingly at Jan. 'Why are you following me?'

She was staring wildly at the penknife. 'Don't hurt me! Please don't hurt me…'

He flicked shut the blade and thrust it back into his pocket. 'I've never hurt anyone with it yet. It's just a deterrent. Up to now it's worked. But I would use it if it were a matter of my life or death. Now why are you following me?'

She blustered, 'I … I was hoping you were going to lead me to somewhere safe to spend the night.'

He stared at her, curious to know why the likes of her needed to sleep out for the night, but his years of living amongst types who held little regard for their fellow human beings had taught him that the less you knew about others, and the less they knew about you, the better. There were those who would happily slit your throat to get that knowledge out of you so as to use it to their own advantage. He told her, 'I travel alone. It's hard enough on the streets without being responsible for anyone else.'

He made to turn away then and continue on his way but Jan pleaded, 'Oh, please don't leave me on my own. I'm not asking you to be responsible for me but I'm scared. At least let me travel with you until we get out of this area.'

He frowned suspiciously at her. 'I've seen the way you look at me. You're seriously willing to be seen in public with the likes of me?'

To be honest, she wasn't. The thought that anyone might class her as a street person like him

25

was excruciatingly embarrassing to Jan. But this man was the nearest she had to an ally in this alien world she found herself in. He knew how to get by here when she didn't have a clue. So she lied to him. 'I haven't a problem with it at all.'

He knew she was being far from truthful but, if he were honest with himself, his conscience wouldn't allow him to walk away from a vulnerable female while she was in a potentially dangerous environment. He said grudgingly, 'It's a free country. I can't stop you walking where you want to.'

Jan was almost grateful the weather was as bitter as it was. The other pedestrians they encountered were far more interested in getting home to pay much attention to the filthy vagrant and the dishevelled woman they passed on the street. Regardless, when Jan saw someone approaching, she hunched her shoulders and lowered her head. They hadn't spoken a word since they had set off. Several times she began to say something, merely to break the silence, but sensed her companion might become irritated by any female chit-chat and demand they part ways, and that was the last thing Jan wanted. She hadn't a clue where they were heading.

The grim back streets they were travelling down were completely unknown to her. Jan hadn't come from the most salubrious area, far from it, but hers was a far cry from here. She vehemently hoped this wasn't where her newfound friend was planning to spend the night, in some rat-infested derelict building or such like, as she doubted the people who lived around here were any more reliable than those who inhabited the arches. She was pleased when it became clear that their surroundings were improving, leaving weed-infested cobbles and red-brick back-to-back terraces for tree-lined streets with gabled houses set back from the road behind large neat gardens. Hopefully there was somewhere around here that he knew of where they could rest. But still they continued walking.

It seemed to Jan that they had been walking for miles. She had hardly had any sleep the night before, staying in a miserable guest house on a flat lumpy mattress, trying to shut out the noises the other guests were making. The landlady had had the cheek to charge her ten shillings for her night's lodging, all the money she'd had left in the world. Now she was struggling to put one foot in front of the other. Never before in all her life had she craved a cup of hot tea and a place to rest her aching body. She was following Glen across a crossroads when, on the opposite corner, she saw a church, light shining through its stained-glass windows. God had played a large part in the situation she found herself in now and she felt that she was finished with religion, but the church itself, a quiet place, seemed to be beckoning to her to take sanctuary.

'Mister! Excuse me, Mister!' she called out to Glen, who was several yards ahead of her.

It took him a few seconds to register who his companion was addressing. He hadn't been called 'Mister' by anyone for such a long time now. He stopped and turned to look back at her.

'We've walked for miles and I'm just about fit

27

to drop. Could we stop and rest for a minute in that church over there?'

He glanced across at it before turning his attention back to her. There was a sharp edge to his voice when he said, 'We've barely walked one mile, let alone miles. You'll have to get used to walking long distances if you're going to survive on the streets. I want to get where I'm heading before anyone else beats us to it.' Then he saw the tiredness in her eyes, the weary stoop of her shoulders, and grudgingly relented. 'All right, I suppose five minutes' rest won't hurt. But no more than five or I'll be off without you. Come on.'

It could hardly be classed as warm inside the thick stone walls but at least they afforded a reprieve from the biting wind. Jan was far too grateful to be resting her aching body to notice she had sat down on a pew close beside her unsavoury-looking companion. It wasn't until she had slipped off her shoes and lifted one leg so she could massage some life back into her foot that she noticed a gathering of people at the top of the aisle. From the way they were acting it was apparent that a wedding rehearsal was in progress. A moment or two's observation told her that the bride-to-be would have been a very attractive young woman, had she not been scowling in frustration as she ordered everyone else about. Most of the party looked mortally fed up with her and none more so than the prospective bridegroom. The elderly vicar, a middle-aged, kindly-looking man, was doing his best to calm the situation.

Suddenly the bride-to-be seemed to sense the presence of others. She turned and looked down the aisle at Glen and Jan, resting in the top pew. On seeing the calibre of the new arrivals, her expression turned to one of absolute horror and she loudly exclaimed, 'What are *those* people doing here?'

The vicar looked down the aisle before telling her, 'This is a church. Everyone is welcome here.'

The soon-to-be bridegroom looked severely embarrassed and said to his fiancée, 'They aren't doing any harm, love. It's bitter outside, they're just having a warm.'

She blurted out, 'Yes, yes, I can appreciate that, but there are other churches they can choose to shelter in. It doesn't have to be this one, and certainly not during my wedding rehearsal.' She eyed the vicar imploringly. 'My parents could arrive at any minute. My father suffers from bad health, and if my mother thought for one second he was at risk of catching anything she would whip him straight back home, rehearsal or no rehearsal. My parents are all the family I've got and if that happened I'd have no one to give me away. Surely in the circumstances you can ban the likes of them from coming in here, just while my rehearsal is taking place tonight.' She fixed her eyes on her fiancé. 'Can't we give them some money and tell them to go and have something to eat ... a bath even, as I can smell them from here? Please, Neil, you have to get rid of them before my parents arrive.'

Despite the distance between them, Jan had heard every word the young woman said and had

29

never felt so humiliated in all her life. She didn't know where to hide her face. She felt a hand touch her arm, turned and saw Glen telling her with the look in his eyes that it was time for them to go. Her shoe was back on her foot and she was out of the church door and hurrying down the path back to the crossroads before he had even managed to ease himself out of the pew.

Joining her outside, Glen said matter-of-factly, 'You're going to have to grow yourself a thicker skin if you want to survive on the streets. That was mild compared to some of the abuse I've had to deal with. Wait until the drunks start spilling out of the pubs. There are always more of them to-wards Christmas.' Then he turned in the direction they had been heading and continued walking.

Jan looked after him, horrified. It seemed to her nothing could be worse than what she had just endured. The thought of going through that ever again, or worse, was unthinkable. She had to get herself out of this living hell in which she found herself. But how she would manage that without any means at her disposal was as insoluble problem.

CHAPTER THREE

Back inside the church, Neil Graham, a tall boyish-faced nineteen year old with a short back and sides haircut and a hint of a quiff in front, was looking very pensive. His fiancée, a pretty girl of around eighteen dressed in the height of fashion, in a full red skirt with layers of netting underneath, a wide black belt around her trim waist and a short-sleeved Peter Pan-collared blouse under a pink cardigan with embroidered black flowers down the front, stood deep in conversation with the frustrated-looking vicar, intent on checking that every minute detail of the forthcoming wedding service was dealt with to her satisfaction. Neil gave a deep sigh, a grave expression settling over his face. There was something he had to do, something he should have done a long time ago ... but each time he thought he had built up the courage, at the last minute it had failed him.

Taking a deep breath, he cupped his fiancée's elbow and said to her, 'I need to talk to you, Cait. Now, please.' Suddenly remembering his manners, he said to the vicar, 'I do apologise for the interruption.'

The clergyman looked relieved rather than offended, and indicated that there was no problem.

Tossing back her mane of long blonde hair, Caitlyn Thomas responded, 'Can't it wait, Neil? I still have a few details I need to discuss with Reverend Harper and...'

He said evenly, 'Cait, you've given your instructions to the Reverend on several previous occasions to my knowledge. I'm sure you don't need to keep going over them with him. Now I do need to speak to you.' He then asked the clergyman, 'Is there somewhere private we can go, please?'

'You're quite welcome to use the Vestry,' Reverend Harper told him. Then he took a quick glance at his watch. 'Er ... will this take long, Mr Graham? Only we're already over-running and I have sick parishioners to visit yet.'

Neil assured him, 'I'll be as quick as I can.'

The rest of the gathering looked on perplexed as he guided a bemused Cait into the Vestry. Once inside, Neil shut the door behind them.

She stared at him expectantly for a moment. When he stared back at her, seemingly tongue-tied, her impatience got the better of her and she snapped, 'Neil, you said what you had to say to me was urgent, so please get on with it. I have a mountain of things still to do and the wedding is only seven days away.'

He had been experiencing feelings of dread, afraid that yet again he was going to back down and not tell her what he knew he needed to, but Cait's reminding him that their wedding was only a few days away hardened his resolve. He blurted out, 'I can't do this any more, Cait.'

She stared at him, utterly shocked, before smiling brightly and telling him, 'Oh, goodness, for a moment there I thought you were telling me you didn't want to marry me! But you mean you can't do any more of this rehearsal tonight as you've arranged to meet your mates in the pub. Surely they'll understand why you're late, though, considering the circumstances. It's not like it's your stag night, is it? That's not until next Friday. And while we're on the subject, Neil, please make sure those mates of yours don't let you drink too...'

He sharply interjected, 'Cait! Will you for once let me finish what I want to say without assuming you know what it is?'

Her mouth snapped shut and her eyes widened in shock. Neil had never used this tone of voice to her before.

Taking advantage of the silence, he told her, 'When I said I can't go on with this any more you were right to think I meant with the wedding.'

Her jaw dropped and she stared at him for several seconds before she whispered, 'You do want to call the wedding off?'

Without hesitation, he nodded. 'Yes, I do. I'm sorry, Cait, I really am.'

She gazed at him a while longer before she gave a knowing laugh, patted him affectionately on the arm and told him, 'Oh, sweetheart, you're just suffering from wedding nerves, that's all. All grooms suffer from them.'

She turned away from him and made to head for the door but he grabbed her arm. When she was facing him again, he said to her, 'I'm not suffering from wedding nerves, Cait. I ... I ... well, there's no easy way of putting this, but the truth is that I don't want to marry you. I can't see a happy future for me with you, Cait, it's as simple as that.'

It was evident that this announcement had stunned her rigid. She stared open-mouthed at him again before she blustered, 'Then why did you ask me to spend the rest of my life with you?'

He sighed heavily, raking one hand through his hair. 'I didn't ask you to, Cait.'

She looked stupefied. 'Yes, you did. In the Chinese restaurant that Saturday night.'

He shook his head. 'No, I didn't. On the table

near us a man proposed to his girlfriend, which we couldn't help but overhear, and you said that you'd like to get married, which I took to mean one day, so I said that I would too, and have a couple of children, and you assumed from what I'd just said that I was proposing to you...'

Her mouth was opening and closing fish-like and she seemed dazed. 'So ... so why didn't you put me right about my mistake?'

Neil was feeling mortally uncomfortable with the way this was going but knew he owed it to himself not to get cold feet now. 'You never gave me the chance to. Next thing I knew you'd got the waiter to fetch a bottle of sparkling wine and were arranging for us to visit jewellery shops to buy an engagement ring – and you wouldn't allow me a word in edgeways. It was like a roller-coaster after that. Everyone knew and the wedding was being planned and I didn't know how to stop it!'

'Well, we were in love. I didn't see any point in waiting.'

He sighed heavily, hanging his head. He hadn't the heart to hurt Cait further by telling her exactly how he felt about her. How claustrophobic it made him feel, the way she clung to him like a limpet whenever they were out together, as though afraid that if she let go of him he'd run off and leave her. He disliked the way she always thought she knew what he wanted better than he did; the way she strove constantly to please him, from the clothes she wore to the way she acted; how she hung on his every word. No matter how much affection he showed her, it never seemed to be enough for her and she constantly demanded more.

When they had first met, he'd enjoyed having a girlfriend who didn't hide the fact she thought him god-like; clung to him as if afraid to let him go; decided what they would do whenever they went out so as to save him the headache. Despite his friends ribbing him that he was under her thumb, Neil felt he'd died and gone to heaven. But then, after her misinterpretation of the scene in the Chinese restaurant, Cait had not given him a chance to put her straight. He'd been swiftly introduced to her parents and with horror saw his own future yawn before him, a pale shadow of a man with a suffocating wife.

After being introduced to her parents, witnessing for himself how her mother doted on her father, pandered to his every whim, made decisions for him without consulting him as if he had no mind of his own, Neil could understand why Cait believed that was how marriage was conducted. And it had shocked him to witness the way her parents, her mother in particular, treated their daughter – with such indifference, coldness even. It was no wonder that she looked to him to supply all her emotional support as clearly she received none at home. But a marriage like that was not for him. He wanted one like his parents shared. Open and loving, each respecting the fact that the other had a mind of their own.

He'd lost count of the number of times he'd tried to tell Cait how he felt and end their relationship, but each time he managed to find an opportunity his courage failed him. Neil was a thoughtful young man and knew how hurt she'd

35

be. But if he did not come clean with her now he might never be able to summon the courage again, and then he'd be stuck for life in a marriage that would be miserable for him.

Neil took a deep breath, lifted his head and looked her in the eye. His voice had a note of finality in it. 'Please accept the fact that I don't want to marry you, Cait. You'll meet someone else who'll love having the kind of wife you'll make him, but what you're offering is not for me.' Having finally said his piece and well aware of the upset his announcement was causing, he felt a sudden desperate need to put some distance between them. He shouldered the door open and left her alone in the Vestry.

Her face ashen, Cait stared after him in horror. Her mind was unable to accept what had just transpired. Neil hadn't ended their relationship, he couldn't have. This was some sort of macabre joke... she was having a nightmare and would soon wake up. Apart from the fact that she loved him so very much, it was imperative that she should be married before her eighteenth birthday only a few weeks away or the consequences would be unbearable. And with that thought fear flooded her, so acute that she started to shake and her thoughts began to whirl. Neil's words had been so final. She had worked so tirelessly hard since the moment she had met him and realised he was the one to make herself indispensable to ... she had tried to become his perfect woman. But obviously she had failed. If she could find out in what way then maybe she could make amends. Surely their relationship

36

was salvageable ... there was still a chance that the wedding would go ahead. With hope rising in her, she made to chase after him but then wondered if it would be prudent to let him cool down for a while before she made any attempt at a reconciliation.

She jumped as the door opened and her chief bridesmaid, Gina, came in. Cait had never been so glad to see her friend in all her life. Gina would advise her on how to handle this situation.

'Oh, Gina, I so desperately need your...'

But before she could say another word, Gina blurted out, 'Neil has just told us all that the wedding's cancelled, Cait. He went off without explaining why. Couldn't seem to get out of the church quick enough.'

Gina looked really upset, which Cait assumed was because she was concerned for her.

'I hope I can still salvage the situation ... it's just nerves. I'm not sure of the right way to go about it, though, and I'd like your advice on whether I...'

Her face sulky, Gina cut in, 'Oh! This means I won't get to wear that lovely dress now, will I? I was hoping that Raymond might propose to me when he saw you two getting hitched. Anyway, I'd best tell the others there's no point in hanging around here any longer. If we hurry, we can still get in at the skiffle club. See you tomorrow at work then.'

With that she spun on her heel and departed, leaving Cait staring after her.

For the second time in less than half an hour she had trouble accepting what had just happened.

Gina was supposed to be her friend, to come to her aid when she was needed, but all she seemed to care about was that she wouldn't get to wear her bridesmaid's dress. And what struck Cait now was the fact that her friend hadn't seemed a bit surprised that Neil had called off the wedding.

There had been far too many times in the past when Cait had felt alone in the world, but never more so than she did now. The tears came then, fast and furious, and she wept unashamedly, feeling utterly bereft. Then, after several minutes of miserable crying, a thought struck her. Wiping her face on the sleeve of her cardigan, she pondered on it. Despite his adamant denial, was Neil only suffering from pre-wedding nerves as she had assumed? Had he come to regret his impulsive actions already? Was he maybe waiting for her outside the church, or outside her house, to beg her to forgive him and put matters right with her? How she hoped ... prayed ... that he was.

Pulling herself together, she made her way back into the church, stunned to find that none of their friends or members of Neil's family were waiting for her. Like Gina, it seemed, they felt no concern for how she might be feeling and saw no need to offer any support, save for the vicar who was waiting for her down by the door, ready to lock up after she had left.

She fought to find something to say to cover the acute humiliation and embarrassment of Neil's jilting of her. But when she drew level with him, she had no words at all.

He smiled sympathetically at her and said, 'In my experience, most weddings have a slight hitch or two before the big day. I'm sure you'll sort your differences out.'

So was Cait, but 'slight hitch' was hardly how she would describe the situation between Neil and her – it was more a cataclysmic event, but she appreciated that the vicar was doing his best to make her feel better. Unfortunately, he hadn't succeeded.

Smiling wanly at him, she went outside. Any hope she'd had that Neil would be waiting there for her was dashed. All she could hope now was that he would call at her house, and with that in mind she hurried off home.

CHAPTER FOUR

Jan had never been so cold in her life. Her bones felt as if they were frozen solid and she was afraid that if she didn't manage to stop her teeth from chattering together they'd smash to smithereens. The bare stone step of the shop doorway was unyielding and, with no other protection against the bitter weather than the clothes she was wearing, getting herself into a position comfortable enough to afford her some sleep was impossible. Very kindly her travelling companion had offered her his blanket before they'd gone into their separate shelters, but at the time she couldn't help but look utterly disgusted by the thin holey material with the vile smell emanating from it. Later she wished she hadn't been so particular as the bit of warmth it would have offered her would have far out-weighed her initial revulsion. The only consolation was that the doorway was deep and so for the most part shielded her from the relentless wind.

It wasn't just the incessant cold and hunger that were getting to her. She felt so terribly vulnerable and her nerves were on edge, the incident in the arches still weighing heavily on her. Even had she been able to make herself comfortable enough to sleep, she doubted she would have dared to render herself so helpless. Another evil-minded person like the one in the arches could easily happen upon her and see her as easy prey, despite the fact that her saviour was only a few feet away in the doorway of the shop next-door.

A picture of him rose in her mind then. The dregs of society, most people would see him as, like she herself had only a few hours ago, but underneath those tattered, filthy clothes and mass of matted hair was a man with some common decency. She had noted too that he did not speak in the thick Leicester brogue of these parts, and his speech was free from swear words. She judged that his background was probably very different from the rest of the lowlifes she'd come across these last few days. She wondered how a man like him had come to end up living on the streets. It was with a sense of shock that she then realised he had saved her from a terrible ordeal and yet she didn't even know his name.

She froze suddenly as she sensed another presence nearby and jerked her head up to look fearfully at the entrance to the street. Her heart thumped, the breath seeming to freeze in her lungs. A shadowy figure seemed to be staring back at her. She immediately assumed an assailant was sizing her up to ascertain whether she was worthy of robbing. Instinctively she brandished her handbag at them, to show that she was armed and wouldn't take an attack on her person lightly. The shadowy figure stepped into the entrance. She opened her mouth to scream blue murder, desperately hoping that yet again her saviour nearby would come to her rescue, when to her utter relief a flicker of light lit the stranger's face and a puff of smoke streamed into the bitter air. Her would-be attacker was just a pedestrian who had stopped to shelter in the shop doorway while lighting a cigarette.

After they had gone on their way it took several moments for Jan to calm herself down enough to try and get some desperately needed sleep, but each time she heard the slightest noise she would sit bolt upright again, eyes locked on the doorway to the dark street beyond. Finally she decided that risking the chance of catching fleas or lice and enduring the foulest of stenches was preferable to causing herself a heart attack with her own jagged nerves.

She struggled up and made her way round to the doorway where her saviour was sheltering. He was staring back at her before she set foot inside.

'Oh, you can't sleep either,' she said to him as she stepped into the long entrance. Shop windows to either side displayed the goods for sale in the establishment – a selection of winter woollens in bright colours which were being promoted as

41

perfect Christmas presents. Jan stopped a foot or so away from where he sat huddled up against the shop door.

He responded a mite grumpily, 'I was asleep until I sensed your arrival. You'll learn to sleep with one eye open and your ears on alert if you want to survive on these streets.'

A violent shiver ran up Jan's spine, which was nothing to do with the freezing weather but more acute fear at the thought of having to spend another night like this. If anyone had ever believed that sleeping rough held an element of freedom and glamour to it, then they were mad. She meant this night to be her one and only experience of sleeping out. She had to stay positive, believe there was a way to get herself out of this situation, it was just that she hadn't thought of it yet.

She said to the man, 'I apologise for waking you.'

He stifled a yawn. 'Well, if you hadn't, there's a good chance I would have been awake soon enough as it's nearly chucking out time ... that's if the coppers haven't moved us on before then. It's rare to get a full night's sleep, what with one thing and another. Did ... er ... you want something?'

She eyed him awkwardly. 'Well ... I was wondering if that offer of the blanket is still open? I ... er ... didn't take it up before as I didn't want to deprive you of it, but ... well ... I'm so cold.'

He knew she wasn't being truthful over the reason for declining his offer and supposed if their roles were reversed he would not have

42

wanted to accept the filthy article either, but the bitter weather tonight was overriding any fear of what she might catch from it. He supposed she didn't give a thought to the way her manner towards him only served to remind him further to what a low state he'd been reduced, for which again he couldn't blame her. Thankfully he had learned over the years to ignore others' negative reactions to him. Pulling the blanket off himself, he held it out for Jan to take. Her slight hesitation before she did so was not lost on him.

'Thank you,' she said, wrapping the article around herself. Then she stood eyeing him awkwardly again for a moment before she ventured, 'Er ... do you mind if I squat down here, only ... I'm ... er...'

Scared, frightened, feeling vulnerable on her own, just like he'd been when he'd first started sleeping rough. Glen wasn't at all keen on the idea of sharing space. He was used to his own company, and it was bad enough having to watch his own back in these mean streets let alone hers as well, which he'd feel obliged to do as he had in the arches. He'd had no choice about losing his self-respect and being reduced to doing things in order to survive that would have absolutely appalled him when he'd been part of normal society, but at least he'd managed to cling on to some of his old beliefs, including the one that a man naturally protects a woman, which was urging him now to tell her to stay. But his opinion turned out to be irrelevant as she was already trying to make herself comfortable on the hard stone floor a foot or so away from him.

43

He watched her for a while, trying to achieve her task but failing miserably. Finally, in frustration that her shuffling about was preventing him from snatching some sleep while he could, he snapped, 'Why don't you take that brick out of your handbag that you just about finished me off with, then use the bag as a pillow?'

'Oh, I never thought of that,' she gratefully responded. 'Thank you.'

He then spent another frustrating few minutes watching her try to get herself into a comfortable position until finally he sat up and said gruffly, 'Look, why don't you swallow your pride and go home?'

Jan stopped her shuffling and sat up to look at him, her face tight with annoyance. She snapped, 'Do you seriously think I'd be willingly putting myself through this ... this ... living nightmare if it was as simple as that!'

'Well, in my experience many people end up on the streets after silly family feuds that go beyond repair because neither side will make the first move to sort things out.'

She eyed him curiously. 'Is that what happened to you then?'

He fell silent for a moment before he said, 'No. It's more complicated in my case.'

'So is my situation.' Jan gave a deep sigh and said quietly, 'My husband's chucked me out. Told me never to darken his door again. He meant it.'

It was Glen's turn to eye her curiously. 'Just like that? For no reason?'

'Oh, he had a reason. Me having an affair.'

'What reason did he give you for believing such

a terrible thing?'

'He didn't need to give me any. He caught me red-handed in bed with another man.'

Glen had heard many dreadful stories about how people landed up in dire straits, but nevertheless he was taken aback by this woman's admission as she didn't seem the type somehow. But then appearances could be deceptive, as he'd found out to his own cost many moons ago. Whether he wanted to know the gory details or not it seemed he was going to be given no choice as Jan continued speaking.

'Harry could at least have asked me what had driven me into another man's arms before he threw me out. Maybe then he might not think so badly of me and would accept part of the responsibility.' She paused for a moment, her eyes growing misty. 'At one time we had a successful marriage. He was a good husband to me and father to our son. The three of us always did everything together ... well, until that horrible evening.'

She paused to flick a tear off her eyelid and there was great sadness in her voice when she carried on. 'I couldn't have wished for a better son. Keith loved his mum and dad and never in all his years did I hear any back chat from him or grumbles and groans if I asked him to run an errand for me.' A smile on her lips, she said, 'He had this shock of thick brown hair, the kind that whatever you plastered on it would not lie down, and a splattering of freckles across his nose ... and such a cheeky grin. He was the happy-go-lucky sort and everyone loved him. I always had a succession of kids knocking on my door, asking for him to come out and play.

'A gang of them come knocking for him that night. They'd all had their dinner but we hadn't. I told Keith he couldn't go out until he'd had his, but then Harry asked me how long it would be before I dished up. When I said about fifteen minutes, he said it wouldn't hurt to let the lad go out meanwhile as long as he came in as soon as he was shouted. I relented and off Keith went. I remember I was singing to myself in the kitchen. I was so very happy, you see. After trying for another baby for the best part of nine years and being convinced it was never going to happen for us again, I had only the day before found out from the doctor that I hadn't got a stomach complaint but was about three months pregnant! Harry was jubilant and Keith couldn't wait to have a little brother or sister.'

She paused to draw breath, pain at the memories she was relaying evident on her face before she went on. 'I was just about to shout through to ask Harry to fetch Keith in when there was this horrendous banging on the front door and I could hear our names being shouted from outside. Harry got to the door first and I was hurrying down the passage when I heard one of Keith's friend's screeching we'd best come quick as he had had an accident. I knew it had to be serious as Keith wasn't the sort to cry over a grazed knee.'

Her voice lowered to barely a whisper then and Glen had to strain hard to hear her. 'He was already dead by the time we got there. Ten years old he was, his whole life in front of him, and it was taken away over some foolish bet. One of his friends had been given an old stop watch and it was decided that they would see who out of them could shin up and down the lamp-post the quickest. Keith had got to the top and, in his haste to get back down, lost his grip and fell off, smashing his head on the pavement. The doctor told us he died instantly. Next thing I can remember is waking up in hospital hours later. I'd gone into deep shock and passed out. Harry, my mother and my two sisters were crying at my bedside. Their tears weren't just for Keith but for our unborn child too. The shock had caused me to miscarry. So, that dreadful night, we'd lost not one child but two.

'I can't remember the next few days. It's like I've wiped out my memories as that time was so dreadful. The funeral is just a blur. I remember finding a small amount of consolation in the thought that Keith was with his little brother or sister and they'd be a comfort to each other. For several weeks afterwards Harry and I just about functioned, both locked in our own ways of dealing with our grief. We barely spoke to one other. Although he never said as much to me, I did suspect he blamed himself for allowing Keith to go out that evening instead of telling him to wait until after he'd had his dinner. Then eventually I began to come out of the fog I was in and to accept that my son was gone from us, our unborn baby too, and whether I liked it or not I was alive and had to get on with life. It was only then that I really saw what was going on with Harry. Just after the funeral a neighbour had come to visit and told us that we might find some comfort in the church. She told us that she had turned to God when her husband died and it had greatly helped her. She left a Bible behind when she went. Neither of us had been the church-going sort before – we got married in a register office – although we never judged anyone else who did and I was surprised when Harry showed an interest in attending the next Sunday service. Of course, I said I'd go with him.

'I rather enjoyed the service, I have to say, and the rest of the congregation were very welcoming towards us, but all the time I was there it was on my mind that I would never get our dinner ready on time for one o'clock when we usually had it ... my mother and sisters and their families were coming that Sunday. I can't say as I took to the vicar either. He's the fire-and-brimstone sort, the type to bully you into believing that it's eternity in purgatory for you unless you live a pure and wholesome life and all your spare time is given up to the service of the church. Harry, though, really seemed to enjoy it, which chuffed my mother very much as she's always gone to church and won't have the Lord's name taken in vain in her hearing. I remember getting a heavy clout around the ear when I was a child when I stubbed my foot and yelped out "Oh, Jesus Christ".

'When Harry announced he was going to go to the next Sunday service, I thought that if he was getting some sort of comfort out of it then I was glad for him, but I told him it wasn't for me and I would be staying home and getting his dinner ready. He didn't seem concerned by that. I got the feeling he was relieved I wasn't accompanying him as this was something he wanted to do by himself. Then he started going every Sunday, not only to the morning service but the evening one too, and I noticed him reading the Bible that our neighbour had left when usually he would have been reading the newspaper and listening to the wireless. We still weren't talking much apart from necessary everyday conversation and we didn't go out together. The only time Harry went out apart from going to work was to church and Bible classes and we ... well ... er ... hadn't had any marital relations since Keith's death, but I put that down to Harry's grieving and still thought that he'd eventually return to his normal self and our life be back to how it was. Well, it would never be the same, of course, but we'd become a proper couple again some time.' She heaved a sigh and said softly, 'But we didn't.

'When that neighbour came round and suggested we try to find comfort in going to church and reading some helpful passages in the Bible, I don't think for a moment she meant it should take over our life. It got to the stage, though, where nothing got in the way of what Harry called his church business. He'd even go without his dinner if it meant he was going to be late arriving for a service or a Bible class or some do-gooding expedition he'd offered to be part of. He started a Bible class of his own in our house, expecting me to provide refreshments, which I did without complaint. The other women who attended used to give me a look because I was Harry's wife yet I wasn't joining in, but I'd just smile sweetly at them and leave them to it while I went back to

49

what I was doing. I tried to talk to him about our marriage suffering because of church activities taking up all his time. His answer really shocked me. He told me he was giving his life to God in an effort to gain redemption for the part he'd played in his son and unborn child's death, in the hope that he would be reunited in the afterlife with his children and gain their forgiveness there. I tried so hard to make him understand that he wasn't to blame, that Keith's death was just a terrible accident, but he said that it was he who'd allowed our son to go out that evening, so the blame did lie with him. And he wouldn't discuss the matter further.

'I spoke to my mother, hoping for some help in persuading Harry that he was going to extremes, to the detriment of everything else. She said that it was as plain as a pimple on a nose how badly he had taken his son's death and the miscarriage, and told me to stop being so selfish and allow Harry to grieve in whatever way suited him and to support him like a proper wife. I should try going to church myself, she said, then I might be a little more understanding – instead of going once and dismissing it. I should have known that in my mother's opinion I'd promised to serve my husband loyally, through thick and thin, when I'd recited my marriage vows. No matter what, I was duty bound to do that until the day he or I died.'

Jan heaved a miserable sigh. 'I tried, I really did. I didn't start going to church with Harry, that wasn't for me and I stuck to my guns there, but I did try and be an understanding wife, never complaining when I was left alone while he went about

50

his church duties. I made his guests as welcome as I could in our house when he held his Bible classes. I was upset but I kept my feelings to myself when he told me that any spare money he had left after paying me my housekeeping and setting some aside for the bills would be given to the church. Harry wasn't mean with housekeeping. I'd always had enough to fund any pleasures I wanted out of it ... meeting my sisters on a Saturday afternoon for a traipse around the shops, a coffee and cake afterwards, occasional trips to the pictures, that kind of thing, although anything like that is no fun on your own so usually I contented myself with reading or listening to the wireless, doing a bit of dress-making. The years went by like that and my hopes that Harry would snap out of this misguided need for redemption and revert back to the man I had married were in vain. We grew further and further apart.

'Last Saturday morning I was hanging out the washing. I could hear the kids next-door playing in their yard. They were discussing what they were hoping to get from Santa this year at Christmas. Then their mother shouted to them from the back door and said it was too early for them to be making their Christmas lists. And besides, if they didn't come in and see to their chores none of them would be getting anything. I remember laughing as I heard all three of them immediately shoot back inside and the back door bang shut after them.

'It wasn't until I was sitting at the table having my elevenses that what I'd heard came back to me. It triggered something inside me, made me see my future, the years stretching ahead in my empty marriage, just making the best of things. It all seemed so bleak that I broke down and sobbed, feeling utterly sorry for myself. Next thing I knew I felt this arm around me and heard someone asking me what on earth the matter was. It was Bernie the window cleaner.

'He's been cleaning our windows for years. He's a nice man, just ordinary-looking, I've never heard him say a bad word about anyone. His wife is a cripple. She had an accident not long after their second child was born, slipped on ice, landed heavily and broke her back. Lying in bed year after year, unable to move, has made her bitter and twisted. She treated Bernie like she blamed him even though he wasn't with her at the time. Bernie has never once complained about his lot in my company but I knew his life wasn't easy, working the hours he does plus caring for his wife and children, although they were both at work by then. He obviously knew about Keith but as far as he … anyone, in fact … was aware my marriage was as it has always been. I was feeling so … so low, I couldn't stop myself. I poured it all out to him, how hard I was finding it, living in a physically loveless marriage. I knew he'd understand, you see, because it must have been the same for him.

'Next thing I knew we were in our bed making love … well, it wasn't love, it was rampant sex we were having, as if both of us were getting rid of pent-up passions we'd kept buried for years. As we fell back on the pillows in exhaustion, I remember thinking that I knew without doubt

52

Bernie had never done anything like this before, nor had I, and nor would we again, despite the way our marriages had turned out. We still loved our spouses, it was just that neither of us had been able to resist the temptation of some physical contact after our years of famine. It was then I sensed someone else in the room. I looked over to the doorway and saw Harry standing there, staring at us both. I hadn't realised the time and he'd returned home from work for his dinner. I can't describe to you the look on his face ... of disgust, hurt, devastation. Before I had a chance to say anything, he'd left. I can't remember Bernie leaving, just my own scramble to get dressed and go after Harry and beg his forgiveness, make him understand why I'd ended up with Bernie like I had.

'He was waiting for me downstairs. The back door was open, my coat and handbag were in his hand which he thrust at me. His eyes were lifeless when he said to me that I'd done the worst thing I could have in God's eyes, committed adultery, and that my actions could be responsible for him being denied his own redemption and the chance to make amends to our son and unborn child, when the time came for him to be reunited with them in heaven. I lost my temper then, shouted at him that I was still alive and had needs that he seemed to have forgotten about in his misguided quest to ensure his own admission through the pearly gates. I asked him how God would view his breaking his marriage vows to love and cherish me, which was what he should be doing instead of turning his back on me.

'He told me how selfish I was being, thinking purely of myself when a man's wife, of all people, should be the one to cast her own needs aside in her duty to support her husband.

'My anger really erupted when he said that. I'd stood by him and not complained once in ten years since he'd joined the church. I told him that this was the damned vicar talking, not him. That man had brainwashed him into thinking as he was, at a time when he knew Harry to be vulnerable. In my eyes he was nothing more than a home-wrecker. Well, I never got any further as Harry manhandled me out of the house then, telling me he wouldn't have that saint of a man spoken about so disgustingly, and I was never to darken his door again. He locked it after me.

'I decided it was best I give him some time to calm down before I tried to talk to him again and I went and sat in the park for a couple of hours. The door was still locked and bolted when I went back, so I knocked. It wasn't Harry who opened it but the vicar. I knew he hadn't any time for me once I'd refused to join his church. I swear there was triumph in his eyes when he told me that I had no place in this house any more after what I'd done, and the church was looking after its disciple in his great sorrow. That vile man then shut the door of my own home in my face.

'She's very old-fashioned and set in her ways is my mother. One of her favourite sayings is, "You've made your bed, now lie on it." I knew she'd hit the roof if I went round to tell her what had gone off and ask her to let me stay there until I could sort things out with Harry, which I still felt I could do once he'd had time to think for himself when that vicar wasn't poisoning his mind against me, so it was my eldest sister I went to see first. I thought I'd get her as my ally, she'd then get my younger sister on board, and we'd tackle Mother together. I've always got on with both my sisters and knew they must have wondered why I hadn't turned up to meet them in town as usual that afternoon. They should both be back home by now, I thought. I couldn't believe it when I walked into my elder sister's house and there they were, the three of them, Mother and my two sisters, having a big pow-wow. That devil of a vicar had wasted no time and been to see my mother with the whole sordid story, even though she didn't belong to his congregation.

'All three of them looked at me like I was something they would scrape off their shoes when I walked in and it was Mother who told me she thought I had a nerve, showing my face here after what I'd done to poor Harry and the shame I'd brought on the whole family. All she was concerned about was how she was going to hold her head up when she went to church after it became common knowledge that she had an adulterous daughter. My elder sister was worried her husband's boss would get to hear and it might affect her husband's promotion. My younger sister just sat nervously looking on, frightened to open her mouth in case she put her foot in it. Anyway, I wasn't given any chance whatsoever to tell my side of the story. No sooner was I in the door than I was herded out, being told never to darken any of their doors again and that they were all going

55

round to offer what support and comfort they could to Harry. With that vile vicar and my own family pecking his ear against me, I knew there was no point in hoping we could work out a reconciliation. So as it turns out on that terrible evening Keith died, in reality I lost the three people I should love most dearly – two children and my husband.'

Jan heaved a deep sigh. 'Thankfully I had a few quid on me from the housekeeping. For the first three nights I managed to get myself rooms in cheap bed and breakfast places, the standard dropping drastically as the days passed and I realised my money was running out. The last place I stayed in ... last night, in fact ... the slovenly landlady had the nerve to charge ten shillings, all I had left, for a damp room no bigger than a cupboard. I swear blind the bedding hadn't been washed after the last person had slept in it and the mattress was that thin I could feel the springs on the bed through it, so I hardly got any sleep. That's why I had no choice but to take shelter in the arches tonight. After leaving that dive I've been wandering around all day, desperately trying to work out what to do next. I'd heard of the arches as somewhere homeless people slept, and that was me, wasn't it?' Homeless. But call me naive, I never expected it to be so bad or that some of the people would be ... well, no better than animals.' She flashed Glen a wan smile. 'Thank God you were there tonight or I dread... Anyway, now you know why I can't go home. I'm not welcome any more. Like you obviously haven't, I've no home either.'

Glen sensed it had done her good to have someone listen to her side of the story, albeit a stranger, when those close to her had not deigned to. He felt it was a pity her family had not given her a chance to explain her actions to them as they might not be viewing her so harshly now if they had. He took hold of his sack of belongings, delved inside and pulled out a crumpled brown paper bag, holding it out to her. 'You must be ravenous, not having eaten all day. You're welcome to this.'

Jan was so hungry she could have eaten a whole horse and for pudding a pig. Regardless, she eyed the bag cautiously. 'Er ... what is it?' she ventured.

It was a half-eaten sausage roll that he'd rescued from a litter bin in the park this lunchtime after seeing it deposited there by the man who had bought it in the first place and eaten the other half. Most of what Glen ate came from bins or from where people had carelessly dropped it on the ground. That was where this woman's meals would mostly come from in the future. It was a whole new way of life she was going to have to learn, where pride didn't figure. He was loath to part with the food, it being the only edible thing he'd unearthed today, but he felt that her need was greater than his. Jan had not had time to learn to live with constant hunger pains gnawing at her stomach, whereas he'd had years of practice. He just told her, 'It won't poison you. It was fresh today.'

Despite how desperately ravenous she was, Jan was very suspicious of just where he had come by this food. Wrapping a filthy flea-bitten old blanket around herself to keep warm was one thing, but putting suspicious food inside herself was another. She said politely, 'I'm not that hungry, but thanks for the offer.'

'Then I hope you don't mind if I do,' he said, taking the roll out of the bag. He took a large bite.

Jan watched him devour the remains of the sausage roll, fighting to keep saliva from dripping out of her mouth. The pastry looked dry and un-appetising but as he hungrily tucked in, hunger pangs exploded within her and she deeply regretted that she had turned her nose up at it.

Glen saw her frown in bewilderment as he carefully folded up the now-empty brown paper bag and put it back in his sack. 'You'll learn not to throw anything away. You never know when some-thing that seems utterly worthless at first will suddenly mean the difference between life and death to you. This bag will come in extremely handy when I go down the market tomorrow evening just on closing, to see what leftovers I can get before the sweepers get hold of them.'

God forbid that she was reduced to eating rotting fruit but Jan's common sense was telling her that it was something she was going to have to do if she didn't quickly come up with a way to get herself out of her dire situation. Desperate to distract herself from thoughts of food and her worrying situation, she said to her saviour, 'So how about you?'

He had been about to settle himself again in an effort to snatch some sleep but at her question stopped what he was doing to look over at her.

'What about me?' he queried.

'How did you come to be homeless?'

He resumed trying to settle himself while saying to her in a dismissive manner, 'Like I said earlier, it's a long story.' Hopefully she would take the hint and drop the matter. It was still very painful to him, how he came to be in the position he was in, despite its happening nearly eighteen years ago.

But Jan, like most women, had a streak of curiosity in her nature. His obvious reluctance to divulge his background only served to heighten this. 'Well, it's not like we've anything else to entertain us, is it? Not like we can put the wireless on or a light to read by ... that's if we had a book between us. So, did you cheat on your wife and she found out, the same as happened to me? Is that it?'

He snapped, 'No. Now if you don't mind–'

But Jan's curiosity was at fever pitch. She cut in, 'Oh, fell foul of the law then, did you, and your family disowned you?'

'No,' he replied, even more brusquely. 'Well, in truth, yes, I did fall foul of the law. But I was innocent. I was framed for what I was put away for. Now if you really don't mind...'

'You're an ex-con? Oh!'

He glared at her. 'Don't look at me like that. I told you, I was framed.'

'Framed for what? And just who framed you?'

Glen sighed. This woman was not going to let it go. She obviously felt that as she had bared her soul to him, it was only right he should repay the compliment. It was apparent he wasn't going to get any sleep until he did. Grudgingly he told her, 'It was a woman who was responsible.'

Jan looked intently at him. 'Oh! What exactly did she have you framed for?'

Glen sighed again as he thought back to a time he usually blanked out. Very quietly he said, 'She got me put away for theft and grievous bodily harm, and at the time I had no idea she was behind it. By the time I did, it was too late. I'd already signed over all my worldly goods to her, as I thought for her to take care of for me until I was released and then return them.'

Jan said, 'Even if you didn't know she had framed you at the time, you must have trusted this woman very much to sign everything over to her for safekeeping?'

'I had no reason not to trust her. She was my wife. She'd never given me any reason to doubt she wasn't as honest as a new-born babe, until I discovered just how devious she was and how naive I'd been.' Glen's face tightened. 'How I wish I'd never gone into that hotel on that particular night. It wasn't one I'd ever been in before and more than likely I never would have again. But I did go in, and by the time I came out my fate was sealed.

'I was a widower with a year-old child. Julia, my first wife ... the love of my life... had died six months before from an embolism on her lung. I was still missing her terribly and the last thing on my mind was finding someone to take her place or be a replacement mother to our child.' His voice grew wistful when he added, 'Lucy was such a lovely child, very placid, always smiling, and I did my best to make sure she didn't suffer from the loss of her mother. I always tried to be home in the evening, to take over from her nanny and give her a cuddle and have a play with her before she went to bed.

'I'd had a particularly trying time of it that day. My father had started the family business just after he married my mother at the turn of the century. He named the company after her. Her name was Rose and so he called it Rose's Bespoke Shoes. Just a small firm employing six people making handmade shoes, which the clients would come in and be specially measured for. I joined him when I left school at fourteen. My mother died three years after that. The doctor said it was from natural causes. She was fifteen years younger than my father, only forty-five. They were devoted to each other, and I know it was a broken heart that eventually ended his life. I'll never change my opinion on that score. They were wonderful parents to me and I still miss them both and always will. The company had grown by then and employed fifty-three people, making handmade shoes for clients right across the Midlands.

'After I'd been at the helm for about three years I decided to expand. As well as making bespoke shoes, we would offer a range of cheaper machine-made shoes and boots to be sold in shops. I also imported them from companies in France, Italy and Spain, to be sold to upmarket stores all over the British Isles. My workforce increased over that time to two hundred workers. Anyway, that day, one way or another, I'd had a particularly trying time and felt the need for a stiff whisky before I went home. That's how I came to be sitting in the bar of that hotel.

'Even though I wasn't interested in women in a romantic way, and was still very much in mourning, I couldn't help but notice that the barmaid was an attractive young woman. She was eighteen years old at the most but had an air of maturity about her. She was dressed in a tight-fitting skirt and low-cut blouse, but looked far from tarty. "Classy" is how I would have described her. After she'd finished serving the customer before me she turned her attention to me, saying that I looked like a man who had had a hard day and was in need of a drink. She asked what could she get me, and before I knew it I was telling her my story. She was very charming and attentive, and I was like a dog with two tails when she asked me if I would show her the sights of Leicester one night as she was new to the area. She seemed really pleased when I agreed. I was far from the tall, muscular, good-looking sort and was astonished that a pretty woman like her wanted to spend time in my company. I had thought that a night out with her would be our one and only date, and was stunned when she made it clear she wanted to see me again.

'When I arrived home after that first date I can only describe that it felt to me like I'd been pierced in the heart by Cupid's arrow. Nerys made no attempt to hide the fact that she'd fallen in love with me. She said my having a young child was of no consequence as she loved children, wanted a horde of her own, and certainly seemed to take to Lucy when I introduced them. Within a matter of weeks we were married. After my first wife had died I'd thought I'd never be happy with another woman. I had to keep pinching myself when I found I was, deliriously so. Nerys was doting towards me, kept the house clean and tidy, was a good cook and I couldn't fault the way she treated Lucy.

'We'd been married barely three months when I arrived at work one morning to find the police waiting for me, a detective and two constables. The detective told me that they'd been informed of suspicious behaviour going on at the premises during the early hours of the morning. A man had seen someone offloading boxes from a lorry and taking them round the back of the premises. The informant, who'd been walking his dog at the time, thought it suspicious for a firm to be taking delivery of goods at that time of night and felt it his duty to report what he'd seen to the police. They were very interested as a lorry loaded with shoes and handbags, which was on its way to Staffordshire, had been hijacked earlier that evening on a quiet country road just outside the city. The driver had been badly beaten with a hard implement, which they hadn't found, and was in a critical condition in hospital. I was deeply upset that I or my firm could be under suspicion of doing the slightest thing underhand. I told the detective to feel free to search the premises from top to bottom as he wouldn't find anything I couldn't account for legitimately. The informant had obviously mistaken my premises for someone else's.

'They eventually found all the cartons from the hijacked lorry stacked in disused outhouses behind the factory, and the key to the padlock and a bloodied crowbar, wrapped in a sack, hidden in the glove box of my car. I was stunned rigid, and had absolutely no idea how the boxes or key and crowbar had got where they had found them. Regardless, I was cautioned and taken down to the station for questioning. Meanwhile all my staff were interviewed. All of them had solid alibis. I was the only one who couldn't prove what I'd been doing. When I'd arrived home from work the previous evening, Nerys had told me she was suffering from a migraine. As soon as Lucy was put down for the night, she had taken a sleeping tablet and gone to bed. She didn't wake until Lucy did, at six-thirty the next morning. She tried to cover for me but as soon as the police started probing about what we'd done that night ... listened to on the wireless, et cetera ... she had to come clean and admit that she had taken a tablet and gone to bed and had no idea what I'd done then. The evidence against me was overwhelming. My insistence that I was innocent carried no weight. Thankfully the driver pulled through so I wasn't charged with actual murder, but I was charged with grievous bodily harm and theft. I received a fifteen-year sentence.

'It all seemed to happen so quickly but all the time I was convinced that the police would realise their terrible mistake, find the real villain and then I'd have my life back. When that cell door closed behind me in prison, I knew that wasn't going to happen. Nerys got a visiting order as soon as she could. I wouldn't allow her to bring Lucy, though, as I didn't want her visiting a place like that. Nerys had made an effort to look nice and be positive when she first arrived for the visit, and I tried hard to assure her that, despite what we'd heard, it wasn't that bad. But she couldn't keep up the pretence for long and broke down, telling me how hard she was finding life without me and that neither of us during the lead-up to the trial had given a thought to how she was going to manage for money, to take care of Lucy and herself. And also, what about the business? Had I someone in mind to run it for me during my absence? Someone that I trusted implicitly.

'I couldn't believe I hadn't thought about such important matters and made proper arrangements. I put it down to my faith in the British justice system and a jury finding me innocent, so that I wouldn't need to consider such matters. In fact, Nerys had been constantly telling me that anyone only had to look at me to see I wasn't capable of doing what I was accused of, and to stop worrying. I trusted all my staff, several of whom had been with the firm longer than I had, but none of them was the right person to head up the business while I was inside. But how was I going to find someone who could do that on my behalf when I was in prison? Nerys said that I needed to put my affairs in the hands of a solicitor, give him my power of attorney, and he could then appoint someone to take care of the business and make sure that she and Lucy were taken care of financially. I felt stupid for not thinking of that myself. I asked her to make a visit to our family solicitor and have him draw up the document-ation, which I would sign the next time she came on her monthly visit.

'When she next visited, against my wishes she'd brought Lucy along with her, telling me that regardless of how I felt about not wanting my daughter to see me in prison, she felt strongly that Lucy needed to see her father and her father needed to see her, and she intended to bring her each time. I was in fact overjoyed to see my daughter, and how well she looked and how Nerys was looking after her. Any worries I'd had that she might already have begun to forget me were unfounded. The smile on Lucy's face when she first clapped eyes on me was a sight to behold. I was glad Nerys had brought her in. These monthly visits from the two women I loved most in the world, and the regular letters Nerys wrote to me in between, would make such a difference to helping me through my period of incarcer-ation.

'Before I knew it the guard was announcing there were only five minutes left. Nerys was crying when she hurriedly dressed Lucy in her outdoor clothes. It would be a whole four weeks before she saw me again, she sobbed, and I was having a job not to weep myself because of the backlash this scene could cause me afterwards with some of the nastier type of inmates. By the time Nerys had finished dressing Lucy, the guard was announcing that visiting time was over and all were to take their leave. We had just said our goodbyes and Nerys was about to go when she remembered she hadn't given me the document

66

to sign for the solicitor.

'The guard was really getting annoyed with the stragglers by now but I knew this couldn't wait for another month ... the business would be suffering without someone at the helm and Nerys needed money to live on. Not caring what trouble I'd get into, I ignored the guard and told Nerys to give me the document. She took it out of her bag, then from the envelope, and turned the pages over to the one I needed to put my signature on. After I had signed on the dotted line, I realised we'd need someone to witness my signature. Thankfully Nerys was able to use her charm on the guard and he obliged, if only so as to be rid of us so he could have his tea break. As I was being escorted out by him I turned and looked back into the visiting room. Nerys was at the exit door, gazing back at me. There was a look on her face ... at the time I thought she was upset to be going off into the freedom of the world, leaving me shut up inside those high walls. But, thinking about it later, I realised how wrong I was. She was saying goodbye to me as she knew she'd never see me again.

'When a week had passed and I hadn't received any correspondence from Nerys and there was no answer when I telephoned her on my permitted weekly call, I was extremely concerned that either Lucy or she was ill. Another week passed and still there was no word by letter or telephone. I became very worried that something awful had happened to them, lots of different scenarios going through my head, none of them pleasant. I couldn't sleep, eat, and was having difficulty concentrating on my job in the prison laundry. When visiting time came around again and Nerys did not appear or send any word to me, I became frantic.

'It was bad enough dealing with the day-to-day living in that place, which was as bad as any stories I had heard, let alone worrying that something was wrong with my family while there was nothing I could do about it. The only thing I could do was write to my solicitor and ask him to find out what was going on. What an agonising wait to hear back from him that was! A week later, when I was pulled off my shift in the laundry as I had a visitor, I knew it had to be important for them to interrupt me at work. I really believed ... prayed ... it was Nerys who'd managed to get special dispensation from the governor to explain to me the reason for her silence. I was terrified it was something to do with my daughter but grateful that I'd be receiving some answers at last. My visitor wasn't Nerys but my solicitor, Charles Gray. The grave expression on his face sent a chill through me.

'He told me he that he was most surprised to receive my letter as he'd not been approached by my wife to have any papers drawn up concerning a power of attorney. After I'd been in touch by letter, he paid a visit to the house. A woman answered the door. When he announced who he was, she introduced herself to him as Nerys Thomas and seemed very surprised when he explained to her the reason for his visit. She told him that I must have had a brain seizure since the last time she had seen me. On her last but one visit I had informed her to contact a solicitor and have her given power of attorney so that she could take care of the business on my behalf and be able to access funds in my bank accounts to look after herself and my daughter. She showed him her copy of the document she'd had drawn up, which I'd signed.

'Having handled not only my affairs but my father's before him, Charles Gray knew my signature well enough to know this wasn't faked. The firm Nerys had used to draw up the documentation and deal with the legalities was a very reputable one.

'Charles then asked her why she hadn't visited me since I'd assigned my affairs over to her and told her that I was extremely worried something had happened to either her or Lucy. He said she seemed really shocked that I was so worried as, after I'd signed the papers and given them back to her, I'd told her that I was handing over everything I owned to her as my way of apologising for the humiliation I'd brought on her by what I'd done. I'd also said that I couldn't expect her to wait ten years for me, so she was to divorce me and feel free to meet someone else. My only stipulation had been that she should raise Lucy on my behalf, with the child believing that her father was dead so that she didn't grow up with the stigma of being related to a convicted criminal. I'd left her in no doubt that I meant what I said as I was going to make sure that she didn't receive any more visiting orders.

'She told Charles Gray that she had done her best to talk me out of it but I wouldn't budge.

Therefore she'd had no choice but to build a future for herself and Lucy without me in it. She asked him to give me her best wishes when next he saw me.

'I was struck dumb by these revelations and started to question if indeed her version of events was the truth and I was losing my mind. Then Charles asked me why, when I'd checked over the document and seen what it stated wasn't actually according to my instructions, I'd still gone ahead and signed. That was when the truth dawned on me. Nerys hadn't wanted me to examine the document before I'd authorised it. She had obviously brought Lucy along with her that visiting time, against my wishes, in order to distract me from the document until the very last minute, so that I wouldn't have time to check through it. Then a terrible thought hit me like a sledgehammer. It could only have been Nerys herself behind my being put away in the first place.

'I could see by the look on his face that Charles was thinking the same as I was, and said as much to him. He asked me just what exactly I knew about Nerys when I'd married her. It struck me it was hardly anything, and what I did know I had taken her word for. I had no choice but to accept that all her words of endearment to me were lies. To her I had been nothing more than a meal ticket. She was obviously on the lookout for a suitable victim to fleece and had found it in me that night I went into the hotel. But all the whys and wherefores ... whether she'd had an accomplice who carried out the attack and theft for which I was framed, or whether she'd paid someone to do it ... were irrelevant now as the document I had unwittingly signed was watertight and there was nothing even a clever lawyer like Charles could do about it. Nerys was now the legal owner of all my possessions.

'No words can describe how devastated and guilty I felt for losing the family home I'd been born in and all the happy memories of life there, along with the business my father had worked so hard to build. But far worse than that was the loss of my precious child. I didn't have anyone else to blame but myself, though, for falling for Nerys's scheme. The only consolation I had was that she must love my daughter as if she was her own or she would have put her in an orphanage.

'I was released on parole after ten years but they seemed like a lifetime to me. I'd had no visitors and no idea how my daughter was faring with Nerys. Release brought me little joy as I'd nothing to come out to. I knew I had no chance of getting back any of my possessions but I badly wanted to see my little girl, even from a distance, just to satisfy myself that she was well and happy. After settling in at a hostel, I paid a visit to my old home. To my shock I found that Nerys no longer lived there and hadn't for ten years. She must have sold up and moved as soon as the house became hers. The present owners had no forwarding address for her. I would have asked Charles Gray's help in tracing Nerys but found he had died years before, and there was no one left working at my old business who would remember me or feel any inclination to help me. I had no choice but to put my past life behind me and get on with the one I had instead.

'The prisoners' welfare people had secured me a job as a labourer at a lumber yard, where I could sleep in one of the outbuildings. That was one of the conditions of getting parole – that I had a job and somewhere to live. I knew from the moment I met my new boss that I was going to hate working for him. He was squat, thickset and brusque, in his late-sixties, and he and his thin, mean-faced wife lived in a ramshackle filthy old place on the premises. I was expected to do as I was told, no questions asked, and be eternally grateful that I had somewhere to rest my head, never mind that it was a rotting shed with just sacking for a mattress. The food I was given was not fit for pigs. My hours of work were from six in the morning until the boss decided I'd finished at night. After deductions to cover accommodation and food I received ten shillings a week, barely enough to buy myself any personal things, let alone clothes.

'I've never had any aversion to hard work, my parents certainly believed in it, but being worked each day until I was fit to drop, and treated like I was the scum of the earth while being expected to show gratitude, was something I wasn't prepared to tolerate. I stuck the job for three months until I'd managed to save up five pounds and walked out of the job without a word to my boss as I didn't believe he deserved an explanation.

'Knowing I'd got to take care of my money until I found another job, I stayed in a hostel for homeless men that night, in a large dormitory surrounded by types as bad as any I'd been in prison with. Next day I spruced myself up as best I could and went looking for work. I wasn't fussy, would have taken anything suitable. All I was asking was to be given enough of a wage to manage on and to be treated like a human being. I was obviously expecting too much.

'Two weeks later I'd visited that many places asking after work I'd lost count, but each time a prospect looked promising, as soon as I told potential employers about my time in prison and that I had no fixed abode, I was shown the door. My money was all gone by this time so I couldn't even afford the two shillings a night to stay in the hostel. I was starting to look really shabby as it's very difficult to keep yourself looking clean and tidy when you've no facilities other than the public baths, for which you need to pay. And I needed money for food more than for hot water. With no job and nowhere to live, I had no choice but to live rough. That was over five years ago.'

Glen's narrative abruptly stopped and he looked at his companion with surprise and shock on his face. He had never told another living soul the whole story of how he'd come to be in the dire situation he was now, he'd kept the whole sorry story locked inside himself. But somehow his subconscious had told him that this stranger would not judge him for his behaviour or use this information she now knew about him to her own advantage.

He took a deep breath and said gruffly, 'Now you know.'

There was a look of understanding and also of great sadness in Jan's eyes when she muttered,

73

'Yes, I do.' She looked thoughtfully at him for several moments before she said, 'I expect you've lived all these years hoping that somehow your wife has been made to pay for what she did to you.'

Glen growled, 'I would be lying if 1 said I hadn't wanted to seek revenge, spent numerous nights trying to find a way to bring that about, but then I realised that all I was doing was making myself more bitter and twisted. Since then, all I've prayed for is that Nerys has kept good her promise to care for my daughter and has raised her to be an honest, likeable young woman with a promising future, as I would have done myself.'

Jan was looking thoughtfully at him. 'It's a pity you can't find out your ex-wife's whereabouts and have your mind put at rest over your daughter. I know you tried to find her when you first came out of prison, but there must surely be some way to unearth where she's living. She installed a manager at the business, didn't she? I realise his first loyalty will be to her, but he has to have a telephone number or some other means of making contact with her if he should need her say-so on a business matter, and they must meet up regularly for her to reassure herself that all is as it should be.' She paused for a moment before adding, 'We need to get into his office and have a rummage round, to see if we can find out where he keeps those details. It's the only way to get a lead on where Nerys is living and for you to have your mind put at rest about your daughter's welfare.'

Glen thought it was generous of her to be

centring her thoughts on him when she had her own worries to face. 'I've been to prison once, I'll not go back again,' he said cautiously.

'Oh, I didn't mean you should break in and run that risk.'

'How then? I mean even if there were a ruse I could come up with to get into the factory, it's not likely anyone would let a vagrant like me into the manager's office unattended.'

Jan responded matter-of-factly, while thinking to herself that it was going to take some doing, 'Then we need to get you smartened up.'

'I'm dying to hear how, when you know I've no money.'

She had no idea at all, considering the circumstances they were both in, but was saved from admitting that to him by noises coming from the entrance to the shop doorway. They both looked over to see several young men leering down nastily at them. They were all either holding bottles of drink or newspaper parcels of chips. It was obvious they were the worse for drink. Jan inwardly froze. Her companion had warned her about possible trouble at chucking-out time, and she wasn't sure what to expect. The men then started shouting abuse at them. It was extremely offensive and hurtful and Jan was ready to answer back, but she felt a hand on her arm and instinctively knew it was a warning to keep quiet. Receiving no response, the men then started throwing missiles. Several bottles fell short of their intended target and smashed on to the concrete floor around them. One did hit home and caught her companion heavily on his shoulder, but he instinctively caught the bottle before it too smashed on the ground. Jan then found herself being pelted with chips, and a half-finished parcel landed beside her. Finally, no missiles left to hand and finding no fresh abuse to hurl, laughing and joking together the men went on their way.

Deeply insulted, Jan snapped, 'How could you just sit there and not retaliate?'

'And give them an excuse to give me a beating? As you know yourself, no one will come to the rescue. When you encounter people like that it's best to do nothing to provoke them further. Then, like those thugs just did, eventually they'll get fed up and move on. Look on the bright side, though.'

She gawped at him, stunned. 'Bright side! What bright side?'

'We've landed ourselves supper,' Glen told her, picking several chips off his coat and putting them in his mouth. He then took a swallow from the remains of the bottle of beer he'd managed to catch hold of. 'That's good. Long time since I've had a drink of beer. Want some?' he asked her, holding the bottle out towards her.

It was just what she needed to help steady her nerves but Jan dreaded to think how long it was since her companion had last cleaned his teeth. She politely refused the beer. The newspaper parcel at her side was a different matter, though. She grabbed it, delighted to see a good portion of chips still left inside, and started ravenously ramming them into her mouth as if she hadn't eaten for months, totally forgetting her manners and to offer a share to her companion as he had to her.

The chips were far from a banquet but enough to take the edge off Jan's hunger. She had to stop herself from licking the last of the crumbs off the newspaper. She made to screw up the greasy paper until she remembered her companion's words that in the world she was in now every object had value, so she smoothed it out and folded it up instead, then handed it to him.

Glen thanked her, saying as he put it in his sack of belongings, 'That'll come in handy to help light a fire with when I'm on my travels in the countryside.' He then suggested to Jan that they move into the doorway next-door because of the danger to them both from the broken glass surrounding them.

Rehoused in their new shelter, Jan once again began to shuffle herself about, trying her best to get comfortable enough to snatch some sleep, her ears ringing to the sound of her companion's snores. Finally, from sheer exhaustion sleep began to steal over her, but just before oblivion hit an idea struck her. Eyes wide open, she proclaimed, 'Well, how stupid of me not to have thought of that before.'

Always with his senses on alert, at the sound of her voice Glen shot bolt upright, one hand automatically diving into his pocket to grab hold of the penknife while his eyes darted round seeking any potential danger. When he realised it was Jan who had woken him, he snapped at her, 'You shouted out. What for?'

She shot him a triumphant look. 'Because I know how we can get you cleaned up.' The only part of his face that was visible, his eyes, told her he was utterly confused as to how and, as exhaustion had overtaken her again, at this moment she lacked the energy to go into detail. Lying back down again, her eyes closing without any effort on her part, she mumbled to him, 'Tell you later.'

CHAPTER FIVE

It was with emotions of sorrow and misery mingled with fear that Cait let herself into the house, a gabled four-bedroomed detached property situated in the affluent leafy suburb of Oadby on the outskirts of the city. She took off her coat which she hung on the antique Victorian stand in the imposing hallway and then made her way into the tastefully furnished lounge where she perched on the edge of a chintz-covered sofa. She looked across at her mother, sitting reading in a matching chair by the side of the roaring fire. Cait knew she was well aware of her daughter's arrival but, regardless, did not acknowledge her.

As she patiently waited for her mother to arrive at a place in the book where she was prepared to stop, Cait studied her. There was no denying the fact that, even though she was approaching her forties, Nerys Thomas was still a very attractive woman. She was tall at five foot seven, and slim. Her fashionably styled dark wavy hair framed a heart-shaped face, and her large almond-shaped eyes were the colour of African violets. Regardless of whatever she was doing she always looked immaculate, as if she'd stepped out of the pages of an upmarket magazine. But strangely she never went out, except to the beauty parlour or to shop for clothes, she had no friends, and didn't invite anyone into the house but would keep any casual callers standing on the doorstep. With her looks her mother could have had the pick of any man she wanted, so why she had settled for a man like Cait's father remained a mystery to her. Samuel Thomas was a small, puny man with thinning fair hair, pale blue eyes and a pasty complexion. He was not a good conversationalist but had a whining way of talking which was extremely irritating, had little sense of humour, and suffered from poor health through having a weak chest and heart. Cait strongly felt that her father thoroughly enjoyed his ill health, basking in his wife's constant attention, and suspected that sometimes he exaggerated his sufferings if he felt he wasn't getting enough of it. Yet her mother was devoted to him, would immediately drop whatever she was doing at a summons from him, fretted and fussed over him like a mother with her young child, and would have no word said against him. Her efforts to look immaculate all the time were on his behalf also.

Cait would often study her own reflection in the mirror and sometimes feel she had inherited her mother's looks, sometimes her father's, but in truth she resembled neither of them so assumed she must take after a more distant ancestor. There was no way of checking that, though, as both her parents were orphans and the past too painful for them to discuss. As far as she was aware her father had never held down a job and it was an inheritance of her mother's that kept the family in the comfort they enjoyed.

Neither of her parents was at all demonstrative towards her. It seemed to Cait that they showered all the affection they had on each other, and had none left to give her. As a young girl she had suffered many rejections by her mother, being told that she was acting selfishly in demanding her time when she knew her father was in need of it, or that Nerys was far too busy suddenly to drop everything on her account. As a result, from quite an early age, Cait stopped asking for any attention from her, to avoid the pain of being pushed away. She did well enough at school but never pushed herself to excel so failed to reach anywhere near her full potential. So long as she got out of the house and went to school, her parents were satisfied. She'd long ago stopped trying to work out what exactly they both found lacking in her that prevented them from showing her any affection, and barely more than their passing attention. Consequently she could only imagine what it would feel like to be hugged and kissed and made a fuss of, allowed into the private circle from which she had always been excluded.

The young Cait had showed all the signs of developing into an intelligent, caring and lovable girl. Unfortunately for her, though, she'd had a mother who stifled all these qualities in her, so the youngster had no choice but to observe Nerys's ways of doing things and follow her example. Her mother was very brusque and matter-of-fact in her approach to others, especially those who worked for her, and would never allow them any sort of familiarity. If they acted informally with her, she always put them firmly in their place. Since Nerys had no acquaintances with children, Cait was a very lonely child, and when it came to going to school had no idea how to make friends. Her abrupt manner did her no favours either.

One day, though, she was in the playground eating some sweets when a girl approached her, and told her that if she would give her one then she would allow Cait to play with her. Cait was a quick learner. This set the pattern for how she would gain friends in future. Most of these relationships were short-lived, but she would regularly entice people to befriend her by offering them inducements she knew they'd be unable to refuse. That was how she had acquired the two friends she palled around with now, Gina and Clare, who worked with her as typists for a fruit and vegetable wholesaler's.

As an attractive girl Cait was not short of admirers, but the only way she knew how to treat them was to behave exactly as her mother did with her father. That had to be the right way, surely. Consequently she smothered any man she went out with, knowing what he wanted or was thinking before he did and making herself indispensable to him.

One day when Cait was sixteen, Nerys had sat her down and bluntly informed her that, although the age of majority was twenty-one, her parents would consider themselves free from any responsibility for her once she reached the age of eighteen. They'd expect her to leave home and make her own way in the world, which was why she was being told in advance so she'd have plenty of time to make arrangements. Nerys informed her that she had been given no choice but to make her own way in the world when she was the same age, and had done well for herself. Now it was time for Cait to do so too instead of always relying on her parents. She had thought at the time that this statement was not entirely true as her mother had had her inheritance to fall back on whereas there was no mention of settling any money on Cait to give her a start. Before she could make any sort of response to this unexpected and shocking announcement, her father had summoned Nerys and without hesitating she had leaped up to see to him.

Cait had been left feeling terrified about how she was going to fend for herself on the money she could expect to earn as a typist. Her mind had turned somersaults, trying to work out how she was going to manage. There was one obvious answer. Whether or not she wanted to tie herself down so young, she had no other choice that she could see but to find a husband to support her.

Through going to the local youth club she met several likely candidates, but they all proved unsuitable. For them marriage was something far away in the future, after they had grown tired of having a good time and sowing their wild oats. With her eighteenth birthday just over a year away, Cait was starting to panic that she'd never find herself a husband before her parents' deadline arrived and she found herself cast out on her own.

By now she had teamed up with Gina and Clare, using her usual method of buying their friendship by paying for most of the drinks and their entry into the dance halls they would all visit together twice a week. Though they had no idea why Cait was so focused on finding a husband, her forwardness with young men was extremely useful to her friends. When Cait spotted a likely prospect and was busy charming him, his mates often turned their attention to her companions and both young women had secured themselves quite a few dates that way. Like all of Cait's other relationships, though, these flirtations were short-lived because most young men couldn't stand her smothering ways and marriage wasn't of any interest to them until way into the future.

It was on a night out with her friends that Cait first noticed Neil. She had just entered the Wine Lodge in the marketplace, a dive of an establishment which still sprinkled sawdust on the floors and sported strategically placed spittoons, but the drinks were cheap and that was why the younger generation were willing to mix with the older clientele whose drinking hole it had been for decades. There was one young man present who stood out from the rest. He was tall, good-looking, had an intelligent air about him and was smartly dressed. Cait was immediately attracted to him.

Heading straight for the part of the bar where he was standing, she purchased drinks for herself and her two friends and she turned purposefully towards him so that she could break the ice by asking him to excuse her. Her ploy worked a treat and moments later she was deep in conversation with him, her two friends with two of his associates. Within twenty minutes Cait had gleaned Neil's name, how old he was, what he did for a living, and was able to calculate his future prospects. She also learned that he lived with his parents in a good area and, the most important bit of information to her, that he had no girlfriend at present. To her relief, she knew she had at last found her man, someone suitable and also someone with whom she knew she could fall in love. She couldn't believe her luck.

Before the two groups of friends went their separate ways Cait had charmed Neil into asking her out on a date the next evening. All she had to do now was pray he fell in love with her and wanted to make her his wife. She knew a proper woman pandered to her man, made him feel like the most important person in her life, was constantly at his beck and call, organised every aspect of his life for him. Well, that was the way her mother treated her father, and he lapped up the attention. Confident that Neil would too, that was how Cait always acted with him.

Five months into their relationship, one evening while they were at a Chinese restaurant, she'd misconstrued a comment Neil made and believed he had asked her to marry him. When Cait broke the news to her parents on arriving home that evening, she had hoped that for the first time ever they would find it possible to lend her some support, especially her mother. Perhaps Nerys would help her organise her big day, like other mothers were delighted to do? Instead, while her father sat coddled warmly in a blanket on the sofa, never taking his eyes off the television, her mother's reaction was to offer lukewarm congratulations, tell Cait not to expect any help from her as all her time was commandeered by caring for her husband, and then return to reading her book. There was no mention of their contributing to the wedding or how much money she could spend on her special day. This troubled Cait. She wasn't in any position to fund it on her wages and nor could she expect Neil or his family to pay for it. This customarily fell to the parents of the bride, as far as she was aware. She therefore assumed her parents would step in.

It wasn't until the bills started to arrive a month or so later that a fuming Nerys informed her daughter that she had no right whatsoever to be spending money that wasn't hers. Just because she had decided to get married did not mean her parents would automatically pay for everything. Thanks to her selfishness a trip to a special clinic in Switzerland, which would greatly have improved her father's poor health, would now have to be put on hold. Nerys didn't seem to consider the fact that Cait had known nothing of this planned trip. But at least she wasn't ordered to cancel all her purchases. Thankfully the ceremony and reception were paid for, her dress and the bridesmaids' dresses, the flowers and transport. Cait strongly suspected this was because her mother would not run the risk of diminishing herself in the eyes of several high-class business people in town by cancelling her daughter's orders.

She became so wrapped up in the arduous task of perfecting her wedding preparations without any help from her mother or her two friends, who always seemed to be busy, and also trying her best to finance these little extra touches out of what little she had left from her own weekly wage once she had paid her dues at home, that she had failed to notice her intended husband was becoming increasingly preoccupied and distant from her as the date for their wedding drew closer.

Learning that the man she loved and had planned to spend the rest of her life with didn't feel the same about her was devastating enough for Cait, without the terrifying prospect of being thrust out into the world to fend for herself on top of it. The only morsel of hope she'd had left was that, despite his denial, Neil was in fact suffering from pre-wedding nerves and might be regretting his actions. So after she'd left the church Cait had gone round to his house, in the hope of a reconciliation.

It was his mother who answered the door to her. Neil had asked her to pass on a message if Cait turned up as he didn't want a direct confrontation with her. She was told that he had nothing more to say to her and that he'd meant what he'd said in the church. His mother sounded sincere and there was a sympathetic look in her eyes when she told Cait to make it easy on herself and accept her son's decision, as he had asked her to.

Cait was in total shock as she made her way home afterwards, dragging one foot after the other, unable to understand why he didn't want to spend the rest of his life with her. Hadn't she done enough to prove to him that she would look after him, run his house for him, take on all the stresses and strains of everyday life by dealing with them herself, just like her mother did for her father? She couldn't leave the situation, walk away from Neil and get on with her life alone. She needed advice on how to put matters right between them. The two girls who were supposed to be her friends had turned their backs on her at this moment of crisis, showing that their friendship was merely superficial and they were only in it for what it brought them. This meant that there was only one other person she could turn to for advice on how to resolve her dire situation.

Waiting patiently for her mother to finish her chapter finally proved too much for Cait. 'I really need to speak to you, Mother,' she blurted out. Before Nerys had chance to refuse, Cait told her that Neil had called off their wedding and asked, 'I treated him like you do Father, and you are both happy together, so where have I gone wrong, Mother?'

If she had been expecting Nerys to impart her worldly wisdom and inform her what she could do to make amends with Neil, then she was to be cruelly disappointed. Nerys's matter-of-fact response was, 'Samuel and I were destined to be together, you and Neil obviously were not. You've got plenty to do before next weekend, to keep you occupied and help you over it. You've still got all your packing to do and things to arrange in the new house, to make it ready to move into.'

Cait stared at her in astonishment. 'Live in the

house that Neil and I were going to share! Oh, I couldn't. It would be too much of a reminder for me...'

Nerys cut in, 'It's a house, isn't it? And you need somewhere to live. If you don't want to live there on your own, find someone to share with you. Be a pity to waste the month's rent that's paid on it, as I doubt it would be refunded.' She then picked up her book and began to read again, her way of informing her daughter that as far as she was concerned there was nothing more to discuss.

Cait lay in bed, staring up at the shadows cast on the ceiling, fighting to concentrate her thoughts on the shifting shapes instead of dwelling on what had transpired tonight and its very serious repercussions for her. She was failing miserably. All the shadows seemed to have Neil's face in them. She heaved a sorrowful sigh, doing nothing to wipe away the flood of tears spilling down the sides of her face. It was ironic that last night she couldn't sleep through excitement and nerves about her forthcoming wedding, and tonight she couldn't because she was feeling utterly desolate that there wasn't going to be one. Neil had made it very clear that there would be no reconciliation.

She wasn't just having to deal with the heart-break of a failed romance either. In seven days' time she would be thrust into the world to fend for herself. Believing she had saved herself from that fate by finding Neil, she had no idea how she would cope with living alone and doing all the things she'd never had to before. This house was the only home she had known. She might most of the time feel like an intruder here, due to the way her parents were, but at least she'd had a certain amount of security, knowing a meal would be on the table for her, her washing done, her bedroom cleaned, albeit by Agnes Dalby, the daily her mother employed, who saw to these household chores.

She felt that she was being forced headlong towards a closed door, her unknown future concealed behind it, with no one to offer her comfort or support, let alone love.

CHAPTER SIX

'Have you got a watch?'

Glen sat bolt upright, still half-asleep but instantly on his guard. He didn't like waking up to find a stranger close to him. No, not a stranger, he realised belatedly. It was the woman he'd saved in the arches the night before – and now she would not leave him alone.

'A watch?' he queried.

His tone of voice left her in no doubt what he thought of her for asking such a stupid question. 'Well ... er ... what I meant was, how do I find out what time it is?'

He glanced out of the shop doorway at the street beyond and answered, 'It's about five-thirty.'

Jan stared at him in surprise. 'How can you possibly know that if you haven't a watch?'

He gave an irritated sigh. 'I can just tell, by the morning air and the colour of the sky, which you'll come to do yourself in time. Now, if you don't mind, I want to try and snatch...'

She interjected, 'We have to go.'

He looked at her incredulously. 'Go where? There is nowhere to go at this time in the morning.'

Jan was desperately trying to stretch the stiffness out of her body so she could get up. She was surprised to find that she had slept for as long as she had, considering the circumstances. 'I told you last night, I know where we can get you cleaned up ... me too. Look, I haven't time to explain – we have to get there before six. Come on.' When she saw he was just looking back at her, befuddled, she urged, 'Come on... What is your name, by the way?'

'Eh? Oh, Glen. Glen Trainer.'

'I'm Janet Clayton. Jan. Now come on, Mr Trainer ... Glen ... we have to arrive where we're going before it gets light, and I've no idea where we are at the moment so I don't know how far we have to go.'

Glen was confused as to where on earth she could be taking him.

Jan was standing up by now, peeling the rotting blanket Glen had loaned her from around herself, conscious that its smell had seeped into her clothes and of her own desperate need to freshen herself up. And there was the fact that she was still so cold she needed to move in order

90

to get the blood flowing in her veins again. Handing the blanket to him, she urged, 'Come on, we really need to be off.'

The conversation they'd had hours before flooded back to him. The woman he now knew to be Janet Clayton had proclaimed that she knew somewhere they could go to smarten themselves up. He was highly intrigued to find out just where the likes of him would be allowed to do that. And besides, he had no clean clothes to change into. But he was wide awake now so he might as well go with her. It didn't look like she was going to take no for an answer.

Out in the street, once Glen had informed Jan exactly where they were, she hurriedly set off. She took him to the town centre then up the high street, crossing the Grand Union Canal over the Richard III bridge, then on up the Narborough Road. It seemed to them that they were the only ones up and about on this bitterly cold early morning. On and on they seemed to go before Jan finally turned down a palisade terraced street. She stopped for a moment by the entry between two houses, taking a good look round to confirm that they weren't being observed from behind any closed curtains before she urged Glen to follow her down the entry.

Halfway down in the near pitch dark, Glen reached out to grab her shoulder. 'If it's your idea to break into a house, then I won't be party to that, no matter how desperate for a wash I am. In all the time I've been living rough, I've never resorted to stealing in any shape or form and I won't start now.'

Jan was insulted. 'I'm not about to break in any-where. I know where there's a key. In the shock of what happened to me, I'd forgotten about it until we were talking last night about the lack of somewhere to spruce ourselves up. She tapped the wall to the right of her. 'This is my house. Well, it was until my husband accused me of having a torrid affair and consequently threw me out. The law would probably be on his side and say he'd every right to throw me out in the circumstances, but he's no right to keep my private possessions from me and I can't be accused of breaking and entering if I have a key to let myself in, can I? And if I happen to invite in a friend and they choose to bathe while they're there ... well, I'd like to see my husband get me slung in jail for *that*.'

A worried expression crossed her face then. 'Just pray Harry's not remembered about the spare key and moved it or that's us snookered good and proper. Anyway, I wanted to get here before it's light so that none of the neighbours spots us and tells him. We'll need to hide in the back yard and be ready to go in as soon as Harry's gone to work. That gives us a good four hours before he's due home for his dinner at one. Oh, come on, time's getting short and we need to hide ourselves before he and the neighbours are up and about.'

The prospect of having soap and water for the first time in an age was hard to resist. Glen fol-lowed Jan down the entry as far as the gate. Deftly lifting the latch, she opened the gate just wide enough to slip through, Glen following close behind. Jan hurried across a small slabbed area

92

and on down a short path, one side of which was lawned, the other a vegetable patch, towards a small brick-built shed which stood against the garden wall. The old door was stiff, its wood having swollen in the wet wintry weather, and Jan had to push hard against it, praying that the noise it made didn't alert anyone. She didn't wait around to find out but gave Glen a shove on his back to urge him inside then quickly followed behind, shutting the door after them.

She breathed a sigh of relief and whispered, 'Well, hopefully we managed that without anyone seeing us. Now we just have to wait until we hear Harry setting off for work.'

The shed was full of gardening equipment and discarded household items, along with the usual assortment of creepy crawlies and evidence of rodents. None of this bothered Glen as he was used to sharing whatever sleeping quarters he could find with such creatures. Jan, though, wasn't so thrilled to be in the dark, dank shed, imagining herself covered in spiders and she constantly gave herself a pat down to remove them, whether they were there or not. The time seemed to pass very slowly. Eventually they heard the welcome noise of the back door opening and closing, then the clomp of hob-nailed boots across the slabs heading for the gate, the latch being lifted then shot back into place moments later.

Jan let several minutes pass to be on the safe side, just in case Harry had forgotten something and returned, before she crept her way over to the shed door. She ran her fingers above the lintel until she felt what she'd hoped to find. 'I've got it!' she whispered triumphantly. She peeped out to check all was clear. 'Come on,' she urged Glen.

Jan took him into a small kitchen, relocking the door after them then drawing the curtains shut before she put on the light. She looked around critically. The kitchen looked immaculate, not a thing out of place. 'Well, for someone who's done the washing up barely a dozen times in all the years we've been married, Harry seems to be managing well enough without me,' she observed.

Meanwhile Glen was feeling awkward to be inside a house for the first time in over fifteen years. It felt a mite claustrophobic to be enclosed once more by four walls. He knew, though, that it wouldn't take him long to shake off these feelings and get used to living in such security again.

While he was lost in his own thoughts, Jan was doing her best to shake off a feeling of desolation, reminding herself that she was in this situation because of her own stupid moment of madness, regardless of what had driven her to it. As far as Harry was concerned, she had betrayed him in the worst way she could and she should not blame him for getting on with his life without her in it.

With forced lightness she told Glen, 'The bathroom is through here. We had the old outside toilet and shed converted into one five years ago. I'll show you how to work the geyser then leave you in peace to have your soak. Oh, look in the cabinet on the wall and you'll find what you need to deal with all that hair on your face.' She laughed before she added jocularly, 'I'll cut that matted mess off your head after you've washed out whatever is nesting in it! I'll get you a sack to put your old clothes in and we'll leave them in the dustbin when we go.' She saw the quizzical expression in Glen's eyes then and knew what he was going to ask. 'Don't worry, you won't be leaving here stark naked. I'm going to sort out some of Harry's old clothes for you that I know he won't miss.'

She led Glen through a door at the back of the kitchen and into a long narrow room with white-washed walls. On one side stood a huge cast-iron bath, on the other a sink and toilet. The floor was covered with black-and-white checked lino. There was a gas heater on the wall above the bath. Above the sink was a white medicine cabinet with mirrored doors. After she'd shown him how to operate the geyser, made sure he had fresh towels and that there was plenty of soap, Jan told him, 'Use as much water as you need. I'll leave you to it while I pack my belongings, sort you out some clothes and see what I can find us for breakfast. Oh, when I've mashed us a cuppa, I'll knock on the door to let you know it's outside.' As she shut the door behind her, she called to him, 'Enjoy yourself.'

Glen meant to. After turning on the geyser which slowly dispensed scalding hot water into the bath, he wasted no time in stripping off his clothes, layer by layer. It was so long since he'd taken them off that they were almost melded together from sweat and dirt. The last layer stuck to his skin, which smarted as he pulled it away.

While the bath was still filling he thought he'd tackle his facial hair. Standing before the misted mirrored cabinet on the wall above the sink, he opened it and took out the items he'd need.

He closed the cabinet doors then wiped a hand over the glass to clear off the mist. On catching sight of the image that stared back at him, he jumped back in shock. He hadn't seen a reflection of himself for many years, purposely avoiding doing so, not wanting to be reminded how low he'd been brought. Of course he'd had an idea he looked bad, but had never thought he'd look quite so grotesque and frightening. No wonder children had cowered in terror behind their mothers' skirts when he had come into view. Blackbeard the notorious pirate would have looked like an angel compared to him if they'd been put side by side. It struck him then that he couldn't even remember what he looked like without a mass of hair and years of grime on his face. Of course, during the many years since he had last seen himself clean-shaven he would have aged; the harshness of the life he was living would have told on him and the lack of proper nourishment drastically affected his weight. He would have to prepare himself for the fact that he might not even recognise himself once he'd finished his ablutions. He picked up the pair of scissors he'd found in the cabinet and set about his task.

Upstairs, Jan was trying to dismiss memories of happier times in this house to the back of her mind as she prepared to pack her clothes and personal possessions. To her shock and dismay, however, she had opened the wardrobe to find empty hangers where her clothes used to hang, and then discovered that the dressing table had been stripped of all the personal items which had cluttered the surface and filled the drawers. Any shred of hope she might still have harboured for a reconciliation evaporated then. She had only been gone a matter of days and already there was no visible sign that she had ever lived here at all. She knew that her indiscretion had caused her husband hurt, but for him to have removed all visible reminders of her so soon cut her deeply. The kind and compassionate man she had married had changed out of all recognition since he had become embroiled with the church and that conniving vicar had got his claws into him. She shut the wardrobe door. She wasn't worried about how she was going to afford to kit herself out with some new clothes, or replace her personal items, or put a roof over her head for the time being until she found a job; she knew exactly how she was going to do that, and to hell with what the vicar or Harry made of it when it came to light what she'd done.

Having sorted out a set of clothes for Glen, she made her way back downstairs, laid them on the floor outside the bathroom, knocking on the door to let Glen know they were there, then went into the kitchen to mash a pot of tea for them both and see what she could find for breakfast.

A short while later, sipping the cup of tea Jan had made him, Glen was revelling in the luxury of feeling hot water lapping gently over him. This was the third change of water, and albeit it was murky it was nowhere near the colour of a

97

muddy puddle as the first lot had been. That had had a thick layer of scum floating on top, which he'd had to scrub away from the sides of the bath before he could refill it. After he had shorn his thick growth of beard close enough for him to shave, he set about removing the rest with a cut-throat razor. He had prepared himself to see a stranger looking back at him from the mirror but he hadn't expected to see someone quite so gaunt with skin the colour of putty, or such deep grooves around his nose, cheeks and eyes where none had been before. If he hadn't known who it was staring out of the mirror, he would never have recognised himself. Between the next change of water he had tackled his mass of hair, shearing it off his head in big chunks, leaving enough hopefully for Jan to shape into a short back and sides. Seeing his reflection when he had done this was another shock and he kept having to remind himself that it really was him.

As he lazed now in what felt like the lap of luxury, aware that he should really vacate the bathroom in order to give his hostess time to use the facilities before they had to leave, the sound of a loud knock on the back door reached his ears. He sat bolt upright, the action causing a wave of water to slop over the sides and on to the linoleum. His heart was thumping madly. Had Jan's husband come back for some reason, having to knock on the door as she had locked it after them? Jan might have a right to be here but Glen wasn't sure where he himself stood. Fear engulfed him that he could be charged with trespass and be facing jail again.

Jan had been frying sausages, about to add the couple of rashers of bacon she had found in the pantry to the pan, when she heard the sound of a key being tried in the back door lock and spun round to stare at it, automatically thinking it was her husband trying to get in. She had told Glen that she had every right to enter the house as she was still technically married to the owner, but in all truth she didn't actually have a clue where she stood legally. Her mind in turmoil, she had no idea what to do. Open the door or stay as quiet as a mouse, hoping Harry would go off to get a locksmith and give Glen and her time to make a hurried escape?

Then she heard a female voice calling out to Harry to let her in. Jan frowned, puzzled. Who was this woman who was familiar enough to be calling him by his Christian name and expecting to be let into the house? Had he recovered from the ending of their marriage so quickly that he had already replaced her with someone else? Then Jan heard the voice again, calling out, 'Are you all right, Harry? I know you're in, I can smell cooking. Are you feeling down because of what happened with your wife? Do you want me to fetch the Reverend to come and talk to you?'

Jan bristled then. So this was a member of the congregation, wasting no time in ingratiating herself with Harry. Saw herself as the next Mrs Clayton, did she? Well, Jan was going to put a spanner in the works!

She unlocked the door, opened it and addressed the woman with a brusque, 'What can I do for you?'

The visitor was roughly in her late-fifties. Hanging down below her coat Jan could see the bottom of a wrap-around apron. Her greying hair was scraped under a scarf tied turban-style. She eyed Jan in amazement and demanded, 'Who are you?'

Jan stiffened and responded indignantly, 'It's you who should be telling me who you are, being's it's my door you're calling at.'

The woman looked shocked. 'Your door! Oh … so you're Mr Clayton's wife. But what are you doing here?' She sneered at Jan in disgust. 'I understood he had turned you out because he caught you fornicating with another man in his bed.'

Jan was very conscious that she was still wearing the clothes she'd been in the last few days and hoped the other woman wasn't standing close enough to notice. She appraised her visitor, looking her up and down. 'You don't look like a woman who believes everything she hears. It was all a misunderstanding that has now been resolved.'

The other woman exclaimed, 'Oh, I see.' She looked most put out. 'But Harry didn't mention he wouldn't be needing our help any more last night at the Church Council meeting.'

She should have known that the do-gooding widows or spinsters among the congregation would have been fussing and faffing over Harry as soon as they caught wind of his misfortune, thought Jan. She planted a smile on her face. 'Well, you have my deepest thanks for looking after him so well while I've been away.'

'And seeing to any washing he needed doing,

and cooking his evening meal ready for him to warm up when he came in from work,' the other woman told her.

Jan thought that the vicar was as cunning as a fox. Why would Harry need to take his heathen wife back when all his housekeeping was being taken care of so conveniently? No fear then of him disentangling himself from the church, and the vicar losing one of his valued followers. 'Well, thank you for that too,' Jan said stiffly. 'You will excuse me, won't you? I was just making my breakfast and I risk burning it.'

'Oh, yes, of course. I'll be seeing you again to-night then, Mrs Clayton, when I attend the Bible class here with the others.'

I shouldn't count on it, thought Jan as she shut the door and locked it again afterwards.

She turned to make her way over to the stove, hoping the contents hadn't spoiled during the time she had been distracted. She meant to knock on the bathroom door and tell Glen to hurry up when out of the corner of her eye she spotted a movement and spun her head to see a strange man standing outside the bathroom door. He looked jumpy and extremely worried. It took her several moments to realise the stranger could only be Glen. What she saw was a hollow-cheeked, pale-skinned man in his early-fifties, though he could be younger given the harshness of the life he had been leading for the last few years. But then, a few home-cooked dinners would soon put some meat on his bones and fill out his cheeks. To her surprise, Jan thought him even now to be quite a handsome man. Out of his

101

ragged dirty clothes and dressed in clean ones, and once she had tidied his shorn-off hair, she wouldn't be at all embarrassed to be seen out in public with him.

'My God,' she exclaimed, 'what a transformation! If I didn't know it was you, I would never think for a minute you were the same man who went into the bathroom a while ago.'

Glen had never been at all vain but after so many years of being shunned by normal society as a misfit, it was good to receive a well-meant compliment. But of more significance were the possible repercussions of the visit to the house. 'Was that caller I heard something to be worried about?' he asked.

Jan shook her head. 'Not at all. Just a woman from the church who's been doing for my husband now he's seemingly helpless with no wife looking after him. I think it's wise we get going, though, before we tempt fate. Do you mind finishing the breakfast? Give the bacon a fry with the sausages, then put them in slices of bread. That you'll find in the pantry, in the bread bin. Behind the curtain under the sink you'll find a couple of brown paper bags that you can put the sandwiches in. We'll eat them in the park. Meanwhile I'll clean up the bathroom after you then take a quick bath myself, and we'll be off.'

He told her, 'I've already cleaned up after me. I used the tin of scouring powder and the scrubbing brush that was behind the toilet.' He didn't tell her that he'd also used the scrubbing brush to help scrub some of the more stubborn dirt from himself, which had hurt like hell. His skin was still tingling.

Jan looked at him, most impressed, that he didn't seem to think all housework was automatically women's work.

A while later, Glen and Jan were sheltering from the icy winter wind under a covered bench area in the Imperial Avenue Park, about a quarter of a mile away from where Jan had once lived. Having finished their meal, they sat back and sighed in satisfaction. Only sandwiches washed down with water from an empty lemonade bottle Jan had found and filled from the tap before they left, but for Glen the best food he'd had for an age, and Jan in days.

Glen's thoughts were racing. He was now in a presentable state, but without the means to keep up his appearance it wouldn't take more than a couple of days for him to start deteriorating again. He ought to make the most of it now, before it was too late. See if he could land himself a casual job that paid on a daily basis. It didn't matter to him how menial the work was, it would at least get him on the ladder to improving his position in life, a chance he'd never thought to have again. With a bit of money in his pocket, he could afford to live in a hostel and hopefully find some more to purchase a change of clothes. Then he'd be able to wash and keep his clothes in a reasonable state until he saved up enough to get himself some permanent accommodation and from there a permanent job. Then he would start searching for his daughter. It seemed that the saying 'one good turn deserves another' was very apt in this case. He had come to Jan's rescue and she had repaid him by giving him a chance to improve his lot. A feeling he hadn't experienced for over two decades buoyed him up. It was one of hope.

Before he could thank Jan for what she'd done for him, wish her the best and take his leave, she said, 'Right, we've a lot to do, so we'd better be off.'

He looked at her, bemused. 'What do you mean?'

She looked back at him, equally bemused. 'You want to try and get your business back from that thieving ex-wife of yours, don't you, and find your daughter?'

He pulled a doubtful face. 'I told you last night that I don't see there's any chance of getting my business back as I signed everything over to Nerys, but I do want to find my daughter.'

'"Never say never" was a saying of my old gran's. Another of her sayings was "Two heads are better than one". And once we put our heads together, you never know what we might come up with as a way to get back what's rightfully yours. Don't concede defeat until we've at least had a go. Now come on, we have to find ourselves somewhere to live before we can do anything else.'

He looked at her, confused. 'But we've no money between us and...'

A wide grin spread over Jan's face as she told him, 'Oh, yes, we have.'

'But how? I mean...'

There was a note of pride in her voice when she told him, 'While you were in the bath I emptied the pot Harry keeps money in to give to the church. I can also pawn my wedding and engagement rings, which should bring us another few quid. And before you start saying I'd no right to help myself to Harry's church money, that money is intended for use in helping the poor unfortunates of this parish ... and you can't deny that we're about as poor and unfortunate as you can get.'

Glen couldn't argue with that. His thoughts whirled. He felt a certain amount of guilt at being the beneficiary of funds gained in this way. But if he let slip this opportunity to improve his life so drastically, there was no telling when, if ever, another would come along.

He realised Jan was nudging him in the side and turned and said, 'Pardon, did you say something?' He then noticed she was holding something in her hand, expecting him to take it. He looked at it in surprise. It was two pound notes.

'A man needs some money in his pocket. If you feel guilty for taking it, knowing where it comes from, you could always make a donation to the church poor box when you're in funds. Now are you coming or what? We've a lot to do today because I don't intend to spend another night staring up at the stars or huddling in a flea-ridden lodging house.'

Glen accepted the money and smiled at her, saying, 'I'm coming.'

CHAPTER SEVEN

Across town Cait was dragging her weary body down the stairs. Her head throbbed, eyes felt sore, and she knew her face was swollen and blotchy from the amount of crying she had done during the night. She was only up now as she was desperate for a drink of water and a couple of aspirin to ease her headache then she planned to return, cocoon herself in her bedclothes again, and nurse the incredible pain of loss and severe worry for her future that seemed to be over-whelming her.

She was so consumed by her own misery she did not see the suitcases piled by the front door. As she arrived at the bottom of the stairs, her mother, dressed for outdoors, pulling on black calf-leather gloves, came out of the lounge.

Spotting Cait, Nerys shot her a disinterested look and remarked, 'So, you've decided to grace us with your presence.'

It was then that Cait noticed the suitcases. She gawped at them. Her mother had told her that the trip she'd planned to take her father to the specialist clinic was off as Cait had spent too much money on her wedding, so where could they be going?

When she asked her mother, Nerys responded briskly, 'I'm taking your father abroad for his health. Not to the clinic of course, as your selfishness has ruled that out, but somewhere warmer than here.' At this Cait frowned. But her wedding had only been called off yesterday evening. There had not been enough time for her mother to arrange a trip overseas at such short notice, surely? Then the awful truth dawned. Her parents had never had any intention of attending her wedding!

Before she had time to deal with the hurt and pain caused by this terrible discovery, her mother's next words reached her.

'When you leave on Saturday make sure you put your keys through the letterbox.'

In the circumstances she was facing, Cait couldn't believe her mother was still expecting her to leave home so soon. She implored her, 'Oh, but Mother, I'm not sure I can go it alone just now... Can't I stay here for a little while longer at–'

Nerys cut in, 'There's no quicker way to get over a setback than keeping yourself busy, physically and mentally. Settling yourself in your own place is just the thing to do that. Staying off from work today, wallowing in self-pity, is not the way to get over a disappointment. You need to pull yourself together, Caitlyn. You're eighteen in a few days and it's about time you started acting like an adult, not a child always looking for sympathy.'

That was one thing she wasn't doing – looking for sympathy where she knew she'd not get any. Cait felt she was not at all ready to make her own way in the world, but at least in her own place she could cry and wail as much as she needed without being made to feel she was being pathetic. She still did not want to move into the house that she and Neil had rented together, but as matters stood it seemed she had no choice until an alternative presented itself. Tomorrow, when she felt a little better, she would write a letter to him, telling him what she planned to do and that she would sort out the change of tenancy with the agents. As for the furniture and other items they had collected together, albeit mostly through presents from his relatives, hopefully he would donate it all to her as he had been the one to call their wedding off. Thinking of him, she felt a fresh flood of tears threaten and took several deep breaths to fight them away, knowing if she did allow them to flow she would only irritate her mother further and receive more unsympathetic words from her, and she'd had enough already.

She asked, 'How long will you and Father be away?'

Nerys looked at her blankly. 'For as long as we need to be.'

'But ... but what about me, Mother?'

She arched an eyebrow. 'What about you?'

'Well, if you and Father aren't here, that will mean I'll be spending Christmas and my birthday on my own.'

Nerys eyed her sharply. 'How selfish you are to be thinking of yourself when your father's health is at risk.' There was a knock on the front door. 'That'll be the taxi. Dalby!' she called sharply. An elderly woman wearing a working dress with a faded wraparound apron over the top, her iron-grey hair cut in a short bob and secured behind her ears with kirby grips, came scurrying out of the kitchen. Nerys instructed her, 'Answer the door to the driver and inform him we won't be a moment, then take the luggage out for him to load.' As the older woman hurried to obey her orders, Nerys told her daughter, 'Go and tell your father that the taxi is here. He's in our bedroom. And don't let the taxi driver see you still dressed like this at this time in the morning.'

Cait turned and ran back up the stairs, out of eyeshot of anyone standing at the front door. She called down to her mother, 'How do I contact you while you're away?'

'You won't be able to. We're going on a tour of the Middle East and will be moving around a lot. Now, I asked you to fetch your father.'

Her sense of loneliness mounted as she went off to do her mother's bidding. Arriving outside her parents' bedroom door, she raised her hand to rap on it just as her father opened it and came out, dressed for travel in a camel cashmere heavy coat over a smart grey wool suit, handmade shoes on his feet, obviously having heard the taxi arrive. He greeted Cait, in his thin weedy voice, with, 'Bring my travel bag down.'

She picked it up and followed him back down the stairs. As she handed it to him in the hallway, she said, 'I hope you have a nice time on your holiday, Father.'

'I'm sure I shall,' he responded shortly as he turned and headed out of the door.

Her mother meanwhile had disappeared into the living room and Cait heard the sound of the key turning in the writing bureau, informing her that Nerys had collected something from inside it. She returned to the hall just as Agnes Dalby came puffing back in after several trips conveying the luggage to the taxi driver to stow away.

Nerys held out a brown envelope towards her employee. 'This is your pay to date. I shall contact you when we get back so that you may resume your duties.'

The older woman looked at the envelope, befuddled for a moment, before she fixed quizzical eyes on her employer and said, 'Er ... you're laying me off while you're away then, Mrs Thomas?'

Nerys gave a snort of derision. 'I'm sure you don't expect me to pay you for sitting around doing nothing.'

With that she turned and walked out of the front door, leaving her daughter and employee staring blankly after her.

A minute or so later, Agnes Dalby was sitting at the worn pine table, sipping on a cup of hot strong tea. She was inwardly seething. Mrs Thomas was well aware that the wage she paid her, which could hardly be classed as generous, was badly needed to supplement her widow's pension and enable her to survive, yet she had thoughtlessly dispensed with her services while she was away and expected Agnes to come scurrying back as soon as she was summoned on their return. How Agnes wished that meantime she could manage to get herself another job so that she would have the great pleasure of telling Mrs Thomas where she could stick hers. The chances of that were slim, though, as few people were willing to take on a woman two years past retirement age, no matter if she was still spritely

110

for her years.

From the first day she had started working for Mrs Thomas and experienced the way she treated those she employed Agnes had deeply regretted applying for the position, but at the time she'd been recently widowed, traumatised by the loss of her beloved husband and, with no skills other than the ones she had acquired caring for her family, had been grateful to be given a job of any kind when she had little money coming in. Despite looking for alternative employment over the years with people who would better appreciate her, she was always pipped to the post by someone younger or with better qualifications. Several years ago Agnes had accepted the fact that unless a miracle happened she was stuck with Mrs Thomas until it was impossible for her to work any longer. Thankfully, over the years she'd had the sense to put away whatever she could spare for a rainy day. It seemed that had arrived so at least she would be able to ride out her monetary famine until her employer returned, so long as she was careful with it.

Movement nearby caught Agnes's attention and out of the corner of her eyes she watched Caitlyn Thomas, back against the sink, face the picture of misery, swallow two aspirin tablets with water. Agnes had mixed feelings about the young woman. She treated Agnes with little or no respect, but then she was only acting towards her as her mother did. She hadn't been taught any better. The girl had been very young when Agnes first came to work for the Thomases just after they had moved here in fact. The child had been such a happy and contented little thing then, reminding her very much of her own daughter, Gladys, who had been just like her as a baby and, under her parents' guidance and nurturing, had grown up into a very kind and thoughtful woman. Unfortunately for Caitlyn, she'd been born to the kind of parents who, in Agnes's opinion, were totally self-absorbed and obviously saw their child as an inconvenience. It had distressed her greatly to witness the way that Mr Thomas barely acknowledged his child's existence, and Mrs Thomas's idea of motherhood was doing the absolute basics for her daughter and nothing more, and even those had halted as soon as the child was old enough to take on the tasks for herself.

Agnes had lost count of the number of times she had had to restrain herself from going up to the nursery when the child's cries went unanswered. Her mother was otherwise occupied with her father, and Mrs Thomas never dropped anything for anyone when her husband was in need of her attention. Agnes wanted to scoop the child up into her own arms and just cuddle her, something she knew the girl was starved of. She dare not, though, in case she was perceived as taking liberties. All she could do was turn a deaf ear to the cries and immerse herself in her work.

The Thomases were an odd couple, to her way of thinking. Mr Thomas she didn't have much to do with so really couldn't make much of. She only saw him in passing as she was performing her duties around the house, and the most she got out of him was a curt good morning or after-

112

noon in that whiny voice of his, and then he would act as if she wasn't there while she carried on her work around him. It had always been a source of great curiosity to Agnes, though, that a woman like Nerys Thomas, who was very attractive with film-star looks in the mould of Elizabeth Taylor, and could have had her pick of men, had settled for a wishy-washy dull little man like Samuel Thomas. But she clearly doted on him, pampered and fussed over him as if he was a china doll, and he certainly lapped up the attention he received and doted as much back on her. For Agnes it was quite nauseating to witness the way they would snuggle close together, she smoothing a tender hand down the side of his face, him simpering back at her. To her it wasn't natural that two people should be entirely caught up with one another, so much so that if one died she had a feeling the other wouldn't last long.

What she couldn't understand either was the way Mrs Thomas hardly ever left the house, except to go to the beauty parlour, clothes shopping, to the library once a week to collect books for them both, and once a month on a Wednesday out for a couple of hours – though where she went, Agnes had no idea. They loved their garden, which was looked after by a man who came in three times a week, and in fine weather would sit together in the shade of the oak tree reading their books, and in winter wrap up warm and link arms, taking slow strolls around the grounds. Apart from that, neither of the Thomases seemed interested at all in the outside world. This holiday they were taking had come as a great surprise to

Agnes as during her time with them they had never travelled before. The concern about Mr Thomas's health must be serious then. To her knowledge they had no friends and made no effort whatsoever to make any. After they'd moved in fifteen years ago, when Agnes had first started employment with them, she had witnessed neighbours round about soon getting the message that any invitations they made to the Thomases would not be taken up, and they'd certainly receive none back. It seemed to Agnes that they were content in their own little world together and neither needed nor welcomed anyone else into it, not even their own daughter.

She was sincerely sorry about the fact that the young woman's marriage had been called off. From what she had glimpsed of Neil when she had answered the door to him, he seemed a very personable sort and Cait herself was clearly besotted with him. However had she managed to explain the reason why he was never invited inside the house, except for once when she had persuaded her parents to allow her to introduce her future husband to them? Agnes had been present, serving the tea, and was struck by the lack of interest the Thomases showed in their daughter's fiancé or in the wedding plans. But from the little she had observed of the way Cait was with Neil, Agnes herself hadn't been surprised that he had called off the wedding. She had never come across a man except for Samuel Thomas who seemed to thrive on having his life organised for him by a woman. She had desperately wanted to take Cait aside and warn her that she could lose her intended through her suffocating behaviour towards him, but she had not dared to do so for the sake of her job.

What was really making Agnes's blood boil now was the glaring truth that the Thomases had never had any intention of attending their daughter's wedding. Holidays abroad took a lot of planning so organising this trip must have started many weeks or even months ago. It was apparent from Cait's reaction this morning that she'd had no idea of this state of affairs. If the wedding hadn't been called off, she would have gone off to work this morning, excited at the prospect of her wedding in a few days' time, only to come home tonight to discover her parents gone. What kind of selfish, thoughtless people acted so despicably to their own child? And if their actions weren't terrible enough, Mrs Thomas herself had been closeted in her bedroom early this morning, making telephone calls, and Agnes had become aware what they were about when Nerys finally emerged and instructed her to box up the wedding gown and bridesmaids' dresses plus the accessories. She had fetched them from Cait's room while she'd still been asleep this morning, ready for collection by a delivery man for return to the suppliers, Nerys obviously meaning to recoup the money she had laid out for them.

And as if that wasn't enough for the young girl to be coping with, the Thomases were still expecting her to leave home and make her own way in the world! Agnes was at a loss to understand just why Mrs Thomas would so blatantly want rid of her own daughter. It wasn't like she was much trouble or they had cramped living conditions and needed the space. In truth Agnes should be glad that with Caitlyn gone from the household it would be one less person for her to be cooking for and clearing up after, but in light of her memories of the sweet-natured child she'd first encountered all those years ago, who'd the potential to grow into a lovely young woman given a little love and encouragement, she couldn't help but feel deeply worried about and sorry for her.

Seeing Caitlyn now looking utterly desolate, Agnes couldn't help but offer the young girl some kind words.

'Forgive me if you think I'm being impertinent, Miss Thomas, as I don't intend to be, but I'm very sorry to hear your wedding is off.' She immediately wished she hadn't spoken as she could plainly tell the young woman was fighting desperately with herself not to break down in front of her. Agnes was well aware that her mother had instilled in Cait the belief that displays of emotion were vulgar. She had to stop herself from going over and putting an arm around the young woman, offering her some comfort, but that would definitely be deemed as stepping out of her place.

Agnes tried to find something positive to say in an effort to cheer her up. 'I'm sorry too that you'll be leaving the house. But having your own place, you'll be able to stay out as late as you like and have no one waiting up worrying about your whereabouts and giving you a telling off when you get home.' Then she could have bitten out her tongue as the look that clouded Caitlyn's face told

Agnes what she herself should have known. The Thomases hadn't cared enough about her to do any such thing.

Deep down, Cait very much appreciated Agnes's efforts to make her feel better. In fact, she would have liked nothing more than to throw herself into the old woman's arms, feel her wipe away her tears and tell her that everything would be all right, but if it ever got back to her mother's ears then she'd suffer Nerys's displeasure. So Cait merely informed Agnes that she was going back to bed and left the kitchen.

Once she had tidied up there was no reason for Agnes to remain here any longer, considering she wasn't being paid. She should be on her way. She'd never had a complete day off in all the years she had worked for the Thomases and would have no trouble filling the days ahead, but she couldn't help but worry how the young mistress was going to cope on her own, facing the prospect she was. She hadn't eaten today and whether she would be bothered to make herself something, considering the dejected mood she was in, greatly concerned Agnes. You shouldn't grieve on an empty stomach, in her opinion. Caitlyn was capable of putting a sandwich together for herself but anything more than that was beyond her as Mrs Thomas had never thought to make it her business to ensure she could cook even the basics, or was equipped to tackle any other household tasks come to that. Putting a meal together for her to heat up later wouldn't take Agnes long and, all her motherly instincts rising to the fore, she decided to do that before she left.

A very short while later, lying in a foetal position, bedclothes cocooned around her, pillowcase soaked with tears, Cait heard the back door closing as Mrs Dalby took her leave. The house fell deathly silent and a dark cloud of loneliness clamped itself around Cait.

CHAPTER EIGHT

'Well, you seem like a nice couple so the flat is yours, if you want it.'

Jan had already explained to Glen that until they were both earning enough to support themselves separately, they would have to share accommodation or the money she had helped herself to from her husband's fund wouldn't last five minutes. Glen's opinion was that if sharing with Jan for however long meant he didn't have to return to his vagrant life, then he would do what it took.

The small two-bedroomed flat they were viewing wasn't in the best of areas and its condition was poor. It had a small kitchen, the grubby gas stove not appearing to have been cleaned since the day it was installed. On it sat a battered, blackened aluminium kettle. Under the window that looked out into a small cluttered back yard stood a cracked brown pot sink with one large cold water tap, turned green with age. Against a wall stood a grubby-looking yellow kitchenette which would hold all their eating and cooking utensils plus their food. Jan wouldn't be able to bring herself to prepare anything in here until she had given all the appliances a good scrub. There were two small bedrooms, each holding a metal-framed bed, rusting in parts, with a thin mattress and tallboy and in a recess by the boarded-up fireplace a clothes rail where they would hang clothes. The toilet was outside in the yard. The wallpaper in all the rooms was very faded, coming away from the wall in places, and the paintwork was chipped and needing a scrub. The furniture had seen far better days. But it was reasonably priced and vacant, and certainly the best out of the four places they had already viewed.

Glen was aware that living here would be a vast comedown for Jan, having seen the home she had been forced to leave, but to him the thought of a chair to sit in, a bed to sleep in, the means to cook a hot meal, and all undercover ... this place was like a palace. He was just terrified it could all be taken away as quickly as it had been handed to him, and that he'd find himself back on the streets. He was also surprised by the fact that after spending so many years keeping himself to himself, he felt comfortable enough with Jan to drop his guard and be open and honest with her, have faith that her only motive in doing what she was for him was because she sincerely wanted to try and help him get his life back on track. She could so easily have used all the money she had taken for herself. She was indeed a special person and he felt it a great pity that her husband hadn't

119

realised that what he had caught her doing was in fact a cry for help from him, to recognise that his wife was a woman with needs of her own, which he seemed to have forgotten in his grief.

'We'll take it.' Without consulting Glen, Jan clinched the deal with the portly, ruddy-faced landlord, who lived in the flat downstairs with his equally rotund wife. They did seem a nice enough couple, though, and not likely to give their tenants any bother unless they didn't keep up with the rent.

'Good, then I'll get you a rent book, you pay me the necessary and you can move in when you like, Mr and Mrs... er...'

'Trainer,' 'Clayton,' Glen and Jan told him in unison.

With the landlord eyeing them both suspiciously, Jan quickly laughed and told him, 'Don't take any notice of me. It's Trainer. We've only been married twenty years and I still keep referring to my maiden name. Give me another twenty and I might accept the fact that I'm not Clayton any longer.'

The landlord laughed then. 'There're times when I wish my wife would forget she's married and where she lives. Anyway, I'll leave you to have another look round while I sort the rent book out.'

Glen and Jan were both extremely grateful that their new landlord was taking them both at face value and not asking for any references.

A few hours later, Jan handed Glen a cup of tea and sat down wearily in the worn brown moquette armchair opposite him, sipping from her own cup.

'Ah, that's better,' she sighed. 'Tea to your liking, husband dear?' she jocularly asked.

He smiled back at her. 'Perfect.' He leaned back in his chair, resting his feet on the hearth of the tiled fireplace. 'I could get used to this.'

She gave a snort. 'I bet you could! I'm not your real wife, though, so housework is shared between us. All right, Mr Trainer?'

'I didn't need to be asked to help you give this place a scrub, did I? It certainly needed it. When I lived rough I'd nothing to clean up but I did my fair share of sweeping, mopping floors and preparing food in the kitchen when I was in prison. Oh, not to forget the latrines and showers. That wasn't a job for the faint-hearted, believe me.'

Jan shuddered at the thought. There was a twinkle in her eyes, though, when she told him, 'Well, in that case, you can prepare our evening meal because after all that shopping we did for our bits and pieces after we signed for this place, and then setting to to rid it from its dust and dirt, I'm fair whacked out. While you're doing it, I'll put away all that stuff we bought from the second-hand and jumble shops. I really would have liked to give the sheets and blankets we got a wash before we use them tonight, but we'll just have to grin and bear it until I can get down the launderette with them.' She gave a laugh. 'They can't be compared to that dreadful thing you loaned me to keep warm in last night, can they?' Then she cast a glance around the bare walls and shelves. 'I would have liked to have bought a few bits to make this place more homely, but at least we've a roof over our heads. I thought we'd have

121

egg and chips for supper. That suit you?'

'Sounds like a feast to me,' Glen said. 'I assume the plan for tomorrow is that we go hunting for work. I suppose the best place to start is the Labour Exchange. I just hope they don't want to delve too deeply into my past. I don't know what kind of jobs they put an ex-con and vagrant forward for.'

'Most people have some sort of skeleton in their cupboards. I doubt they'll want to know what you were doing twenty years ago, but for the last ten you can tell them that you worked for a firm doing … I don't know … whatever comes to mind … but the owner died and the firm folded so that's why you can't provide any references. It's a lie but told with the best of intentions.' Jan looked thoughtful then. 'I've been thinking about the work situation. Since what we're doing is all in aid of trying to come up with a way for you to get your business back and find your daughter too, would it not be a good idea to check out if there's any work going at your old firm? We might be lucky. After so many years, I doubt there's anyone still working there who would recognise you. But if one of us was working there we might be able to fathom out a way to get ourselves into the boss's office and have a look through his private files for information on your ex-wife's whereabouts. If she has sold the business on, we'd still need the new owner's personal details so we could pay them a visit, using some excuse or other, and get them to part with information about the person they bought the business off.'

Glen looked back at her thoughtfully. 'Mmm, I

see your logic. I don't know how I'd feel, working in the firm I once owned, but I'd lump it if it meant I found out where Lucy was. I still don't think I've a chance in hell of getting my business back, though.'

'Well, you never know, we might find out something about your ex-wife we can use against her – blackmail her into handing everything back. My old gran used to say, "Nothing ventured, nothing gained",' Jan told him.

He smiled. 'Your old gran used to have a lot of sayings, didn't she?'

Jan smiled back at him. 'She was a lovely old dear. Kind-hearted and very compassionate. I miss her so much. She wouldn't have called me a harlot and turned her back on me without hearing my side of the story, like my mother and sisters did. Mother certainly doesn't take after Gran, that's for sure. But as my old gran used to say, "Every cloud has a silver lining". In your case that's true, isn't it? If my mother hadn't done what she did then I wouldn't have been seeking shelter under the arches last night and met you.'

Glen whole-heartedly agreed with her. As he sipped his tea a feeling of trepidation mingled with excitement filled him. Tomorrow could prove another red-letter day for him, should luck be on their side and his old family firm have a vacancy he'd be deemed suitable for. He could, in fact, do any job that was being offered there as after all he used to run the place, but of course they must never become aware of that or it could scupper his chances of finding out any information about Nerys and his daughter.

123

CHAPTER NINE

The next evening Cait sat at the dining table, head in her hands, tears dripping on to a plate of congealed food. The previous evening, when she had finally dragged herself out of bed desperate for a drink, she had been stunned to find a meal left under a plate, ready for her to warm up. Agnes had prepared it for her before she left. Cait couldn't eat it then, the thought of food making her feel sick, but Agnes's show of thoughtfulness towards her, when no one else seemed to care whatsoever, had brought her to tears. She slept deeply from sheer exhaustion and woke the following morning feeling just as wretched as she had when Neil's rejection of her first sank in.

Acutely aware that she would already be in serious trouble for taking a day off work yesterday, and fearful of losing her job, she had forced herself to get up, dressed and go to the office. She hadn't thought that life could get any worse for her, but she had been wrong. All the girls at work had found out that her wedding had been called off and, on top of her heartache, Cait had had to cope with a day of pitying glances and sympathetic words plus the odd snide remark or two.

Not much sympathy from the two girls she palled around with, though. They were both clearly miffed that no wedding meant that they weren't after all going to get the opportunity of bowling over their boyfriends in the type of dress they'd never be able to afford themselves, both secretly hoping that the wedding of their best friend would prompt their two men into proposing also. Neither of them spared Cait's feelings when they made it clear to her that their loyalties now lay with Neil because they didn't want to jeopardise things with their boyfriends. She'd need to look elsewhere now for friends to support her through this rough time.

Her boss, a sour-faced spinster, would not accept the calling off of her wedding as an excuse to take a day off work and informed Cait that her wages would be docked accordingly. The next time she took a day off for such a paltry reason, she would be dismissed.

She had visited the house agents at lunchtime, just catching them before they closed, to request she take over the tenancy of the new house by herself, only to be informed that the landlord would not accept a single tenant whose wage wasn't sufficient to cover the rent and bills. Her sharing with another girl was not an option as the landlord did not want his house ruined by possible parties or strings of boyfriends coming and going, which could upset the neighbours. The only property they had that was in Cait's price range was a miserable tiny bedsitter in a slum area, where those with any sense did not venture during the day, let alone after dark. It seemed the only option she had left was to find herself affordable lodgings.

On arriving home that evening she had gone straight up to her bedroom to change out of her work clothes and, for the first time, noticed that her wedding dress and the bridesmaids' Christmassy red and green gowns were no longer hanging on her wardrobe door. She hadn't moved them so it seemed her mother had wasted no time in recouping what she could of the wedding expenses before she had left on her trip. Cait had no doubt she had cancelled and demanded refunds for everything else she had laid out for too. She'd dragged herself back downstairs and into the kitchen where she went to fetch more aspirin from a shelf in the pantry, along with a glass of water to wash them down with. She spotted another covered plate on the table, with something propped against it. Agnes had written a note to say that she had made herself a cottage pie for dinner, had made too much and brought it round to save Cait from cooking for herself when she got home from work. It just needed heating up.

The tears flowed again. Why was it that their cleaner showed more consideration and sympathy for her than either of her parents seemed able to do? With no stomach for food still, the meal went the same way as the one Agnes had prepared for her yesterday, into the bin. Cait sat down at the table, rested her head on her arms and sobbed until she'd no more tears left.

It was a good while later before she lifted her head and wiped her wet face with the already sodden handkerchief she was clutching. It was pitch dark outside and an icy wind was whistling through the wintry garden. The night stretched endlessly ahead of her. She was in no mood to

126

watch television, listen to the radio or read a book. What she really wanted to do was seek the sanctuary of her bed, hopefully to sleep dreamlessly for a few hours and be released from her heartache and worries. But that would not find her somewhere to live. She had bought the *Leicester Mercury* on her way home. The sensible thing for her to do now would be to scour the accommodation advertisements, to see if anyone was offering lodgings she could afford in a suitable area. But before she could get up off her chair to fetch the newspaper from the table in the hall there was a rapping on the front door. Her heart pounded. Dare she hope that her caller was Neil?

Jumping up, she dashed to the front door, yanking it open, the look of expectancy on her face rapidly fading to one of confusion when she found a middle-aged man facing her.

'Miss Thomas?' he asked.

Warily she answered, 'Yes.'

He pointed to a large carton standing on the step. 'Delivery for you.'

He made to turn away, but with a bemused look on her face Cait stopped him. 'What's in the box?' she asked.

He looked at her as though she was stupid. 'How should I know? I'm just the taxi driver delivering it to you.'

She stared at it for several moments, wondering what could possibly be inside. There was only one way to find out. The box was large and heavy and she had to heave it inch by inch over the doorstep and into the hall, damning the driver for showing no manners and leaving her to struggle.

The box was taped up and she had to go and fetch a knife from the kitchen. She was very curious indeed by now as to what the box held. On opening the cardboard flaps, she stared at the contents with her emotions raging. Was someone having a joke with her, sending her items of household equipment when it must be common knowledge by now that she and Neil were no longer setting up home together? Then she saw an envelope with her name written on it sticking out from under a pile of tea towels. Pulling it out, she opened it up and her stomach dropped. It was from Neil's mother, telling her that he had asked for help in clearing out the house they would not now be occupying and this box contained all the items Cait had personally bought. She finished off by saying she hoped she hadn't missed out any and wishing Cait the best for her future.

A flood of fresh tears rolled down her cheeks. Receiving back the items that she had saved up for and bought so excitedly to help her look after Neil as she felt a wife should was like another nail in her coffin. She couldn't take any more disappointment today. She ran upstairs to her room where she pulled off her clothes, leaving them heaped on the floor, flung herself into bed and cocooned herself inside the covers.

CHAPTER TEN

Glen's stomach was churning as they turned the corner of the street where the factory stood. He was willing there to be a vacancy that would get him inside legitimately and his quest off to a start, otherwise he had no idea how they would ever unearth Nerys's whereabouts.

As they had travelled here old habits had surfaced. Without his thinking about it, whenever they had encountered other pedestrians Glen had automatically ducked his head and made to give them a wide berth, to save himself the embarrassment of their doing so, until Jan had pulled him to a halt and reminded him in no uncertain terms that he was no longer the filthy individual of yesterday morning but now a smart-looking man. Although the shirt, suit and raincoat he was wearing were all second-hand, he felt he was the smartest he'd been since swapping civilian clothes for a prison uniform. His shoes were a little tight, though, and pinched his toes. He also felt naked without his thick covering of facial hair which, in weather like this, had kept his face warm. It would take him a while to get used to being clean-shaven.

As they drew closer, a young woman came out of the door leading into the reception area to stand in front of a glass-fronted box attached to the wall. Opening it up, she took out several cards then replaced them with a few others.

Glen said to Jan, 'The vacancy box is being updated.'

She said enthusiastically, 'Seems we've arrived at the right time then.'

They slowed their pace until the woman had finished her task and returned inside. They then hurried through the big iron gates and across a cobbled forecourt to the box where they scanned the contents. There were five vacancies in all.

Jan said, 'Well, I'm starting to think there is a God. Two of the vacancies are right up our street! The general dogsbody for you, only they've labelled it maintenance man, and canteen assistant for me.'

Glen looked at the cards thoughtfully. It was a job he could do thanks to his father, who had made him learn the business inside out, from top to bottom.

Jan was saying, 'Maintenance man is perfect as you'll have free licence to roam as you like under the pretext that something needs fixing. As a canteen assistant, hopefully I'll get the job of taking the tea trolley round the offices for elevenses and afternoon tea, and then I'll get the opportunity to have a nose around the boss's office when he's not there. So, ready to go in and apply?'

'As I'll ever be,' he told her.

It was like stepping back in time for him as they entered the reception area. The place hadn't changed at all. If he recalled correctly, the same paint was on the walls, although it looked tired, scuffed and chipped in places and cried out for redecoration. In front of them a staircase rose up to the second floor where the offices were. A door to one side of the staircase led to the factory part of the building and the store rooms. To the other side of the staircase was the desk where the receptionist sat. Behind her, set against the wall, was a small six-line plug-type telephone board. Further down, a row of six straight-backed chairs was placed against one wall for visitors to sit on while they waited to be seen. With her headset on, a plug cord in her hand, her back to them, the receptionist was busy telling a caller to hold the line for a moment while she connected them. That done, she swivelled around in her chair to continue typing a letter on the Imperial 66 typewriter that stood on the desk, which she'd been in the process of doing before the switch-board had bleeped. She jumped, on spotting the two arrivals, not having heard them come in.

She was a young girl, twenty at the most, dressed smartly in a plain navy skirt and white blouse under a pale blue cardigan, her brown hair fixed neatly in a French roll. She looked very efficient. She smiled politely at Jan and Glen and asked, 'What can I do for you?'

It was Jan who took the lead. 'I've come to apply for the job of assistant in the canteen.'

'I'd like to apply for the position of maintenance man,' Glen told her.

'You'll have to make appointments. I'll call the manager's secretary to see to it for you. Could I have your names, please?'

When they had given them to her she turned to face the switchboard again, dialled an internal number then after a moment spoke into the mouthpiece, eventually writing something down on a notepad. Swivelling back, she told Jan and Glen, 'The manager is very busy now but if you're prepared to wait, he'll be able to fit you in in about an hour.'

'We'll wait,' Jan told her.

They took chairs in the waiting area, Jan wishing she had brought a book with her to while away the time, Glen thinking that these chairs were the same ones that were here when he was in charge of the place. If Nerys did still own the firm she certainly hadn't authorised any expenditure towards the upkeep of the premises, it seemed. He also wished right now that he smoked, as he could do with something to calm his nerves.

Their thoughts were suddenly distracted when the door opened and a middle-aged woman came in. She wore a shabby black coat, the Crimplene dress she had on underneath hanging down several inches below its hem. Her thick stockings had many snags in them and her shoes were scruffy and down-at-heel. She wore a turban-style scarf on her head, several pink rollers showing in the middle of her forehead.

The receptionist greeted her with the same courtesy she had shown to Glen and Jan.

Jan frowned when she heard the woman tell the receptionist that she wanted to apply for the job of canteen assistant. To Jan she didn't appear to have made any effort to impress a prospective employer with the way she dressed. She was, though, mortally glad that as she had arrived first, she'd get first shot at landing the job. It was up to her to make sure she did.

Having called the boss's secretary, the new arrival was told by the receptionist that if she was prepared to wait, then the manager would interview her for the position after he'd seen the couple already waiting.

The woman shambled over and sat herself down beside Jan, saying to her, 'You haven't come about the job in the canteen, have yer?'

Jan looked at her, wondering what it had got to do with her. 'As a matter of fact, I have.'

The woman folded her arms under her ample bosom and, with a smug look on her face, said, 'Then yer wasting yer time, me duck. The job is mine. Me friend works in the canteen, she's in charge actually, and she's recommended me for the job, so there's no chance of you gettin' it.'

Jan eyed her sharply. 'We'll see about that.'

There was a look of challenge in the other woman's eyes when she retaliated, 'Yeah, we bloody well will!'

It was Glen who was called for first by the manager's secretary, a pleasant-faced, middle-aged woman dressed in a tweed suit and stout shoes. She came downstairs to fetch him. As he got up he flashed a look at Jan as if to say, 'Wish me luck,' before following the grey-haired woman back up the stairs, along a corridor and into the office with a plaque on the door announcing 'Manager'.

Glen knew this office like the back of his hand. It had been his father's first, then his. It hadn't changed one bit. The walls were still lined with oak panelling; it had the same large mahogany desk and cracked red leather wing-back chair

133

behind it. A very comfortable chair, Glen remembered. The same large worn Chinese rug covered most of the dark-stained floorboards. The only change that Glen could see was that the old portrait of King George had been taken down from the wall and replaced by one of the young Queen Elizabeth II, showing her on her Coronation Day two years ago in 1953, having succeeded to the throne on the death of her father. In the leather chair where by rights Glen should have been sitting was a besuited man of about sixty. He had a strained expression and a tired look in his eyes, but regardless he smiled a welcome at Glen and stood up to shake his hand. 'Reginald Swinton, Manager,' he introduced himself.

Glen said a silent prayer before he responded, hoping his name meant nothing to Reg Swinton. 'Trainer. Glen Trainer. I'm pleased to meet you, sir.'

Reg looked taken aback for a moment. 'Trainer? Same name as the man who owned the company before my boss bought it. He turned out to be a rum character indeed. Seems he wasn't happy with the profits the firm was making him and was caught using the place to store goods he'd stolen from a hijacked lorry, critically injuring the driver in the process. He served quite a lengthy sentence for what he did. Could still be inside, for all I know. Looking at you, though, I can see you're no more capable of doing something like that than I am, and it's just a coincidence you share the same name. Right, let's get down to business. Please take a seat.' He

134

waited while Glen settled himself before continuing. 'So, Mr Trainer, I understand from my secretary you've come about the maintenance position?'

Glen was very relieved that he'd got over the name hurdle and hadn't had to lie his way out of it. He nodded eagerly. 'Yes, that's right, sir.'

The other man grinned. 'I'm not titled gentry, Mr Trainer. Please just address me as Mr Swinton.' Reg Swinton then ran his fingers inside the collar of his shirt. 'It's hot in here, isn't it? Do you mind if I open a window?'

Glen didn't think it was hot at all, but Mr Swinton did appear flushed. He told him he had no objection and tried not to shiver as an icy draught blew through the open window, seeming to make straight for him.

Back in his chair Reg Swinton said, 'Right, what I'm looking for is someone who's capable of fixing the machines in the factory when they break down and seeing to all the other maintenance work in the place, down to changing light bulbs. Question is, are you the man I'm looking for?'

Glen responded without hesitation, 'I'd say so, Mr Swinton. There's nothing I can't tackle, from unblocking toilets to sweeping up if the cleaner is off for any reason. And there's nothing about the machines in the factory that I don't know about and can put right.' He could have kicked himself for adding that.

Reg looked at him sharply. 'I haven't shown them to you yet so how do you know that? Have you worked here before? If you have, it was before my time as I pride myself on knowing all my employees.'

Glen blustered, 'No ... no, I haven't. I was just assuming the machines were the same as I looked after in my old job for a shoe firm. Made by the British United Shoe Machinery Company on Belgrave Road. But, of course, one machine is not unlike another when it comes to repairs.'

'Well, I can't repair machines so I wouldn't know and will have to take your word on that,' Reg told him. 'You say you worked for a company similar to this?'

How Glen hated lying but it was so important to his cause that he landed this job. 'Yes, in Northampton. Ten years I worked for them. They made bespoke shoes but didn't import from other countries like Rose's does.'

Reg looked impressed by this. 'You have done your homework, knowing we import shoes as well as make them. So why did you leave your last post?'

Glen couldn't help but notice that his prospective employer was sweating profusely now, had taken a large handkerchief out of his jacket pocket and was wiping beads of moisture from his face with it. He wanted to enquire of him if he was all right as in truth it was really quite cold in here now and he should by rights be shivering, as Glen was trying hard not to do. But that could be seen as impertinence and he didn't want to risk losing the job because of that.

'Had no choice, Mr Swinton,' he said. 'The old man who owned the firm died, and with no one to take over the reins it just folded. That's why I can't give you any references, I'm afraid.'

'Well, I'm not sure references are worth the paper they're written on myself. Any boss can write down that the employee he's referencing is the best he's ever had, trustworthy and reliable, when in fact they are nothing of the sort. It's just that they're wanted rid of, and sometimes the best way to do that is to try and help an un-wanted worker get taken on somewhere else.'

Glen sighed inwardly with relief that he seemed to have passed that hurdle, then held his breath and crossed the fingers of both hands in the hope that the question he feared he would be asked next didn't come: whether he'd ever been in trouble with the law.

Reg Swinton obviously thought he looked honest enough not to insult Glen by asking him such a thing. Instead he asked, 'If you're from Northampton, what brings you to Leicester?'

Glen hadn't anticipated that question and his mind went blank for a moment before he blurted, 'Oh, er ... just a change of scene.'

Reg seemed to think that reason enough. 'Well, I need to fill this vacancy as soon as I can as my last man left yesterday without warning. Got an engineering job elsewhere with an immediate start. He was a good man and I didn't like losing him.'

He studied Glen for a moment. 'I like the look of you, Mr Trainer. You don't seem to me like a man who says he can do something when he can't. I really should show you around the place before I ask you to make a decision, check that you're happy with what you see, but I haven't got the time right now. Other people to interview for the jobs we have going, and I've a customer coming in at eleven, too. Would you consider taking the job, though, with a view to starting tomorrow if you can?'

Glen fought with himself not to jump up and give the man a hug of gratitude. Regardless of his main reason for wanting a job with this particular company, he still needed one in order to survive and he liked this man, felt he'd be a good boss to work for. They went over a few formalities, then shook hands on the deal.

Glen made his way back down the stairs. When he saw Jan, she was looking up at him with an enquiring look. He flashed her a brief smile, hoping that would tell her that he'd been successful. Reg Swinton's secretary was now hurrying past him, on her way to bring Jan up to the office. As she passed Glen at the bottom of the stairs, he whispered to Jan, 'I'll wait for you down the road. Best of luck.'

While she made her way up the stairs behind the secretary, Jan was aware that the other woman who'd come after the canteen job was looking daggers at her.

Fifteen minutes later she came hurrying down the street to join Glen, who was waiting for her perched on a low wall. She had a worried expression on her face and he automatically took that to mean she had not been successful. As she reached him Jan gave a violent shiver and said, 'Brrr! It was as cold in that office as it is out here. Did Mr Swinton seem all right to you?'

Glen frowned. 'He had a good sweat on and I'd

say he looked tired, but apart from that he seemed all right.'

'Mmm, I think he's sickening for something myself,' Jan mused.

'Well, your concern for the man is commendable, but I take it from the look on your face that you weren't offered the job?'

She smiled triumphantly. 'I certainly was. Start tomorrow. I'm looking worried as I'm concerned about our new boss. He seemed like a really nice man to me. I don't think the woman who came in after me is very happy, though. She was of the opinion that the job was hers as her friend already works in the canteen and has recommended her. Well, she shouldn't have taken it for granted, should she?' Jan rubbed her hands together and said gleefully, 'Anyway, Mr Trainer, seems like the first part of our plan has worked.'

Glen was just happy at this moment to have been given gainful employment and could keep up the new life he was living. The thought of returning to his previous existence did not appeal one little bit. 'I didn't like deceiving Mr Swinton as to the reason why we wanted jobs with this particular firm.'

Jan slapped him on his arm. 'Sometimes we have no choice but to do things we aren't happy with. That's life. Come on, let's get out of this cold and go and celebrate with a cup of tea and a slice of cake in a café. I think we should splash out now we're both earning and have pork chops for our dinner tonight.'

Glen wasn't sure whether the money she'd taken had been meant to be spent on such luxuries. Nevertheless, his mouth watered at the thought of a pork chop – something he hadn't had for years.

He hurried after her.

CHAPTER ELEVEN

The next day at work seemed to drag on for ever to Cait, each minute seeming like a hundred. Her sour-faced boss had still not forgiven her for taking a day off without just cause, as well as for the fact that she hadn't as yet caught up with her work. Last night yet again her sleep had been anything but restful, and so her day had been one long struggle. She was mortally relieved when home-time came as she was desperate to leave, make herself a cup of tea and drink it while she scanned the Accommodation pages in the *Mercury,* hoping to find something that was suitable for her. Then she'd have a long soak in the bath and go to bed.

As she let herself in at the front door she heard movement coming from the kitchen and froze rigid. Her parents were away, the daily laid off until they came back, so the house should be empty. There was no other explanation for a presence in the house other than burglars. She felt a rising sense of panic and decided she needed to alert the police. Cait made to depart for the telephone box at the end of the avenue, but the clanging of a cup on a saucer and the tinkling of a teaspoon made her stop in her tracks. Was the burglar making themself a cup of tea? Then the appetising aroma of beef stew reached her and she realised that the 'intruder' in the kitchen had to be Agnes Dalby. Had she forgotten she was not supposed to be here?

Hearing the front door, Agnes came scurrying out of the kitchen to find Cait taking off her coat and shoes. She had a worried expression on her face as she said, 'Oh, Miss Thomas, you're home at last.'

'This is my usual time for getting home,' Cait reminded her as she put on her slippers. 'More to the point, what are you doing here?'

Agnes had fully expected this question and was prepared for it. 'When I got home yesterday I remembered a few chores I hadn't done that couldn't be left until your parents came back, so I came in to see to them. I thought while I was here I might as well see to any laundry you had and cook you a meal, Miss Thomas.'

The thought of food had made Cait feel sick recently, but she was surprised to find that this time the appetising smell of the stew was making her mouth water and stirring pangs of hunger in her stomach.

Before she could make any response, Agnes was saying to her, 'I must tell you, Miss Thomas, that there's been an extremely urgent telephone call for Mrs Thomas, and as she's not here, I need to tell you about it.'

Cait asked her, 'Who was it from?'

'A woman. She said she was calling from the company.'

141

Cait stared at her, non-plussed. 'What company?'

Agnes shrugged. 'I don't know. The woman just said she was calling from Mr Swinton's office at the company. She said something terrible had happened that only Mrs Thomas could deal with and she needed to come in as soon as possible. I told the woman that Mrs Thomas was away abroad and I wasn't sure when she'd be back. She said the situation was urgent and would we send Mrs Thomas's representative. As Mrs Thomas's daughter that would be you, wouldn't it?'

Cait was bemused by it all. 'What company could possibly have such a dreadful problem that only my mother could resolve it? This has to be a mistake,' she told Agnes. 'Either you got the wrong end of the stick or the person on the other end has mixed my mother up with another Mrs Thomas.'

Agnes tried to hide how insulted she felt to be told she wasn't capable of taking a simple message. 'I can assure you the message I've given you, Miss Thomas, is exactly as it was given to me. I did actually ask if a mistake might have been made and it was another Mrs Thomas she was after. The woman told me she found Mrs Thomas's contact details in Mr Swinton's private files, so she did have the right person. She has called three times since to check when Mrs Thomas's representative will be arriving to deal with matters. She sounds more frantic each time. I kept telling her I'd get you to telephone her as soon as you came home. I've been in such a quandary as to whether or not to telephone you at

142

work, Miss Thomas, but I knew you wouldn't be allowed private telephone calls there and could get into trouble, so I had no choice but to wait until you got home this evening.'

Cait didn't feel in the mood to deal with anything other than running herself a bath at the moment, but supposed she really ought to get to the bottom of this situation. She stepped over to the table with the large black Bakelite telephone on it, a pad and pencil by the side. Seeing nothing was written on the pad, she turned back to face Agnes. 'Where is the woman's telephone number?'

'She didn't give me one.'

Cait snapped at her, 'Then how am I supposed to telephone her back?'

'Oh, I assumed Mrs Thomas would have it in her telephone book.'

Something that Nerys never let out of her sight, though Cait had always suspected that all it held were the numbers for her hair stylist and beauty parlour as those were the only people she had ever overheard her mother calling. 'Which she will have taken with her,' Cait retorted now. 'Well, no matter how critical this woman's situation is, I can't do anything about it. Should she telephone back tomorrow, please ensure you get a number from her this time.'

Agnes hoped the sarcasm didn't show in her tone of voice when she responded, 'I'll make sure I do. I'll go and put your dinner out then I'll be off home.'

Her mother would never consider it proper to thank an employee for doing anything for her as

143

they were paid to do so. But what Agnes had done today for Cait she wasn't being paid for, and Cait felt the least she could do was show the older woman she appreciated her thoughtfulness.

She called after her, 'Thank you for cooking for me amid all your other chores.'

A shocked Agnes froze in her tracks for a moment, thinking she was hearing things, before she turned and smiled at Cait and said, 'My pleasure.' In her surprise at actually being thanked for something she had done after all the years she had worked here unacknowledged, she nearly forget herself and added 'love', but remembered her place just in time and instead said 'Miss Thomas'.

A while later, feeling lonely in the eerily silent house and wishing Agnes were still here to afford her some company, Cait sat at one end of the large scrubbed pine table in the kitchen, forking small pieces of stew and potatoes into her mouth, surprised to find she was actually enjoying the meal. A copy of the local evening newspaper was open before her. Had her parents been here she would never have dared eat at the kitchen table, let alone read at the same time, but it was far warmer in here than in the large imposing dining room in which she felt overwhelmed. It also felt good to be doing something she wanted to do instead of having to abide by the house rules set by her mother. Her mind, though, was not on the print she was scanning but on the conversation she'd just had with Agnes. Cait couldn't work out why her mother's presence was needed so urgently to resolve a problem at a company. She wasn't aware, had no inkling whatsoever, that her mother was involved in any way in business. But according to Agnes there had been no mistake. Her mother's details had been found in the private files. It was all very confusing but equally intriguing.

Cait frowned. But then, what did she really know about her mother ... about both her parents? Nothing much except that they were orphans and neither of them needed to work as her mother had a private income. She had long accepted that the past was too painful for them to talk about. But surely she had a right to know some bare facts about her own background, no matter how painful it was for them to tell her. Her need to find a place to live was suddenly overridden by a great curiosity about her own family background. With her parents away, this might be her only opportunity to see what she could uncover.

Her parents must both have birth certificates. At least from those she would be able to find out the names of both sets of grandparents, which was more than she knew now. There might even be a photograph or two so she could see what they'd looked like. But where would important papers like that be kept?

When she had needed her own birth certificate to show the vicar before the wedding, her mother had told her she was busy and would get it for her when she had the time. She hadn't been busy at all, was just arranging some flowers she'd cut from the garden. Cait had apologised to her for not asking for it before but said she really did need it right then as Neil and she were off to see the vicar, and nothing could proceed apparently until he had seen her birth certificate. So Nerys had gone upstairs to her bedroom in a mood, telling Cait to wait down here. So that was where she obviously kept things of importance – somewhere in her bedroom.

Her parents' bedroom had always been out of bounds to Cait. She was never allowed in there except when her mother expressly sent her up to do something for her. She had never dared venture into that private sanctuary unbidden before, for fear of the repercussions should it come to light, but now she had nothing to lose, had she? And there was no one here to witness her intrusion. As long as she left the room exactly as she had found it, no one would be any the wiser. Except herself if she was fortunate enough to find the information she was seeking.

Leaving the kitchen, Cait went upstairs and along the landing to stand outside her parents' bedroom door. She reached out to take hold of the knob but withdrew her hand in a flash as a vision of her mother's face swam before her, a look of severe reprimand on her face, reminding Cait this room she was about to enter was forbidden to her. Nerys was hundreds of miles away by now, but regardless her grip on Cait was still an iron one. Nevertheless, Cait's need to fill in the blanks of her past spurred her on. Defiantly she grabbed the knob, turned it and walked purposefully inside the room.

The moonless evening was dark. Light from the street lamps did not reach the house as it was set

146

well back from the road. Despite the fact there was no one to witness her intrusion into her parents' private sanctum, Cait still felt guilty and went to pull the curtains tight across before she dare switch on the light, blinking to accustom her eyes as light flooded the room.

Then she cast her gaze around. It was a large room, the size of two bedrooms in most people's houses. The paper on the wall behind the bed was of roses in shades of pink. The rest of the walls had been lined in heavy Anaglypta paper painted cream. The thick carpet on the floor was cream also. The furniture was all of matching light oak. A big solid wooden-framed bed dominated the back wall. To each side of it stood a small table with a lamp, the shades the exact colour of the heavy green satin counterpane covering the mattress. Two large wardrobes stood against one of the side walls. Obviously one was her mother's, the other her father's. Under the wide window on the wall opposite was a large mirrored dressing table with an assortment of jars of face cream and several perfume bottles arranged on top. It had three deep drawers down each side and a pink covered stool tucked into the gap in the middle.

Cait imagined her mother sitting at it every morning, applying her make-up and attending to her hair before she came down; cleaning her face and brushing her hair before she retired to bed at night. For a moment she wondered what it would have been like to have been allowed to sit and watch her mother, learn tips from her on how to look after her skin, instead of having to glean information for herself by looking through her mother's discarded magazines.

She gave herself a mental shake. She had intruded into this room for a purpose, and moping over things that might have been would not help her achieve that aim.

The dressing table was the obvious first choice. Cait worked her way through the drawers. Two were devoted to silk underwear, a third filled with scarves of every colour and pattern a woman could possibly need. Another held unopened bottles of perfume, face cream, make-up and hair products. It was apparent her mother didn't like to run out of anything. Of the last two drawers, one was filled with packets of seamed stockings in every colour that was made. The last drawer was devoted to jewellery ... rings, necklaces, bracelets, brooches, hair slides. Not all of it was gold but the costume pieces were so well made they would have been taken for real.

The dressing-table drawers did not contain what Cait was seeking.

After checking each drawer to make sure not one thing looked as if it had been disturbed, she went over to the wardrobes. One was slightly shorter than the other and only had one large door; the other side held drawers, eight in all. It was a man's wardrobe. The larger one had double doors and no drawers. A woman's wardrobe. Opening that one, she stared in shock at the number of clothes hanging inside. There was an item for any occasion. Cait was aware her mother had an extensive range of clothes, judging by those she'd seen, but not on this scale. Flicking through them, it struck her that more than half the items here she had never seen Nerys wear. Anger started to flare within her. On Cait's starting work her mother had stopped buying her clothes, telling her that was now her own responsibility. Nerys knew she struggled to clothe herself well on her wages, but had never offered to help her. Her mother used to dress her expensively so having to lower her sights had not been an easy thing for Cait to come to terms with, having to shop at places such as C&A instead of Marshall & Snelgrove. She had been told by Nerys that funds would not stretch to an elaborate wedding and had lowered her sights accordingly, settling for an off-the-peg dress not a specially made one to her own design, the same for the bridesmaids, and a Daimler to ferry her to the church instead of the coach and white horses she would have liked. The reception was booked for the Bell Hotel and not the Grand ... and yet her mother seemed to find the funds to clothe and adorn herself with the best money could buy.

Again Cait reminded herself what she had come into this room for. The bottom of the wardrobe held nothing but a dozen or so pairs of handmade shoes neatly lined up, each pair with a matching handbag. Shutting the doors, she turned her attention to the hat boxes arranged on top. Each held only what it was intended for. Expensive creations, one of which wouldn't have looked out of place in Buckingham Palace, in Cait's opinion. All these clothes and accessories for a woman who never went out socially or entertained, just so she could look good for her husband.

Shutting her mother's wardrobe, she then turned her attention to her father's. Again the clothing was all of top quality, shoes handmade, an array of tasteful cufflinks and tie pins, all gold and jewel-encrusted, but nothing Cait found was of interest to her in her quest. Nor was there anything in her father's tallboy. The only place left in this room where she felt important things might be hidden was under the bed. Down on her hands and knees, she peered under it. To her disappointment there was nothing, not even a speck of dust thanks to Agnes's thoroughness.

It seemed her mother did not keep important documents in her bedroom. The only other place that came to mind was the attic. Cait was back on her feet now and giving a violent shudder. She had only been in there once, as a child. The door to it was always kept locked and her childish imaginings viewed this inaccessible place as somewhere magical where fairies lived, a wonderland such as she'd seen in pictures in her books. She was to find out that it was anything but. One day when she was about six, having been left alone for hours to entertain herself, she had ventured out of the nursery in search of a drink to find the door to her wonderland ajar, and noises coming from up above. Excited that she was about to enter a magical world, she slipped inside and climbed the stairs. She arrived at the top to discover her wonderland looked nothing like the ones in her books. It was a dim cavernous place, curtains of cobwebs hanging from the beams, most of the dusty floor filled with equally dusty discarded furniture, which her mother had got fed up with and replaced, and trunks of old clothes. From a wire in the ceiling above her head hung a single bulb. There was another at the far end of the huge room where the noises she had heard downstairs seemed to be coming from.

Then she froze rigid, her heart thumping in her chest, when behind a broken curtain of cobwebs loomed a huge figure, heading towards her. Cait wanted to run away from this monster that she knew would gobble her up, but her feet wouldn't move. As it neared her, the terrifying figure suddenly stopped and seemed to be staring at her for a moment before a voice boomed, 'This is no place for a little 'un like you, love. Now back down yer go. I've nearly finished fixing the leaking water tank then I'll be out of here meself. For as big and ugly as I am, I can't abide spiders and there's an armyful in here.'

Her monster was just a plumber and her wonderland just a dirty attic where unwanted items were stored. Cait's disappointment had lasted for weeks. She had never been up there since and didn't at all like the idea now, but it was either that or abandon all hope of finding out something about her ancestry.

After taking a look around to make sure nothing seemed amiss, she was heading for the door when she stopped short on spotting a small half-door in one corner of the room, on the wall opposite her parents' bed. It must be a cupboard. She hadn't noticed it before as it was painted the same colour as the Anaglypta wallpaper. Her hopes escalated. This looked promising. She went over, bent down and pulled on the small knob. The door did not budge. Then she noticed the keyhole. Her hopes rose further. Surely this

151

cupboard door would only be locked if what was kept inside was important enough to be kept safe. But where could the key be?

She hadn't come across one when she was searching the room. Cait gave a sigh of frustration as her mind sparked into action. The only option open to her was to make another close search.

She had tried everywhere and just about given up when she pulled too hard on one of the two smaller drawers at the top of her father's tallboy and it fell out, scattering the pile of folded socks and packets of new ones inside on the floor. She was left holding the handle of the tipped-up drawer in her hand. Issuing a loud sigh of annoyance with herself, she knelt down and put the drawer on the floor, proceeding to pick up the scattered socks and hoping her father would not notice anything amiss when he next used the drawer. It was then that she noticed that on the side of the drawer facing her was taped a small key. She had found what she was looking for.

After carefully lifting the tape enough for her to get at the key, she crawled over to the cupboard, put the key in the lock, then turned it and opened the door. Cait stared at what it contained in surprise, not having expected this. It was a small safe. Very solid-looking. She tried the handle, not surprised to find it was locked. Sitting back on her haunches, she scowled as she tried to fathom just where the key for the safe would be secreted. Could it possibly be taped to the side or back of one of the other drawers in her father's tallboy? It wasn't but she did eventually find it behind a loose bit of skirting board to one side of the safe itself.

Her parents seemed to be going to a lot of trouble to hide from prying eyes what they kept in the safe.

Cait found her hands were shaking when she put the thick key into the lock, turned it, then pulled down the heavy lever to open the thick metal door. Her eyes widened when she saw what was inside. The bottom of the safe, at least eight inches thick, seemed just to be a solid metal block, which to Cait was wasted space unless it was there to make the safe much heavier to move should it be discovered by undesirables. It was the piles of bank notes arranged at the front of the metal shelf that first held her attention. There were three of them, in denominations of ten shillings, one pound and five pounds. She took a guess that there must be at least a hundred pounds here altogether, a small fortune to Cait who earned three pounds a week. It was too soon for her mother to have regained anything from her cancelled wedding so this money must just be what was kept in the house for general use. Then she noticed the wooden box tucked away at the back of the shelf. She reached inside and took it out. This must contain what she was seeking.

Sitting back on her haunches, Cait opened it up, thankful that this box wasn't locked either. For a moment she stared at the contents in surprise. Not the documents she had expected to see but something wrapped carefully in tissue paper. Putting the box down on the floor in front of her, she carefully lifted out the tissue-wrapped parcel, then equally carefully unwrapped it. What it revealed made her eyes widen. Several items that must have belonged at one time to a baby. There was a tiny pair of knitted bootees, a white cotton nightdress and a knitted matinee jacket in the same fine wool the bootees were knitted from. These must have belonged to her when she was a baby.

Then she noticed a folded piece of paper inside the box which the tissue parcel had hidden. She picked it up and opened it. It was her own birth certificate The things had been put away in this memory box with such love and care that Cait believed her mother must once have adored her. Why then had that love come to fade and be replaced by the indifference she had showed ever since Cait could remember?

After wrapping the baby mementoes carefully and replacing them inside the box on top of the birth certificate, she locked the safe and returned both keys to where she had found them.

Cait left the room no wiser about her own past than she had been on entering it.

CHAPTER TWELVE

Glen strode purposefully into the reception area at seven-thirty prompt the next morning. Regardless of his own reason for choosing to work here, he was determined to earn his money and not make Reg Swinton regret taking him on.

The factory manager had instructed him to arrive via the works entrance, accessed from the canal tow path, and make his way through to the reception area from there. He would be met and taken down to the maintenance office to be introduced to the other men. As Mr Swinton hadn't arrived yet Glen took a seat to wait for him. As he did so he wondered how Jan was getting on.

Jan had been told to make her way to the canteen kitchen and report to a Mrs Digby who was in charge and would be expecting her. Jan lost her way a couple of times before finally finding her destination and going inside. Her first impression of her boss, Hilda Digby, was not favourable. On Jan's arrival her new boss had been in the process of putting on a clean white overall in the small room at the back of the canteen where the staff kept their personal belongings. She was the sort of woman people think of when picturing a cook: as round as a beachball, with a smaller ball for a head. She appeared to have no neck as it was hidden by heavy jowls. On hearing someone arrive, she turned and looked over. Seeing it was the new recruit, she scrutinised her with small shrewd grey eyes.

Jan immediately judged her to be hard-faced, the type to sit on her fat backside barking out orders while her underlings ran around like headless chickens, doing all the work for which she took the glory. She had wanted her friend to get the job as she was operating money-making scams with the other canteen workers in which her friend was willing to participate, and that might not be the case with a complete outsider coming in. She would make Jan's working life a misery in order to get her to leave, then do her best to ensure it was her friend who was hired this time.

But Jan was working here for something more than a canteen assistant's wage. She was helping a very deserving man try to get his life back together, a man to whom she owed a debt of gratitude because he had saved her from a terrifying situation. In return, she was concentrating all her efforts on helping his rehabilitation and would deal with the consequences of her own marital failure after that. She wasn't going to allow this bully of a woman to jeopardise her future.

Before the cook warned her off, she decided to get in first and warn her instead.

In a meaningful tone of voice, Jan spoke out. 'I got this job fair and square. Your friend shouldn't have taken it for granted she'd be given it just because you'd promised it to her, and she should have arrived early for the interview to avoid the risk of someone else getting in before her. I did, and that's that. What you and the other staff have going on between you here is nothing to do with me. I just want to get on with my job. And you can give me the evil eye like you've just done as much as you like, but you won't scare me. When I leave here it'll be under my own steam, not because you've hounded me out.'

She was then very embarrassed to find out that her assumption about her new boss was completely wrong.

The other woman stared blankly at her for a moment before she said, 'I have no idea who this so-called friend of mine is. It's an old trick though that, love, to frighten off the competition. I haven't

156

the jurisdiction to hire and fire. Only the powers that be have that. If you thought I was giving you the evil eye then I'm sorry. I was just sizing you up for an overall. Size fourteen is my guess. Actually I was wrong to do that first – I should have introduced meself before I did anything else.' She held out her hand in a friendly fashion. 'I'm Hilda – Digby is me last name but we're all on first-name terms here.'

Mortified, Jan accepted her hand and said weakly, 'Pleased to meet you. Janet Clayton. Jan.'

'Was I right?' Hilda asked her then.

Jan looked puzzled. 'About what?'

'Size for your overall?'

Jan smiled in embarrassment. 'Yes. Fourteen it is.'

Kitted out and ready for the off, Hilda took her into the main kitchen area while explaining that there were two other women working alongside them, both part-time from nine until one. In the kitchen, Jan took a good look around. The equipment was old but spotlessly clean. A large gas stove dominated the back wall. Sitting on top of it was the largest frying pan she had ever seen. To each side of the cooker were metal tables; on the shelf underneath one was stacked an assortment of saucepans all larger than the biggest pan in a normal household. Under the other table was an assortment of mixing and preparation bowls. There was a huge metal table in front of the cooker on which all the food preparation was carried out. A door at the far side of the room led into a walk-in larder and cold store. Over the other side of the room, filling its width, was a large counter with various warming trays set inside to keep the food hot during service. At one end of the counter was a shelved glass cabinet holding filled cobs, crisps, chocolate bars and biscuits. At the other end stood a large brass till. To the far side of the counter was a large area filled with Formica-topped tables and wooden chairs, where the workers sat to eat their food.

While Jan had been taking a look around, Hilda had gone off into the cold room and arrived back with an armful of sausages and a stack of rashers of bacon. She gave a jolly chuckle, making her fat jowls wobble, seeing the look on her new recruit's face.

'Yes, it really does look like we cater for the forty thousand in here. You'll soon get used to it. Now let's set to and get these sausages on the go as the daily bread delivery will be here in a minute and I'll show you how we check that off. And best you know ... Bert Braddock – or Bert Bread as we call him – thinks he can charm his way into any woman's underwear with the promise of half a dozen fancy cakes. He probably has ... he's not a bad looker is Bert ... but I'll warn yer, not that I think you're the type that would fall easily for a flirty wink from a good-looking man, Bert's got a wife who'd not think twice about knocking you into next week if she got just an inkling you had designs on him. Thought I'd better mention that.'

She reached over and picked up two knives from a tray at the back of the counter, giving one to Jan. 'Right, first we need to separate the sausages. Like this,' she said, slicing the twisted gut between six of them in a flash quicker than lightning. A

158

thought then seemed to strike her and she stopped what she was doing and looked at Jan questioningly. 'Er ... just what did you mean by *"what you and the other staff have got going on between you here is nothing to do with me"?*'

Jan gawped at her for a long moment before she blustered, 'Oh, er ... did I say that? I don't remember.'

Hilda shot her a look that said: I know you did. 'Well, let me tell you, nothing untoward goes on in my canteen. My books will stand up to any scrutiny. I can account for the last pea. Any wastage, of which there's very little, is marked down too. If any of the staff were caught with light fingers, they'd be reported to the management and got rid of. I'm glad to say in all the years I've been running the canteen, I've never had cause to report anyone. I hope my record won't be broken,' she said to Jan meaningfully.

She responded with conviction, 'Not on my account.' Inwardly she hoped that she didn't end up getting the sack for snooping around before either Glen or she had found out what they were after.

Back in the reception area Glen was becoming concerned. It was approaching eight and Mr Swinton had not yet turned up to meet him. Glen wondered if he'd forgotten, but he hadn't seemed like a man who would forget an arrangement he'd made. Maybe something urgent had come up that was keeping him. Just then he heard the door the other side of the stairs open and someone come in. When they came into view at the bottom of the stairs he saw it was the young receptionist who had dealt with him and Jan yesterday when they had first arrived to apply for the jobs. But instead of the cheery smile her pretty face had sported yesterday, today she seemed very subdued, upset even. Glen wondered if she'd had an argument with her boyfriend the night before.

As she approached her desk she looked surprised to see someone sitting there before she said, 'Oh, yes, of course, you're our new maintenance man. I'd best telephone up to Miss Trucker and ask her what we're to do with you in the light of what's happened. Just give me a moment while I take the switchboard off night service and open the main door.'

Glen felt he had been right after all, judging by what the young woman had just said, and that something had happened that was commanding Mr Swinton's full attention. He watched her as she took a set of keys from a drawer in her desk then hurried over to the reception door, unlocking it. She returned to her desk, sat down in the chair, replaced the keys in the drawer, then swivelled around to face the switchboard. She flicked off the night-service switch, then put on her headset, pushed a plug into a hole and dialled a number. After a few moments she spoke in hushed tones into the mouthpiece then listened for a few moments. Pulling out the plug from the hole, she swivelled back round to address Glen.

'Miss Trucker has asked me to apologise but she's tied up at the moment and can't take you to the maintenance room. She's asked me to telephone Harry Owens the store man who'll be

160

expecting you and will give you a walk around the place so you can familiarise yourself with it. The jobs that are outstanding you'll find written down in a book on the desk in the maintenance room. Just get on with them. Miss Trucker said she'll try and get down later if she can, to find out how you're settling in and answer any questions you might have.' She then proceeded to instruct Glen on how to get to the maintenance room, which of course he already knew, but regardless listened intently.

As he made to depart he thanked her before adding, 'Would you please tell Miss Trucker that it's apparent to me something major has happened that needs all Mr Swinton's attention and he can rely on me to sort myself out.'

To Glen's shock he saw the young woman's eyes fill with tears, her bottom lip tremble. She then uttered, 'Oh, of course, how stupid of me! You wouldn't know, would you? I'm still so upset myself that the fact never even crossed my mind. You see, Mr Swinton...' She paused for a moment to pull a handkerchief out of her cardigan sleeve and blow her nose before she continued. 'Such a lovely man he was, everyone liked him. He won't half be missed. 'Course, it's selfish of us all, we know, but we're all worried about just who will take his place ... well, we could get a right tyrant and...

'Oh, I'm sorry, I'm going off at a tangent, but Mr Swinton had a heart attack yesterday morning. Just after ten-thirty it was. He was found by one of the workers collapsed at the bottom of the back stairs, obviously on his way back to the office

161

after his walk around to see that everything was as it should be in the factory. He died before we could get the ambulance to take him to hospital. We're waiting for Mrs Thomas, she's the owner of the factory, to come and deal with things.'

CHAPTER THIRTEEN

It was the muted shrilling of the telephone down in the hall that jolted Cait out of sleep at just after eight that morning. She had slept badly again and now she had overslept. She was too late to get herself ready and off to work and be there for eight-thirty. This on top of the day she'd taken off without permission would surely result in her dismissal. At this moment, though, she felt so low, she didn't actually care whether she lost her job or not, regardless of the consequences. She could no longer hear the telephone ringing so she turned over and closed her eyes.

An urgent rapping on her bedroom door had her sitting bolt upright and staring over in fright. She was alone in the house so who could possibly be knocking on it? Her answer came in the form of Agnes Dalby, who came bustling in to stand at the bottom of her bed. She had a look of concern on her wrinkled face.

'I'm sorry to disturb you, Miss Thomas, but I was worried about you not coming downstairs this morning at your usual time, being's it's a work day. I was worried you might be ill.' She scrutinised Cait's face. 'You don't look good, Miss Thomas, not good at all. Shall I call for...'

Cait exclaimed, 'You frightened the life out of me! You're not supposed to be here. What are you doing?'

Agnes wanted to tell this angry young woman that she herself couldn't get off to sleep last night for worrying how she was coping, rattling around in this big house on her own, with no one to help her through the disappointment she had recently suffered or check whether she was feeding herself properly, but she didn't know how Cait would respond to this so she lied. 'I realised when I got home last night that I had left my umbrella here. I'll more than likely have need of it before your parents return so I came to fetch it. When I came in, there was no sign that you had been up and about getting ready for work or had any breakfast, just last night's dishes still on the table, so I was worried about you.'

The mention of the dirty dishes brought home to Cait that now she no longer had Agnes to see to all the mundane household tasks, it was up to her to tackle them in the future. The thought of how to go about cooking and laundering and other household chores when she had not a clue how to do them troubled her. She wished she could ask Agnes to show her the basics but daren't risk her mother finding out she had been familiar with the hired help. 'I'll tidy the kitchen later,' she told Agnes.

'I'll see to it while I'm here, Miss Thomas, and I might as well see to cooking you your meals and anything else that needs doing. I've nothing else

163

to do with my time at the moment so it'll be a favour to me to let me be here, instead of twiddling me thumbs at home.' This was another lie Agnes was telling as her daughter in Nottingham had pleaded with her to come and stay for a week or so and spend time with her grandchildren – that was after she had voiced her feelings over her mother's employer laying her off unpaid and without warning. But as much as Agnes loved her daughter and grandchildren there was a great need in her to make sure that this vulnerable young woman was coping on her own before she felt she could go off and enjoy her short period of freedom. Looking at Cait again in concern she said, 'As I said when I came in, you don't look good at all. Shall I telephone for the doctor to come and have a look at you?'

'I doubt he has a magic cure for what I'm suffering from, so don't waste his time,' Cait snapped back, just wanting Agnes to leave her alone so she could snuggle back under the covers and be left with her misery.

The older woman did not look convinced but said regardless, 'If you say so, Miss Thomas. There was another reason I came up to see you. That woman has been on the telephone again. The one who called several times yesterday. She said their situation is getting critical now.'

Cait heaved a frustrated sigh and said irritably, 'And just what *is* their situation?'

'Oh, Miss Thomas, I didn't feel it my place to ask. I did get her name and number this time, though. She's a Miss Trucker and she's calling from Rose's Quality Shoes and Leather Goods.

They're on Bowman's Lane, off Frog Island. It'll be one of those factories backing on to the canal. Miss Trucker ended the call under the impression she would hear shortly when Mrs Thomas's representative will be paying a visit.'

Rose's Shoes? The name sounded familiar to Cait. She had seen it somewhere recently. Then she remembered. Printed inside her father's shoes when she had been rummaging around his wardrobe, looking for family documents. So this critical problem was nothing more than a mix-up over an order for shoes for him? From the number of them in his wardrobe he was obviously a good customer of theirs whom they didn't want to lose. Though why he needed so many pairs when he rarely left the house was beyond her. A thought struck her then. If she resolved this issue on her mother's behalf, maybe, just maybe, it might help to rebuild the bond they had shared when she was born. It was worth a try. Besides, the Trucker woman obviously wasn't going to give up badgering them until someone representing her mother had paid a visit.

First, though, Cait had to build the momentum to get herself out of bed, which was the last thing she felt like doing at the moment.

She instructed Agnes, 'If the woman telephones again, tell her I'll call in to see her later. Oh, and while you're at it, telephone my boss at work and tell her ... anything you can think of that will be accepted as an excuse for my absence today.'

With that she turned over in bed and pulled the covers over her head, signalling to Agnes that this conversation was at an end.

CHAPTER FOURTEEN

Glen was trying his best to listen to Harry Owens as the man gave him a brief overview on what to himself were the important matters of tea- and meal-break times, and where the canteen and toilets were. Glen's insides were turning somersaults. Thomas had been Nerys's maiden name; she had obviously reverted to it after she had obtained a divorce from him. That was why Charles Gray couldn't find any trace of her after she had sold their house and moved to another. At any time they were expecting his nemesis to arrive. If they crossed paths and she recognised him, that put paid to any plan of finding out where she lived so that he could visit the house and be reunited with his daughter. All he could hope was that, should they come face to face, either Nerys wouldn't take much notice of a mere factory worker or else he'd changed so much since she'd last seen him that she wouldn't recognise him.

He realised that Harry had stopped talking and was looking at him curiously. Glen said, 'I'm sorry, I didn't catch that.'

'No, miles away, you were, mate. You look a bit green around the gills to me. Are you all right? Only one death in this place is enough for one week.'

Glen managed to say jocularly, 'Oh, I'm fine, just got a lot to take in as you can appreciate,

166

starting a new job, getting used to new ways and people. It all seems a bit overwhelming right now.'

'No different to what I felt when I first started here, and everyone else who starts a new job. It will soon slot into place and you'll feel like part of the furniture. I can only tell you it's a good place to work ... well, it was under Reg Swinton, but of course it depends now on who's brought in to replace him. I expect the owner will have to run it meantime. Such a shock, Mr Swinton going so swift like that. I'd only seen him a couple of hours before it happened. He was doing his inspection round to make sure all the workers were okay and everything was running smoothly before he went up to his office for a client meeting. At the time I did notice he looked tired and had a bit of a sweat on him, but I put that down to the pressure of getting our orders out in time for Christmas.'

Glen tentatively asked, 'What ... er ... is the owner like?'

Harry pulled a face and shrugged. 'Dunno. Never seen her in all the seven years I've worked here. As far as I know she comes here once a month to go over matters with Reg Swinton, but she's never graced us lot on the shop floor with her presence. Those that have had the privilege of crossing her path said she looks a stuck-up cow and acts like she's royalty. In all the years Nell Green took a tray of tea through to the office with a plate of best butter shortbread, she never once heard a thank-you from her. There wasn't ever any acknowledgement when she retired after

167

forty-odd years of service.

'Anyway, I think I've shown you as much as I can and the rest you'll have to find out for yourself. I must get on, the shoes won't box themselves, and it don't look like I'm gonna get much help again today, same as every day, from that lazy sod of an assistant I've got. If he don't buck his ideas up soon I'm off up to see the hierarchy about getting him replaced by someone who isn't work-shy. So excuse me, mate, won't yer?'

Glen thanked him for his time then made his way into the maintenance room which was hardly bigger than a small cupboard, lined with old wooden shelving that groaned under the weight of the assorted tools and paraphernalia needed to carry out his work. A well-worn desk was rammed in one corner with a rickety-looking chair at the side, allowing just enough room for Glen to sit on while he answered any summons on the scuffed black Bakelite telephone. The room didn't even have a door on it. He knew from what Harry had told him that any supplies he needed were ordered through the stores department, but all orders then had to be sanctioned by the works manager before they were placed with their suppliers. Until Reg Swinton's replacement was on board, he'd have to make do with what supplies he had. Glen was just mortally relieved to learn that he wouldn't personally have to approach the owner for their approval and wouldn't come into contact with Nerys that way while she was running the place until a replacement for Mr Swinton was found.

On examining the jobs book, it seemed to Glen

that the last maintenance man had been very diligent. Apart from a couple of light bulbs that needed replacing in the gents toilets, situated in the clocking-in area, and a twice-daily replenishing with coal of the huge cast-iron boiler in the basement, it seemed at the moment that he wouldn't be anywhere near the offices or in danger of bumping into Nerys. He was going to be eased into his job gently. But that was to change.

The telephone started shrilling. It was the factory foreman. A belt needed replacing on one of the stitching machines. Would Glen come straight away to avoid losing more production time? Grabbing the tool box and taking several belts of different sizes out of the stock on the shelves, to make sure he was carrying the right size replacement, he set off, praying that repairing machines was just like riding a bike. Once mastered, never forgotten.

Over in the canteen, Jan, who hadn't worked for twenty years, was already feeling the strain and she'd only been at it two hours. Frying up two hundred sausages, then the same amount of rashers of bacon, cutting open and spreading margarine on a hundred cobs, readying the fat in pans for the fried eggs to be cooked fresh as required, and opening catering-sized tins of tomatoes and beans for those who wanted them on top of their sausage or bacon, grating cheese, slicing shoulder ham and tomatoes and onions for those wanting cold sandwiches ... all this just to satisfy the appetites of the factory workers at ten o'clock, when they'd all swarm in demanding to be served quickly so as not to waste a second of their twenty-minute break. And there was still the dinner to be prepared yet, which today was cottage pie, peas and chipped potatoes, jam roly-poly and custard for pudding. In between this it was her job to take the trolley around the offices at eleven, but first she had to load it with the urn of boiled water for coffee and the huge pot of tea, plus a selection of filled cobs.

Jan was just putting the last of the cooked sausages and bacon in the oven to keep hot when Hilda wobbled up to her. 'You've done a good job there, Jan. Some of the sausages are a bit burned, but then some of the blokes like 'em like that. Used to the burned offerings their wives dish up to 'em,' she added, laughing. 'You've earned a break. Fifteen minutes. Help yourself to a cup of tea and a cob with whatever you want in it, then sit and enjoy it at the table where Maggie and Dilys are sitting. I'll be joining you all in a minute. Today we must be back ready to serve on the dot of ten. Not that we never are but we'd best be diligent. Mrs Thomas, the big cheese, is expected. She's never condescended to show her face on the factory floor let alone in here before, but you can never be sure that she might not decide to lower herself. I don't want her to have any cause to pick fault, and the new manager that's brought in led to believe I don't run a tight ship in here.'

She paused for a second as a thought struck. Her voice grave, she said, 'Oh, of course, you wouldn't know, would yer? Reg Swinton, the manager that interviewed you for the job yesterday, had a heart attack and died. So sad, such a lovely man. He'll be a hard act to follow.' Hilda wiped a tear from her eye and gave a sniff. 'Right, come on, breaktime will be over before we've started ours.'

As Jan made herself a bacon cob, then poured tea into a cup, adding milk and sugar, she wondered if Glen had heard the news about Reg Swinton and that the owner was on her way, only she wasn't a Mrs Trainer but a Mrs Thomas. That must mean that Glen's ex-wife had sold the business after all, and Jan wondered where that left them in their search for his daughter.

CHAPTER FIFTEEN

Cait shivered as a blast of icy wind caught her on alighting from the bus, the second she'd had to catch to reach her destination. She had desperately tried to get back off to sleep after Agnes Dalby had left her bedroom earlier that morning, but had failed miserably. What had finally got her up and dressed was Agnes once again coming up to inform her that Miss Trucker had called yet again for information as to when they could expect Mrs Thomas's representative to visit, and it became apparent to Cait that the woman wasn't going to give up until she had been to see them.

There was a freezing mist swirling over the murky canal waters when she made her way over the small hump-backed bridge and down the steps at one side, on to the slippery cobbled path that led to the dozen or so factories and warehouses backing on to the canal. It was only then that she realised she had arrived at the workers' entrance to the premises and had to retrace her steps, go further up the main road and down the next road off it which led her to reception at the front of the premises, She found herself facing an old building with a tall chimney rising from it and a faded sign on its front: Rose's Quality Shoes and Leather Goods, Established 1921. It nestled between a coal depot and a tea warehouse. When she arrived in the reception area, the young girl behind the desk wished Cait a good morning and asked what she could do for her.

Cait had barely finished telling her who she was when, much to her surprise, the other girl fairly jumped to attention, as if she had just announced she was royalty, and blurted out, 'Oh, please go straight up, Miss Thomas. I'll telephone Miss Trucker to meet you.'

By 'straight up' Cait assumed the receptionist meant she was to make her way up the stairs. At the top, she found a middle-aged woman hurrying down the corridor to meet her. She wore a harassed expression on her face but there was also an element of surprise mingled with it when her eyes fixed on Cait.

'Good morning, Miss Thomas. How very nice to meet you. I'm Jane Trucker, Mr...' she paused for a moment, realising what she had been going to say before she changed it to '...the manager's secretary. I'll show you through. I wasn't sure whether you'd prefer tea or coffee so I've ordered both. As soon as you're settled, I will inform the kitchen you're here and have it sent up. I hope that is acceptable to you?'

Cait was wondering why on earth she was being treated like a very important person. Perhaps her mother demanded such attention from those she dealt with here.

Now in the manager's office, Jane Trucker was standing by the chair to the front of the desk, it being obvious she was expecting Cait to take the seat behind it. Cait thought that was odd, but had no objection to sitting in the red leather chair behind the desk. It might be well-worn but looked to be far more comfortable than the chair opposite.

With a sad expression on her plain face, hands clasped tightly in her lap on top of the shorthand book and pencil she had brought along with her, Jane Trucker said to Cait, 'I hope you don't object to my handling this situation, Miss Thomas, only Mrs Thomas usually dealt with Mr Swinton himself. As his personal secretary I did have a certain amount of contact with her too so...'

Cait didn't care at this moment who she dealt with, she just wanted to get this over with and go home. 'Just what is this urgent matter only my mother can resolve for you?' she demanded.

Miss Trucker paused for a moment. Obviously what she was about to divulge was causing her distress. 'Miss Thomas, it's my very sad task to inform you that Mr Swinton passed away yesterday morning. He suffered a massive heart attack. Obviously we needed to inform Mrs Thomas as soon as possible, as you can appreciate. I have

173

informed Mr Swinton's widow of the reason why Mrs Thomas hasn't yet been in contact with her to offer her condolences, but now that you're here I expect you'd like to be in touch yourself and speak on behalf of the family. I know Mrs Swinton would appreciate that. I have her details.

'As soon as the funeral arrangements have been finalised, I'll inform you. We office staff are having a collection for flowers and the factory workers are having a separate one. If you wish me to arrange a wreath on the family's behalf, I'll be happy to do so. The more senior staff, myself included, would like to attend the funeral, but we need to ask you first if you have any objection to our taking the time off? Oh, also, I'd appreciate if you'd tell me if you wish me to arrange a car to take you to the church and then the funeral tea afterwards. I understand Mrs Thomas isn't expected back for two or three weeks, so as her representative I assume you'll be attending on her behalf? Unless you have managed to contact Mrs Thomas since my telephone call this morning and she's making her way back as we speak?'

Cait was staring at the woman blankly, wondering why she was telling her all this. Although it was sad, what did it matter to her mother that the manager of the firm that made her husband's shoes had died? And why was this woman seeking Cait's approval for the senior staff to attend the funeral? Something odd was going on here, something she couldn't grasp. She asked, 'Are you making special arrangements to go to the manager's funeral for all your best customers?'

Jane Trucker looked a mite embarrassed that

she hadn't thought to do that. 'I will certainly contact them and make arrangements for those who wish to attend.' She picked up her notebook and pencil and made a reminder note to herself.

It was Cait's turn to look at her in surprise. Why had the woman responded as if she were obeying an order? The throbbing headache she had woken up with that morning was returning with a vengeance. 'Look,' she said briskly, 'can we just get on with whatever you called me in here for?'

Jane looked taken aback for a moment. Reg Swinton had always treated her with the utmost respect and courtesy, no matter how fraught he felt. As a professional, she managed to keep her feelings to herself and responded evenly, 'Yes, of course. Would you like me to ask the senior staff to come up now?'

Puzzled, Cait asked, 'What for?'

The other woman looked surprised. 'Well, for you to introduce yourself to them, Miss Thomas, as their temporary boss until Mrs Thomas returns. Presumably then she will let us know if she's going to be running the place herself as its owner or if she will be looking to find a replacement for Mr Swinton.'

Cait stared at her, stunned by this revelation. Surely she had misheard the woman. But she knew she hadn't. She had definitely just said that Nerys was the owner of this company. Why had she never mentioned anything about it? She needed a few minutes to herself to digest this information. 'I need some time on my own. You must have work to do,' Cait said shortly.

Another show of rudeness towards her proved

too much for Jane Trucker and she responded brusquely. 'Yes, of course. I do appreciate Mr Swinton's death must have come as a great shock to you, considering how long and how tirelessly he worked for your family.' She rose from her chair in a dignified fashion. 'I'll go and check where that tea and coffee has got to. Please call me on the intercom if you require anything or when you're ready to continue, Miss Thomas.'

Cait waited for a few seconds after Jane had closed the office door behind her, listening to her stout brogues thudding along the corridor as she made her way down to her own office, before she let her shoulders slump and dropped her head down on the desk. She hadn't the least idea what was going on. She had never heard that the private income her mother lived on came from the profits of this business. But that was far less of a concern than the fact that it was obvious she was expected to run the company until her mother's return.

Cait raised her head and sat up straight, staring blindly across the room. Did she come clean to Miss Trucker that she had no idea how shoes were made, let alone how to manage the people who made them?

But if her mother returned from her travels to find that her daughter had successfully dealt with this major crisis on her behalf, she couldn't fail to see Cait in a more positive light. And then another thought struck. How hard was it to run a company anyway? After all, the workers did everything, didn't they, and the boss just kept an eye on them to see that the profits were rolling in.

If she made a success of running the business on her mother's behalf, how could Nerys not allow her to keep the position permanently?

She leaned back in the chair to rest her head against it, thinking how to proceed from here.

According to the girls she worked with, it was the menials that did the brunt of the work and kept the business profitable, while the big boss and senior managers barked orders at one another, sitting on their backsides all day behind closed office doors, drinking tea and coffee and planning their expensive holidays. The life of a boss sounded good to her. No sour-faced supervisor breathing down her neck, making sure she did her quota, berating her loudly in front of everyone else for any mistakes, monitoring the times she arrived and left. Cait could come and go as she liked as the boss.

She suddenly realised she was hungry. She could go to the canteen and see what was on offer. But then it struck her that a boss wouldn't be expected to eat with the workforce. She couldn't see her mother doing that anyway. There must be a separate canteen that catered for those in charge. She would need to ask Miss Trucker where it was. She supposed first, though, she ought to introduce herself to the senior staff. She had no idea what she would say to them, though.

Then another thought occurred to her. Her clothes hardly reflected her new managerial status. In her hastily pulled-on thick jumper and black slacks, she wasn't dressed in any manner to gain respect from the workforce. She needed to buy herself some smart new outfits, things that suited the boss of a company. But she hadn't the sort of money that would take; for the last year all her spare cash had gone on buying things towards the house she and Neil had been going to share after their marriage.

Then a picture of that pile of notes in the safe in her parents' bedroom floated tantalisingly before her. Cait focused on that vision for several long moments while she came to a conclusion. Surely, in the circumstances, she would be doing the right thing, using some of that to kit herself out with? Her mother always looked immaculate, and as her representative Cait would be expected to do so too. But how did she explain away finding the secret safe and the keys to access it? She was no nearer coming up with a plausible explanation than she had been earlier. But her parents weren't due home until after Christmas at least, so she'd time on her side.

Excited at the thought of her shopping trip, she was about to pick up her handbag from the side of her chair and get up to go when the door opened and she looked over to see a woman wearing a white overall, with a white net hat concealing her hair, backing her way in, holding a laden tray. She swung around and hurried over to the desk, grateful to be putting the tray down on top of it. She then exclaimed, 'Phew, that was heavy! I worried all the way from the kitchen I was going to drop it.'

Jan looked appraisingly at the young woman on the other side of the desk and frowned. She was sure she'd come into contact with her – or someone very similar-looking – before, though she couldn't remember where. She said to her, 'You're new, aren't you? Just like I am today. And got yourself lost, did you, like I've just done?' There was a chuckle in her voice when she carried on, 'I thought it was bad enough finding myself in the cutting department. Felt a right idiot with all them faces looking at me wondering what I was doing in there, but you'll really get it in the neck if any of the hierarchy find you in here. This is the big chief's domain, love. This is my first day, but from the little bit of gossip I've heard about the owner she's far too high and mighty even to introduce herself to any of her employees, except for the manager and his secretary, so if her daughter is anything like her, you could be for the high jump if she finds you in here. Come on, let's get out of here before she comes back.'

Cait was staring at her stony-faced. If her austere supervisor at work heard one derogatory word said against the boss she would waste no time in disciplining the guilty party. Cait realised she should take the same stance. 'How dare you speak about Mrs Thomas in such a way? It amounts to no less than ... than treason.'

Jan gawped at her, stunned. 'Treason! She's not the queen...'

Cait interjected, 'But she *is* your employer.' Her mind then raced to come up with a suitable punishment and the only thing that came to mind was, 'Go and collect your cards and leave the premises. And don't expect to be receiving a reference.' She then cringed inwardly. She had gone too far. This woman didn't really deserve to be sacked just for speaking out of turn, but if Cait backtracked now it wouldn't do her credibility any good.

Just then the door opened and Jane Trucker appeared. She said to Cait, 'I'm sorry to bother you...' then stopped talking on spotting Jan. 'Oh, you've brought the tray up, thank you. You can leave us now.'

Jan seized the opportunity to make her escape. She scooted out of the door.

Cait said to Jane, 'I've sacked that woman as she was extremely rude about my mother. Now, if you'll excuse me, I have somewhere important to go. I'll be back in the morning. I'll introduce myself to the senior staff then if you'll arrange to have them come up to the office ... shall we say about ten o'clock?'

She made to walk out then but Jane stopped her with, 'Oh, but Miss Thomas, I'm here to tell you that Mr Lakeland has just arrived. I took the liberty of explaining to him about Mr Swinton and he's deeply upset, having dealt with him for many years now. He's asked me to let his secretary know where the funeral is to take place so that he can travel down to pay his respects.'

Cait looked non-plussed. 'Who is Mr Lakeland?'

'A very important customer of the company's. He's the owner of several shoe shops in and around London and the home counties. He's here as he has become good friends with Mr Swinton over the time he's been dealing with us and was passing through Leicester on his way to visit his daughter who lives in Sheffield. Mr Swinton told him that if he wanted to break his journey and drop in, he would show him an early preview of our spring range and offer him refreshments.'

Cait froze, a wave of terror rolling through her. She was in no position to entertain clients, let alone a very important one. She'd be asked questions she'd not be able to answer and make herself look stupid. Neither was she dressed for the part, something she felt was of paramount importance. She blurted out to Jane, 'I have a really important appointment now that I cannot miss. You'll have to deal with him yourself.'

Giving the other woman no opportunity to make any response, she grabbed her handbag and coat and rushed out of the room, leaving a dumb-struck Jane Trucker staring after her.

When Jan arrived back in the kitchen, Hilda was stirring a huge pot of gravy with a large metal spoon. She called over, 'Oh, yer back, lovey. I was just about to send the huskies out for yer. Got lost, I gather. Well, it's n'ote we've not all done when we first started here. The place is like a rabbit warren. You found the boss's office eventually?'

Jan nodded. 'Eventually. I had a funny experience when I did, though.'

Hilda frowned at her. 'What d'yer mean?'

'Well, there was this young thing in there, looked no more than seventeen, and I took it that she was a new employee like me who'd got herself lost. I told her where she was and that she'd better scarper quick before the boss came back in, because if she was as snooty as I'd heard

181

she was then the girl would be for the high jump. Well ... then she started spouting off about me committing treason, speaking about the boss like that, and told me to collect my cards. Luckily for me the boss's secretary came in ... the lady who fetched me when I came for the interview. She thanked me for bringing up the tray and told me to go. I didn't need telling twice and left her to deal with ... well, I suspect that young girl is an escapee from the loony bin, or if not she needs locking up. She's obviously not right up top to be thinking she can go around accusing people of treason and believing she has the authority to sack them.' Jan suddenly remembered where she'd first come across the girl. It had been when she and Glen had stopped in the church to rest on the night they'd first met. The girl had been throwing her weight around then too – she obviously made a habit of it.

Hilda was looking at her thoughtfully. If the gossip she had heard had an ounce of truth in it, then she feared her new recruit had just come face to face with the owner's daughter, who was standing in for her mother while she was away. This probably did mean that the young woman was in a position to sack whoever she liked, whether it was justified or not. Judging by her performance up to now, though, Jan looked as if she would shape up to be an asset and Hilda didn't want to lose her. As it was, no one had officially told her that a member of her staff had been dismissed for what was perceived as insubordination, although to Hilda all Jan was guilty of was passing on gossip to the wrong person – hardly a sacking offence, in her eyes. Until she was told officially, she wasn't prepared to take action. She decided not to tell Jan who the young woman she had crossed swords with in the office actually was, in case her new recruit decided to leave anyway. In a very short time they would have a horde of hungry workers descending on them and Hilda needed every staff member she could find to help deal with them.

She told Jan, 'Well, hopefully, as we speak she's being carted off back there. Anyway, I'll send Maggie out with the staff trolley for a week or so until you've got your bearings.' She felt this was best, just in case Jan ran into the owner's daughter again and she wondered what Jan was still doing here. 'Can you help Dilys peel the spuds for the chips, and when you've done that could you go outside and check all the tables have the right condiments? Salt, pepper, tomato and brown sauce ... and make sure they're all filled up. You'll find what you need to do that in the pantry.'

On the factory floor, Glen had just finished putting a new belt on a welting machine in the Welting, Rounding and Stitching Department. The operator was a thirty-something man who had just returned from having a cigarette outside while his machine was being fixed. Glen said to him, 'That's you as good as new. I can't find the guard, though. It wasn't on when I stripped it down to change the belt.'

'That's 'cos I took it off,' the man told him. 'It's easier to operate my machine without it. It's just a bloody hindrance.'

183

'It might be,' Glen told him, 'but it's there for a reason. To save you from getting hurt.'

'Yeah, well, I'll take me chances. It's harder to do me daily quota with it on.'

Glen eyed him closely. 'Have you any children?'

His unexpected question surprised the man. 'What that's got to do with ... but, yeah, I have. Five, if yer want the exact number.'

'Not much work going, I wouldn't have thought, for a man with a mangled hand or worse. So how will you provide for your five children and wife then?'

The man eyed him blankly. That thought hadn't occurred to him. Most of the other men, apart from a handful of old-timers, thought guards were for the lily-livered. But now the thought that through his own neglect he could be responsible for ruining his family's future, all for the sake of being able to ease back a little on his working pace, seemed daft to him. He opened a metal drawer on his machine bench, rummaged around in it until he found what he was seeking, and handed it to Glen.

He took it and patted the welter on his shoulder, saying, 'Good man.'

Having finished his task, and with the man now back working on the machine he'd just fixed, Glen packed his tools away, picked up the metal tool box and made to return to his office. A man of about his own age stopped him, holding out his hand to introduce himself. 'Alf Bisson, foreman of this department. I'm also the works union representative. I'm very impressed with you. I've been trying to get the men who've taken

184

off their guards to put them back for their own safety ever since I started here ten years ago. In your first morning as maintenance man you've managed to achieve more than I've ever done. It's a big issue with the union, is safety, but trying to get the men to be responsible for themselves when their daily quotas are at stake is another, despite me warning them if 'ote did happen to them while their guards are off there'll be n'ote the union can do for them by way of compensation. How yer fixed for getting the others to put theirs back on too?'

'I'll try my best. I've witnessed with my own eyes what can happen. When I...' Glen just stopped himself in time from saying 'when I owned this place'. He quickly changed it to: '...was working at my last place, I saw a man trap his arm in a machine with no guard on as there weren't such things in those days. I've also seen men chop fingers off. After the incident with the arm, I ... the firm insisted that all machines where possible had guards fitted to them and they stayed on, whether the men liked it or not.'

'I don't like talking ill of Reg Swinton as he was a good man to work for but it was his opinion that the men knew what was at stake if they chose to work without their guards on. To me, though, some rules need to be clad in iron, for the good of all.'

Glen nodded his agreement.

Alf smiled at him. 'You'll do. If you fancy joining my table in the canteen at lunch, I'll introduce you to the other foremen.'

Later that evening Glen pushed away his bowl and said to Jan, 'That soup was good. Thank you.'

She smiled with pleasure. 'Yes, it wasn't bad, if I say so myself. Vegetable soup and bread is not what I'd call a proper meal after a hard day's graft, but we have to watch the pennies until we both get paid. And our first pay packet will be short three days, being's we started on a Thursday.' She gave a chuckle as she added, 'As my old gran used to say after what she called a make do and mend meal, "It filled the 'ole."'

'Well, it certainly filled mine,' said Glen, chuckling. 'Now why don't you go and put your feet up while I clear up the kitchen?'

'Sounds like luxury to me. I'm not used to being on my feet all day and my ankles have swelled up like balloons. I'm going to give my feet a soak in a bowl of hot water.'

A short while later Glen joined Jan, taking a seat in the battered armchair opposite hers next to the fire. Her feet in the bowl of now-tepid water, she was resting her head on the back of the chair and had her eyes closed, appearing to be asleep. Careful not to rouse her, he gently opened out the evening paper he had bought from a corner shop on his way home, but before he could begin reading, Jan opened her eyes and said to him, 'I've been dying to ask how your day went but I thought I'd wait until dinner was past because, you see, well … I don't know whether you've heard about Reg Swinton and that the owner's due in to see to things until a replacement is found? Only the owner's name isn't

186

Trainer, apparently, it's Thomas.'

'My ex-wife's maiden name,' he told her. 'Either it's a huge coincidence that the person she sold the business on to had the same name or Nerys changed her name back when she obtained her divorce from me. My gut feeling is it's the latter. She obviously wanted to disassociate herself from my surname in case people frowned on her for being the wife, or ex-wife, of a criminal. Or perhaps she wanted to make it difficult for me to find her when I was released from prison.'

Jan thought about this for a moment. 'Or, of course, she could have got married again. I know it would be a coincidence, but Thomas isn't an uncommon name, is it? One of my schoolfriends was called Diane Brown and she married a man called Archie Brown, so it does happen.' Jan looked at Glen in concern. 'So how do you feel about the possibility of bumping into...' she was not sure how to refer to Nerys Thomas – as the ex-wife, that woman, the conniving bitch? So she just said '...her while you're going about your job?'

Glen sighed. 'Well, it worried me that I might, and if so would she recognise me, but thankfully if she did come in today, she never showed her face where I was working. Although I did hear that in all the time she has owned the firm, she's never once been seen on the shop floor.' He thought back to the young Nerys Thomas he had met and fallen in love with. He had found her then to be a warm, caring, honest person, one who had never acted as if she would deem a shop floor as beneath her or its workers as inferior. But

187

from what he knew now, that side of her had been all an act. Of the real Nerys, he realised, he knew nothing at all.

Jan was sighing with relief to hear that he'd been spared such a shock. 'I looked out for you in the canteen at lunchtime, to try and have a word in case you hadn't heard what had gone on, but I didn't see you at all.'

'I didn't feel like any lunch today. Was too churned up after hearing about Reg Swinton and the fact that Nerys was expected in. I didn't know how I felt about maybe seeing her swanning about as the big I am, knowing just how she'd got the business. And I was also racking my brains as to how I could best pick my moment to go and tackle her about seeing Lucy, before she had me thrown off the premises and I lost my chance altogether.'

At that moment Jan was far more concerned to hear that he had gone for over nine hours without any food inside him. 'You will waste away if you carry on like that, going without any lunch!'

'I told you, I wasn't that hungry. And don't forget, I'm not used to eating three square meals a day yet.'

'No, I suppose not. Anyway, as terrible as it is of me to say, Reg Swinton's death is a Godsend to us.'

Glen looked at her sharply. 'It is? How?'

'Well, your ex-wife's coming in to manage the place until she decides what to do saves us from risking our necks, getting information from the private files. We can just follow her home one night, can't we?'

'Oh, of course, I never thought of that.' Then a thought struck Glen. 'It might not be as easy as it sounds.'

'Why?'

'It's hardly likely Nerys will travel by bus, is it? She'll either drive herself or have someone drive her. We can hardly follow a car on foot.'

'Oh! How stupid of me not to have thought of that. Do you drive? No, don't bother answering that as it's irrelevant. We can't afford to buy a car anyway.'

'Well, I've decided that Nerys actually coming to the works herself is the best opportunity for me to get Lucy back. As soon as I hear she's on the premises, I shall go and confront her and demand she allows me to see my daughter – and I won't leave until she does.'

'There is a risk to that. I know how important finding your daughter is to you, Glen, but if you do what you plan to, you'll definitely lose your job. Nerys won't allow you to carry on working there once she knows who you are.'

He nodded. 'I know. But I can only hope that as Reg Swinton gave me a job, another firm will too if I use the same story about my background.'

'Well, at least I'm earning. It will be very tight but we'll just have to manage on what I'm paid until you get set on again.'

He looked at her, stunned. She was prepared to make such a sacrifice for him? She was indeed a special woman. How would he ever repay her for what she was helping him do?

Jan was saying, 'Anyway, if she didn't come in today then it's Saturday tomorrow so I can't see her coming in until Monday now. That gives you two days to plan what you're going to say to her when you go and confront her. I had been going to suggest that we get a tin of white-wash at the weekend and give this place a freshen up, but in light of the fact we might be living on the bread-line for a bit, we'd better conserve every penny we can.'

The water in the bowl was by now stone cold. Jan took her feet out of it, and was drying them on one of the cheap thin towels they had bought from the second-hand shop when she asked him, 'A walk in the park doesn't cost anything, does it? Weather permitting, how do you fancy that on Sunday afternoon? Make a change from us staring at these four walls.'

Glen was thinking to himself. The more he was getting to know Jan, the more she reminded him of his beloved first wife, Julia. Both were caring women, very easy to be around, respected the fact that he was entitled to make his own decisions. He felt so comfortable sitting here with her that as far as he was concerned their living arrangement could go on for ever. But he knew it would end when their reason to be together no longer existed, whether it had a successful outcome or not. She'd want to go her own way then to build a new life, like he supposed he would. This time last week he hadn't known she existed, but he did know that when it came time for them to part company he would miss Jan. Hopefully she would want to remain friends with him.

He smiled at her. 'I'd like that very much, Jan.'

Very much indeed, he thought.

CHAPTER SIXTEEN

The following Monday morning Cait studied her reflection critically in the wardrobe mirror. The navy, pin-stripe suit, with its pencil-style skirt finishing just above her calves with a kick pleat at the back, short fitted jacket and crisp white blouse underneath, all made her look much older than she was and feel very sophisticated, so she was happy that she had created the look she had set out to. She did not feel that her hairstyle did her new look justice, though, and decided to deal with that at the first opportunity.

After her shopping expedition on Friday that had extended into Saturday too, she now had three more suits and a selection of blouses for work, and three evening dresses ready for when she received invitations to the posh dos she was expecting to attend in her newfound position, especially the Christmas ones since the day itself was only three weeks away. All she needed now were shoes and handbags to complete her outfits. She had been tempted to buy those, having spotted quite a few suitable styles, but then it had struck her that as the boss of a company that produced such items, she wouldn't be perceived as championing them by parading the competition's wares. She hadn't paid attention to the make of her mother's shoes when she'd rummaged through her wardrobe, but she assumed they were all Rose's.

A feeling of nervousness rushed through her. She was used to being instructed as to what to do, not instructing others. Then she inwardly scolded herself. What had she to be nervous about? She was the boss, the company figurehead. It was her job to make sure all the workers were earning their pay, keeping her mother's profits coming in. That was what paid for the big house, the holiday, and all the smart clothes. There was one thing she should do before she went to Rose's, though, and that was to sever her employment with the wholesale fruit and vegetable company. What a relief that was going to be! And there was part of her that was going to enjoy seeing their expressions when she informed them just what her new position was to be.

In the kitchen doorway Agnes Dalby did a double take when she spotted Cait make her way across the hallway into the dining room, to take her seat at the table. If she didn't know better she would have thought Cait had an elder sister she hadn't known about, and a very smart, sophisticated-looking young woman at that. With a fresh pot of tea in her hand, Agnes hurried after her. 'Good morning, Miss Thomas. I have to say, you do look extremely smart today. I haven't seen that outfit you're in before. Is it new?'

Cait had too much on her mind today to question Agnes as to just why she was here when Nerys had laid her off. It would never have occurred to her that it was because she cared deeply about Cait's welfare. It was nice, though, to be complimented on her appearance after working so hard to transform it. 'Thank you. It's one of several I've bought since I took over my new position,' she told the daily.

Agnes turned the cup over in its saucer and poured a cup of tea for her. 'Oh, you have a new job, Miss Thomas? Many congratulations. May I ask if it's a promotion within the company you're already in or with another firm?'

Cait opened her mouth to tell her then snapped it shut. For whatever reason, her mother had kept it a secret that she owned a business. What her reaction was going to be when she did arrive back and discover that her secret was out Cait wasn't sure. Although Cait felt sure that Nerys wouldn't fail but be impressed with her daughter for having risen to the occasion and stepped into her shoes during her absence, she was fairly confident her mother would not want her blabbing about their private affairs, so she avoided the question.

'Thanks, Dalby. I'll just have toast this morning.' Which was more, in fact, than she could actually face given her apprehension about the day ahead, but Cait knew it would be foolish to take on a big day on an empty stomach.

Agnes registered her evasion of the question about the job and left the room to attend to her tasks.

A while later Cait alighted from the bus and stood before the building she now saw as her ex-place of work, savouring the thought of what she was about to do before she opened the door leading into reception. She ignored the shocked look that the middle-aged receptionist shot her. Employees, they both knew, were meant to arrive

193

by the back entrance. Instead Cait walked across the foyer to go through to the offices.

Outside the general office door, she paused just long enough to draw breath before she turned the knob and made her way purposefully inside. She immediately saw that her sour-faced supervisor was at her own desk, taking work to be done out of her in tray to distribute it around the other typists. She must have realised that as it was now approaching nine-thirty Cait wasn't turning up for work again. By now several of the other clerks and typists had noticed her, staring at her agog as she weaved her way through their desks.

Hearing the sound of heels approaching on the hard floor, Sylvia Grey looked up. Her eyebrows rose when she saw it was Cait. If she noticed her smart new look she didn't make any comment, just said evenly, 'Good morning, Miss Thomas, so good of you to grace us with your presence. Would you like to come into my office? We need a private talk.'

It gave Cait great pleasure to reply to her, 'What I have to say to you can be said here.'

Sylvia Grey shot her a knowing look, interjecting before she could add another word, 'Don't try to offer me any more unacceptable excuses for your absences, Miss Thomas. The person you got to telephone me yesterday told me you were in bed suffering from women's problems. We are all women in this department, and if we all took time off when we suffered from our so-called problems then this firm would grind to a standstill. You don't look to me like you're suffering from anything debilitating. In fact, I'd say you're positively glowing. I doubt there is any acceptable excuse for your lateness today.'

She shook her head sadly. 'I'm afraid we've arrived at the stage where your behaviour can no longer be tolerated. It isn't fair to the rest of your colleagues who have to share your workload while you take days off, as and when you feel like it, as well as keeping up with their own. We won't be asking you to serve out your notice. It's a shame it has come to this as I did have high hopes for you.'

This statement stunned Cait. 'High hopes! But you were forever singling me out to criticise my work and passing me over when it came to promotion.'

The older woman eyed her meaningfully. 'Constructive criticism, Miss Thomas. It's my job to point out mistakes made by all my charges, spurring them on to improve themselves. I singled you out no more than you deserved, which in truth wasn't very often. On the whole your work was of an acceptable standard since you've greatly improved from when you first joined us here. As for passing you over for promotion, you aren't ready for that until such time as you temper your attitude, young lady.'

'There's nothing wrong with my attitude!' Cait exclaimed, insulted.

Sylvia Grey eyed her. She had in fact tried to speak to Cait on numerous occasions about her annoying and unnecessarily superior manner. 'And while you believe that, Miss Thomas, you'll never achieve any higher status than that of typist. In this company or any other.'

Cait puffed out her chest. Well, that's where the old dragon was wrong and it was going to be a great pleasure to tell her that there was no higher position in a firm than heading it up as the daughter of the owner. She wanted everyone in the room to hear what she was about to divulge. In a loud voice she began, 'For your information, Miss Grey…'

She was interrupted by the arrival of Sylvia Grey's assistant, a tiny mousy woman who in a squeaky high-pitched voice announced: 'Sorry to disturb you, Miss Grey, but Mr Cummings has asked for one of the girls to be sent to him for dictation. I took the liberty of answering your telephone as you were otherwise occupied. He says it is urgent.'

Miss Grey thanked the woman and said to Cait, 'I'll have your wages and cards made up ready for you to collect next Friday from reception. Please clear your desk of any personal belongings and be on your way.'

With that the older woman hurried away, leaving Cait fuming that she'd been cheated out of her moment of glory.

The personal belongings she had kept in her drawer – a nearly empty bottle of hair lacquer, hairbrush, couple of lipsticks, clear nail polish for halting runs in her nylons, a packet of Fox's Glacier Mints, a half-eaten packet of custard creams – she threw in the bin as she felt they weren't worth filling her handbag with, even though she meant to swap it for one of far higher quality as soon as she took up her new position. She was conscious that all the girls were secretly watching her, knowing they were highly amused by the way in which Miss Grey had dismissed her. Still, this was the last time anyone would dare treat Cait in such a manner.

A while later, as she walked purposefully through the main entrance into the reception area of Rose's, it didn't escape Cait's notice that the young receptionist sat up to attention the moment she saw her and called over 'Good morning, Miss Thomas', in a very respectful manner.

At the bottom of the stairs Cait hesitated for a moment, worried that her journey and diversion might have ruffled her appearance in some way. She was about to ask the young woman if she looked all right then remembered that she was temporarily the boss of the company so needed to act at all times as if she was in charge. That meant not showing anyone she was feeling in any way out of her depth, even though she was.

It was apparent that the receptionist had alerted Jane Trucker of Cait's arrival as the older woman was waiting for her in what was now her office, notepad and pen in hand.

If she was surprised by the transformation in Cait she didn't show it, just said a pleasant 'Good morning, Miss Thomas' as Cait took off her smart new red coat. Before Jane Trucker could say anything else, Cait told her, 'I could do with a cup of tea first and then I'd like you to arrange for me to see a sample of all the court shoes and handbags we stock.'

Jane told her, 'Miss Thomas, we have a room set aside with samples of all our merchandise out

197

on display for our customers to view and select from. I appreciate that you want to familiarise yourself with the stock and can take you down there later when we've dealt with all the matters that need your immediate attention. If I could take the liberty of using your telephone, I'll order the tea and then we can get down to it.'

Her mother, Cait knew, would not have stood for what she would have perceived as someone ignoring her wishes. Cait feared that if she didn't stand her ground this time they would think her a pushover and never take her seriously.

'May I remind you, Miss Trucker, that I am in charge of this company and expect you to obey my instructions,' she said. 'Now, if you would arrange for me to view our stock of shoes and handbags, as I asked, I'd be grateful. Size five for the shoes.' She hoped the secretary could not tell that she was inwardly shaking at having to remind her of her place. Then her misguided beliefs as to how the owner of a business should act made her add: 'Have them brought up here for me to look over.'

Jane Trucker had worked for the company for many years, had more than proved her loyalty and commitment to it, and did not at all appreciate being treated in this fashion by a young chit of a girl, even if she was the owner's daughter. And she was cross to discover that the girl was after some shoes and bags for herself rather than familiarising herself with their stock. To her credit Jane kept these feelings to herself and replied: 'I'll see to it immediately, Miss Thomas.' She turned back as she remembered she had something important to relay to her new boss. 'The arrangements for Mr Swinton's funeral have been finalised, Miss Thomas. It's to be at two-thirty at St Peter's on Thursday afternoon. I'll order a car to collect you at two.'

Downstairs in the stores, as Glen was making his way back to his office after attending to a broken fluorescent light strip in a corridor, he heard Harry Owens grumbling loudly in annoyance. As he arrived near him, Glen asked, 'Something upset you, Harry?'

'You could say that,' he spat back. 'That little madam upstairs has only demanded a pair of every style of courts and a sample of all our current range of handbags to be delivered to her office. What's wrong with her getting off her arse and paying a visit to the viewing room like everyone else does when they want to view the products? Little upstart, she is. As if I haven't enough to do with six orders to get out by tonight, and a delivery from Italy and one from Northampton to check in. Jeffrey!' he shouted. When he received no response, he angrily snapped, 'Now where's the little sod got to? Out the back for a crafty fag, I bet, while I was getting me instructions from Miss Trucker. Well, he made it clear from the moment he started here that the word "work" was a dirty word to him. Reg Swinton is ... was ... usually such a good judge of character, he should have seen what Jeff was like at his interview and not taken him on, but he's the grandson of one of the old stalwarts in the factory and Reg agreed to give him a try from respect for the old man.

'Well, he'll have to go. I'm not prepared to carry him any longer. I'd already mentioned my feelings to Reg when he asked me how the new recruit was getting on, and he agreed that if Jeffrey hadn't pulled his socks up by the end of the week then it was his cards for him. I shall have to go and see *Madam* to have her sort this out if she expects this department to keep up with the workload.'

Glen thought it strange that Harry was referring to Nerys in this way. 'Maybe Mrs Thomas didn't realise she was heaping such a task on you when she asked for the samples to be taken up to the office. I mean, she wouldn't know that your junior storeman is such a shirker, would she? Not until you tell her, that is.' He was not defending Nerys but attempting to dampen Harry's anger as he wouldn't like him to approach Nerys in his current frame of mind and risk losing his job.

Harry thought about this for a moment and said, 'I suppose you have a point. Anyway, you obviously haven't heard ... it ain't Mrs Thomas herself honouring us with her presence. Apparently she's on holiday somewhere exotic, a place the likes of her employees can only dream of going. It's her daughter who's representing her meantime. I ask yer, a lass hardly out of her nappies running a place like this, even if it is only temporary ... well, it beggars belief, so it does.'

But Glen had stopped listening when Harry had announced that it was Nerys's daughter that was up in the office. His thoughts ran out of control. He was having difficulty believing that his beloved daughter, whom he had missed terribly during his enforced separation from her, was now in the same building as he was. He had to fight to stop himself from charging up there, begging her to believe that he was neither dead – if indeed Nerys had told her that – nor the murderous thug she may have been led to believe. But her office was hardly the place to spring such a shock on her. Now he knew where she was he needed to plan meticulously just how he was going to break the news to her. He needed Jan's help on this.

In the meantime he would settle for just a glimpse of Lucy so that he could see what she looked like now, whether she took more after her mother or himself. But to catch that glimpse posed him a problem. A lowly maintenance man such as he had to have a reason to visit the offices, and he didn't have one. He was unaware that Harry was staring at him and looking perplexed.

Having finally got his attention, Harry said in concern, 'This is the third time I've asked you, mate, but are you all right? Only you're as white as a sheet and you look like you've just had some shocking news.'

Glen gave himself a mental shake, forcing a smile to his face. 'Oh, I'd just ... er ... remembered that I was asked to get some potatoes on my way home tonight. Don't know what made me remember that while you were carrying on.'

Harry eyed him knowingly. 'Ah, well, when the wife's given you her orders it's best not to forget or it'll be the evil eye for you all night, me lad. I speak from experience.' Harry's expression then changed to one of curiosity. 'Rumour has it that you're rather pally with the new woman in the canteen that started yesterday, the same as you? In fact, it's said that you came in to apply for the jobs together.'

Glen smiled to himself. So the rumour-mongers were as active today as they had been when he had owned this place. Not wanting to have Jan perceived as a woman of loose morals, he lied. 'We happen to live opposite each other. Mrs Clayton knew I was looking for work, as she herself was, and so when she saw on the vacancy board that Rose's was in need of a maintenance man as well as someone for the canteen, she rushed back to tell me in the hope no one beat us to it. We travel back and forth to work together now. Whatever the gossips are saying, I can assure you we're nothing more than friends.'

He couldn't help his thoughts from returning then to the problem of how to get himself upstairs so that hopefully he could catch a glimpse of his daughter. Like a thunderbolt the perfect excuse suddenly struck him. He could have hugged Harry's missing assistant for handing it to him. 'Just let me check with the receptionist that she hasn't any requests for urgent work to be done and then I'll give you a hand taking the shoes and handbags upstairs.'

Harry slapped him gratefully on his back. 'Thanks, mate. That means we can load both trolleys at the same time and take 'em up together in the service lift. That'll save me two...' He stopped abruptly as a figure appeared around the metal shelving at the end of the room and started slowly heading their way. Harry bellowed, 'And where the hell have you bin?'

Glen turned his head to see who Harry was addressing and his heart sank to see a thick-set youth, his whole manner betraying the fact that he'd sooner be anywhere else but here. Reaching them, he responded in a nonchalant tone, 'I had to rush off as I needed the lavvy bad. Got stomach trouble. Must be summat I ate last night.'

Harry scowled darkly at him. 'Do I look like I came up the Clyde in a banana boat? You stink like an old ashtray. I guessed you'd disappeared off for a crafty fag while me back was turned, and I was right. You can make the time up out of your dinner hour. Twenty minutes, I make it.' Ignoring the sulky look his assistant shot him, he ordered, 'Now go and fetch both trolleys. You can help me stack 'em with stuff that's wanted upstairs and then take 'em up. Get yer skates on, lad,' he barked.

As the youth shambled off to do his boss's bidding, Harry said to Glen, 'Might as well try and get him to earn some of his pay, at least while he's still here. I do appreciate your offer, mate, and if I can return the favour sometime, don't hesitate to ask.'

Glen heaved a sigh as he went off into his own cubby hole, silently praying that another reason for him to take himself up to the office would present itself soon.

A short while later, sitting amid at least fifty open shoe boxes, Cait stuck out both legs and admired the black suede, high-heeled, peep-toe court shoes on her feet. She thought she looked stunning in them and they were far more expensive than she could ever have afforded on a junior typist's wage. 'I'll have these too,' she said.

Jane was inwardly fuming at being used by her new boss like a lowly assistant in a shoe shop, not the fully qualified personal assistant that she was. She had to stop herself from snatching off the shoes and throwing them back in the box to join the nine other pairs Cait had chosen for herself already. Then she realised the girl was waiting to be handed another pair.

'You've seen them all now, Miss Thomas,' she said politely.

Cait was pleased with her choices so far. All she needed now was to select a handbag to go with each pair.

It was nearly dinnertime before she had made up her mind which handbag went with which pair of shoes, and all her chosen items were stacked up ready for her to take home. The discarded ones were back in their boxes, all courtesy of Jane, and ready to be returned to the stores.

Jane said, 'Shall we get down to business now then, Miss Thomas?'

Cait looked at her, bemused. 'What business?'

Jane looked back at her, equally bemused. 'All the things we need your decision on, Miss Thomas. Mr Gates ... he's our designer ... needs to see you urgently so you can okay and sign off on the new designs for the autumn collection. Mr Owens, who's in charge of the stores ... you met him this morning when he brought up the stock for you ... has a staffing problem that needs resolving. Mr Roberts has an issue with the last batch of leather we had delivered...'

Cait felt it wasn't her job to get involved in such petty matters. Hers was to make sure they were all earning their money and not dodging work. 'I'm sure these people can manage to sort out their own problems without involving me.' Her stomach was telling her it needed attention. 'I want some lunch. What's on the menu today? I'll need you to explain where the senior staff canteen is.'

Jane was gawking at her, astounded that she was expecting the heads of the various departments to make such important decisions unsupervised. Should they make an error of judgement, there could be far-reaching consequences for the company. These sorts of decisions were usually for the general manager or the owner of the company to make. The staff in question were not going to be at all happy about this turn of events. And what could Miss Thomas mean by 'senior staff canteen'? There was just one canteen for everyone, and if she felt herself above eating with the rest of the employees – which Mr Swinton certainly hadn't – she'd have to eat in her own office.

A thought suddenly occurred to Cait. Now that she had her new wardrobe and accessories, what was needed to complete her transformation was a new hairdo. She would pay a visit to her mother's hairdresser that afternoon. There was no time like the present.

She said to Jane, 'Forget lunch, I'm off. Please have the shoes and bags delivered to my home by taxi.' Picking up her handbag, she put on her coat before disappearing out of the door, while Jane stared after her.

Five minutes after the hooter had boomed its announcement that it was home-time, Jan caught a glimpse of Glen's pensive expression as he made his way over to where she was waiting for him on the canal tow path.

As he joined her she laid a reassuring hand on his arm and said to him, 'Let's get home and we'll have a good talk about it.'

He flashed her a wan smile and nodded his agreement.

The meal Jan prepared, of faggots, mashed potatoes, tinned garden peas and gravy, was very tasty, although hard as she might try she could not achieve the same smooth, creamy texture to her mash as her mother always produced. Jan had long ago accepted that this was one culinary skill she would never master. Glen had eaten every scrap on his plate and expressed appreciation to her for his meal, but it was Jan's opinion that with what she knew was on his mind he hadn't tasted a morsel of it. Having eaten they both sat nursing cups of tea in the sagging armchairs by the blazing fire that Glen had made while Jan had been clearing away. She looked at him in concern, gazing mesmerised into the flames. She thought it best to wait for him to speak first.

It was twenty minutes later when he finally looked across at her and said softly, 'Lucy was so close, Jan, but she might as well have been a million miles away. I had the golden opportunity to try and catch a glimpse of her snatched away from me...' He proceeded to tell her what had happened. 'I prayed another chance would come along but it hasn't. I had no jobs outstanding and nothing came in so I spent the rest of the day tidying the shelves in the maintenance room and checking if I needed to order anything, in an effort to occupy my mind.'

'It must have been purgatory for you,' Jan responded understandingly. 'But, you know, there was an excuse you could have used to get you in that office.'

He looked quizzically at her. 'There was? I racked my brains for one and came up with nothing, so I'd like to hear what it is?'

Jan smiled. 'You men aren't as devious as us women, that's why it didn't occur to you. You could have just made out that you'd heard on the grapevine a radiator was leaking. Or maybe that a window was cracked and you needed to measure the glass to replace it, something like that, then when you were told that there wasn't anything amiss, you could just put it down to receiving the wrong information from whoever it was that passed it on.'

'Well, I have to say, that simple idea never crossed my mind.' Then Glen heaved a forlorn sigh. 'Trouble is, Jan, I'm having a struggle with my conscience. You know how much I want to see my daughter. To have the opportunity to try and make up for all the years we've lost, just hold her in my arms for a second, would mean more than anything to me. But to my mind the workplace isn't the right place to break the news to her of who I am or explain to her that the woman who's raised her isn't the wonderful

207

mother she thinks she is. Getting her to believe my story when I have no proof of what Nerys did to me is another problem. And, of course, I have no idea what Nerys has told her about me. But when all's said and done, what she's about to learn is going to devastate her, isn't it? I'm not sure I can do that to her, Jan.'

'Listen, Glen, when my son was alive, I wanted to protect him from everything that might cause him hurt or heartache. But you can't ... it's impossible. Life has its ups and downs, its good times and its bad, and as we're growing up we have to learn to deal with them and the things that happen to us.' She leaned forward, eyeing him earnestly, and spoke with conviction. 'Your daughter needs ... deserves ... to know that her father is alive and well and that he loves her. She needs to know the truth about why you disappeared from her life, Glen, no matter what pain it causes her.'

He looked at Jan for several long moments before he said, 'But what if...'

She cut in, 'Life's full of *what ifs*, Glen. Mine certainly is. What if it had been pelting with rain that night and my son had not gone out at all? What if I'd dished the dinner up earlier and we'd been eating when his friends called? What if Bernie hadn't been my window cleaner? What if Harry hadn't come home when he had and caught us ... I could go on.

'Stop thinking about the what ifs, Glen, they might never happen. Let's just deal with things as they come, eh? I agree that the workplace isn't the right one to divulge the type of news you have to give your daughter, but as things stand it's the only option open to you. Or, just an idea, you could always wait for her to come out of work and waylay her then – tell her you have some very important family news and ask her to go somewhere you can discuss it. A nearby pub perhaps. But, look, first things first. Why don't you decide just what you're going to say to her first, before when and where you're going to do it?'

It was good advice Jan was giving him and he smiled at her. 'Yes, I will.' He took several sips of his tea, which was now cold, before he looked across at her again and tentatively asked, 'Did ... er ... you happen to see Lucy when you were taking the tea trolley around today? If you did, what's she like?'

Jan had been waiting for this question. It wasn't until dinnertime when she had been wiping down tables near a group of women from the offices upstairs that she had overheard them discussing the fact that it wasn't the actual owner who had come in to run the business but her daughter. That was when she had realised that the young woman she'd had a run-in with yesterday morning in the boss's office had had every right to be in there, and every right also to dismiss Jan for speaking as she had about her mother. Jan just hoped that she didn't come face to face with her again until sufficient time had passed for her to have forgotten the incident. But then, how could she tell Glen that what she'd thought had been her first impression of his daughter hadn't been at all favourable? When she'd seen her in the church, Jan had thought her far too full of her own importance and her manner certainly left a lot to be desired. She just couldn't tell the truth, though. Hopefully, she had caught the young woman at a bad time.

She lied to Glen. 'I've not been out of the kitchen. Hilda's decided it's best I learn the ropes in the canteen first.' She wanted to ask him how his day had gone but Glen was staring into the glowing coals in the fireplace again. It was obvious his thoughts were fixed on his daughter and how best to handle the delicate situation with her.

Jan sat back in her own chair and rested her head, stretching out her feet to prop them on the hearth. She found herself thinking about her husband and for a moment was transported back to a time when they had all been happy. After dinner had been cleared away, the three of them would sit together in the living room, she with her knitting or the latest book she was reading, Harry with his newspaper, Keith with a comic or toy, the radio playing in the background, all relaxed and content in each other's company. She'd believed this state of affairs would go on until Keith grew up and left home, and then it would be just herself and Harry, happy in each other's company. Never for a moment had she any idea that fate would play its hand and rip their lives apart.

She wondered what Harry was doing now. Then she realised she didn't need to. After eating a meal cooked for him by the do-gooding women of the congregation he would be at the evening service or attending a meeting on church matters, maybe planning for Christmas which would be on them shortly. At the thought of the festive season her eyes strayed to Glen, still lost in his own thoughts, staring into the fire, and she wondered what Christmas last year had been like for him. The same as all the other Christmases for the five years since leaving prison, she suspected, spent scavenging for something to eat, then searching for somewhere to keep warm. No festive cheer for him.

For the last few years her own Christmases hadn't been the joyous occasions they were meant to be. The family get togethers, joining her mother and sisters at one of their houses or at her own in yearly rotation, she had put a stop to, not feeling it right to inflict on them the tension between herself and Harry at a time when families should be enjoying themselves. After breakfast Harry would go to church then afterwards join members of the congregation in visiting the needy and elderly members of the parish, delivering the boxes of food that had been collected over the weeks leading up to the holiday via kind donations from the general public. Then there were the fund-raising events which Harry was always in the thick of. She was never sure what time he would get back for his dinner but she cooked it anyway and would then sit staring at the Christmas tree and paper trimmings gathering dust – those being her own efforts to inject some Christmas cheer into her home – waiting for him to return and doing her best to ensure their meal wasn't ruined mean-time. They would then sit opposite each other at the dining table, both fighting to make conver-sation but failing since neither had anything to say to the other. They had stopped buying gifts for one another, even token gestures, as Harry was resolutely of the opinion that any spare money they had should be put towards benefiting those less fortunate than themselves.

Well, this year, unless something happened to see them parting company by then, she was determined to make sure Glen and she had some Christmas cheer. A good meal and a little present to open at least. And perhaps, if all went well, Glen might have a special visitor to entertain.

CHAPTER SEVENTEEN

Agnes Dalby sighed with relief to hear footsteps descending the stairs at long last. She scurried out of the kitchen to greet Cait. 'Good morning, Miss Thomas. I was getting really worried about you. It's well past your normal time for leaving the house to go to work and you haven't even had any breakfast yet.'

At the bottom of the stairs Cait looked over at the woman, feeling perplexed. Agnes had been in every day since her employers had left, continuing with her duties despite the fact that she wasn't being paid. Cait couldn't at all understand why she was acting this way and not off enjoying her leisure.

'You did understand my mother's instructions to you when she left?' Cait asked her now.

She nodded. 'Perfectly. Mrs Thomas laid me off until she comes back.'

212

'Then why are you still working here when you're not being paid?'

'Because if I didn't, who would look after you, Miss Thomas?'

Cait felt shocked. Was this Agnes Dalby's way of telling her she cared about her? If so, why was it that she could when Cait's own parents couldn't? She didn't know quite how to respond to this so just said, 'I would like some breakfast, Agnes. Tea and toast will be fine.'

It wasn't lost on Agnes that Cait had addressed her by her Christian name for the first time, and wondered if the girl had realised. She felt warmed by it. 'I'll have it ready in a jiffy.'

As Agnes bustled back into the kitchen she fought down her desire to ask Cait just where she was getting the money from to buy the smart new suit she was wearing, different from yesterday's, not to mention pay for the new hairstyle she was sporting, which was clearly from an expensive salon in town, the sort her mother frequented. Then there were the dozen or so boxes of new shoes and handbags that Agnes had helped the taxi driver bring in when they'd been delivered yesterday afternoon. Even if she landed herself a new job, it couldn't pay on such a munificent scale, and besides she hadn't been working there long enough to have been paid her first wage packet. And, more surprisingly, this new job didn't seem to require her to work normal office hours either as she was home by four yesterday afternoon and had time to have her hair done first. It was after nine o'clock now and Cait seemed in no hurry to be at her new workplace.

But it wasn't Agnes's place to query that, she decided.

There was a question it was her place to broach. As she was putting Cait's breakfast before her Agnes asked, 'Miss Thomas, do you know what your plans are for Christmas yet? Have you had any word whether your parents will be back by then? Only there isn't much time if I'm to make a Christmas cake and pudding, mince pies et cetera, and also what I'm needed to prepare in advance for Christmas Day. I can order all the provisions from the butcher and grocer, of course.'

Cait looked back at her blankly. Christmas Day had never proved any fun for her in the past, her parents not at all the type to make merry, and she had been so much looking forward to a different sort of holiday this year, surrounded by Neil's family and friends, which wasn't going to be now. Still, there was time for her to meet someone else ... maybe she could find a way to entice someone new to ask her to join them for the day. She told Agnes, 'I've been invited out for Christmas Day so there's no need for you to prepare anything special.'

The motherly side of Agnes was relieved to learn that the young woman was not spending the day alone. No one should be left solitary on the Lord's birthday, in particular a young girl who was not only getting over a broken engagement but also coping with the fact that her self-centred parents hadn't showed any consideration or compassion for her when going off on holiday, knowing her emotional state at the time. Looking forward to taking one day off at least, Agnes went back to the kitchen to clear away.

Cait finally arrived at the factory at just after ten. When she arrived she saw the young receptionist laughing with another girl. Both of them were in her own age group, fashionably dressed and looked the friendly sort. Here was an opportunity to make some new friends, a chance to ingratiate herself with them and hope one of them would invite her to join them on Christmas Day.

But then Cait remembered her position in the company, and her mother's belief that it wasn't the done thing for the hierarchy to fraternise with their employees. In future the type of friends she needed to make for herself were the type who mixed in the same social circles as she did now. She hoped she'd be invited into those circles by the company's customers and suppliers who would want to build good working relationships with her.

As she had been yesterday, she was greeted in her office by the efficient, unflappable Jane Trucker.

'Good morning, Miss Thomas,' she greeted Cait in a businesslike manner.

Cait flashed her a critical look as she took off her coat and hung it up on the coat stand behind the door. She considered Jane to be a plain woman who did herself no favours by wearing such matronly, old-fashioned tweed suits, high-necked blouses, thick stockings and sturdy shoes. But today she looked even more dour, dressed as she was all in black. Then it struck Cait that she was all dressed like that because she was attending a funeral. A funeral she herself was supposed to be attending, representing her mother! Inwardly she heaved a sigh. A funeral was the last thing she felt like attending, though it seemed she'd have to as her mother's representative.

She said to Jane, 'I could do with a cup of tea, if you'd order it for me.'

That wasn't what the secretary had been waiting for Cait to speak to her about, but regardless she said, 'I'll see to it, Miss Thomas.'

Cait shivered and said, 'It's chilly in here.'

Jane did not fail to notice the couple of magazines Cait took out of her handbag and put on the desk, and wondered whether this meant she was going to sit and read them all day or if she was actually going to make some contribution towards keeping the company profitable. She told Cait, 'The radiators in the whole place have a mind of their own, I'm afraid. One day they're boiling hot and the next stone cold. The boiler is really long overdue for replacement. In fact, the whole system needs renewing as it must be over fifty years old. Half the maintenance man's week is taken up with plastering over its cracks, so to speak. I know Mr Swinton had spoken to Mrs Thomas about it a few times over the last few years, and we're waiting for her decision.'

Cait knew better than to go over her mother's head. 'I expect there are a couple of electric heaters around somewhere. Will you find me one and bring it in? Oh, and you won't forget about the tea, will you?'

Jane inwardly sighed. This young woman

seemed to think that a secretary's job was purely to run about seeing to her every whim, when in truth she had a mountain of important work to do – much of it work that Cait herself should be attending to. Jane did have some important information she needed to tell the young woman, but supposed she ought to see to her requests first then hopefully she would be more receptive.

Five minutes later Jane returned armed with a plug-in heater which she then spent several minutes moving around the room until Cait was satisfied she was receiving the full benefit of it. The tray of tea was delivered meantime and as Cait poured herself a cup Jane said, 'I need to warn you, Miss Thomas, to expect all the foremen to visit you at eleven.'

Cait looked up, a blank expression on her face. 'What for?'

'I passed on the instructions you gave me yesterday and they aren't happy.' Flabbergasted at first then fuming was the truth of the matter, once Jane had informed them of their extra responsibilities.

Cait fought to hide her alarm. She didn't like the thought of several burly men descending on her, obviously aiming to intimidate her into backtracking on her instructions. If she allowed them to force her to countermand her orders, where would her credibility as a boss be?

And, of course, there was the problem that she had delegated the work to them in the first place because she herself wasn't capable of tackling it. Should that come to light she'd become a laughing stock around the factory. She had to make a stand here, show these men that she may be young but she was the boss and what she said went. It was very important that her mother returned to find the company prospering in her daughter's capable hands. Then she would see Cait in a new light and that wouldn't be the case if she found the workers running rings around her.

She said to Jane, 'Inform the men that I have given them my instructions and have nothing more to say on the matter. Did you need me for anything else?'

Jane did. The same as the foremen, her workload had already been more than enough for her to cope with, without the extra burden that Cait should have been dealing with heaped on her as well. Like the foremen, she was neither qualified nor remunerated enough to make such critical business decisions, and was worried just who would be held accountable if errors were made. But if Cait didn't see fit to listen to the foremen's legitimate reasons for refusing to take on the extra responsibilities, then she was unlikely to pay attention to Jane either.

She excused herself and left the office.

A while later Cait had finished reading the magazines from cover to cover, the articles not as interesting or informative as she had expected, and was leaning back in her chair, wondering what to do with herself now. She heaved a deep sigh. Being a boss had not proved as exciting as she had thought it would. According to the girls she had worked with in her previous job, the owner would sit in his inner sanctum on his fat arse telephoning around his business colleagues, arranging social events ... lunches, games of golf and the like. As matters stood she had no business colleagues. That would surely change, though, once word spread that a new female boss was in place at Rose's who needed wining and dining in order to secure business deals. In the meantime she needed to fill her day, which seemed to be passing too slowly. It really was no fun having nothing to do. Cait was surprised to notice that she was missing being kept busy.

She suddenly realised that she had not yet taken a tour around the factory. Righting herself in her chair, she made to lean over and press the button on the intercom to summon Jane Trucker to escort her but then thought better of it. She would have to make small talk with the older woman as they went around, and Cait felt she had nothing in common with her and didn't relish awkward silences. She hadn't yet asked Jane where the executive dining area was. Hopefully she would find it herself on her travels and have some lunch there.

On leaving her office Cait decided to take the stairs leading down to reception. Then she saw a door to the side of her that she hadn't noticed before and decided to investigate where it led. There were more stairs behind it. She deduced that this must be the back entrance to the offices, avoiding the reception area. Descending them, she found herself in a short corridor with one door on her right and another at the end. The sign on the door informed her it was the customers' viewing room. Making her way over to the door at the end, Cait opened it and found it led to a wide area she assumed was the workers' entrance as on the wall was a clocking-in machine along with a clock-card holder on the wall to one side of it. She could see the signs for male and female lavatories and there was another door opposite that had no sign on it.

Cait went across to that and had a peek through. It led into a large cobbled area, with several separate old-looking two-storey buildings grouped on the other side. The site the company occupied appeared far larger than she had envisaged. It was now possible for her to see that the building she was in was two-storey at the front with a single storey extending quite a distance off the back.

She took a look around. Several people were in the process of crossing the yard, obviously on works business judging by what they were carrying. But then she saw a couple of groups of men and women huddled in the doorways opposite, smoking cigarettes. When she looked back and down both sides of the main building this side of the yard she saw a couple of other groups of workers, also smoking while they laughed and chatted between themselves. She watched as members of each group, having finished their cigarettes, threw their butts on the ground then disappeared back inside. Seconds later other workers arrived to take their places. This practice was the same as in her last job. The warehousemen smoked in the yard under whatever cover they could find, while the office staff sat smoking at their desks. Now Cait was in charge, though, she wasn't sure how she felt about the practice continuing. After all, the workers were taking unofficial breaks when they should in fact be working.

She decided to go across the yard to visit the outlying buildings first, finding herself intrigued to know just what went on in there. She began to cross the cobbled yard. With everyone else dressed in work clothes, she suddenly felt very self-conscious and out of place, dressed in her expensive suit and suede court shoes. Although she kept her eyes straight ahead she was acutely aware some people had noticed her and were looking at her curiously. She didn't doubt that by now word had spread through the company that the owner's daughter was taking care of business until her mother returned from holiday, and she suspected the people watching her were wondering if this was her. She wished now she had asked Jane to accompany her. At least then people would know for certain that she was the new boss and not just an over-dressed new clerk in the office.

She was barely a quarter of the way across when she heard a loud wolf whistle then a male voice shout: 'Well, look what we got here! A new doll in the offices. 'Bout bloody time. Already shagged 'ote worth having.' Then another voice shouted, 'Eh up, what yer doing tonight, gel? Fancy the back row of the flicks? I promise I won't keep me hands to meself.' The first voice snapped angrily, 'Keep yer hands off, Jez. I saw 'er first.' The man addressed as Jez then retorted, 'As if a babe is gonna look at you when I'm around, yer dozy git.'

Cait spun on her heel to face the two young

men responsible. One of them was extremely good-looking, almost as good-looking as Neil, and normally she would have been flattered to have captured his attention. The youth who had caught her eye was tall, his dark hair slicked back at the sides, long quiff fashioned into a DA. Under his gaping brown work coat, his clothes were Teddy boy-style. Like the majority of women Cait revelled in being found attractive by men, but she reminded herself that she wasn't one of the girls in the office any longer but the boss and should conduct herself accordingly.

She felt it best to ignore the men so turned around and made to continue on her journey when another comment made her spin around once more. 'Did you just call me a stuck-up bitch?' she called angrily.

Jez, pretending to look around innocently, then brought his gaze back to her. 'Who else d'yer think I'm talking to, yer daft cow? Look, no need to act shy with us, gel.' A twinkle of mischief sparked in his eyes. 'Fancy five minutes around the back of the bike sheds?'

She temporarily forgot that these two men would not know who she was and snapped angrily, 'How dare you speak to me like that? Don't you know who I am?'

It was Jez's mate who answered. 'Some frigid tart that thinks she summat she ain't, dressed like a dog's dinner.' He poked Jez in the ribs. 'Yer wasting yer time, mate. Yer'll be lucky if the haughty bitch will allow yer to hold her hand, let alone get any further.'

Jez laughed. 'Yeah, yer right.' He smirked at

Cait. 'I'm hung like a donkey so it's your loss, doll.'

'How dare you...'

The scene was cut short by a middle-aged, balding man who poked his head out of the door behind the two young men. He addressed them both with an annoyed, 'Oi, you two! You both asked to go to the men's, not to go out for a crafty fag. Now get back inside. We're still behind with the boxes for the order that's due to go out...'

He was interrupted by Cait who demanded: 'Are you in charge of these men?'

For the first time he noticed her. He looked startled for a moment before he responded, 'Yes, but what has that to do with you, young lady?'

'I'll tell you what it's got to do with me. I'm Caitlyn Thomas.'

Fred Holt's face turned pale and he gulped audibly. 'Oh!'

'These men have just insulted me. I want them disciplined. Severely.' Before she could stop herself, Cait blurted, 'They're both to be sacked. I want them off the premises right away.'

Astounded, Jez exclaimed, 'Eh, now, hang on a minute! We weren't to know who you was. 'Sides, it was only a bit of fun we was having. In't right being sacked for having a bit of fun.'

'Yeah, that's right,' piped up his worried mate. 'Just a bit of fun we was having. All the other gels here lap it up.'

Cait knew the two men had only been amusing themselves but felt that should she retract her decision, the rest of the workforce wouldn't take her seriously. She couldn't afford to back down now. 'Well, I'm not one of the other girls. I didn't find your way of talking to me a bit funny.'

Fred pleaded, 'Oh, now, Miss Thomas ... these two are good lads. They'll apologise for upsetting you, I'm sure. Promise not to do it...'

Cait still felt that the men should be disciplined for their unwarranted rudeness to her, but deep down she knew she had reacted too harshly. But to relent and lighten their punishment would be to show that she was out of her depth, which in truth she was. 'I've said all I have to say on the matter,' she announced.

Not wanting to risk finding herself in the middle of another such situation, she decided to go back to the office and ask Jane to take her on a guided tour.

As she arrived at the secretary's office, she found the other woman bashing out correspondence on her Remington typewriter. There was a harassed expression on her face when she said to Cait, 'What can I do for you, Miss Thomas?'

'I'd like you to show me round the factory.'

'Oh, er ... you mean right now, Miss Thomas? Only I must get these letters out today. They really should have gone yesterday but I didn't have time...'

'Don't you have a typing pool to see to that?' Cait asked her.

'No, Miss Thomas. Each department has their own clerk-typist to deal with paperwork.'

'Oh, I see. Then I suppose my walkabout will have to wait for when you aren't so busy.' She remembered something she needed to speak to the other woman about, but the shrilling of the telephone stalled her. Jane excused herself to answer it. Cait could tell that the conversation was not going to be a short one so left her to it.

Back in her office, she flopped down on her chair and leaned back in it, giving out a long sigh to find herself back where she'd started just ten or so minutes ago.

She glanced idly around the office. To one side of her desk, against the wall, was a large bookcase crammed with dusty-looking volumes, their titles telling her they were all to do with the shoe trade over the ages, along with numerous copies of shoe-trade magazines and brochures from other firms. Normally such tomes would not have interested her in the slightest but it suddenly occurred to Cait that she should find out a little about the industry she was now in, if for no other reason than being able to converse knowledgeably on the subject when she was socialising with others in the trade, which she hoped to be in the future. She got up, went across to the bookcase and selected a book at random, taking it back to her desk. Much to her astonishment she found herself quickly becoming absorbed in the history of the shoe trade, astounded by the fact that until the middle of the last century all footwear was made by hand in people's homes, wives working alongside their husbands and children until the invention of machines took the trade into factories, which were mainly in the Northamptonshire area. Before she knew it Cait had read the whole hundred pages and the hooter was sounding to announce to the workers it was dinnertime. She realised she was hungry herself.

She still hadn't asked Jane Trucker where the boss's dining room was but the thought of eating alone either there or in her office should she have a tray sent up did not appeal. She decided she would go out for lunch. There must be a decent place to eat around here. As boss she wasn't confined to just an hour so she would string it out for as long as she could to while away some time. That just left the remainder of the afternoon to get through. She supposed she could try another book from the collection here but felt she'd read enough about the shoe trade for one day. Then a thought struck her. As boss she was at liberty to come and go as she pleased so she really didn't have to come back to the office this afternoon if she didn't want to. There was a film she was keen to see at the pictures, *The Ladykillers*, a crime comedy with Peter Sellers and Alec Guinness amongst other big-name British stars taking part. There was no reason why she shouldn't go and see it this afternoon.

On her way out she was passing Jane Trucker's office when she remembered there was something she wanted to speak to her about so made a detour.

Jane was just replacing the telephone receiver and it was apparent she was working through her dinner hour as a plastic box containing a sandwich and an apple stood open on her desk. She smiled a greeting at Cait and said to her, 'Miss Thomas, I'm glad you've come in. I was just speaking to one of our suppliers of hides about a batch that's late being delivered, which could disrupt our production schedule. It's my guess what's happened is that the firm has had an urgent order come in from another company, who have threatened to go elsewhere for their hides if they don't receive supplies urgently. So what they've done is given them our order to keep them sweet, giving us a fabricated tale about the reason for the delay in our delivery. They never would have dared act this way with us before Mr Swinton died. Anyway, I'm waiting for a call back from their sales director with a firm delivery date, but it would carry much more weight if you'd be good enough...'

Cait knew the woman was going to ask her to speak to the supplier's sales director and the thought terrified her. She couldn't bring herself to tell Jane this so replied, 'Well, if you're waiting for a call I'll make this brief. I want you to inform the foremen as a matter of urgency to pass on to the workers that in future there'll be no more toilet breaks during working hours.'

Jane looked taken aback. 'But people can't be denied a toilet visit when they need one, Miss Thomas.'

'It's not the toilet they're going to, though, is it? I witnessed that myself this morning when I went for a short walk and found several couples canoodling around the side of a building, two women having an argument, several other groups of people laughing and joking and smoking cigarettes ... all on the firm's time. So from now on the workers will visit the toilets before they start their shifts and during authorised break times only.'

Jane opened her mouth to inform Cait that all the workers in the production departments were on piecework, so weren't paid if they weren't physically producing anything. Those who did have an impromptu break would be up to their daily quota level as none of the workers would risk taking home a short pay packet at the end of the week. She could also assure Cait that those not on piecework were closely watched by their superiors, whose job it was to keep them in line. None of them were going to risk their jobs by turning a blind eye to shirkers. But before Jane could enlighten Cait on this, she was saying as she headed out of the office, 'I'll see you in the morning.'

Jane immediately called after her, 'Oh, but Miss Thomas … what about Mr Swinton's funeral this afternoon?'

But Cait did not hear her. She was already out of earshot.

Jan could tell immediately she clapped eyes on Glen as he made his way over to where she was waiting for him on the canal tow path that evening that he had heard the same rumours she had. There was a grim, worried expression on his face. This, though, wasn't the place to discuss matters, and Glen would talk about it when he wanted to. In a repetition of the previous night, they were both seated by the fire after dinner had been cleared away before he gave a heavy sigh and looked across at her, so many emotions blazing from his eyes it would be impossible to name them all.

In a helpless tone he said, 'I don't know what to do, Jan.'

'About what?' she asked, as though she had no idea.

'Have you heard the rumours going around about Lucy?'

She could tell by the look in his eye, the tone of his voice, that he was hoping she hadn't, meaning that matters might not be as bad as he feared they were. Just a few of the staff disgruntled by his daughter's idea of leadership, not the majority. Jan nodded and said gravely, 'According to what's being said, your daughter doesn't seem to be making herself very popular, does she?'

He shook his head, grim-faced. 'Not from what Harry Owens told me, no, she isn't. According to him she's acting like she's the queen bee and all the workers better do as she says or suffer harsh consequences.' His face screwed up into a mask of mortification. 'And apparently she's really upset everyone because she didn't attend Reg Swinton's funeral. Never even showed her face or sent an apology. His widow was extremely upset, as you can imagine, Reg having worked tirelessly for the firm for the length of time he had. Harry said that it was very embarrassing for the staff who attended.'

'Oh, dear,' Jan mused. 'That really is unforgivable of her. Anyway, in respect of the way she's lording it about, in all fairness, Glen, she's only sixteen.'

'Seventeen in January,' he corrected her.

'Then she's still sixteen now. When I was her age, I thought I knew everything. Wouldn't listen to any advice my elders tried to give me but believed everything people of my own age told me, even things that my own common sense should have told me were complete bunkum. One of the things I believed was that the top brass sat in their ivory towers all day, waiting for us minions to keep them in champagne and caviar. Of course, it wasn't until I grew older and wiser that I realised the truth of what the bosses really got up to when I thought they were idling: handling critical day-to-day issues that affected the success of the company. Didn't you think that too before you wised up?'

'No. My father made sure I knew everything about running a successful business. The moment I was old enough, I was shown what went on behind closed doors.'

'Oh, yes, of course.' Jan folded her arms under her shapely chest and said matter-of-factly, 'Well, your ex-wife is to blame for letting your obviously grossly inexperienced daughter have free rein with the company while she's swanning around on holiday, not giving a damn. Serves her right if she comes back to find the place has gone to the wall.'

Glen eyed her sharply. 'Wouldn't be much help to the people who rely on their jobs to keep a roof over their family's heads and food on the table, would it? I couldn't bear to see the company suffer, and especially not at the hands of my daughter with her daft ideas about running it. Her grandfather started that company from scratch, put his last penny into it, built it up by working all hours ... to provide for his family and have something of value to hand over to me when he retired. Or, as it turned out, died. I worked hard

230

to build on what he'd left me. When Lucy was born I vowed to work even harder, to ensure she had a good inheritance. I can't just stand by and say nothing when she's doing so much damage.'

Jan frowned. 'What do you propose then, Glen? If you want to have any hope of building a relationship with Lucy, you need to pick your time and place carefully and be very sensitive in your approach.'

Glen stared at her blindly. His emotions were in turmoil. He might not have set eyes on his daughter for fifteen years but his love for her and sense of parental responsibility had never diminished. He was torn now between a desperate need to protect Lucy from the vicious tongues that would be lashing her for the way she was acting, excuse her behaviour, blame himself somehow for it, while the other part of him wanted to demand from her just why she thought she was a superior being with the right to treat those she saw as beneath her as if they didn't matter. He vehemently hoped that Lucy's behaviour was just the result of her immaturity. She was obviously not equipped for the role she'd been forced into. Jan was right and Nerys must be out of her mind to think that a girl of such tender years could do what was being expected of Lucy, just because she herself didn't want to cut short her holiday.

A wave of weariness swept over Glen. For the first time since he'd been rescued from his miserable life on the road, he wished he was back there now with only the task of keeping himself alive to worry about, a monumental problem to him at the time but one which seemed to be paling into insignificance compared to what he was facing in his new life.

Jan meanwhile was feeling sorry for her new friend. She had known him for only a short space of time but it had very quickly became apparent to her that Glen was a highly moral man who, despite the terrible situations he had found himself in over the last few years, had never lost his principles. It must be destroying him to have learned that his daughter had developed into such an unattractive individual. Jan, though, felt that the young girl couldn't be held entirely responsible for her outlook on life. She wouldn't say as much to Glen, though. He would be feeling enough guilt already for the way his daughter had been raised.

Leaning forward, she told him, 'Look, Glen, I know how important the business is to you, but you need to remember it's no longer yours. If it suffers in any way from the workers deciding to strike, then that's on Nerys's head alone. What you need to be concentrating on is making a plan for how you're going to approach your daughter and break the news to her. And you need to decide on that quickly, before Nerys comes back and you lose your chance.'

Glen looked at Jan thoughtfully. She was right. The business his father had started was important to him, along with keeping the workers in employment, but far more important was reinstating himself with his daughter, which was going to be hard enough in itself, hoping she would believe his side of the story against the one Nerys must have told her.

CHAPTER EIGHTEEN

The next morning Cait stared at her own reflection in the bathroom mirror. It would take a lot of carefully applied make-up to disguise the bags under her eyes after her lack of sleep. Her afternoon out the day before hadn't proved to be as much fun as she had thought it would be. It had been no fun eating by herself in the restaurant and no fun either watching the film by herself, not able to get out of her mind the fact that the last time she had visited the cinema Neil had been with her. Tomorrow would have been her wedding day and at the moment she had no idea how she was going to get through it.

Today she really didn't feel like going into work. The only reason she was, was the thought that should her mother decide for whatever reason to cut her holiday short and return home for Christmas, this very day even, and find Cait wallowing in misery huddled on the sofa, leaving her company without anyone at the helm, then her one chance of proving herself a worthy daughter would be doomed to failure. She was worried that she hadn't as yet come up with anywhere near a plausible explanation for rummaging around in her parents' bedroom, finding the safe and helping herself to the money inside, but was dearly hoping that once she had delighted her mother by rising to the challenge and doing such

233

a commendable job of overseeing her business, then that misdemeanour would be overlooked.

Cait heard the padding of footsteps coming down the landing and turned her head to see Agnes heading to her bedroom with a cup of tea for her. It struck her that she had grown fond of the old woman recently and she knew she would never have got through the last few days without Agnes's motherly fussing and care of her, something she could easily get used to but daren't because as soon as her mother returned, providing Cait was allowed to stay here at home and would not need to leave to live in a place of her own, Agnes would have to revert to Nerys's rigid house rules: that she was employed purely to cook and clean and not in any way act familiarly with the family. Cait wished she could bring herself to go against her mother and tell Agnes she appreciated her thoughtfulness towards her; tell her of the times she'd had to restrain herself from throwing herself on her shoulder. How she longed to feel the comfort of a pair of motherly arms around her. But she was prevented from admitting it by a strong sense of her mother standing behind her, eyes boring into the back of her head, tapping her on her shoulder, daring her to defy her rules. Maybe one day Cait could find the courage to do so, when she felt it was right to, and give Agnes due thanks. But at the moment she couldn't.

A short while later Jan and Glen wished each other good day as they went their separate ways after clocking in at the factory. It didn't escape either of them that the majority of those clocking in at the same time didn't look very happy. They both hoped that this was because they faced another long day at work when they'd sooner be somewhere else, and not for any other reason.

As he had lain in bed the night before, Glen had taken Jan's advice to him seriously and realised he needed to come up with a plan for how to meet Lucy away from the workplace. It had to be before Nerys returned or he could lose his chance. He had decided that tonight he would wait for her to come out of work and approach her in the street, tell her that he was an old family friend and he had something important to tell her. He felt sure she would be intrigued enough to hear what he had to say, and agree. He had told Jan of his plan that morning over breakfast and she had thought it a good idea.

When Glen arrived at his room he was surprised to find no sign of Harry Owens. His assistant, Jeff Briggs, though, was living up to the nickname that Harry had bestowed on him. Lazybones was sitting on a chair at the packing counter, engrossed in a copy of that morning's *Sketch* when he should have started work by now.

As he took off his coat and hung it up, Glen asked him, 'No Harry today?'

Without lifting his head, Jeff shrugged. 'Ain't seen him this morning.'

'Oh, well, maybe he's just a bit late for some reason and will be along any minute. Haven't you anything to be doing?'

Jeff gave a nonchalant shrug. 'Yeah, I 'spose, when I've finished this.'

Glen shook his head at the young man. He wanted to say something to him, remind him that if he didn't buck his ideas up soon he'd be finding himself looking for another job. But it wasn't his place. He went into his room to check what jobs he had on for today, collect what he needed to carry them out and be on his way. He had several routine tasks but one needed to be seen to first. The night watchman had written down in his book during his shift last night that as he'd been doing his rounds he'd noticed that one of the trees at the back of the building, in the strip of wasteland between the factory and the disused outbuildings, was half-uprooted. Glen was reminded then of the case the police had brought against him. He was alleged to have hidden the spoils of his 'robbery' in those outbuildings. According to the night watchman, the tree was at risk of toppling straight into the back of one of the buildings edging the cobbled yard. There was no telling what damage would be caused then, not only to the building itself but to the workers inside if it fell during the daytime. High winds were making it more unstable. Picking up a sturdy rope and a saw, Glen wrapped himself up warmly then went off to deal with it.

Only seconds after Cait arrived in the office that morning at nine-thirty, Jane Trucker tapped on the door. As soon as Cait called out for her to enter she came in, holding a leather folder. Her voice was noticeably clipped when she said, 'Good morning, Miss Thomas. I've some letters that require your signature.'

Having taken off her coat, Cait made her way around the desk and sat down. She took great pleasure in saying, 'Leave them with me. I'll sign them later.'

Jane Trucker decided Cait Thomas was just a child in an adult's world.

As Jane still hadn't made any effort to leave the office, Cait tersely asked, 'Was there something else?'

'Well, yes, there is, Miss Thomas,' she said in her usual businesslike manner. 'I just wondered if you were feeling better?' Jane saw the look of bemusement on her young boss's face and continued, 'We all thought you must have been suddenly taken ill yesterday afternoon as you didn't come to Mr Swinton's funeral. Mrs Swinton was very upset but I assured her that it was obvious something serious had happened, to keep you from coming.'

Cait looked back at her blankly. She had forgotten all about the funeral. Feeling ashamed, she said, 'Yes, it was something serious that stopped me from coming.'

It was apparent to Jane that was all the explanation she was going to get for her non-attendance. Gut instinct told her that the truth was the young woman had completely forgotten about it. To the rest of the workers, this thoughtless act was the final straw in a long list of misguided decisions Cait had made in the short time she had been in charge of the company. To them enough was enough, as Miss Caitlyn Thomas would very shortly find out.

Cait was saying to her, 'I'd like you to escort me

round the factory this morning.'

Jane looked flustered. 'Oh, er ... I'd be glad to, Miss Thomas, but I really haven't time this morning. Well, all day really. In fact, I'd be hard pressed, as matters stand at the moment, to tell you when I'll have any free time. I've got such a lot of work on, you see.' She hoped that Cait would take this as a hint and offer to help.

But her hopes fell flat when Cait responded coldly, 'I trust you'll let me know when you do find you have the time. When you return to your office, would you order me a tray of tea?'

Through gritted teeth, Jane responded, 'Of course, Miss Thomas.'

In her own office Cait took a pile of magazines from out of the handbag at the side of her chair, selected Woman's Own, placed it on the desk before her and was soon engrossed in its pages.

Meanwhile in the canteen, buttering a mountain of cobs and slices of bread, Jan was craning her neck to look over at the four men sitting around a table at the far end of the room, smoking endless cigarettes, deep in conversation. She had a worrying feeling she knew who they were and what the topic of their conversation was, but was hoping she was wrong. She would have asked Hilda but she was busy in the cold store making a list of supplies. One of the other canteen assistants was coming her way, armed with a tray containing a huge pile of sausages and bacon, and Jan waylaid her as she passed by.

'Dilys, do you know who those men are around the table?'

Dilys Brennan was only a couple of years older than Jan and had been a pretty young girl when she had married the handsome, charming William Brennan, twenty years before. But after giving birth to eight children, two of whom had died at birth, and putting up with a man who had turned out to be work-shy, liked his drink and thought that his wife was a punchbag after a session on Saturday nights, she now looked and acted twenty years older.

Dilys put down the heavy tray for a moment. Frowning, she replied to Jan, 'Keeping our jobs safe, I hope, ducky. But without taking the serious action I fear they may be planning, which would affect our wage packets. If that happens, I don't know what I'll bloody do this Christmas!' Picking up the tray again, she went on her way.

Jan's worried eyes were directed back to the men. So they were who she suspected them to be. She wondered if Glen had heard that a union meeting was in progress, and like her was deeply concerned about the outcome and what it would mean for his daughter.

The meeting had hardly been in progress for ten minutes when the men all scraped back their chairs and stood up. The one who seemed to have been leading the meeting said something to the other three, which Jan couldn't hear, then the other men left and the leader walked over to the counter and asked to speak to Hilda. Jan was nearest to the cold store and so went over and gave her a shout that she was wanted. She had obviously been waiting to learn the outcome of the meeting taking place in her canteen. Her face was screwed in worry when she came bustling over to the counter where the man spoke to her in low tones before he turned and left.

Hilda said loudly, 'Right, girls, listen up.' She paused for a moment while her staff all stopped what they were doing. When she had their full attention, she continued, 'The union has called a meeting in the yard in fifteen minutes. I don't think I need to tell you what it's about. Right, carry on what yer doing until then. Regardless what the outcome is, we'll still have hungry mouths to feed.'

Jan wasn't in the union, and neither she suspected were the other canteen staff, but like them she knew it was in her best interest to go along with the rest unless she wanted to suffer the consequences of being seen as a blackleg.

The telephone in Hilda's office shrilled out and on her way back into the cold store she about-turned and hurried off to answer it. Several moments later she came out and said to the rest of the staff, 'That was Jane Trucker asking us to take a tray of tea up for *Madam*.' Her mouth split into a broad grin. 'Well, she can wait until we find out the outcome of the meeting.'

Glen agreed with the night watchman that the tree needed to come down before it did untold damage. He'd sawed off some of the lower branches, and realised he should have brought ladders with him to tackle the ones further up so as to lighten the tree before he tried to pull it down using the rope. He was making his way down the narrow opening between two buildings

240

that led back to the cobbled yard when the hum of voices reached him, growing louder the nearer he drew to the front of the buildings where the yard opened out before him. He was stunned to see that the voices belonged to dozens of the workers already gathered in the yard. Others were coming out of the main works entrance and also from the buildings to the side of him, huddling into groups where they conversed with each other, their breath forming clouds as it hit the icy air. On a small platform that had been erected nearest the huge entrance gates, using several sturdy wooden crates, stood four men. They were talking amongst themselves. One was holding a megaphone. One of them was Harry Owens.

Glen's heart sank. A representative had obviously approached the union late yesterday. A meeting of the shop stewards had been called first thing this morning, and that was why Harry had been absent from his post. They had agreed what action needed to be taken against Lucy's way of running the firm and were putting it to the workers now for them to vote on. Over by the entrance, Glen spotted Jan standing with a group of women. He could see she was scanning the crowd, looking for him. Weaving his way hurriedly through the throng, he went over to her.

'Oh, there you are, Glen,' she exclaimed the instant she spotted him. She then said gravely, 'I hope we're not going to be asked to vote on what I think we are. Well, we can't vote, can we? We're not in the union. But all the same, we'll have no choice but to go along with what the members decide.'

Glen just looked back at her grimly.

Meanwhile, upstairs in the office, the muted sounds of many voices reached Cait's ears, filtering through the window which overlooked the yard. For a moment all went silent, then a louder voice erupted. She got up and went to the window to look out. When she saw all the workers she assumed a fire drill was in progress as she couldn't think of any other reason for the whole factory to be congregating in the yard. They'd had a couple of fire drills while she was working at the wholesaler's. They always seemed to take place in the depths of winter, all the staff left standing outside, freezing, until the all clear was announced. Well, sooner them than me, she thought as she returned to her desk, assuming she hadn't been expected to take part because of her status.

Outside Glen looked on in dismay as the raised hands were counted. In reality they didn't need to be. It was apparent even to the dimmest of those present that those agreeing to strike action outnumbered those who didn't by at least twenty to one.

Jan touched his arm and whispered to him, 'Well, hopefully this will make Lucy take notice and change her ways.'

He sighed heavily. 'Despite the damage a strike will do the company, and what it will mean for us all, especially at Christmas time, I can't help feeling responsible for her and the way she's behaving. After all, she is my daughter. And what about my responsibility to her, as her father? I can't just stand by and leave her to deal with this on her own. I can't, Jan.'

Before she could stop him, he hurriedly stepped over to the workers' entrance to the building. Stopping long enough to make sure all the workers' attention was fixed firmly on the union representatives, not on him, Glen quickly disappeared inside.

CHAPTER NINETEEN

Outside the manager's office he paused briefly, praying that Lucy was indeed inside and hadn't left the premises. According to rumour she had a habit of coming and going as she pleased. He'd lifted his hand to rap on the door when suddenly realisation hit him and he withdrew his hand as if he'd been struck by lightning. He was about to come face to face with his daughter for the first time in more than fifteen years and this was definitely not going to be the reunion he had planned.

Taking a deep breath, he finally rapped purposefully on the door and, without waiting for a response, went inside.

Thinking that at last her tray of tea had arrived, Cait looked up from her magazine and was shocked to see a man dressed in a brown work coat walk in. She was in the middle of a gripping short story and resented being unceremoniously disturbed just when she had reached a poignant scene. She snapped at him, 'How dare you come in here before I give you permission? What do you want?' The significance of the tool box in the man's hand then registered and she added, 'You've come to fix the radiators? About time.' By way of getting her own back on him for entering her office without leave, she childishly continued: 'Now isn't convenient. I'll tell Miss Trucker to contact you when it is. And make sure you knock next time.' With that she returned her attention to the magazine.

Glen's eyes were fixed on the young woman's face. So his and Julia's beautiful baby girl had grown up into this very attractive young woman. She had Julia's eyes, her bow-shaped mouth and the same colouring. Her pert nose she had inherited from his own mother. Glen couldn't see anything of himself in her at that moment, but there had to be something. It was a pity her manner wasn't as appealing as her outward appearance. He couldn't help feeling, though, that he had encountered her somewhere before.

Aware the man was standing staring at her, Cait jerked up her head and snapped, 'Are you deaf? I told you to go away and come back when it's more convenient for me.'

Her rude retort snapped Glen out of his trance. 'I really need to talk to you, Lucy.'

She scowled at him, bemused. 'Lucy! Why are you calling me by that name? My name is Cait ... Caitlyn ... but it's Miss Thomas to you and don't you forget that. I could sack you for such insubordination. Whatever the problem is, speak to your foreman about it. Now, if you don't leave as I asked, you will be looking for another job.'

Glen was furious that Nerys had taken it upon herself to change Lucy's name. Julia and he had agonised over numerous choices for their beloved new baby, wanting to find the one they felt suited her perfectly. They'd felt happy that they had. Before he could stop himself, he retaliated. 'If you carry on sacking people at the rate you are, then very soon you'll have no staff left, young lady. Is that how you believe the boss of a company keeps the staff in line – by threatening them with the sack should they act in any way you don't like?'

Cait was startled by his unexpected harangue and couldn't help but defend herself. 'My mother instilled in me the fact that familiarity breeds contempt. She owns this company and I'm running it the way I know she would, keeping the workforce in their place and earning their money.' She jumped up from her chair then, eyes darkening thunderously, and wagged a warning finger at him. 'What right do you think you have to come in here challenging me? If you don't leave now, I'll have you thrown bodily off the premises.'

Glen was busy thinking. So Jan was right again and his daughter's abrasive, self-important atti-tude was all down to Nerys. What a good actress that woman was to have kept her true nature so well hidden from him. Sheer guilt for being blindly sucked in by her and allowing this state of affairs to happen flooded him. Without thinking he blurted, 'I have every right to speak to you in any way I feel fit as I'm ... I'm...' Then his nerve completely failed him and he ended up saying instead, 'I've come to help you as a friend, Miss Thomas. Believe me, you need a friend right now.'

She laughed mockingly. 'I have enough friends of my own, thank you very much, so I certainly don't need the likes of you...' she flashed a derogatory look over him before adding '...an odd job man as one.'

He shook his head sadly. 'I'm surprised you have any if you treat them the way you do the people who work for you.'

Cait's eyes narrowed darkly at what she saw as his impertinence. Reaching over to the intercom on the desk beside her, she smacked her hand down hard on the button and yelled, 'Miss Trucker, get in here now and bring some strong armed men with you. Miss Trucker, are you listening to me?' Receiving no response and thinking, Where the hell is the woman when I need her? she shot out from behind the desk and went over to the door. She yanked it open and yelled down the corridor, 'Miss Trucker, get in here now.'

Glen realised that strong action was called for if he was going to get his daughter to listen to him, and time wasn't on his side. In a commanding tone he told her, 'Shut the door, sit back down and listen to what I have to say to you. It's in your own best interest.'

Cait spun round and stared at him, speechless. She made to retaliate in her usual manner but was stopped by her instincts screaming at her that this man was putting his job at risk in order to get her to listen to what he had to tell her, so whatever it was it must be important. She really ought to hear him out. As she silently made her way back into the office to retake her seat behind the desk, it struck her that she should feel extremely wary of being alone in here with a man she did not know, but strangely she didn't. Fixing his eyes with hers, she snapped, 'Well, what's so important then?'

He sat down on the chair in front of the desk, putting his tool box to one side of him. Fixing her with his eye, he told her, 'This is not the Dark Ages, Lu– Miss Thomas. It's nineteen fifty-five. Unions fought for the rights of workers to be treated fairly.'

She shrugged her shoulders. 'What's that got to do with me?'

'You aren't treating your workforce at all fairly. Of course, you never should have been put in charge of the company, even if it's only until your...' he had difficulty saying the next word but he forced himself to '...mother returns from holiday. Sixteen should never have been considered–'

'I'm eighteen,' she sharply corrected him. 'Well, I will be in a few days' time.'

Glen looked at her for a moment before saying, 'No, you're sixteen, seventeen at the end of January. I should know as I am your–'

She cut in, 'I know when my own birthday is. I have a certificate to prove it. I'm eighteen on the twenty-eighth of December. I don't know why you should think I'm only sixteen and my birthday is at the end of January.'

The breath left his body and he was staring at her blindly as the significance of what she had just told him registered. This young woman wasn't his

247

daughter after all. He felt as if someone had punched him hard in the stomach. But that meant that all the time Nerys was with him, she must have been hiding the existence of her own daughter. Why would she do that? He had a child when they had met, so why would he have had any objection to her having one? But this posed the question of just where his own daughter was. He realised that Cait was waiting for an answer and said awkwardly, 'Oh, I ... er ... I must have overheard someone talking and thought it was about you.' Then a thought struck him. 'They must have been talking about your sister.' There was a hopeful note in his voice.

'I haven't got a sister. I'm an only child.'

Again he stared at her, frozen, his thoughts desperate. The only other answer was that Nerys must have had his daughter adopted. Her promise to him to look after her while he was serving the sentence he hadn't deserved had been just another of her lies. It had been bad enough thinking for all these years that his beloved child was being raised by the woman who was capable of doing what she had, but complete strangers... More importantly, the only way he was going to find out what Nerys had done with Lucy was to tackle her himself. But what if she wouldn't tell him? His anger was running high, not at the young woman before him but at her mother for making his life a misery still after all these years. He couldn't help but bang his fist on the table and say harshly, 'You are far too young and in-experienced, even at eighteen, to be expected to run a company. Your mother must have been out of her mind to think you were up to keeping this place going until she returned from her trip.'

He stabbed a finger at the pile of magazines on the desk in front of her. 'Is this how you think a boss runs a company, reading magazines while his staff do all the work and you just pocket the profits? What have you inside your head, young lady, cotton wool? As the head of this business it's your responsibility to keep the work coming in and deal with all the problems that arise. And, most important, do all you can to make sure your workforce is happy. And you don't achieve that by willy-nilly putting controversial rules in place without union agreement first, or by passing all your work on to others who are neither skilled enough nor paid to do it and who already have enough on their plates doing their own jobs. As for sacking those who happen to look at you in the wrong way... You might believe the myth that bosses sit on their backsides all day long with their feet up on the desk, taking the occasional tour around just to remind the workforce that a beady eye is being kept on them, but a myth is all it is.

'A boss should work harder than any of his workforce, roll his shirt sleeves up when the going gets tough and do all he can to ensure he has work for them every day. *That's* how he gains their respect and loyalty. Now listen to me, young lady, the workforce have had enough of your behaviour and aren't going to take any more of it. You risk ruining the company and losing them their jobs. The final straw was the fact that you never showed your face at the funeral yesterday.'

'I can't see what difference that made. I didn't know Reg Swinton,' she told him defensively.

He gazed at her incredulously. 'Reg Swinton had worked for your mother for many years and done a splendid job of running her company. You should have dropped everything to show your respects to him. The staff who attended were extremely embarrassed by there not being any appearance by the owner's representative. I can't imagine how let down Mrs Swinton felt. A union meeting was called this morning and a vote was held on what action should be taken to put a stop to your nonsense.'

Cait gasped. 'That wasn't a fire drill going on in the yard but a union meeting!'

He eyed her, stunned. 'You didn't take the trouble to go and investigate, to make sure just why all your employees had downed tools? You just assumed you knew. A proper boss would know everything that's going on in his factory before it happens. You have such a lot to learn if you ever want to manage a business successfully, Miss Thomas. Anyway, the union representative and shop stewards will be paying you a visit very shortly to deliver you their ultimatum: either you step aside and someone more qualified is put in your place until Mrs Thomas returns or the workers are downing tools until you do agree to their terms. If the strike goes ahead, the repercussions for the company could be irreversible and there's more than a probability that your mother will return from her trip to find she has no company any longer. Now you were the cause of this present situation and only you can put a stop to it before it's too late.'

Cait was far too shocked by what had been said to offer any response. She sat staring blindly at the man before her, trying to digest it all.

But getting no reaction from her whatsoever, Glen took it to mean that his words to her had fallen on deaf ears. His effort to make her see the error of her ways and put matters right was just a waste of his time. Grabbing up his tool box, he stood up and walked out, pulling the door shut behind him.

As she heard it shut, a rush of sheer panic filled Cait. Emotions were raging through her: humiliation, shame, hurt, anger, but none of them was as acute as the fear filling every fibre of her being at the thought that her mother could return to find Cait's irresponsible actions had resulted in the ruin of her company. Her ambition to show her mother she was a daughter to be proud of would not come about if she didn't heed that man's words.

Jumping up from the chair, she bolted to the door and ran out into the corridor.

Glen, feeling utterly helpless and deeply saddened that he had failed in his attempt to make Nerys's daughter see reason, was about to descend the stairs when he heard a shout.

'Mister ... Mister...'

He turned his head to see a frantic Caitlyn Thomas beckoning him back. He stared at her. Did this mean she had after all taken on board what he'd said to her and was prepared to try and put a stop to the strike? Full of hope, he hurriedly retraced his steps.

She had disappeared back into the office by the time he got there. He followed her inside and looked at her expectantly. She was standing by the desk, wringing her hands. 'Mister... Oh, please, my mother can't come back and find I've been responsible for ruining her business. You must help me stop that happening. I'll make it worth your while. Twenty pounds ... thirty ... whatever you decide. But you must help me.'

Glen was appalled that she felt she needed to bribe him to help her but, conscious that the delegation would be descending on them any minute, he asked, 'You're prepared to agree to the union's demands then?'

She nodded her head vigorously. 'Yes, you go and tell them that.'

Glen shook his head. 'That's for you to do, not me, Miss Thomas.'

Cait looked horrified at the thought but they had no time to debate the issue as there was a loud knock on the door. They both looked across at it. Glen then glanced at Cait's fear-stricken face and said, 'It's up to you now. Just remember, though, that the men need to feel you're sincere in what you say, so no high-handed attitude.'

She gulped as she turned back to face the door, hesitating for a moment before she called out, 'Come in.'

She immediately felt intimidated by the four middle-aged men who entered the room to stand just inside the door, eyes fixed on her. She dearly hoped they could not see that she was shaking.

Harry Owens was among the delegation and noticed Glen who had moved to stand over by

252

the window. He looked surprised. 'What are you doing up here, man? You're not working, I hope, in light of what's going on?'

All four men were looking at him suspiciously. He thought it best not to divulge the true reason he was up here as they could see that as interfering with union business. He lied, 'I was up here having a look at the radiators and left my tool box behind to attend the meeting. I was just collecting it.'

They all seemed happy with that explanation and it was the union representative, Alf Bisson, who told him in an authoritative tone, 'Well, you can leave now as we've private union business to discuss with Miss Thomas.'

Cait inwardly froze. They were telling that man to go ... she didn't even know his name yet she felt he was the only ally she had. She didn't feel she could do whatever she had to without knowing he was nearby, lending her strength. 'Whatever is said in this office will be common knowledge when you go and report it back to the rest of the workforce so it's of no consequence if he stays,' she announced, inwardly quaking. Then, desperate to get this over with before she lost her nerve, and reminding herself of Glen's words of advice to be careful of how she addressed the men, she took a deep breath and in a pleasant and sincere tone said, 'I'm ... I'm sorry ... very sorry for the way I've been acting. I admit I wasn't thinking straight to believe I had what it takes to run this company. I was just trying to help my mother out while she's away, that's all. I'm sure you can all appreciate that.'

She paused for a moment to draw breath before she continued. 'All the new rules I've put in place, well, you can forget them. And the men I sacked are reinstated. I'll do my best to find someone else to run this place as a matter of urgency, so if you'd just bear with me until then...'

The men all looked astonished, her apology and her behaviour the last things they'd been expecting.

Alf Bisson, a militant at heart, was not as happy as the other three that a strike had been averted. In all the years he had been union rep for this company, he'd only had what he perceived as petty problems to deal with and had been looking forward at long last to showing the workers that he was more than a match for the hierarchy. He was annoyed that this young woman had thwarted him. Another chance like this to show his mettle might never come his way again, considering that this company in all its history had never had a strike. Reluctantly he said, 'Well ... er ... right you are then, Miss Thomas. We'll take this back to the staff and get their vote on it.'

As soon as they had departed, Cait let out a huge sigh of relief and said to Glen, 'Did I do all right?'

He smiled at her. 'More than all right, Miss Thomas. You should give yourself a pat on the back. That couldn't have been easy for you.'

'No, it wasn't, but at least now my mother isn't going to return from holiday and find her business in ruins. How much do I owe you?'

He frowned. 'Owe me?'

'For helping me?'

'But I don't need paying. I was only too glad you did let me help you or I dread to think what the consequences might have been.'

She looked most surprised. 'Oh! If ever I've got anyone to do anything for me before, I've always had to make sure it was worth it to them.' Then she remembered all the things he had said to her so bluntly and her bottom lip began to tremble, tears to prick her eyes. 'You said some horrible things to me.'

She was obviously very upset by his remarks, but if she was expecting him to apologise for what he had said to her then she would wait a long time. 'What I told you were some home truths, Miss Thomas. I couldn't see any other way to get you to take notice than to be brutally honest. And a bit more advice... If you carry on the way you are, turning people away from you with your manner towards them, then you're going to end up a lonely old woman. Unless, of course, that's what you want for yourself, so you purposely treat people with disdain, to stop them getting close to you for some reason?'

Cait was stupefied. No, she certainly didn't want to end up alone. But she was only taking her lead from her mother and *she* wasn't a lonely old woman. She frowned, confused. Something struck her. The man had just said that by acting the way she was towards people, she was in fact pushing them away. She hadn't realised that; had always assumed she should speak to people like that because her mother did. But was it just her mother's way of informing other people not to try and get close to her? Her life was complete the

255

way it was and she didn't need anyone else in it? Now Cait thought about it like this, it made sense as her mother never made any effort whatsoever to make friends or even acquaintances.

A vision of her parents rose before her then. They would sit side by side on the sofa, chatting and laughing together at their own private jokes, not sharing them with her, seemingly oblivious to the fact that she was sitting in an armchair nearby. They lived in their own little world that no one else, except under exceptional circumstances, was allowed into. And that was the way they liked it. In the light of this realisation, Cait now knew that all her efforts to regain her mother's affection and be allowed into their inner circle had been a total waste of time. There were two people only in that circle and no room for any more, not even her, no matter what she did. Maybe her parents had not planned to have her in the first place, she'd just been a mistake, and the mementoes in that box in the safe were not hers at all but her mother's from when she was a baby.

And then a really awful thought struck her. Having seen the way her mother was with her father, and not having any other couples in her life to judge by, she had assumed that that was the way all women should behave to their men. So when she'd been asked out by a boy she liked the look of, she had always emulated her mother's behaviour in every way. But suddenly she realised that just because her father was content to have a woman who devoted herself to him, did not mean to say that every man did. It was obvious to her now that Neil hadn't.

A wave of great sadness overcame her then. Why couldn't she have had parents who at least took the time to offer her some guidance in life, instead of leaving her to her own devices? Then maybe she wouldn't be in such an awful mess now. And suddenly she didn't care about putting the money she'd taken back into the safe, as what did it matter if her mother discovered she'd been snooping? What would she do to Cait? Throw her out, that's what. Well, she'd already done that. And it wasn't as if she would miss her parents' loving arms around her and their support because you never missed what you'd never had, did you?

She didn't realise that she was crying until Glen asked her, 'Are you all right, Miss Thomas?'

Cait shook her head, tears rolling down her cheeks. 'Not really,' she uttered. 'This is all so awful. I feel so ... so...' The floodgates opened then. Sobbing, she told him, 'I lied to you. I haven't got lots of friends. I haven't got any. I don't want to end up a lonely old woman. I want people to like me and want to be my friends but I don't know what to do about it.' She raised her head then and looked at him imploringly. 'Help me, will you? Tell me what to do to make people like me.'

His heart went out to her then and he dearly wanted to go to her and put his arms around her, give her a comforting hug. But that wouldn't be the right thing for him to do. She was, after all, the daughter of the owner of the business and he a mere worker. He felt very uncomfortable with this situation. It was one thing, putting a young

257

woman right on her mishandling of the business, but quite another dealing with a distraught one who needed advice on how to change herself into a better person. Women were better at this sort of thing anyway. He vehemently wished Jan were here now as she'd know how to handle this. But she wasn't and he couldn't leave the distraught girl without offering her some sort of help.

Glen said, 'It's not easy changing the habits of a lifetime, but if you really want to then the best advice I can offer you is to remember always to treat people in the way you would wish to be treated yourself. Then you won't go far wrong. Another thing is to take just a second or two to think before you speak, so that to the best of your knowledge what you are going to say isn't going to offend or hurt someone, and also the manner in which you say it.'

Cait seemed to digest his words of wisdom for a moment before she flashed him a wan smile. 'I'll remember, I will.' She could see a battle before her, though, constantly having to watch everything she said and did in order to become the better person she wanted to be. And how was she going to convince all those who knew the old Caitlyn and gave her a wide berth unless they had no choice that she wasn't that selfish person any longer, and make them give her a chance to prove it to them? And how on earth was she going to look her parents in the eye now that she had had her eyes opened to the fact that they had no love for her, only for themselves?

She suddenly felt a desperate need to return home, pack her things and go somewhere far away, another town where no one knew her and where she could make a fresh start. She could take the rest of the money from the safe to set herself up with a home and she felt sure she wouldn't have much trouble getting another job. But then to turn her back on the business, leaving the staff struggling to keep it going without any guidance, would not be trying to make herself a better person, would it?

She gave her wet eyes a wipe with the back of her hand, sniffed and then looked at Glen for several moments. It didn't feel like it at the moment, considering what she was facing, but in the future she knew she would owe this man a debt of gratitude for the risk he had taken today in coming to tackle her. She looked at him quizzically for a moment as several things about him didn't seem to sit right. 'I can't understand why someone like you is just working as an odd job man,' she queried.

'It's as good a job as any.'

She eyed him searchingly. 'You look and dress like an odd job man would ... but ... well ... I can't put my finger on it, but I can only say you seem to know more about the running of a business, and certainly how to handle the union men, than I'd have thought an odd job man would. You certainly dealt with this situation as if you've handled similar ones before. You speak well so I know you've come from a good background. I might only be young and inexperienced in the ways of business but I haven't got so much cotton wool in my brain...' she flashed a quick smile at him when she said that, to let him know she was

259

making light of what he'd accused her of earlier '...that I don't know when I'm in the company of someone who is better than they're making out they are. How did someone like you end up being an odd job man? And what is your name, by the way?'

Glen stared at her blankly. He couldn't bring himself to tell her the whole truth as that would run the risk of breaking a young girl's heart by informing her that the kind loving person she doubtless considered her mother to be was in fact a con artist, and the lifestyle she herself was living was all based on the proceeds of trickery. It wasn't fair that he lie to her either. He'd been very fortunate up to now that the people he had come across in the company either weren't aware of its history or, if they were, hadn't considered that the Glen Trainer who used to own the company and himself were the same man. He dearly hoped this situation would remain the same until he was ready to leave. He doubted Nerys would have told her daughter the truth of how she'd come to own Rose's so felt he was on safe ground telling Caitlyn his name and the diluted version of how he came to be working here.

He walked across to the window, turned his back to it, then began speaking. 'My name is Glen ... Glen Trainer.' He paused for a moment with bated breath to see whether the name meant anything to her, and inwardly sighed with relief when she made no comment. He continued, 'I've not always been an odd job man. I used to run a company once, a business similar to this in fact...'

He was stopped in his tracks by a thud on the door, the sound made by the toe of a shoe hitting it.

Cait looked over at it for a moment before she called out, 'Come in.' It seemed she had temporarily forgotten her new resolve. Her tone was curt.

There were fumbling sounds from the other side of the door and Glen realised whoever it was was having trouble turning the door knob. He went over, turned the knob, and opened the door to find a woman outside, attempting to balance a laden tray which she was struggling to keep steady with one hand while the other was trying to open the door. She had her head bowed, a white net cap pulled down right over her forehead to cover her eyebrows, as if she was trying to hide her face. Of course he knew it was Jan.

'Why are you...' he started to say.

Righting herself, the tray now held in both hands, her head came up and with her eyes she silenced him. Then she bowed her head again and he stood back, watching in bemusement, as she hurried with the tray over to the desk, set it down and mumbled, 'Your tea, Miss Thomas. Sorry for the delay.' She hurried back towards the door. Just as she passed by Glen, she lifted her head and shot him a look that told him not to talk to her and also that she was desperate to know what was going on, then she was off down the corridor.

Cait said to Glen, 'You were telling me?'

'Pardon? Oh, yes. The fact is that the owner died and the son sold up. The new owner decided he didn't want a manager running the place as he was going to head it up himself. I felt I'd had enough of the responsibility of that kind of job anyway and got myself something back on a production line. It was a huge drop in salary but I was happy to be sleeping well at night. I was ready for a change when I saw the maintenance man's job advertised and thought I'd apply and … well, here I am.'

Noises from outside in the yard made him glance out of the window. 'Seems people are returning to work.' He turned back and walked over to his tool box. He picked it up and said to Cait, 'Well, I'd better get back to it myself.'

She looked aghast. 'But you can't leave me. I mean, I don't know how to go about finding a replacement manager like I promised the union men I would.'

'Miss Trucker will help you with that. From the dealings I've had with her, she seems like a very capable woman.'

Cait sighed. And she herself hadn't treated her very civilly. More apologies were necessary it seemed.

Glen appeared to read her mind. 'She doesn't come across to me as a woman who bears grudges. You'll be fine.'

Another thought struck Cait then. 'Oh, but wait a minute. We don't need to look for a temporary manager to run this place. You've run a business. You're qualified. You could do it, couldn't you?' Then she wouldn't need to hang around here and could get on with starting her new life.

Glen hoped he wasn't showing the horror he felt

262

at her suggestion. The job he could do easily. The company still seemed to be running along the same lines as it had when he had owned the place, maybe a few administrative changes but it wouldn't take him long to get to grips with those, but there were reasons why he couldn't, wouldn't, accept her offer, the main one being that if he were ever to head up this company again it would not be as a manager but because he owned it. And that he never would as it was highly unlikely Nerys would have her conscience pricked after all this time and hand it back to him. But the main reason was that she could come back at any moment and, if she found him running the place, all hell would break loose.

He smiled at Cait and told her, 'Thanks for the offer, Miss Thomas, but I like the job I'm doing. I wouldn't fancy all the responsibility of managing again. I really must get back now in case any machines have broken down. Wouldn't do for me to be responsible for holding up production.'

Cait sat staring at the closed door for several moments after Glen had shut it behind him. She felt physically and emotionally drained and wished more than anything that she could climb into bed, pull the covers around her and sleep for eternity. But she had meant what she'd said. She no longer wanted to be the person her parents had made her into, and if she was serious about making herself into a better person she had better make a start. She knew it wasn't going to be easy for her, Glen Trainer had told her that, but she was determined she was going to change the habits of a lifetime.

She thought of Glen again. She had read somewhere that people could sometimes appear in your life for a very short space of time, then leave just as quickly, but the impact of their visit could be significant. She knew she would be forever grateful to him for taking the risk of coming to talk to her, indebted to him in fact – but it was a debt she doubted she'd ever be able to repay.

Cait sat upright in her chair and took several deep breaths. Time to make a start. After first rehearsing what she was going to say and how, as Glen had advised her to do, she reached over to press the intercom buzzer and said politely into it, 'Miss Trucker, when you're free, would you please come into my office? I would like to ask your advice.'

She could only imagine the look of utter astonishment on Miss Trucker's face at having received such a civil message. But she imagined it correctly. It took the secretary several moments to accept that it had indeed been Caitlyn Thomas whose polite tones she had heard over the intercom and not someone playing a joke on her.

CHAPTER TWENTY

After the day he'd had, Glen felt the need for a drink stronger than tea and had gone off to the local corner shop to treat himself and Jan to a couple of bottles of beer each. He had to admire her self-control. She obviously knew that the strike had been staved off in some way and Glen knew she was desperate to hear his account of what had happened when he had paid a visit to the office today. And, of course, how he'd got on with Miss Thomas. Had he told her who he was, and if so what had her reaction been? When he returned with the beer and they were seated opposite each other in the fireside chairs, he'd be ready to tell her all.

Back at the flat, Jan vigorously wiped away at burned splashes on top of the old enamel cooker, which helped to ease the frustration slightly. She was desperate to hear from Glen how his visit to Lucy had been. She stopped her rubbing and frowned as she heard a purposeful knock on the door to the flat. That was quick, for Glen to have got to the shop and back so soon. He'd hardly been gone a minute or so. She could have sworn, though, she had seen him take his key off the hook by the door before he left. As she reached it and noticed his key wasn't there, she assumed he must have lost it.

Opening the door, she said, 'Challenging Roger Bannister's record for the one-minute mile is...' Her voice died away as she pulled the door fully open and saw who the visitor actually was. 'Harry!' she uttered, shocked.

He walked past her into the front room. Jan stood staring after him blankly for a moment. When she'd recovered herself she found him standing in the living area, waiting for her to join him. As soon as she did he said darkly, 'So Mrs March was right and it *was* you she saw coming in here one night when she was visiting a needy parishioner. She knew who you were from visiting our house when you opened the door to her.' His tone accusing, he continued: 'While you were trespassing there recently you stole money that was intended for the needy. Money that generous people had donated, some going without themselves in order to do so. How can you live with yourself, knowing you've done such a despicable thing?'

Jan raised an eyebrow at him. 'Er ... just remind me again, Harry. That money *was* intended for people in desperate need, wasn't it?'

'Yes, it was.'

'Well, *I* was one of those people after you threw me out without anything more than the clothes on my back. So it went to a needy person, didn't it?'

He looked stunned but found he couldn't argue with that, so didn't. 'You took some of my clothes too.'

She gave a nonchalant shrug. 'Because I knew someone else in dire need, and in the circumstances I didn't think you'd mind.' Over her shock now, Jan folded her arms, looked him square in the eyes and said, 'So Mrs March is the name of your do-gooding friend, is it? Is that all she does for you, Harry, a few cleaning jobs around the house and cook you a meal?'

He shot her a disapproving look. 'No need for that attitude, Janet. I won't have you speak about Mrs March that way. I wouldn't have managed to keep house without the help of the good ladies of the congregation.'

She responded sardonically, 'No, you wouldn't have time for housework, would you? Not with every minute taken up with helping the deserving.'

He ignored her jibe and said, 'Mrs March also noticed a man coming in here with you that evening. She said that by the way you acted together, you obviously knew each other well.'

Jan scowled angrily at him. 'Not in the way that you're implying we don't!'

'So you deny you're living together, even though there are signs of a man all over the place,' he said, casting his eyes around, noting Glen's slippers by a chair, the unread evening newspaper over the arm of it.

'Actually we are living together but as friends, clubbing together to fund a place to live in because otherwise we couldn't afford it. We sleep in separate bedrooms,' Jan added defensively.

He cast his eyes around again before bringing them back to her. 'How can you live in a place like this? It's barely more than a hovel.'

'Like this! Let me tell you, it might not be Buckingham Palace but it's a far cry from living on the streets.'

'I grant you that much. But it can't be compared to the house you left.'

'The house you threw me out of and told me never to darken the door of again, you mean?'

His face tight, Harry snapped, 'I found you in bed with another man. What did you expect me to do ... make you both a cup of tea?'

Jan shook her head sadly at him. 'You still haven't accepted any responsibility for driving

267

me into another man's arms, have you, Harry? I'm sure God is very grateful for your dedication in serving him and I hope, like you do, that his reward to you will be a place in heaven where you can make your apologies to Keith for allowing him out on the night that he died. But in the process you've turned your back on the people who loved you ... on me ... starved me of love and affection, giving it all instead to the people you were helping while I became nothing more than a housekeeper to you.'

'I asked you to join me in becoming a servant of the Lord, Janet.'

She said in all sincerity, 'Oh, I would have been quite happy to do some good turns for the needy now and again, but I wasn't prepared to give up my life to it, like you were.' She gave a deep sigh and looked at him tenderly. 'We used to be so close, did everything together. You were constantly telling me how much you loved me and physically showing you did too, like I did then. Where did that Harry go?'

He looked her in her eyes and said flatly, 'He died the night our son did, Janet.'

She heaved a deep sad sigh then asked, 'Look, why are you here exactly?'

'Well, you never came back to beg my forgiveness ... but then I know you can be stubborn. So I've come to say I forgive you and tell you you can come home.'

'Oh, I can, can I? You really think I'm going to come home just to be your housekeeper again?'

'You're my wife and a wife's place is by her husband. You made vows before God to honour me until death parted us, remember that, Janet.'

'It was a different man I made that promise to, Harry. You've already told me that man is dead so there's no point in my coming back in the hope he might return one day.'

'Are you telling me you're not coming back?'

'Not to live like I was before, Harry, definitely not. I can't, I'm sorry.'

'Well, in that case, I want a divorce.'

She felt stunned for a moment, not expecting to be asked that, then she forced a laugh. 'Oh, so you can make an honest woman of Mrs March, I take it?'

'I told you, I will not have you speak about her like that, Janet. Mavis is a good woman. She's as committed as I am to the church and we get on very well together.'

Jan had a vision of them both sitting by the fire at night after returning from distributing food to the homeless in the city or attending a church service, reading passages from the Bible together as they sipped their hot milk. She heaved a deep sigh and refused to think about that any more. 'Look, Harry, we were very much in love, had a wonderful marriage and were both happy believing we'd end our days together, but unfortunately we had a terrible tragedy to deal with and we've ended up going our separate ways. It's a very sad business. I don't begrudge you your happiness, Harry, and if Mrs March can be the kind of wife you want for yourself now, then I won't stand in your way. I'll sign the divorce papers as soon as I get them. I couldn't find my belongings at the house – I assume you've packed

269

them up ready for me to collect. I'd appreciate it if you'd get someone to bring them here for me when you can. And, Harry, I do wish you every happiness.'

She stepped over to him and gave him a peck on his cheek.

He looked surprised by her gesture. Tears glinted in his eyes momentarily. He flashed her a wan smile and said softly, 'I wish you every happiness for your future too. Goodbye, Janet.'

She followed him to the door and saw him out. They were both aware it was doubtful they would see each other again. They moved in different circles now.

Jan dashed out to meet Glen the moment she heard his key in the lock. He hadn't even got through the door before she was saying to him, 'Give me one of those bottles, I really need it.' Taking one from his hand, she dashed back to the kitchen with it. Glen followed her, feeling bemused. Something was obviously amiss with her, but considering he'd not been gone more than fifteen minutes he couldn't imagine what. He watched her snap the cap off the bottle. Not even taking the time to pour it into a cup – they had no glasses as yet, feeling they were a luxury to be afforded when they got paid again – she raised it to her lips and took several long gulps. Then she gave a loud burp, reddened in embarrassment and said, 'Pardon me.'

Frowning at her, he asked, 'What's going on, Jan?'

She took another long swallow from the bottle

before she told him. 'Harry came round. You've not long missed him.'

Glen was surprised. 'Harry Owens was here?' He couldn't understand what the man would need to see him about that was urgent enough to pay him a visit at home. How would he know his address anyway as Glen hadn't told him?

Jan shook her head. 'No, not him. My husband Harry ... the last person I expected ever to knock on the door. It's shaken me up. He told me that one of his fellow church members was visiting someone around here on a mercy mission and recognised me as I came home one night.' She took another long swallow from the bottle before she continued, 'He came to tell me he'd forgiven me and he was allowing me to go home.'

Glen was shocked by how much this news unsettled him. Just as shocked to realise he would miss her, and not just a little. Regardless, he wouldn't be much of a friend if he didn't show her he was happy for her. He forced a bright smile to his face and told Jan, 'Well, I wish you the best but I'm sure you won't need it.'

'I'm sorry to disappoint you but I'm not going back, so you can take that happy expression off your face.'

He was shocked at himself again when he realised how glad he was to hear that she was not going back to her husband. Glen had no choice then but to admit to himself that, in the short space of time he had known her, he'd grown very fond of Janet Clayton.

She was continuing, 'Our marriage was over the night Keith died and Harry and I both know

271

it now. He's met someone else, someone who suits the man he has become, and he wants to marry her. I've told him he won't have any trouble from me over a divorce. Anyway, I don't want to talk about his visit any more. Now I think I've been patient enough! I want to hear your account of what happened at work today.' She drained her bottle and picked up another, parted it from its top and this time picked up a cup to fill as well. She handed these to Glen, telling him, 'Go and make yourself comfy in your chair while I sort myself out another drink. I'll follow you through.'

A minute later Jan sat looking expectantly at him. 'So how did Lucy take the news that you're her father? I bet she was shocked.'

He took a long swallow of his drink then shocked Jan by telling her, 'She's not my daughter, Jan. She's not Lucy.'

'She's not! Then ... then who is she?'

'Her name is Caitlyn Thomas.'

'Oh! Well, that doesn't mean she isn't Lucy, Glen. Nerys just changed her name, that's all.'

'That was my immediate thought, but I managed to find out that she's eighteen just after Christmas, and Lucy would only have been seventeen at the end of January. And she has a birth certificate to prove it.' To Jan's distress she saw tears glinting in Glen's eyes when he continued, 'I still see so much of Julia in her, though. She has her eyes, her hair colour...'

Jan cut in gently, 'That's because you want to see Julia in her, Glen. We can all see what we want to at times, even when it's not really there.'

He nodded. 'Yes, I realise that.' He took a deep breath and gave himself a shake. 'This means that Nerys had a year-old daughter herself when we met and I can't understand why she hid the fact from me. After all, it wasn't as if I had an aversion to children, not with one of my own, was it? And who was looking after her while Nerys was with me?'

Jan's mind was turning somersaults and she was talking to herself more than to him, trying to get them in order. 'So this Caitlyn Thomas would be Lucy's elder sister ... well, not her real sister ... but they might not know they're related or even if they did...'

'Jan, Caitlyn told me she hasn't got a sister. She's an only child.'

'Oh! Oh, I see. But then that means...'

'That Nerys must have had Lucy adopted or put in an orphanage.' Deep sorrow filled his face as he uttered, 'I'll never find her now.'

Her face stern, Jan wagged a finger at him. 'Eh, now, don't you dare give up hope. We'll find Lucy, if I have to break into the archives at City Hall myself to get her records and find out where she is.'

Glen could not help but smile at the vision that rose before him of Jan kitted out all in black, her face blackened with boot polish, skulking around City Hall looking for the best place to break in.

She was saying, 'Despite the fact that the authorities won't tell you who adopted Lucy or her whereabouts, I'm sure they would pass a letter on from you to her, and then it's her choice whether she contacts you or not. Which of course she will, Glen. Any child would want to meet their natural parent, even if it's just from curiosity; but I'm sure Lucy couldn't fail to want to get to know you better, once she'd met you. Anyway, there's also the chance that Nerys had her privately adopted and that means she will know the names of the people and where they are ... or where they were if they have moved since, but it shouldn't be that hard to track them down. If she did have Lucy privately adopted then it wouldn't be any skin off Nerys's nose to tell you who she gave her to after all this time, would it? She's got what she wanted from you after all, and I doubt the couple who took Lucy can do anything to prosecute Nerys as it would all have been off the record and might not even have been legal, if you see what I mean?'

Jan saw hope return to Glen's eyes. He said to her, 'Nerys can't stay away for ever, can she? I'll just have to bide my time until she gets back and tackle her then for the information I want. If she's got an ounce of common decency in her, she'll tell me.'

'*We'll* go and tackle her,' Jan told him. 'Two people standing firm against her won't be as easy to get rid of as one. Anyway, that's sorted. Like you said, all we can do now is wait patiently until she gets back from her jaunt.' She drained the last drop of beer from the bottle, drank it back then got up. 'Ready for another?'

He nodded. 'Don't mind if I do.'

'Me neither. Then you can tell me what happened in the office when you went up. Oh, I've just remembered, I've already drunk my share of the beer. It's not that I'm a drinker, but it's been slipping down so well.'

He grinned. 'You can share my other one with me.'

She smiled back at him. 'You're a gent, Glen Trainer, and don't dare let anyone tell you otherwise.'

After sharing the bottle equally between them and having settled comfortably back in her chair – or as well as she was able to in the lumpy old thing – Jan said to Glen, 'Right, I'm all ears.'

A troubled expression clouded his face. 'Well to tell you the truth, Jan, I might have got Miss Thomas to see sense, but I'm not proud of myself for the way I managed it.'

A picture flashed into her mind. He had tied Caitlyn Thomas to a chair and was standing over her, gun in hand, threatening to kill her if she didn't do what was necessary to put an end to the strike. Then she gave herself a shake. She might not have known Glen long but she knew he wasn't the sort to hurt a fly. 'So what did you do, then?'

With his eyes fixed on the glowing wood in the grate, he said, 'As soon as I discovered she wasn't in fact Lucy, the need to save the factory from possible ruin and the workers from losing their jobs was paramount. I was very conscious that I hadn't much time before the union chaps would be knocking on the door delivering their ultimatum, so I went in all guns blazing, so to speak. I really gave her some home truths, Jan. Was very blunt with her.'

'It wasn't her you were angry with, though, was

it, Glen? It was her mother you wanted to set straight, having just learned the latest lie in a long string of them. She promised to care for Lucy, didn't she, raise her as her own while you were inside ... and she didn't at all but passed her on to strangers.'

He nodded. 'Yes, it was all that in my mind and it was wrong of me to take it out on Caitlyn Thomas. But still, my harsh words did seem to make her take a good look at herself and she couldn't have liked what she saw as she told me she didn't want to be that person any more. So some good might have come from it. I think out of all I said to her, what had the most impact was when I told her that if she didn't do something to change her ways, she'd end up a lonely old woman. She was crying, Jan. It didn't make me proud to see I'd made a woman cry. And the worst thing of all was when she asked me what she should do to make herself into a better person. I did my best by telling her a couple of things she could do but said that the only person who could really help her was herself. Once she'd dropped her superior attitude, I found her to be a very pleasant young woman.'

Jan looked thoughtful. 'Do you think she will manage to change herself? I mean, leopards don't change their spots, do they?'

He pondered this for a moment before he said, 'I agree that as a general rule they don't, but there is always the exception. Miss Thomas was adamant that she didn't like the person I'd made her see she was. I warned her that it's not going to be easy for her, changing the habits of a lifetime, but I did get the impression she was determined to. So hopefully she will succeed, Jan.'

'Well, from the gossip I heard in the canteen, she's certainly trying, I'll give her that. Dilys came back from delivering the afternoon tray of tea up to her in the office and told us that she found Miss Thomas and Miss Trucker deep in discussion. Well, it was Miss Trucker that was doing all the talking and Miss Thomas was listening to her apparently. Dilys got the shock of her life because Miss Thomas actually thanked her for the tea. I heard via the union representative when they came back and told us the outcome of their visit to the office that she'd agreed to all their terms, admitted to them she wasn't up to the job and promised to get a temporary manager in to run the place until her mother gets back. You could tell they were all shocked by this turnaround in her.'

'She offered me the job of manager.'

Jan exclaimed, eyes lighting up with excitement, 'She did? My God, this is the answer to your prayers, Glen! Just accept it long enough to have a good rummage through the files, Nerys's address has got to be in there somewhere, and with a bit of luck you might find something incriminating you can use against her to make her hand back the company.'

He tutted at her. 'Jan, if Nerys was clever enough to plan and carry out her scheme to frame me, she isn't going to be daft enough to leave any incriminating evidence around, is she?'

She conceded this. 'Well, thinking about it, not

in the office admittedly, but somewhere at her house ... and as manager you can find her address in the private files without having to use any underhand means.'

'And then we break into her house? Come on, Jan, look at us, two middle-aged people who have never broken the law in their lives ... well, I certainly haven't, although there were times when I was close to it after not eating for a few days. But I still couldn't bring myself to steal from anyone. I'd have been too worried I'd taken food from a child's mouth. I doubt you've ever done anything wrong either.'

A guilty look crossed Jan's face. 'Well, I have actually.' She saw Glen glance at her in surprise and with a twinkle of amusement in her eyes, told him, 'I'm ashamed to admit that I stole a penny out of my mother's purse once to buy some sweets. I was only seven at the time. And then I felt so guilty I couldn't eat the sweets so I gave them away and never did it again. And before you say anything ... as far as I'm concerned, that money I took from Harry's church fund was not stolen as it was used for the purpose for which it was intended.'

'You have a point, I suppose, but despite the fact we wouldn't be sitting toasting ourselves by this fire and have a bed to sleep in tonight if you hadn't helped yourself to that money, I still don't feel comfortable about it. I will make donations to the church when I can afford to. I suppose as you've admitted your crime-ridden past then I should too.'

She eyed him, intrigued. 'Oh, what did you do

that was illegal then?'

'Not exactly illegal but I did blatantly lie to my father once. I'd told him I was going to a friend's to study for my exams, which was where I was going, but it wasn't to study as he was having a party while his parents were away. I was fourteen at the time.'

'Did your father ever find out?'

Glen nodded. 'I got as drunk as a lord on my friend's father's best Scotch and passed out on the sofa. When I didn't come home at the time I should have my father became worried and came to collect me, found me in the state I was in and banned me from going out for a month. He showed no sympathy whatsoever for the dreadful hangover I suffered, which it took me days to get over.

'Anyway, neither of us deserves jail, Jan, but if we got caught breaking into Nerys's house, well, that would be different. I've been in jail, remember, and I wouldn't recommend it. And there's a problem about me taking the manager's job even for just long enough to have a look through the files. It would be just my luck if Nerys chose that moment to return and caught me behind the desk. She could have a field day then. Throw me out without a by-your-leave, accuse me of taking advantage of the situation to extort money or steal goods, and have the police brought in to investigate. Don't forget, I've already got a criminal record. Although they won't find any wrongdoing this time, I'd still be out of a job.

'And don't forget also, Jan, some people at work know that you and I are good friends and live in the same building. They could even know it's the same flat we live in together and believe we're a couple ... you know how nosy folk are. That means you would automatically be seen as my accomplice, be thrown out as well, and in the circumstances I can't see them paying us for the days we've worked, can you? So we'd both have no jobs at a time when it's hard to get another, being close to Christmas. There's no way we could pay the rent on this place, which is due next Friday, so where would that leave us? Back where we were just days ago, in that shop doorway.'

The look on Jan's face told him that was unthinkable to her.

Glen continued, 'I know it's pathetic, but can you imagine what it would be like for me, managing a company I used to own and for the woman who stole it from me? For just that reason alone I couldn't take the job, Jan. My male pride, you see.' He paused for a moment to drain his cup of beer, then tip the remains of the bottle into it. 'I've been giving my position a lot of thought. Up to now I've been lucky that the people I've come across in the factory have accepted my explanation about my name, but I haven't been everywhere yet and there's a chance that there might still be people working for the firm who worked for me. If they recognise me and start talking about the past, it will get back to Nerys and she'll cause trouble.

'Being realistic, Jan, I think I'd best find another job before she gets back. I don't need to work at the firm any longer, do I, as I've found out the information I needed and can't get any further in my search for Lucy until I can tackle Nerys face to face about it.'

Guilt flamed in Jan's eyes and she said reproachfully, 'I never stopped to consider the consequences there could be for you when I bamboozled you into working at Rose's.'

'I'm just as much to blame because neither did I at the time. Too bent on finding Lucy's whereabouts to think further than that.' He smiled at her. 'You were just trying your best to find a way to help me, that's all.'

Jan looked thoughtful. 'Well, now we've got to make a plan for how we're going to get you up to the office to tackle Nerys when she does come back. I suppose I'll have to ask permission from Hilda to use the telephone as I have an emergency, then get hold of you at your new workplace as soon as I hear word Nerys is on the premises. Then you'll have to make up some damned good excuse to your new boss and hope he'll give you permission to go out, then get over to the factory as quickly as you can, hoping Nerys doesn't leave meantime. It's going to be like planning a military operation.' Jan heaved an exasperated sigh. 'God, all we want is the chance for you to talk to the bloody woman. How hard can it possibly–' She stopped dead in mid-flow and, to Glen's surprise, started laughing.

'What's so funny?' he asked her.

'Us. We're still not thinking clearly. Pair of old duffers we are. The answer is staring us in the face. We follow her daughter home after work. She's not old enough to drive so keep everything crossed she doesn't catch a taxi or get the family car to pick her up. Hopefully she catches the bus like the rest of us menials.'

Glen was feeling mortally inadequate for not thinking of this solution himself but he was glad Jan had. It seemed to have the best potential for his achieving his goal. He said enthusiastically, 'I'll do it tomorrow night. I'll...'

Jan piped up, 'You can't be the one to follow her, Glen. Caitlyn Thomas knows you, and if she catches sight of you tailing her she could get suspicious. I need to be the one to do this. Tomorrow's Saturday and the office staff don't have to work like us factory lot do so I doubt she will. It'll have to be Monday night. Oh, dear, seems like a long weekend's in front of us. Anyway, I'll tell Hilda I've got somewhere important I need to be straight after work so I'll have to leave as soon as the hooter blows. I'll hide somewhere I've got a good view of the factory gates and as soon as I see Miss Thomas coming through them, I'll tag on behind her, keeping at a safe distance. Hopefully she'll be in too much of a hurry to get home to take much notice of what's going on around her. And it's dark that time of night, so that's on our side...'

The plan sounded a good one to him but, regardless, several problems struck him. He said to her, 'But, Jan, you'll have been on your feet all day and be tired. And it's freezing weather. You could catch your death if for some reason Caitlyn Thomas stays late in the office.'

She told him, 'Well, I'll be sitting down on the bus, and I'll make sure I wear two pairs of knickers.'

He grinned. 'Well, it seems it's all go then.' Another thought struck him then. 'But Caitlyn knows you too, Jan. You brought a tray up to the office this morning so she's seen your face, hasn't she?' He eyed her quizzically. 'Er ... by the way, why were you acting so oddly when you brought it in this morning?'

She looked at him for a moment before shifting awkwardly in her seat. 'Well ... er ... you see, I wasn't entirely honest with you... I didn't lie, but I didn't tell you either as I didn't want to upset you since you believed at the time that the young woman in the office was your daughter. If I had told you I'd met her, you would have asked me what she was like, and I didn't want to tell you so–'

He cut in, 'You're babbling, Jan. What is it you're trying to tell me?'

'Just that I crossed paths with ... well, the girl we now know is Nerys's own daughter, not yours, the first morning she came in. In fact both of us have come across her before. She was the girl in the church who kicked up a fuss when we went inside that night to rest.'

The incident came back to Glen. 'Well thank goodness she hasn't recognised us this time around, considering the state we were in then. She'd know the information I've told her about my background is a pack of lies.'

'No one would realise the man that was in the church is the same one sat opposite me now,' Jan said. 'There's no comparison. In my opinion she was too concerned at the time that we'd spoil her wedding to take much notice of us. At least, I assume it was her wedding, only as she's still a Miss, something must have stopped it happening. Perhaps her fiancé didn't like her attitude and called it off before it was too late. If that's the case I do feel a bit sorry for her. She will have had a hard lesson to learn.'

Jan paused for a moment. 'That first morning, I had a run-in with her and she ended up sacking me. Accused me of committing treason! Thankfully the boss's secretary arrived then and I made a quick exit, glad the young woman hadn't asked for my name. I did tell Hilda what had happened but she just told me to get on with my work and she'd deal with it. Thankfully I heard no more. I was acting strangely this morning because I was concerned she might recognise me and remember, but I don't need to worry about bumping into her now with the union agreement to reinstate those she sacked unfairly, do I?'

Glen smiled. 'I wondered why you were behaving differently. Now I know.'

'Please don't hold it against me for not telling you what she was like. How could I tell you that the daughter you were longing to get to know again was ... well, as I thought at the time, a nasty piece of work who had escaped from the lunatic asylum?'

'Jan, if the roles had been reversed, I wouldn't have been able to tell you either. I only hope I can sleep tonight, thinking about what we hope to do on Monday. I do hope nothing happens to put a spanner in the works.'

She nodded in agreement. 'Me too. I think some hot milk is called for. Hopefully between that and the beer we'll both get a good night's sleep.' When she returned with cups of warm milk, Glen thanked her for his and said, 'Tomorrow afternoon I thought I'd come home and get changed then take a trip around the area and have a look at the factory vacancies boards, to see if there's anything suitable going.' He would have liked to ask Jan to accompany him, but didn't want to in case she preferred to have some time to herself while he was out. He would have been very surprised to have learned how disappointed Jan was that he didn't ask her.

CHAPTER TWENTY-ONE

Earlier that evening Cait put the key in the lock and let herself into the house. After today's revelations she found she could no longer consider this as her home. Home was a warm, welcoming place, and she now realised she had never known anywhere like that. If she had children of her own, she vowed, she would never make them feel like intruders in their own home, only to be tolerated until they were old enough to make their own way in the world. Until she got her own place, though, which she meant to do as a matter of urgency, she had no choice but to stay here.

As she closed the front door behind her, she flattened her back against it and heaved a weary sigh. She had never meant anything so much in her life as when she had said she didn't want to

285

be the old Cait any more but a much nicer person. It was such hard work, though, constantly having to think about what she was going to say before she said it, and in what tone of voice, and the only thing that kept her persevering was the vision Glen Trainer – or her saviour as she now saw him – had conjured up for her of herself as an old woman, sitting by herself with no one in the world to turn to, no one caring whether she was alive or dead. The thought terrified her.

As exhausting as she had found it, she had to admit that making her apologies to Jane Trucker for her previous appalling behaviour had made her feel a bit better about herself. When she had asked the capable secretary if she would be willing to help source a temporary manager as Cait herself had no clue how to proceed, and also to talk her through anything else that was required of her in order for the company to keep running in the meantime, it had been surprisingly uplifting to see the lines of strain fade from the older woman's face. Jane's shoulders had sagged in relief on hearing she was no longer expected to shoulder the burdens she had been carrying for the last few days, and her gracious response to Cait had been that it would give her pleasure to help in whatever way she could.

Hearing her arrival, Agnes came to greet her, saying, 'Oh, I'm glad you're home, Miss Thomas. I just wanted a word before I left for the night. I've banked up the fire for you and your dinner is keeping hot in the oven.'

Cait had expected the daily to have gone home by now and desperately wanted to start running herself a bath as the sooner she did, the sooner she could get into bed and fall sleep after her tumultuous day. Agnes's waylaying her caused her to forget her resolve to change her attitude. 'Just what is it you want to speak to me about, Dalby?' she replied carelessly.

It was the hurt look in Agnes's eyes that reminded Cait if she carried on like this she would indeed become that lonely old woman Glen had prophesied. To Agnes's surprise she followed up her rudeness with, 'Forgive me, Agnes, I've had a tiring day. What was it you wanted a word about?'

'Well, it's just that you know I usually finish on a Saturday the same as Sunday, after I've cleared up dinner about two o'clock, and the rest of the day is me own? Well, I'm ... er ... very aware what day tomorrow should have been for you and it could be difficult for you to get through it on your own. So what I'm trying to say is that with your parents not being here, I'm willing to stay on in case you might feel the need for someone to talk to. I can do the same on Sunday if you'd like me to.' Agnes hurriedly added, 'Please don't think I'm being impertinent, Miss Thomas, 'cause I don't intend to be. What I am is concerned for you, that's all, one woman to another.'

Not that she was a woman who deserved Agnes Dalby's concern after the way she had treated her since she'd come to work for them, Cait thought, overwhelmed with shame. She realised now just what the poor woman had had to put up with, being treated with such hostility by her employer in order to see that she stayed in her place and did not feel at liberty to poke her nose into their affairs. But now Cait wondered just why her mother had felt such a need to keep people at arm's length. It had to be her ownership of the factory since it was never mentioned, but just why she felt the need to keep that a secret Cait couldn't fathom.

Because of the events of today and the exhaustion she was feeling, she had temporarily forgotten that tomorrow should have been her wedding day. It was going to prove a hard day to get through. Although the new Cait she was desperately trying to turn herself into should grab Agnes Dalby's offer of friendship, she felt the need to be on her own so that she could cry and wail for as long and loud as she liked, hoping this would help her over her grief for the loss of Neil and allow her to move on into the new life she was going to make for herself.

'Thank you, Agnes, but I'll be fine. Now why don't you get off home? You've not been paid to be here, remember.' She smiled and added, 'But I want you to know I'm grateful for what you're doing for me. Goodnight.'

With that she turned and made her way upstairs, leaving a very confused Agnes wondering if she had misheard her expression of gratitude. Uppermost in Agnes's mind, however, was a feeling of amazement at the change in Cait's behaviour. What could possibly have happened to the girl today to bring about this miraculous change in her personality?

As soon as Cait woke the next morning, the significance of the date hit her and a vision of

288

Neil swam before her. She wondered how he was feeling right now – more than likely celebrating his lucky escape from her, she thought – and at this her face crumpled and a flood of tears began to flow. She had never felt so lonely and desolate in all her life. Then suddenly some words Glen Trainer had said to her resounded in her mind. *The only one who can help you is yourself.* She wasn't doing anything to help herself lying here thinking of painful things that could only make her miserable. She couldn't stop painful things happening to her in the future, but she could make sure that when they did she had her own circle of friends around her to turn to for comfort. The first thing she must do was find herself a place to live so that the new Cait she was more than ever determined to become had somewhere to invite new friends back to.

She had just arrived at the bottom of the stairs, intending to make herself some toast then go to the nearest newsagent's and buy a copy of the *Mercury,* when she froze as she heard a key being inserted in the front door. It opened and to her surprise she saw Agnes walk in.

She couldn't fail to spot the worried expression on the old woman's face, which immediately turned to one of relief when she saw Cait.

'Oh, you are up and about, Miss Thomas. I ... er ... I'm so used to working I didn't know what to do with myself. I thought I'd just drop by and ... er ... fold that washing I put on the pulley in the utility room yesterday. And I might as well iron it while I'm at it. While I'm in the kitchen I could mash a pot of tea. Would you like a cup,

289

Miss Thomas?'

Cait smiled at her. 'I know you're really here because you're worried about me, and I appreciate that. Yes, I'd like a cup of tea, Agnes, thank you.'

The old woman smiled back at her before she went off to mash the tea.

Cait stared thoughtfully after her. This turn of events had come about because of her own small display of consideration for Agnes last night. Agnes wanted to repay her by showing some back. Cait felt she now understood how friends were made. Suddenly she didn't feel so alone any more. She had made her first friend.

CHAPTER TWENTY-TWO

At mid-morning the following Monday, Glen was fighting to keep his concentration focused fully on the bags of coal being emptied down the chute into the boiler room, in an effort to stop himself from worrying over the outcome of Jan's planned escapade tonight. He was desperate for its success, not relishing at all the prospect of a repeat performance should it fail. He didn't think his nerves would stand that. He was going to have to be patient, though, as by his calculation it was going to be at least seven o'clock before Jan got back to the flat. And that was provided she didn't face any setbacks during the operation. He was thankful that he had spotted a couple of job vacancies while he'd been out walking at the weekend. He was going to go straight after work tonight, not only because he really needed to find himself another job but because applying for them would help occupy some of the time, instead of pacing the flat, waiting for Jan to come home.

Meanwhile, upstairs in the office, Jane Trucker was telling Cait, 'There's many in the company that *think* themselves capable of running this place...' She suddenly realised what she had inadvertently said and vehemently hoped that the young woman she was addressing didn't see it as a jibe against her, as Jane hadn't intended it to be. Thankfully there was no sign from her demeanour that she had and Jane hurriedly continued: '...but no one who could step into Mr Swinton's shoes and carry on where he left off. Maybe Mr Harris the accounts manager, Mr Gerrard the foreman over at the main factory, and a couple of the other foremen have the skills between them to do the job, but I can just imagine what trouble that would cause, each of them fighting to be top dog. So that leaves us with the only other option of advertising for someone, though this near to Christmas and the job only being short-term, I can't see us getting anyone.'

Cait thought about this for a moment before she replied, 'But if that's the only option then we have to give it a try. And in the meantime we struggle on the best we can.'

Jane Trucker nodded in agreement as she closed her notebook, picked up the bulky folder

291

of letters that she had asked Cait to sign and said to her, 'I'll go back to my office and telephone the newspaper office. Our advertisement should go in tonight's *Mercury*.'

Cait watched her as she began to make her way to the door, and frowned. She had been very mindful today to watch exactly what she said and how she said it, but regardless all through their meeting this morning Cait strongly sensed that Jane wasn't quite sure yet that the young woman she was dealing with had indeed had a change of heart. It was apparent that the formidable secretary wasn't going to be so easily won over as Agnes had proved to be.

Cait's brain cranked up a gear, whirling frantically in her effort to decide what she could do to convince Jane there'd be no going back to her old ways. Something else Glen Trainer had told her gave Cait an idea. *At busy times even the owner or manager will roll their sleeves up and get stuck in to help out.* She was well aware the secretary was over-burdened with work, trying to cover much of what a manager would normally deal with. She had a strained look about her. Perhaps Cait could offer to ease her workload by doing what she was capable of?

Jane had opened the door and was just about to step out when Cait called to her, 'Miss Trucker, is there anything else I can do for you?'

She turned back to look at Cait. 'We've covered everything for now, Miss Thomas.'

'I mean, work that you need help with? I know you're busy coping with some managerial stuff that I really should be doing but can't, but I am

292

a good typist and a dab hand at filing.'

The woman's jaw dropped. 'Oh! It is very kind of you to offer but ... well ... you're the owner's daughter, Miss Thomas. It wouldn't be right for you to be doing that kind of work.'

Cait smiled at her. 'Well, as I see it, you have been good enough to help me out, so I'd really like to repay the compliment.'

Jane's shock was such that she stuttered, 'Well ... well ... I am rather behind. I do have some correspondence I would welcome a hand with, and a huge pile of filing, and that would free me up to attend to other matters that need my attention.'

Cait smiled warmly at her as she stood up and walked over to join her. 'Lead the way.'

Sitting on the bus on her way home that night, Cait was pleased with her efforts at self-improvement today and felt she had made a favourable impression on quite a few people. Jane Trucker was still being guarded towards her but had readily accepted her offer to help again tomorrow. Cait nearly let herself down on only one occasion when a young clerk from the general office had come into Miss Trucker's office to bring her some stationery she had requested. On spotting who her helper was, bashing away on the typewriter, she was so surprised to see the boss's daughter that she bumped into the desk and knocked over the remains of Cait's cup of tea. It spilled over two letters she had just finished typing. Cait automatically started to retaliate in her old way but thankfully managed just in time to stop herself, instead smiling at the offender and telling her that no real harm was done as she could retype the letters.

She was so consumed by her own thoughts Cait had not noticed the middle-aged woman sitting several seats behind her, watching her surreptitiously, having followed her from a safe distance ever since Cait had left the factory.

Since arriving back at the flat at six-thirty that evening, Glen had managed to keep himself busy making up the fire, having everything ready to mash a pot of tea, and potatoes peeled and shaped into chips ready to cook when Jan came home. Now it was approaching seven and he was anxiously sitting in his armchair, wondering why she wasn't back by now and worried something had happened to her ... the temperature today had been far too low to melt the hard frost of last night and it was slippery out tonight. He feared she might have met with an accident. Or maybe Miss Thomas had spotted her and Jan was down at the police station now, having to explain away her actions. It was seven-forty-five by the time he finally heard her key in the lock and jumped out of his chair to greet her.

'I was so worried about you,' Glen told her, helping her off with her coat and hanging it up for her along with his own on the hook on the back of the door. 'I was convinced you'd had an accident, slipped on the ice or something. Or that you'd been spotted by Miss Thomas.'

Jan was rubbing her hands and stamping her feet in an effort to bring life back to them. She smiled up at him and through chattering teeth quipped, 'Nice to know you care. Now get out of my way so I can reach the fire. I'm frozen to the marrow.'

He was so relieved to see her safely back, he realised that he cared more for her than if she was just a friend. He would have been even more shocked if he'd had any notion that Jan felt just the same about him.

By the time he came through with a cup of tea for them both she had just about thawed out and was ready to talk. Before he could ask her anything she put him out of his misery. 'Nerys lives across the other side of town, that's why I've been so long. It's two bus rides away and they don't run so regular after rush hour is over. I had to wait longer for the return journeys. It's off the London Road ... Elms Road it's called ... in a gabled house, four bedrooms at least with a huge garden. Mind you, it's small compared to some of the huge places on that street and round about. You could have six families living in some of those. I wouldn't like to be employed as a cleaner in one of those places. Anyway, goal achieved.'

He visibly sagged with relief. 'With no mishap to you?' he asked in concern.

'None apart from frostbite. So there's nothing else we can do now except wait patiently until Nerys gets back.' She intuitively read the expression that crossed Glen's face then. 'Look, I know she didn't show any thought for you whatsoever when she was carrying out her despicable plan against you, and obviously hasn't since, but even Nerys has to have a morsel of compassion in her somewhere. Anyway, let's stop talking about her for now. You went to apply for those jobs you told me you saw advertised on Saturday afternoon. Any luck?'

'Well, I thought I might be in with a good chance at one factory. The manager was still in his office when I got there and agreed to see me, and the receptionist let slip when she was showing me to his office that they hadn't had anyone suitable apply yet. The interview seemed to be going well, I told him the same background story as I did to Reg Swinton, but this man did ask me if I'd had any trouble with the law in the past. I suppose I should have said I hadn't and risked them not doing any checks on me, but I decided they just might. As soon as I told him I had, and what for, even though I tried to convince him I was innocent, the interview was terminated.'

'Oh, well, his loss,' said Jan reassuringly. 'There are other Reg Swintons out there, Glen, who'll only have to look at you to know you're just not capable of doing what you were accused of. Someone will take you on. Look, as I've told you before, should something happen which means you have to leave your job immediately, then my wages will just about cover the rent and food, as long as you have a real passion for bread and lard. We'll cope until you're working again. Oh, thinking of food, I'd best get cracking on some dinner for us,' she said, reluctantly withdrawing her legs from where they were resting on the hearth.

Glen was staring at her thoughtfully. If Jan was prepared to make such a sacrifice for him, did he

296

dare hope that meant she cared for him as more than just a friend?

Slippers on and cardigan pulled tightly around herself to ward off the cold air in the kitchen where the heat from the fire didn't quite reach, she made to rise. Glen stopped her, saying, 'You stay put. I've got the meal under control. Won't be a banquet but even a mere man like me surely can't make a muck up of egg and chips.'

As he went off into the kitchen, Jan slid off her slippers, resting her feet on the hearth and settling back in her lumpy chair, issuing a contented sigh. Before their son's accident, Harry had been a wonderful husband, but like most men he'd believed cooking was a woman's job. She had agreed with him then, he was out at work all day providing for his family and it was her job to look after them, but she had been tired too occasionally ... men never did appreciate that running a house was just as hard as labouring over a machine in a factory. After a particularly gruelling day labouring over the washing tub and mangle, it would have been nice if Harry had offered to see to their evening meal once in a while so she could put her feet up and read the evening paper. She would like to think she could get used to having Glen cook for her now and again, but she couldn't because sooner or later he would be in a position to fund a place of his own and then they'd part ways. Hopefully they'd still remain friends, though, and see each other now and again for a catch up. She wanted Glen to get on and build a good life for himself. God knew he deserved to have the best future possible, considering he'd been callously robbed of all he'd had. As a moral and compassionate human being herself, Jan would do all she could to help him achieve that for himself, but selfishly she hoped that it would happen later rather than sooner.

CHAPTER TWENTY-THREE

Three days later, Jane Trucker took a sip from her tepid cup of tea and said to Cait, 'Until a temporary manager is appointed you're still in charge, Miss Thomas, so it's down to you who we select out of this lot.' She inclined her head towards the pile of application letters they had just been opening together. 'I'm surprised we've received so many, considering the post was advertised as only temporary, but word has probably got out on the grapevine about Mr Swinton's death and the applicants think that temporary in this instance refers to a trial period. I expect they're hoping if they prove themselves, the job could become permanent.'

Cait looked down at the forms for a moment before she shrugged her shoulders in a helpless gesture. 'Well, you're far better qualified to know than I am.'

Jane shook her neatly kept crop of iron-grey hair. 'I'm not qualified enough to make major decisions such as this one, Miss Thomas, and neither is anyone else in the factory. I'm afraid this is one only you can make.'

Cait sighed heavily and looked pensive. The applicants all professed to have the necessary skills and experience, but she was aware that not every prospective employee told the truth. She herself hadn't been entirely honest when she had applied for the job with the fruit and vegetable wholesaler's after passing her exams at secretarial college. At her interview she had unashamedly claimed that she had often worked for a novelist at weekends during her training, although she never had, but felt this was bound to make her look like a better prospect than an applicant with no experience at all. Of course she'd covered herself by saying the author had since passed away, in case they decided to check on her.

But even if Jane Trucker and she set about the huge task of checking out every claim on the application letters, to ascertain the applicants were being honest and above board, she had no idea what questions to ask when interviewing them or what traits to look for in them to determine whether they'd be the right sort of person to manage Rose's. Much to her surprise, she did now actually have some feelings for the staff, and wanted to assure them all of a decent future.

She needed someone who had managed a factory to help her choose the right man for the job, and where on earth was she going to find anyone with those credentials?

Then she knew exactly where she could.

Gathering the application letters together, Cait said to the older woman; 'Leave this with me, Miss Trucker. I know just the person who can help me with this.'

Thinking it must be a friend of the Thomas family, she said, 'Very well.'

Application letters secured in a manilla folder, Cait went in search of Glen. Not knowing exactly where the maintenance room was situated, it took her a while to find it by asking directions en route. It was apparent to Cait that everyone she approached was aware of who she was by now, but judging by their guarded manner towards her they were still extremely wary of her. She hoped that by being polite towards them and showing her appreciation she would start to win them over. She finally found the maintenance room but to her dismay it was empty. And it could hardly be called a room either as it was no bigger than a large cupboard and crammed so full of all manner of items, stacked along the shelves lining the walls, that there was hardly room for the small desk and chair. She was pondering how to find out where Glen was now when someone came in.

'Looking for Glen to report a repair job, love?'

Cait turned around to see a middle-aged man struggling under the weight of a pile of shoe boxes. She assumed he was heading for the packing area, which she had spotted to the right of the maintenance room on first arriving. From a distance, Harry Owens couldn't see the features of the young woman in Glen's office, but as he drew closer recognition struck. Realising just who it was he had spoken to so casually, he spluttered, 'Oh, it's you, Miss Thomas. I thought you was one of the gels from up in the main offices, wanting something fixing.'

He turned the corner at the end of the rack of shelves, went over to the counter, put the boxes down on it and retraced his steps to stand just outside the maintenance room.

The man was familiar to Cait, they had obviously met before, but for the moment she couldn't place him.

He put her out of her misery. 'Harry Owens, Miss Thomas. We met ... er ... when ... er...'

She remembered him. He was one of the four union representatives who had given her an ultimatum last Friday. She could now smile at the fact that it had taken four burly men to band together to face a young woman less than half their age, regardless that it hadn't been at all funny for her at the time. She could see Harry Owens himself was feeling uncomfortable at the way they had first met, worried that she might be harbouring ill feeling towards him. After all, she was still the boss and at liberty to find a way to make him pay, if she was so inclined.

Having thought carefully about what she was going to say, Cait responded to him in a pleasant manner. 'Oh, I remember you now, Mr Owens. Nice to meet you again.'

He was mortally relieved that it seemed there'd be no repercussions for his involvement in Friday's stance against her. He could barely believe, in fact, this was the same young woman that all the employees had been so willing to strike against. Miracles did happen, it seemed to Harry.

Cait assumed he was wondering just what she was doing, dealing personally with a mundane

301

task when she had an assistant at her disposal. She thought she'd better offer him a plausible explanation, feeling she could be subjecting Glen to unnecessary suspicion from the type of fellow worker who took a dim view of employees and bosses appearing to be in cahoots. So she told Harry, 'Miss Trucker is very busy and I didn't want to burden her with something I could easily take care of myself.'

The look on his face told her he thought it very commendable of Cait to show such consideration towards her staff. He said, 'Mr Trainer said before he went off to see to his first job this morning that he had a full day of it today, jobs to deal with all over the factory, he might not even come back to his room until knocking-off time. If the repairs are urgent, I could get word around you're looking for him. Ask him to come up and see you in your office, Miss Thomas?'

Inwardly Cait was very cross with herself. If she did as Harry Owens was now suggesting then Jane Trucker would become suspicious as to why she and the maintenance man were deep in discussion in the office. She knew she would have to get Glen on his own so she could put her proposition to him, although she wasn't quite sure yet how.

She told Harry, 'Well, the work to be done is not at all urgent. It will wait until Mr Trainer hasn't so much on. Between me and you, Mr Owens, I was using the excuse to get out of the office for a bit.'

He laughed. 'Oh, most of us are guilty of doing that at some time or other.' He then realised what he'd said and almost fell over himself to add, 'Oh, not that I'm saying we're all looking for excuses to skive. Not at all I'm not!'

She reassured him, 'I'm sure you weren't, Mr Owens.'

On her journey back to the office her mind was occupied by trying to work out the best way to speak to Glen without any of the three hundred people who worked here being aware of it. There was only one place really where she could talk to him with no risk attached, and that was at his home. Cait had arranged to go and view a small one-bedroomed flat which she had spotted advertised in last night's paper, straight after work. She would go and visit Glen afterwards, she decided. She had discovered that the filing cabinet in her office had not been used purely to hold bottles of drink and glasses to entertain Reg Swinton's guests when they paid him a visit, but was crammed with personnel and customer records. This meant she could ascertain Glen Trainer's address without arousing any suspicion from Jane.

Back up on the second floor Cait called into the ladies' toilets before she dropped the folder of applications off in her office to take home that night. She was in a cubicle when she heard the door open and at least two sets of footsteps then the taps being turned on.

Two woman began talking and Cait couldn't help but overhear.

One of the women said to the other, 'That damned ink off the Banda machine is almost bloody impossible to get off me hands.' She must have given herself a look in the mirror then as she let out an anguished wail. 'Oh, look, me cheek is covered in it!'

The other woman spoke then. 'Well, if you can't get it all off just cover it with extra panstick tonight when yer getting ready to go out. What time are we all meeting at Timmy White's again? Seven-thirty or eight, I can't remember?'

'Seven-fifteen. We're going to the flicks, remember, to see *The Ten Commandments*. Oh, that Yul Brynner certainly tickles my fancy.'

'How can you fancy him? He's bald.'

'Don't care. I only have to hear his voice and I get shivers up me spine. What I'd give to find him wrapped up under the tree for me on Christmas Day! Oh, talking of Christmas, we mustn't forget to get the tickets for the Palais on Christmas Eve else we won't get in. We'd better decide on that tonight when we meet up with the other gels, who's going to collect the money off us all and go and get them, though I suppose it'll be down to me as usual.'

The other woman was obviously not listening but thinking of the night itself. 'I can't decide what to wear ... me red or me blue dress. I get more offers of dances in me red dress, but when I wear me blue I usually land meself a fella. Never the man of me dreams but better than n'ote.'

In the cubicle Cait was sitting with her elbows on her knees, chin resting in her hands, the conversation she was overhearing making her wonder what Christmas and New Year's Eve would be like for her this year. Christmas Eve was only days away now and as matters stood it seemed a very remote possibility that she would be planning what to wear for a evening of fun as she'd no one to go out with, male or female. Neither had she anyone at home to celebrate the day with either. Not that previous Christmases could ever have been described as fun. Since there were only the three of them, and her parents weren't the greatest communicators at the best of times, Christmas Day had seemed like Sunday to Cait except for the fact that they swapped gifts. Last year she'd received five pounds to buy herself something with. She now realised it was because her mother did not think it was worth trailing round the shops to find something Cait would be thrilled to receive. She herself always looked for a special something for them both, but from their noncommittal reactions on opening the gifts she was never sure whether they were pleased or not. She wasn't hopeful that her mother had thought to leave anything for her this year.

Cait knew she didn't have to spend the forthcoming festive evenings alone. She could go out right now and charm those two girls into inviting her along with them. She now knew, though, that it wasn't the way to make lasting friends. Those she made in future should be made in the proper way: by waiting to be invited to join their group because she was liked, and not as she had done before by buying friendship for the short time it lasted until the other person could no longer endure Cait's self-absorption. This year she would have to spend the festive season content in her own company, but hopefully next year would be a different matter so long as she continued to keep working hard on herself, which she definitely meant to do.

She waited patiently until the two girls had gone before leaving the toilets herself, not wanting them to know that she had been listening in.

CHAPTER TWENTY-FOUR

At approaching seven-thirty that evening, Jan was showing Glen an uncompromising side to her nature he had not witnessed before.

'A bit more to the left. No, not that much. To the right a bit. A bit more. No, that's too much. A bit to the left...'

Having patiently endured what he felt was Jan's misguided need for perfection for the last half an hour, he finally snapped at her in frustration, 'What does it matter if it's not perfectly straight?'

'It matters to me,' was her terse reply.

'But this chair I'm standing on isn't in the best of condition. I can feel it shaking beneath my weight. If I don't get down off it soon I fear it will collapse and I'll end up breaking my neck, not to mention having nothing to sit on.'

'Well, the sooner you get it right, the sooner you can get down, can't you? Now a bit to the left ... a fraction more ... another fraction more. Yes, that's it! Push the drawing pin in quick before you move it again.'

Having satisfied Jan at long last, Glen clambered down off the rickety chair before she changed her mind and took it back into the kitchen.

Jan meanwhile walked over to the other side of the room and stood looking at it admiringly. 'Looks very festive, don't you think?' she called to Glen, even though she knew that he disapproved of her spending just the couple of shillings she had out of the money she had taken from her soon-to-be-ex-husband's poor fund, on the red and yellow rolls of crepe paper which she had twisted together to form ceiling decorations. Money was still tight for them as although they had been paid for the first time last Friday by Rose's, their pay had been short as they'd only worked two days of the previous week and Rose's paid a week in hand. It had just been enough between them to cover the rent and not much more. The pitiful-looking two-foot Christmas tree placed in front of the window, kept upright by mud packed around it in a rusting tin bucket that had been discovered under the sink when they'd moved in and draped in the remains of the crepe paper, was already beginning to shed what needles it had left on its spindly branches.

Having replaced the chair, Glen made his way over to join her. Regardless of his feeling that they should hang on to all the money they could, he had to admit that the bit of colour the trimmings and the tree provided did help bring a touch of cheer to the otherwise dull room. But he had more important things on his mind than Christmas decorations. He had something to tell

307

Jan and she hadn't given him chance so far, having commandeered him as soon as their evening meal had been cleared away, to help her with the decorations.

He said now: 'That hand-delivered letter that was waiting for me when we got home... I opened it while you were cooking dinner.'

Jan looked at him keenly. She suspected this had something to do with the job he had gone after during his dinner hour yesterday, a storeman's place at Byford's clothing factory. She had been itching for him to open it and tell her the outcome. Typically Glen wanted to wait until they were seated by the fire before they discussed anything of note.

'Did you get the job or not?' she demanded.

He smiled. 'I did. Their present man is retiring in the middle of January. They want me to start the week before so he can show me the ropes. Thankfully in the interview I wasn't asked whether I had a criminal record. I presume they thought this would have been checked recently if I was already employed by a reputable company, and they accepted my excuse that I was only considering leaving Rose's so soon because their job was better.'

'Well, this means you can stop worrying about Nerys suddenly returning and discovering you in the building. It doesn't matter if she sacks you now as you've another job to go to. Oh, this calls for a celebration! Pity we've no spare money for beer. We'll have to make do with a cuppa. I'm certainly ready for one after putting up those decorations.'

He started to remind her that in fact it was he who had done that while she had stood issuing instructions, but before he could there was a knock on the door. They both looked at each other, wondering who could be calling on them at this time in the evening. They hadn't made any new friends yet who would pay them a social call.

Then Jan thought she knew who their caller was. 'It'll be the landlord come to check if we've settled-in all right. We haven't seen him since we took on the flat, have we?' As she headed for the door, she added, tongue in cheek, 'Maybe he's going to offer to give the place a freshen up? Replace the lumpy sofa and armchairs with something even a bit more comfortable.'

Glen thought he'd tidy away the debris from the decorations while she saw their landlord in. Jan opened the door, prepared to greet their landlord, but instead gawped in surprise to see Cait.

She meanwhile was hoping this visit would be more productive than her last had been. Whether the flat had been just perfect for her or not at all suitable, she had no idea. She had arranged to meet the landlord at six outside the house. By seven, when she was unable to feel her feet and hands for cold, he still hadn't turned up and Cait concluded that he'd already let it before she arrived and hadn't had the courtesy to stay around and tell her. She was disappointed at losing the prospect of her own place but also glad not to have got it because if the landlord didn't give a thought to leaving someone out in the bitter cold waiting fruitlessly for him, then how would he treat his tenants? This did bring home to Cait, though, the fact that she needed to be free during the day in order to apply for accommodation as soon as she saw it advertised. She needed to seek a new job for herself, too, and attend interviews. The sooner a temporary manager was found, the better as far as she was concerned.

When she arrived at Mr Trainer's door she was relieved to see a light shining and hear voices inside, as by now she was desperate to warm up. She smiled at the woman who answered the door to her and was just about to announce herself when a thought struck her. Cait knew she'd met this woman before, had some sort of dealings with her, but for the moment couldn't place her. She said to Jan, 'I really am so sorry to bother you but I need to speak to Mr Trainer about an urgent matter.'

Jan was having no trouble at all remembering her previous encounter with this young woman. It certainly hadn't been a pleasant one. She wondered just what was so urgent as to bring the likes of Caitlyn Thomas out on a bitter night like this, and what the young madam would make of their humble surroundings.

She stood aside, saying to her visitor, 'Please come in.'

Cait was only too glad to.

It was Glen's turn to be surprised when he saw Cait arrive in the living room. He stood staring at her blankly for a moment, the same questions going through his mind. He noticed she was holding a bulky manilla folder and wondered what was in it. 'Miss Thomas, very nice to see you,' he greeted her politely.

She noticed Glen was holding some scraps of crepe paper and a pair of scissors. 'Oh, I've disturbed you putting up your decorations,' she said apologetically.

Jan shot him a look, telling him not to dare say that two strips of crepe paper and a spindly tree was it.

'You haven't at all, Miss Thomas. We'd decided we'd had enough tonight and would finish it off tomorrow evening.'

She said then, 'You'll be wondering why I've called. Well, I need your help, Mr Trainer, on a matter it wasn't wise to discuss with you at work.'

He was intrigued. 'Let me take your coat for you,' he offered. She took it off and handed it to him. 'Please, take a seat.' He indicated the sofa, hoping she chose to sit on the part that wasn't quite so worn and uncomfortable as the rest.

'Would you like some tea? Jan offered, hoping Cait wouldn't notice that the patterns on the second-hand cup and saucer did not match and nor did she have any biscuits.

Cait replied with enthusiasm, 'I would very much, thank you.' She took a seat on the sofa, far too glad to be near a fire after being out in the cold for so long to notice how uncomfortable it was.

Since she always had the kettle simmering on the stove, just off the boil, it didn't take Jan long to make the tea. When she came through with two cups for them she said politely, 'I'll leave you to talk,' and went into her bedroom.

After taking a much-needed drink from her cup

311

and replacing it in its saucer, Cait said to Glen, 'I'll get to the point, Mr Trainer, as I don't want to interrupt you for too long.' She then reminded him of her agreement with the unions to put a qualified person in charge of the factory and explained that the post had been advertised in the *Mercury.* The responses were in the manila folder she had with her. Cait ended by telling him, 'Obviously I have no idea what qualifications I should be looking for in the candidates, so I wondered if you would take a look and indicate those you think have what it takes to fill the role. I'm sorry to put you to this trouble only you told me you'd run a business like Rose's in the past and I haven't anyone else I can turn to who knows the ins and outs like you do, Mr Trainer.' She tentatively held out the folder of application letters towards him.

Glen made no attempt to take it from her, just looked at her thoughtfully for several long moments before saying, 'In my opinion what you're doing is a waste of time.'

She looked taken aback. 'I don't understand. I said I'd find someone better equipped to head the company in order to avoid the strike.'

He nodded. 'Yes, and at the time I believed that was the right thing to do. But I don't need to sift through these letters to know that none of the applicants will prove suitable. Any man with the right credentials to head a firm like Rose's will already be employed in a similar capacity, and would only consider moving to another company if the job offered were a step up for him: bigger firm, more money, that kind of thing. They would

312

not even consider leaving a permanent job for a temporary one that might only last a few weeks, on the remote chance it might be longer. I can guarantee you that all the men who have applied are shop-floor workers who think they have what it takes to run a company. One or two might even be right, but there'll be no one with relevant experience. For the rest, the only reason they're willing to take a temporary job is so they can make themselves a bit of money before their incompetence is found out. And even should I be wrong and one or even more of the applicants is just what the company needs, I doubt it's possible to have someone in place this side of New Year.

'By the time you've interviewed them and checked their backgrounds, if they are in work they'll have to give notice and then you're looking at the middle of January at least before they can start. Mrs Thomas will surely have returned from her holiday by then and might not approve of the man you've taken on or else decide to run the place herself, then the poor chap will be out of a job before he's even started.' Glen saw an opportunity to find out when Nerys planned to return and hoped he'd put his question to Cait in such a way she wouldn't suspect there was anything more behind it than he was superficially asking. 'Have you had word from Mrs Thomas as to when she plans to come back?'

Cait wondered why he would want to know, but regardless couldn't bring herself to tell him that her mother wouldn't consider her plans any of her daughter's business. Besides, Nerys believed that she had moved out of the house by now, and was living independently, so her return wouldn't be of any consequence to her daughter anyway. Cait shook her head.

Glen was sure he'd seen a momentary flash of sadness in the young woman's eyes and wondered if matters were all as they should be between mother and daughter. Whether they were or not, though, was none of his business. He was just disappointed that he was still having to hang about for Nerys's return before he could tackle her about Lucy. He said to Cait, 'Well, I've never been abroad but I understand it's not at all easy to telephone back home. Maybe Mrs Thomas has tried but couldn't get a connection.'

She smiled. 'Yes, that's most likely the reason. My mother will have her hands full, though, as my father is not a well man and needs a lot of looking after. They've gone to a warmer country at this time of year, in the hope it would do him some good.'

So Nerys had married again. Seemed a bit of a coincidence, though, to Glen that the man she had married just happened to have the same surname as Nerys's maiden one. He smiled at Cait. 'Hopefully it will.' He looked thoughtful. 'When the union reps insisted you step aside for someone more capable of overseeing the company, they weren't meaning you should go to the lengths of employing someone new. You could just appoint someone already employed by the company as caretaker till your mother's return.'

Cait eyed him sharply and told him with conviction, 'Mr Trainer, I may be young and

314

naive but I did manage to work that out for my-self. I asked you if you'd take on the job after finding out that you had the relevant experience, but when you made it clear you weren't interested I asked Miss Trucker for her advice on who else she thought might fit the bill out of the current employees. It was her opinion that there wasn't anyone. I didn't know what else to do but look outside for the right person, in order to honour my agreement with the union.'

Glen inwardly smiled to himself. It was readily apparent that Caitlyn Thomas had been true to her word and had worked hard to change herself into a much more affable person, but he was glad to see that in the process she had not lost her spirit and did after all seem to have more than empty space in her head. He felt that with the right guidance and training, she showed the potential of being capable of running a business such as Rose's. When he had owned the firm, like his father before him, he had always kept an eye on the younger members of staff and if any showed signs of possessing the ability to further themselves, he would encourage them to do so. Some had gone on to manage other firms, a couple even ran their own businesses. He won-dered why Nerys hadn't already begun the process with her daughter, starting her at the business and allowing her to work from the bottom up as his own father had done with him. Nerys must have had her reasons, he supposed.

Sensitive to her own behaviour nowadays, Cait was feeling mortified about the way she had just spoken. She had slipped back into her old haughty ways. She blurted out, 'I'm sorry, Mr Trainer, I didn't mean to speak so rudely to you.'

He smiled at her. 'You didn't. You were under the impression I wasn't giving you credit for having any intelligence, you were insulted and decided to put me right. You did so very eloquently, without any show of your old attitude at all. You were obviously serious about changing your attitude and have worked hard on yourself to make that happen. To have come so far in such a short space of time, you deserve a pat on the back. Anyway, it should be me apologising to you for not giving you the credit you deserve for thinking of advertising the job when there was no one suitable to fill it in the company. It's very commendable you wish to honour your agreement with the union.'

She sensed from his tone that, regardless, he did have an alternative suggestion. 'I get the feeling that you think there is another choice, Mr Trainer? If I'm correct, I'd like to hear it, please.'

So she was astute as well, it seemed. She had been hiding all these good qualities in herself under a misguided display of superiority to others, but at least they were surfacing now. To Glen's way of thinking it was better late than never. He hadn't at all liked this young woman when he had first met her but found he was quite warming to her now. 'You're right, I do have another suggestion. Just carry on as you are until Mrs Thomas comes back. Now that you have started to work with the staff and not against them, the company isn't suffering. From my observation as I go about my work in the factory,

316

the foremen are keeping the workers in line and the workers are more concerned with their plans for Christmas than with what's going off upstairs – and with keeping their noses clean so as not to risk losing their Christmas bonus. I'm sure Miss Trucker has her eye on the office staff, making sure all the work is kept up to date there. At this time of year most businesses are winding down until after New Year, except for the shops, of course. After New Year it's slow for a few weeks while the retailers are getting rid of their old stock in their sales. Things don't usually pick up until about mid- to end-January when some of the staff at Rose's will be kept busy making sure the orders for the new spring stock are packed up and delivered to the customers in time. The rest meanwhile will be busy making summer shoes and ordering in the ready-made stock from abroad, while others are showing buyers our autumn designs for them to place their orders. The factory starts making those as soon as they've finished on the summer range. It's a never-ending cycle, Miss Thomas. Your mother will surely be back by then.'

Cait looked confused. 'But what about my agreement with the union representatives?'

'Well, they're under the impression that you're doing your best to find someone suitable so, as far as they're concerned, you are honouring your agreement with them. As long as the men they represent are happy with the way things are in the workplace, then they have nothing to grumble about.'

At the thought of the implications for herself of

what Glen was suggesting, she said without thinking, 'Oh, but then that means...' Cait's voice trailed off as she realised just what she'd been about to voice. That she wouldn't be free to start getting her new life off the ground. Worse, that she'd have to stick around and see how her mother reacted to discovering she had dared defy her by staying in the house, and had even rummaged round in her parents' bedroom as well as helping herself to money she had found in their safe. She just didn't want to see them again, not now she realised how little they thought of her. Cait had never felt able to open up to others about her personal life, though, abiding by her mother's rule that it was no one else's business. Although she would very much have liked to share her burden with someone, hear that it wasn't her fault her parents didn't love her but a lack within them, she just couldn't bring herself to.

She realised Glen was looking at her quizzically, waiting for her to finish what she had been about to say. She gave a small laugh and told him, 'I'm sorry, my mind has just gone blank. I can't remember what I was going to say.'

He would have believed her had she looked at him when she said it, but she didn't, addressed the fire instead, and he noticed the look of great sadness in her eyes. He wondered what she could possibly be so sad over? Then he remembered Jan's speculations about the called-off wedding, and wondered if it could have anything to do with that. He smiled and told her, 'It happens to the best of us.'

Meanwhile, sitting in her bedroom, the blankets wrapped tightly round her to ward off the bitter chill in the unheated room, Jan wished the pair sitting by the fire, all snug and warm, would hurry up and finish their conversation so she could return and join them. She'd only been sitting on her bed at the most for twenty minutes but to Jan it felt like twenty hours. When she had made Glen and Caitlyn a cup of tea she had not been able to bring one with her into the bedroom as they only had two cups, and now Jan was desperate for a hot drink. Until their visitor showed signs of making her departure, though, it would be rude of her to go and interrupt them.

Taking her blankets along with her, Jan crept over to the door and put her ear to it. She could hear the muted sound of voices, which told her that Glen and Caitlyn Thomas were still deep in discussion. Then an idea struck her as to how she could have her cup of tea without appearing intrusive. She wasn't being a very good hostess, was she, if she didn't offer their guest another drink? Then, while she was making it, she could have one first, drink it quickly, then wash out the cup, refill both of them and take them through. Jan thought this was an ingenious idea.

Shrugging off the blankets, she came out of her bedroom and made her way to the perimeters of the living area. 'Excuse me butting in; I just wondered if either of you would like another drink?'

She had crept in so quietly that neither of them had heard her. They turned their heads in surprise for a moment then both of them smiled at her.

Glen told her, 'We've finished what we were talking about, Jan, so you're not intruding.' He flashed a look at Cait then. 'We are finished, aren't we? There isn't anything else you need help with?'

She shook her head. 'No, there isn't, thank you. I can see the sense of what you advise.' She looked at Jan, considering her question. It would take her at least an hour, maybe more, to get home, and Cait suspected it was colder now than it had been when she'd arrived. Having another cup of tea before she left would certainly help her brave the weather. 'I hope I'm not overstaying my welcome, but I'd really like to accept your offer of another cup of tea before I set off home.'

Jan assured her, 'Of course you're not overstaying your welcome. It's quite a journey to your house from here, isn't it?' Then she could have kicked herself, realising what she had thoughtlessly said, and knew she'd better say something more to cover it up before Cait asked her how she knew. 'I mean, on a freezing night like this, any distance at all seems too long, doesn't it?'

Cait nodded. 'Yes, it does.'

Jan said, 'I won't be long with the tea.'

Glen got up from his chair and said to her, 'You come and sit by the fire while I make the tea.' He gave her a look that told her he'd already had one whereas she hadn't.

Desperate for a warm, Jan didn't argue with him. Sitting on the edge of an armchair, she held out her hands towards the fire for a moment then gave them a rub together before withdrawing them to rest demurely in her lap. She shot Cait an awkward smile. She wished now that their visitor hadn't accepted the offer of another cup of tea and was on her way home so Jan herself could take off her slippers and rest her icy feet on the hearth, then lounge back in her chair to read an old magazine one of her colleagues at work had given her. She was also intrigued as to why Cait had called and hoped Glen would put her out of her misery soon. She'd no idea how to make small talk with someone half her age, and the boss's daughter to boot. She could hear Glen clanking around in the kitchen and wished he would hurry up.

Cait meanwhile, with acute embarrassment, had finally recognised Jan as the woman she had sacked for speaking out of turn about her mother that first morning she had gone into Rose's. She wanted to apologise to Mrs Trainer for her own inexcusable behaviour. She took a deep breath and said, 'I recognise you now, Mrs Trainer. You work at Rose's too, don't you? Look, I need...'

Jan was reluctant to revisit their unpleasant initial meeting so hurriedly replied, 'Yes, I do. In the canteen. Next time I bring you up a tray of tea, I'll make sure I add a nice cake for you.' Then to change the subject, she said, 'I think we're in for some snow. It's certainly cold enough for it, in my opinion.'

Cait was astute enough to realise that the older woman did not want to talk about their first encounter, so responded, 'I wonder if we'll have a white Christmas this year then?'

Jan nodded. 'Mmm, yes, that would be nice. Traditional like.'

They both sat in silence for a moment, each seeking something to say next. It was Cait who

321

thought of something first.

'Have you finished all your present shopping or have you still some to do?'

Jan wanted to buy something for Glen. This would be his first proper Christmas since Cait's mother had ripped his life apart so she was determined to make the day as special as she could for him. She was certainly looking forward to seeing his face when she told him on Christmas morning to look under the tree and see if Santa had left him anything, but just what that gift would be depended entirely on how much money she had left from her first full wage packet. There was barely anything over from the money she had purloined from Harry's fund for the needy. She just responded, 'Still got a bit to do. What about yourself?'

Cait had no one to buy a present for as matters stood. Then it struck her that maybe she should get a little something for Agnes as a thank you for all her kindness in Cait's time of need. She responded to Jan, 'Like you, still have a bit to do.'

The Thomases had money to spend so Jan assumed their Christmases would reflect that. 'I expect Mrs Thomas pushes the boat out at this time of year, entertaining lots of family and friends.' Then she remembered that Glen had told her Nerys was an orphan and Cait an only child, and forgot she wasn't supposed to know this. In her need to keep the conversation flowing and avoid any awkward silence, she continued, 'Oh, of course, your mother being an orphan and you an only child, I expect you'll be going to a friend's this year, won't you?'

Cait frowned at her quizzically. 'How did you know that my mother is an orphan ... both my parents are, in fact ... and that I am an only child?'

Jan stared at her. How careless not to watch what she was saying 'Er ... well ... you told me, didn't you?'

Cait shook her head. 'No, I didn't.'

Jan gave a nervous laugh. 'Well, I must have heard it at work. You know how it is, people like to gossip ... makes them feel superior letting others know they know something the rest of us don't.' She hoped her explanation was enough to placate Cait and, not wanting her to think too deeply about it, asked again, 'So friends, is it, you're spending Christmas Day with?'

Cait could have lied to her, but what did it matter to this woman what she was actually doing on Christmas Day? 'No, actually. I've decided to have a quiet time on my own this year. I'm really looking forward to it.'

But Jan noticed the way she averted her eyes to look into the fire when she said this, which made her wonder whether Cait was being truthful. To Jan's way of thinking someone being on their own, whether by choice or not, on Christmas Day was a bleak prospect.

'Christmas is a time for spending with others. It won't be any fun eating dinner on your own ... and who will you pull a cracker with?' she protested.

Cait didn't want to discuss this topic any longer as it was only serving to remind her that she was virtually alone in the world, except for her fledging friendship with Agnes. 'Honestly, I really am looking forward to spending the day quietly, Mrs Trainer,' she insisted.

Jan wasn't convinced. 'I don't like the thought of anyone spending Christmas Day on their own, so all I'll say is, if you should change your mind, then you are more than welcome to come here. Please don't forget as I mean it. It won't be the sort of day you'll be used to, no expense spared so to speak, but we can at least provide company for you.'

Cait was very touched by Jan's invitation. It was the first genuine offer of company she'd had. 'Thank you, Mrs Trainer.'

Jan was feeling uncomfortable. 'I have to tell you that I'm not Mrs Trainer, so it's not right to let you keep calling me that. My name is Clayton. Janet Clayton. I prefer Jan to Janet, though. Me and Glen, well, we live together. I'm sure some people who know at the factory think we live in sin, but we don't. We're just friends, nothing more. We each have our own bedroom. We found ourselves in a position where we both needed somewhere to live but couldn't afford places on our own, so we pooled resources.'

Cait was looking at her with interest. 'What a good idea. Better than having nowhere to live.'

Jan said ironically, 'Just a bit.'

The girl then mused to herself, 'I shall have to consider getting someone to share with me if I can't find a decent place I can afford on my own.'

She was speaking louder than she'd realised and Jan heard her. 'You're surely not thinking of leaving home just yet? You're far too young to be fending for yourself.'

Cait stared at her blankly for a moment before she responded, 'Well, we all have to make our own way in the world at some time, don't we?'

Jan gave a shrug. 'I suppose so. Your mother might not see it that way, though. I doubt she'll let you leave without trying to get you to wait a little longer.'

An expression flashed over the young woman's face then, one that Jan couldn't quite read. She had no time to decipher it. As quickly as it had appeared it was gone. But she had definitely seen sadness and fear, she realised.

At long last Glen arrived with two steaming cups of tea rattling in their saucers as he tried not to spill any. Jan had never been so relieved to see him, grateful that her fight to keep the conversation flowing was at an end and now he could take over.

Ten minutes later Cait thanked him again for his help, and both of them for their hospitality, and took her leave.

After seeing her out, Glen returned to sit back in his armchair and looked at Jan for a moment. She was staring into the fire, seeming very thoughtful. Finally he asked her, 'You all right, Jan?'

'Eh? Oh, no, I don't think I am.'

'Have you a headache? I can pop to the corner shop and get you something for it, if you have.'

'Ah, thanks, Glen, I appreciate that, but no, I haven't got a headache. It's just that...'

'Just what?'

She sighed. 'It's just that I don't think all is well there.'

He looked confused. 'All's not well where, Jan?'

'With that young woman.'

'In what way?'

'Well, I can't pinpoint it exactly. Just a couple of times when we were talking, I felt that she wasn't being truthful.'

'She was lying, you mean?'

'No, she wasn't lying. But, like I said, not being entirely truthful either.'

'You're making no sense to me,' Glen told her, befuddled.

'Well, for instance, we were discussing Christmas and she told me she really wanted to spend the day on her own, was looking forward to it, but all my instincts told me that she wasn't one bit. That's what I mean.'

Glen frowned thoughtfully. 'Well, she told me that day in the office that she hadn't got any friends. I suppose she hasn't anyone else to spend Christmas Day with. She obviously felt embarrassed and didn't want you to feel sorry for her.'

'Mmm, yes, I suppose. I did say she was welcome to come here if it was company she was after, but I don't expect she'll take it up since we're old enough to be her parents. But she's also thinking of leaving home and I sensed that the thought of fending for herself terrified her. So why is she even thinking of doing it? And, Glen, that young woman has an air of great sadness about her. What could she have to be sad about? I mean, to me she's living a charmed life. A nice house to live in ... her mother looking after her.' Jan's face darkened then. 'More than she's doing for your daughter, Glen, after she promised you she'd take care of Lucy.'

He was thinking the same. 'And all I want to do now is find my daughter and put this all behind us. Try and do everything I can to make up for lost time with her.'

Jan smiled at him. 'Yes, you're right. Hot milk?'

'Yes, please. While you do that, I'll see to heating the stone bottles to warm up the beds.'

CHAPTER TWENTY-FIVE

On turning into the main street after leaving the road Glen and Jan's flat was on, to Cait's utter dismay she saw a bus pulling away from the stop. The bitter cold was already seeping through her thick winter coat and chilling her bones. She was also very hungry and tired, having had nothing to eat since a cheese cob in the office, and did not at all relish the thought of the wait that lay ahead of her until the next bus arrived, then another wait on top of that for the second bus that would ferry her home. Dragging her feet, she walked the rest of the way to the bus stop and leaned wearily against the post. She looked around. A shop front directly opposite caught her attention. It belonged to a taxi firm. She smiled to herself. She would get a car home, and in a very short time be sitting tucking into the dinner Agnes would have put in the low oven to keep warm for her.

She darted across the road and into the taxi

office. At the counter she gave her address and was told a car would pick her up in ten minutes. Cait took a seat on a red plastic-covered bench that ran under the shopfront window and picked up a tattered magazine to look through while she waited. The wall-mounted radio was playing a selection of Christmas songs: 'I Saw Mommy Kissing Santa Claus' and 'Winter Wonderland' – in case anyone needed reminding what time of year it was.

Lost in the article she was reading, Cait wasn't aware of another customer coming in until she felt the pressure of someone sitting down nearby her on the bench and automatically looked up to see who it was. As her eyes met the newcomer's she froze. He looked shocked too. They both stared at each other for several long moments before Neil looked away, got up, spoke briefly to the man behind the desk then made his way outside. Cait turned her head to look through the window and saw him leaning against the window of the shop next-door. She felt a great need to apologise to him for what she now realised must have been a very difficult time. She needed him to know that the person he thought her to be no longer existed, in the hope that he might not feel so embarrassed by the situation then.

Saying she would be outside for a few moments should her taxi arrive, she went to join him.

As soon as he saw her come out of the door, Neil said to her awkwardly, 'Look, Cait, I know you must be hurt by the way I finished our relationship–'

She cut in, 'I was, Neil, very much so, and also

328

very confused. I couldn't understand what I'd done wrong, but since our breakup a lot has happened to me. I'm now in a position to see myself as others did. I loved you so very much, Neil, but I now know that the person I was then wasn't very easy to love back or to be around either. I wanted you to know that I am very sorry for putting you through what I did.' Just then a voice called out from the taxi office next-door that her car was arriving. Simultaneously, it drew up at the kerbside. For Cait it had arrived at just the right time. She had said all she wanted to and hopefully now Neil wouldn't remember her quite so bitterly.

She made a dash for the taxi, yanked open the door and jumped inside, turning her head to look out of the opposite window so that Neil could not see her tears of deep regret as the car pulled away.

CHAPTER TWENTY-SIX

In two separate households, roughly four miles apart, two entirely different Christmas Days were being experienced.

Inside the shabby flat, standing beside Jan near the fireplace, a blazing fire burning brightly inside it, Glen was staring at the gaily wrapped parcel he was holding. Jan meanwhile was looking on, silently urging him to open it so she could see by his face whether her choice of gift had been a good one. Finally she could stand it no longer and snapped at him, 'Oh, for goodness' sake, stop staring at it like the village idiot and open the damned thing!'

He lifted his eyes from the parcel and grinned at her. 'Don't be a spoilsport, Jan. It's been many a long year since I've had a present to open on Christmas Day and I want to savour every moment.' Then he looked at the brown paper-wrapped parcel she was holding and urged her, 'You open yours first, then I'll do mine.'

She chuckled, saying, 'Oh, you're acting like a big kid. Tell you what, we'll open them together.'

'All right,' he agreed.

Jan was desperate to find out what he had bought her and had the paper off before Glen had even made a start on his. Inside was a pair of brown woollen gloves. Jan didn't know whether to laugh or cry. Laugh because she had bought Glen exactly the same thing as he had, to keep his hands warm in this bitter winter weather they were experiencing. Cry because although they were just friends, and although she hadn't ex-pected a gift from him at all, she had foolishly hoped for something pretty that would make her feel more feminine. Her clothes consisted of two gabardine skirts, one black and the other dark green, two plain blouses and two brown cardi-gans, along with a change of unflattering under-wear. She had bought them all from the second-hand shop to tide her over until their monetary situation improved or Harry found time between his work and church duties to send her belong-ings round.

Glen was saying to her as he was still trying to

get the paper off his gift, 'You needed gloves, didn't you? I noticed how cold your hands get on our way to and from work. Have I got the right size?'

Jan suddenly felt guilty for being disappointed with her present. In truth he'd got her exactly what she needed, and thanks to his thoughtfulness her hands would now be warm and cosy while she was out in the wintry conditions. Throwing the paper into the fire, she pulled on the gloves then wiggled her hands at him. 'They fit perfectly, thank you,' she said sincerely.

Glen managed to rip off the remainder of the paper and started to laugh when he saw the gloves Jan had bought him. 'Great minds think alike,' he said, also throwing the paper into the fire and pulling them on. 'Just what I needed – and a perfect fit too. Thank you.'

She told him, 'Well, I noticed the way your hands got cold too.' Then she said, 'It's time for me to get the dinner on the go or it won't be cooked for three.'

Christmas Day fell on a Tuesday this year and last Friday night, after receiving their first full wage packets, Jan and Glen had sat down and calculated what each of them needed to put in for their share of the bills, including a little extra for festive food which Jan would bargain for on Christmas Eve. She had been delighted to find that she did have enough left from her wage not only to pay for her own personal needs, but also a small gift for him too.

On Christmas Eve all the employees were allowed to leave early, and at just after three-thirty Jan hurried out of the gates along with the rest of the workforce, heading straight for the town centre, in particular the market, on a mission to secure some bargains. Glen had offered to accompany her, to help carry the groceries home, but she had waved off his offer with a flap of her hand, telling him that he'd only hinder her and she would much prefer it if he had a roaring fire ready to greet her along with the singing of the kettle when she returned home.

It was a jubilant Jan who had walked wearily through the flat door at just after seven that evening, laden down with brown carrier bags filled with last-minute buys she had fought with other bargain hunters to acquire, sporting several bruises and a pair of laddered stockings to prove it. Having told her to sit down in her armchair by the fire and rest her aching feet while he made her a cup of tea, Glen also unpacked the bags. With all she had bought piled on the table, he stood and stared at it. At the battered-looking clementines, bruised apples, netting bag of nuts with smashed shells, wilting vegetables, and especially the sorry-looking chicken that had been flattened due to being at the bottom of a large mound of ready-plucked ones the market-stall butcher had got ready in the early hours of that morning, ready to serve his never-ending stream of customers. He'd been glad to sell it to Jan for a couple of shillings sooner than get nothing for it by throwing it away. For a man who over the last five years had never known where his next mouthful of food was coming from and often went for several days at a time without any at all, the sight before Glen was one to behold. He was looking forward to sitting down for his first Christmas dinner for many a long year and eating it in Jan's good company.

As she made to go into the kitchen area and begin preparing the food, Glen stopped her, saying, 'Just a minute, I think you've missed something.'

She looked at him, puzzled. 'Such as what?'

'Something else under the tree for you.'

Her eyes lit up. 'Something else for me?' She dashed over to the tree and bent to look around the rusting bucket, but saw nothing. She was about to scold Glen for having a joke with her that she didn't at all find funny when she spotted a small wrapped package sitting on top of the soil in the bucket where he had hidden it, hoping she wouldn't see it until he was ready to tell her about it. She snatched it up and started squeezing the parcel. It was soft and immediately her excitement began to mount. Ripping off the paper, she stopped short to stare at what she'd found inside. It was a silk scarf, brightly coloured in rich shades of blue and green. Had she had a choice, she would have picked this one for herself. She looked at him, astonished, and uttered, 'Oh, thank you so much, Glen. It's beautiful. But you shouldn't have. It must have cost you...'

He put his fingers to his lips to tell her not to continue. 'I wanted to get you something nice by way of showing you my appreciation for everything you have done for me, Jan.'

Trouble was, she wanted him to have bought

her this gift because he cared for her as more than just a friend.

She told him, 'I shall wear it all the time,' and again started to make her way into the kitchen, but again he stopped her.

'I'm not quite finished yet. There's another present. This one I bought for us both.' While she looked on speechless, he went over and bent down behind his armchair. When he righted himself he was holding a large wooden box-like object in his hands.

Jan clapped her hands together in delight. 'It's a wireless. Oh, Glen, you've bought us a wireless. Oh, I have so missed listening to it. Put it on now and let's liven this place up. It's Christmas Day after all.' Then she looked at him quizzically. 'How did you pay for my scarf and the wireless?'

As he was plugging the wireless into the electric socket and tuning it in, he told her, 'Well, I get paid more than you and so I had more left over after taking out the money for my share of the bills and food. The wireless, as you can tell, is second-hand, but you're not the only one who can strike a deal. The bloke wanted seventeen and ninepence for it but I knocked him down to fifteen.' After a lot of hissing and crackling, Glen hit the BBC Home Service and lively dance-band music boomed out loud and clear.

Jan loved to dance. Impulsively she grabbed Glen's arm and started waltzing vigorously around the room with him, both of them laughing as they did so, until the tune finished and they collapsed on the sofa together, still laughing.

'Oh, that was fun,' she spluttered.

Glen nodded. 'It was. I can't believe that after all these years I still remember how to do it.'

'Well, I suppose it's like riding a bike. Once learned, never forgotten.'

Glen then looked searchingly at her for a moment before he tentatively suggested, 'When we've afforded ourselves some decent clothes maybe we could both go to a dance one night at one of the halls?' He was worried then that Jan might think he was asking her out on a date. If she didn't think about him in that way he feared he might have put her in a compromising situation, so quickly added, 'Be nice to go out as friends.'

Oh, why did he have to go and add that when she'd just had her hopes lifted that this was Glen's way of telling her he saw her as more than just a friend? She said lightly, 'Yes, I'd enjoy that.' Then she got up, saying, 'Right, we really must make a start on the dinner. Come on, you can start peeling the potatoes while I fish the giblets from the chicken to make the gravy with.'

Meanwhile in another household across town Cait sat staring out of a window which looked onto a sweep of neatly kept front garden. But she was not seeing how beautiful it looked, with the frost sparkling like miniature diamonds on the blades of grass and leaves and bark where the weak December sun touched it. She was far too miserable to notice.

She had thought she would get through the day fine, sleeping late and then occupying herself reading through the pile of magazines she had bought, watching what she wanted to for a change on the television and not what her mother and father dictated, but she hadn't bargained on feeling so very sad, lost and lonely, with no heart to do anything whatsoever, the neverending day stretching before her.

Her desolate state had nothing to do with the absence of her parents but was all to do with Neil. Their chance encounter had resurrected all the feelings for him that she had been trying to bury.

She had firmly told Agnes not to come in today, and to enjoy being with her family and friends, but still she had insisted on preparing a meal that would just require heating up, so at least she knew Cait was enjoying a proper Christmas dinner. She had also been overwhelmed with the small gift that Cait had bought her: a bar of lavender-scented soap and matching talcum powder. Never having received so much as a token from her employers before after years of loyalty to them, from the way she'd responded an onlooker would have thought Cait had given her the crown jewels.

She had slept badly the night she had bumped into Neil, unable to get him out of her mind, and her only respite since had been while she had been occupied at work. But immediately Agnes had departed at six on Christmas Eve, leaving her entirely on her own, memories of Neil, and her own pain and heartache at losing him, had flooded back with a vengeance and not left her since. That morning, feeling wretched and exhausted, Cait had dragged herself out of bed and moped aimlessly around the house. She was

336

still in her dressing gown, unwashed, her hair dishevelled. It was now after two o'clock and the meal Agnes had prepared her was still sitting untouched in the fridge where she had left it yesterday, Cait having had no appetite since her unexpected meeting with Neil.

She knew she wasn't helping herself by wondering who he had held in his arms for the last dance on Christmas Eve; who he had kissed under the mistletoe; who was sitting by his side at the dinner table today, sharing jokes with his family; who he had bought a special Christmas present for.

She knew she was upsetting herself unnecessarily, and that she needed something to occupy her mind and take her thoughts off Neil, even for a short while.

What, though? There was nothing in this house that would provide the distraction she needed. She knew it would be easier for her when she returned to work the day after Boxing Day, but that didn't help her right now. If only everywhere wasn't closed. With somewhere to go, the cinema, a museum, a browse around the shops, she would at least have had other things to think about.

Cait heaved a deep forlorn sigh as she watched a robin fly from branch to branch, vehemently wishing she was just a bird with only the problem of where her next worm was coming from to think about. Then unexpectedly a memory popped into her head. But she did have somewhere to go. Somewhere where she had been told she'd be welcome. That was an invitation whichever way she looked at it and there was no reason to believe it wasn't genuine. All thoughts of Neil were suddenly replaced by ones of what she would wear, how she would get there and what to take with her as she couldn't go empty-handed.

It took her several telephone calls to find a taxi firm that was providing a skeleton service that day. An hour later, carrying a bottle of five-star Napoleon brandy she had taken out of her parents' drinks cabinet and wrapped up in brown paper and tied with a ribbon, Cait went out to meet the taxi as soon as she heard its tyres scrunching on the gravel drive. Settling herself in the back of the car, she informed the driver of Glen's and Jan's address and they set off.

At just after twelve that night, three people climbed into their beds, tired but happy. Glen had thoroughly enjoyed his day. He had been in very pleasant company ... had been most surprised when Caitlyn had turned up, but pleased she had taken Jan's invitation seriously and didn't mind sharing the day with two people old enough to be her parents. The food Jan had prepared had been sumptuous and he was stuffed to bursting with it. He'd also enjoyed several small tots out of the bottle of brandy that Cait had brought with her. He'd never been a willing participant in parlour games in his younger days, much preferring to sit back and watch everyone else play their part, and laugh at their antics. Jan, though, was having none of it. She had left him with no choice but to act out several charades for Cait and her to guess the answer to, and then do likewise for him. He had also been roped into taking part in games of I Spy, Blind Man's Buff, and Guess the Famous Person, and sing along to carols being played on the wireless during the evening service. All in all, he had been most surprised to find how much he had enjoyed himself.

Only one thing marred what would otherwise have been a perfect day and that was his wish to be reunited with his daughter.

Jan's idea of a perfect Christmas Day was plenty of tasty food, good company, and having some fun and laughs – the latter two being the things sadly lacking from her life over the last ten years. But today she felt she couldn't have bettered the company she was in, and she couldn't remember when she had last laughed so much over other people's antics. They'd played a selection of parlour games, her voice was hoarse from singing along with the wireless, and she'd certainly enjoyed the treat that Cait had brought along with her.

There was only one thing that was missing from her day, and that was the fact that Glen had not been reunited with his daughter.

A day that had started out so miserably for Cait had ended with her feeling far more positive about her future. Glen and Jan between them had provided just the distraction she had needed to free her mind for long periods of time of all thoughts of Neil. She had been reluctant at first, in her low mood, to participate in the parlour games Jan suggested they play, not having the energy to do anything more than to sit and watch. Jan, though, was not taking no for an answer. If she and Glen were going to be making fools of themselves then it was only fair that Cait did too. She was surprised by how much she had enjoyed herself. By the time she finally departed for home that night her only regret was that she hadn't gone to visit Glen and Jan earlier in the day.

CHAPTER TWENTY-SEVEN

Cait's birthday several days later passed uneventfully. No one at work knew what day it was and she didn't enlighten them. In fact, had it not been for Agnes's thoughtfulness in buying her a card there was a strong probability she would not have remembered what day it was herself until after the event. She had believed that New Year's Eve would prove equally uneventful and prepared herself to spend it quietly at home by herself. But to her utter shock and joy, and without her having to manoeuvre others into anything, she was offered an invitation because the young woman issuing it had taken a liking to her and felt she was just the type who would fit in nicely with the group of girls she socialised with. All Cait's hard work in changing her attitude was rewarded and New Year's Eve was not the quiet lonely occasion she had prepared herself for.

The invitation had come about the evening before when she had arrived at the bus stop in town to await her journey home. It had started to pour down and, having no umbrella with her, she'd started to get soaked. Next thing she knew she was being asked by a young woman of around her own age, who had noticed her predicament, if she would like to share her umbrella with her until either of their buses arrived.

Cait had noticed her while they had been waiting for their respective buses. She'd liked the look of her, and whereas before she wouldn't have hesitated to acquaint herself with the girl and do her best to engineer a friendship, the new Cait held herself back and allowed the girl to make her own approach if she wanted to. The bad weather had created the perfect opportunity for that to happen. Cait was only too glad to accept the offer and soon found herself falling into easy conversation with her rescuer. She took an instant liking to the bubbly young woman and tried not to hope she might feel likewise, for fear of being disappointed. But she obviously did because before they parted company, Cait's bus thankfully arriving first as it was still pouring down, the other girl Cait now knew to be Belinda had given her her address and invited her to come round whenever she liked, which a jubilant Cait had enthusiastically agreed to do. As she had stepped on to the platform of the bus Belinda had called out to her that if she wasn't doing anything better, she was welcome to join her and her other friends on New Year's Eve. They were all meeting at the clock tower at seven-thirty and going to see in the New Year at a skiffle club.

Cait was waiting at the clock tower for Belinda

341

and her other friends to arrive at a quarter past, not taking any risk she might be delayed and miss them. Belinda's other friends, three of them as it turned out, were a bit wary of her at first, but soon warmed to the new Cait's friendly, unpushy, easygoing manner. Before the evening ended she had become the fifth member of their group, her vision of herself as a lonely old woman beginning to fade.

CHAPTER TWENTY-EIGHT

Cait had never before seen Jane Trucker in a flap, but she was certainly seeing her in one this morning.

In a complaining tone while making a list of things to do, she was saying, 'Oh, if only the secretary had remembered her mistake yesterday and not when she realised Mr Bowden was already on his way! She'd forgotten to inform us last week that he is planning to visit us today to view our summer collection and make his order ... he's getting married at the end of February so will be away on honeymoon when we normally have all the buyers descending on us. He's visiting all his suppliers early and is expected here at twelve today so we've got less than two hours to get everything ready for when he arrives.'

Cait asked her, 'Who is Mr Bowden?'

Jane smiled. 'He's a nice young man. Not long since taken over the family business when his father retired. He's been here a couple of times accompanying his father as his second-in-command, but he told me once when I was chatting to him while his father was with Mr Swinton that when he was a young boy, his father used to let him take a day off school and as a treat bring him along to meet some of the suppliers. He came to Rose's several times then. Bowden's are amongst our best customers and we push the boat out for them. The family own several high-class shoe shops in towns and cities up north, all patronised by the well-to-do of those areas who buy only our most expensive handmade range, so we really can't afford to upset them.' Jane paused long enough to look at her wrist watch. 'Goodness, time is moving on.'

Cait was bothered on two fronts by this unexpected visit. The first reason she did not voice to Jane. She'd have to cancel her own arrangement with another landlord to view a flat he was letting. She had meant to go in her dinner hour, desperate to be the first in the queue this time. At least it wouldn't affect her arrangement to visit Belinda at her house tonight, for a girlie get-together. The second concern she had she did voice to the older woman. 'I'm worried I'm going to make a total hash of this and look a real idiot. Mr Bowden is bound to ask me questions about the stock he's interested in, and I won't be able to answer.'

'Stop worrying. There's nothing he'll ask that I can't answer. If I see you struggling, I'll step right in.'

Cait was mortally relieved to hear this. She

asked Jane, 'What would you like me to do to get things ready for his arrival?'

Jane consulted her list. 'Hilda Digby needs informing she'll be required to provide a cold buffet for us in the entertainment room – that's the room off the viewing room where we take customers after they've decided on their selections, where they can relax with refreshments while we do the rest of the business. Hilda is not going to be at all amused at the short notice we're giving her, but knowing her as I do I expect she'll do her best to put together a good spread.'

'Would you like me to speak to her?' Cait asked.

Jane smiled gratefully at her. 'If you don't mind, yes, please. Oh, and can you ask them to prepare a tray of tea and coffee ready to bring up to your office the moment we get word Mr Bowden's arrived. And if you could ask April on reception to keep her eyes peeled for his car in the car park and let us know immediately she sees it.'

Cait chuckled. 'It's like organising a military operation.'

Jane nodded. 'Isn't it just? I'm sure our customers have no idea how much trouble we go to to make them feel welcome and valued.' She looked down her list again. 'After you've dealt with the telephone calls, would you be kind enough to check the viewing room? See that the cleaner has given it a dust and polish recently as we haven't had a viewing for a couple of months. The shelves and what's on them could be in need of a dust. If so, let me know and I'll do it myself if

I have time. Or maybe I can find someone in the factory to do it.'

Cait had no intention of putting any more pressure on Jane. If the room needed dusting she would do it herself.

Jane remembered something else then and said, 'Oh, and another thing to add to the list. Check the gents' toilets are clean and there's a fresh bar of soap and clean towel available. Then have all the men up on this floor told to use the one in the workers' entrance until Mr Bowden has left. Can't risk him using the facilities after the disgusting state some thoughtless men leave them in, can we?' She said this as she added more tasks to her list. 'Right, I think I've thought of everything. First of all I'm going to arrange for Harry Owens to check his inventory. All the outside manufacturers' samples of the new range should be unpacked and on display. If not, he needs to see to that urgently. I already know that all the samples of the designs we produce ourselves are displayed. Just before Mr Swinton died, he took all the office staff down with him to have a look at them. He felt it was important for all the employees to know just what the company sold.' A momentary look of sadness crossed Jane's face at that memory but she quickly reverted to her efficient self.

Cait rose, telling her, 'I'll get back to you as soon as I've dealt with the jobs you've given me – see if there's anything else I can do.'

Jane stared at Cait as she hurried away. After the young woman's disastrous start, she was proving to be quite an asset. She would willingly accept instructions from Jane, and had not once reverted to her old superior ways. Jane couldn't fault the work she produced either. She knew she'd be sorry when eventually a permanent manager was in place and Cait returned home. She assumed the family couldn't be short of a bob or two, considering the way the factory had always done well since she'd been employed here. No doubt Cait usually spent her time in leisure pursuits. It was a shame, she felt, that the girl had not shown any interest in joining the company in a junior capacity as it was apparent to her that Cait had a good brain in her head and, with the right training and encouragement, could go far.

The shelves and stock did after all need a thorough dusting. Cait knew the cleaners kept their materials and equipment in a cupboard next to the ladies' toilets by the clocking-in machine. After collecting what she required, she set about the task. Half an hour later she was still in the showroom, giving the shelves and the display of shoes and handbags on them a proper dust, doing her best to make sure they were all arranged in a way that showed them off to their best advantage.

Harry Owens did a double take when he bustled in a short while later, pushing a trolley with a dozen or so boxes holding the samples of shoes he'd not yet had time to unpack and check off. The owner's daughter was standing there with a cloth in one hand, a shoe in the other, giving it a vigorous rub.

Looking at her incredulously, he said, 'You shouldn't be doing a job like that, Miss Thomas.

We have cleaners to see to that sort of thing.'

Cait wiped her forehead with the back of one hand. 'The client is due very shortly so we had no time to locate them. It's all hands to the pump. Miss Trucker is running around, trying to get everything organised in time like her tail's on fire, and I don't mind at all what I do to help.'

Harry looked impressed. Tongue-in-cheek, he said, 'Well, when you've finished, my office could do with a once over.'

She laughed. 'I'll see what I can do.'

A while later Cait was down to her last two shelves. Having picked up one of the shoes it held, she had given it a thorough dusting and was just putting it back when she felt the heavy wooden shelf wobble. Then, to her absolute horror, it broke away from its moorings in the wall and clattered to the floor with a crash, narrowly missing her feet. It collided with the one below, bringing that down with it and scattering all the shoes that had been arranged there.

Cait stared at the chaos surrounding her for several long seconds before panic reared within her. The customer was due shortly and what impression would he receive if he walked into this mess? She couldn't tell Jane about it as she'd already got her hands full. Cait needed to sort this out herself. Her brain sprang into action. She needed Glen Trainer up here, and quick, to repair the shelves while she checked all the shoes over for any signs of damage. There must be a telephone extension nearby for the customers to use. Maybe in the entertainment room next-door. She was relieved to see she was right when she

347

popped her head around the door a moment later. Dashing into the room and over to the table, she picked up the receiver.

When the receptionist answered, in an urgent tone, Cait said, 'This is Caitlyn Thomas. Please locate the whereabouts of Mr Trainer of Maintenance and have him come to the viewing room urgently. I can't stress *urgently* enough.'

Immediately it sank in with the receptionist just who her caller was, she snapped to attention and responded, 'I'll get on to it straight away, Miss Thomas.'

Cait replaced the receiver in its cradle and headed back to the showroom.

Glen's and Cait's paths had not crossed since Christmas Day, though obviously due to her position she knew he was leaving soon for a better job with more prospects. Just before the hooter blew that evening, when she knew he'd be clearing his desk for the new man who'd replace him, Cait had meant to telephone him discreetly, to wish him the best in his new venture and to thank him for what he'd done for her personally. But while he was here she could do that in person.

When Glen came charging into the room ten minutes later, breathless from running, he found Cait on her hands and knees picking up the shoes and inspecting each one as she did so, putting any marked ones aside to attempt to disguise the defects using an assortment of pots of shoe polish and buffing cloths which she had discovered in a drawer beneath the display shelves.

She was mortally glad to see him and exclaimed, 'Oh, thank God you're here! I'm sorry about this as I know it's your last day with us and this is all you need. But you can see for yourself what's happened and we have a customer ... a very important one ... descending on us any minute to view our summer range and make his order. We can't show him in here to this mess, can we? He's expected to arrive around twelve and that's less than an hour away.'

Glen quickly weighed up just what needed doing then assured her, 'It'll be tight but I reckon I can have this back to what it was by that time. I'll do my best anyway.'

She thanked him enthusiastically. Side by side they worked together, Cait continuing to inspect the shoes and clean those requiring it, Glen fixing the shelves securely back in place. She had just finished her task and Glen was tackling the second of the shelves when the telephone in the next room shrilled. Cait went to answer it.

Before she could announce who she was into the mouthpiece, Jane Trucker asked in an urgent manner, 'It's that you, Miss Thomas?'

'Yes, it is, Miss Trucker.'

'Have you finished down there? Is it all ship-shape? Only I've just had a call from reception. Mr Bowden's car has pulled up at the front entrance ... well, by now he'll be out of it and heading inside. You need to be back up here ready to greet him when I escort him to the office.'

Cait rested the receiver on the small table and dashed back into the viewing room, to whisper urgently to Glen, 'Miss Trucker's on the telephone. The customer has arrived and is heading for reception right this minute. Miss Trucker wants me back up there now. But we're not finished here!'

Glen told her, 'Another fifteen minutes at most is all I'll need. Don't worry, I'll be out of here long before you bring him down. After his journey he's bound to want to freshen up and then a cup of tea or coffee and to pass some pleasantries with you before getting down to business. Take the back way and then you won't bump into him in reception. I'll finish off here and put the rest of the shoes back, make sure it all looks as it should.'

Cait smiled gratefully at him. 'Thank you so much, Glen. There's not time now but I'll speak to you before you leave tonight, to say my good-byes.' With that she spun on her heel and dashed back into the entertainment room to pick up the receiver again and say into it, 'Sorry about that, I just had to check something. I'll be straight up, Miss Trucker.'

Cait had just arrived back in her office and managed to flick one hand over her smart skirt to rid it of any evidence of her scramble over the floor. She straightened her jacket, smoothed a hand over her hair and hurriedly applied a fresh coat of lipstick. After a tap at the door Miss Trucker walked in, followed by a tall good-looking man in his late-twenties. He was wearing a trench-style coat over a smart suit, and a trilby hat set at a jaunty angle covered his head of thick dark brown hair.

Jane made the introductions. 'Mr Bowden, Miss Thomas. Mrs Thomas, the owner of the factory, was away abroad when Mr Swinton passed away so unexpectedly. In fact she isn't back yet, so Miss Thomas is in charge of the place until her mother returns.'

Smiling, Mr Bowden walked towards her with one hand outstretched in greeting. After they had shaken hands he took off his hat and coat, which he gave to Jane to hang up for him, he said to Cait, 'I was sorry to hear about Reg Swinton. He was a good man, a pleasure to have dealings with. I've never met a member of your family before so it's nice to at last. Your mother obviously gives you far more credit that my father did when I was your age. He would never have allowed me the sort of responsibility your mother has given you in running this place. He wouldn't even let me choose styles from our suppliers until he retired. Anyway, you're obviously doing a first-class job of deputising for your mother as the firm seems to be running very smoothly to me.'

Cait told him, 'I can assure you that it is only through the valiant efforts of Miss Trucker and the rest of the staff.'

Jane flashed a look at Cait which told her she appreciated this public recognition of what she was doing, over and above the call of duty. Then she asked Mr Bowden, 'May I offer you any refreshments?' She held out her hand to indicate a tray on Cait's desk, holding a pot of tea and one of coffee, along with everything else needed to serve the drinks.

He shook his head. 'No, thank you. If it's all right with you, I'd prefer it if we got business out of the way first then I can relax while we have some lunch. I'm assuming you have laid on lunch as you always do?'

Jane told him that of course they had.

Cait meanwhile was inwardly panicking. Barely ten minutes had passed since she'd left Glen and he'd told her that he'd need fifteen to finish the job. If they went down to the showroom now he could still be working in there, and that wouldn't do. Her mind raced for some way to keep Mr Bowden in her office for another five minutes but it was too late for that as he and Jane were already heading for the door, obviously expecting Cait to follow them.

Worried Glen would still be working away when they arrived and she'd have to make excuses for his presence to Mr Bowden, Cait was mortally relieved to see him exit the room, carrying his tool box, just as they were approaching it, the three of them walking side by side, Mr Bowden in the middle of the two women. Jane had also seen Glen come out of the room, was bothered by the fact that he'd been in there at all, immediately thought that when the canteen ladies had delivered the food after Cait had left a short time ago they must have noticed something wrong and called him to sort it out. She picked up speed and hurried ahead to check that all was in order, regardless of the fact that it was too late now to do anything about it as Mr Bowden and Cait were only seconds behind her.

Meanwhile Cait realised that Mr Bowden was no longer beside her and stopped to see where he had got to. It was with surprise that she saw him standing looking past her and down the corridor.

She turned to look that way also, to see what had caught his attention. All she could see was the back of Glen as he disappeared through the door leading to the main factory part of the building. Mr Bowden seemed to be frowning. She walked back to join him and asked, 'Are you all right, Mr Bowden?'

He pointed down the corridor. 'That man I saw come out of the showroom and walk along the corridor. He looks different somehow but I know his face. I just can't think where I know him from.'

There had only been one man Cait had seen so she said, 'You mean Mr Trainer, our maintenance man?'

He looked at her thoughtfully for a moment. 'Trainer? The name rings a bell. Oh, of course, maybe I came across him when I used to come here as a child with my father.'

'I'm sorry, Mr Bowden, but you couldn't have. Mr Trainer has only worked for the company for a few weeks.'

'Oh, then it must be somewhere else I know him from.' He shook his head. 'No, but it's not. It was here I remember seeing him. He wasn't a maintenance man then, though, because I remember he was wearing a suit. He gave me ... something what was it now? I know, it was a bag of bulls-eyes because he knew they were my favourites.'

Just then Jane came back out into the corridor looking for them, wondering why they hadn't joined her by now, and all thoughts immediately focused on the matter in hand.

Just over an hour later, business in the viewing room had been concluded very satisfactorily and Jane was leading them into the entertainment room for refreshments where hopefully Mr Bowden would make a sizeable order.

Dotted strategically round the walls was an assortment of framed photographs, all of scenes related in some way to the shoe industry. As well as a large mahogany table where the buffet had been set up, there was the smaller table which held the telephone Cait had used earlier along with stationery, pens and ink for the customer's use. Opposite the mahogany table were several comfortable chairs which Jane now settled Mr Bowden and Cait into while she served them their food and drinks. As she approached the table she realised that in her rush to get everything ready on time she had forgotten to send down the selection of wines she kept locked up in her office, so as to be able to provide a drink stronger than tea or coffee to their prestigious clients should they wish it. She was cross with herself for her lapse but as ever appeared calm and efficient as she made a suitable excuse for leaving the room and went off to fetch them.

Meanwhile, Cait and Mr Bowden fell into easy conversation. She was listening to him telling a funny anecdote about one of the customers who patronised their Leeds establishment, a titled lady who felt it was beneath her to visit the shop in person when she required a new pair of shoes, but would give the manager of the shop a brief description of the style she was after then expect him to visit her with a selection of shoes to choose from. Suddenly he stopped in mid-story and exclaimed: 'I've suddenly remembered more about what I was talking about earlier, in the corridor. I remember it vividly in fact.'

It took Cait a moment to recall what he was talking about but she listened carefully as he went on speaking.

'I would have been about fourteen or fifteen at the time and we were at the breakfast table. My father was reading the morning newspaper when suddenly he said to my mother something like, "My God, Mildred, I don't believe it. You remember Trainer from Rose's? You met him at one of the Christmas trade dinner dances we were invited to a couple of years back. He was there with his wife, she was pregnant at the time with their first baby. Well, it seems Trainer's up before the beak for hijacking a lorry for its load of shoes, nearly killing the driver in the process.

'"A man saw a lorry being unloaded at the back of Rose's as he was walking his dog down by the canal and thought it suspicious enough to report to the police. In light of a hijacking incident earlier that night, the police took him seriously. They made a search of the premises the next morning and in one of the outhouses they found all the stolen goods from the hijacked lorry. The key to the padlock securing the outhouse door and the bloodied crowbar used to attack the driver were discovered in the glove box of Trainer's car. Also, he exactly fitted the description of the man seen by the passerby to be unloading the lorry. He can't produce an alibi for the night in question."

'I remember my father being very shocked by this news. He couldn't believe that Trainer was responsible for committing such a vicious crime, not the man he knew so well – or thought he did. And he couldn't understand why Trainer would need to do something like that for the money, as Father said he hadn't heard any gossip that the company was in financial trouble. In fact, to his knowledge it was prospering. But all the evidence pointed to Trainer so he must have been guilty. Anyway...'

Cait had been listening to him intently, but one particular comment he'd made, made her interrupt him. 'Did you say, *his company?*'

He nodded. 'Yes. Trainer owned the business back then. My father didn't talk about it any more within my earshot, so that's all I know or remember. Your mother must have bought the business after Trainer was sent down. I'm surprised she never told you the story about the previous owner.' He adopted a thoughtful expression. 'I do wonder what Trainer's doing working back here, though? Can't be easy for him, odd jobbing for a firm he used to own. In fact, just how did he wangle a job for himself back here, all things considered? I'm surprised a reputable firm like Rose's is employing a man with his criminal background. Oh, but maybe he's recently been released from prison and, with hardly any chance of getting a job elsewhere, convinced Reg Swinton that he was a reformed character and should be given a chance to prove it. From what I knew of Reg, he would be just the sort to give anyone the benefit of the doubt. To me, though, a eopard rarely changes its spots so if I were you I'd have a beady eye kept on Trainer, just in case he's not a reformed character. He could secretly be up to something which you should put a stop to before it's too late.'

He then pulled a worried expression. 'Mind you, I could be branding some poor man a vicious criminal when in fact he's not that Trainer at all, just looks like him and happens to have the same name. I mean, it's got to be fifteen years since I last saw him and much water had passed under the bridge since then. I should consider whether the old memory bank is playing tricks on me. Oh, here are the drinks,' he said, rubbing his hands together as Jane returned, carrying a bottle each of white and red wine. He jumped up from his seat and strode over to her, offering, 'Let me do the honours and uncork the wine for you.'

This information about Glen had shaken Cait to the core. Her thoughts were flying around like bubbles in a vigorously shaken bottle of lemonade. This had to be a case of mistaken identity. The Glen Trainer she knew couldn't possibly be a vicious criminal, not a nice man like him. He was her saviour. He had risked his own job to talk sense into her and save the company from possible ruin and the workers from losing their jobs. To her those weren't the actions of a thoughtless, violent man but of a caring, thoughtful one. She had socialised with Glen and never noticed the slightest thing about him to arouse her suspicions. But then Mr Bowden had told her that everyone who had known him at the time had been under the same impression about him as she was now, only to discover when he was caught that they'd been duped by him. Like she had been.

Then an awful thought struck Cait. What if Mr Bowden was right and Glen Trainer had come back to Rose's to attempt to make money for himself? She had seen where he lived, noticed what kind of clothes he wore, the food that had been served up to her at Christmas. If he was indeed the same Trainer who had owned the company, then this was a man who had once been able to afford the good things in life. Maybe he wanted that life-style back for himself. He would never afford it on the wages of a maintenance man, and with his record never be able to climb the promotional ladder much higher than that. So the only way he could achieve a better standard of living for himself was to do it illegally.

She started wondering about that morning she had believed Glen had risked his job to talk to her about the firm and the workers' security. What if that had been just a ruse to cover up his true motivation? That if the firm went under through a long-drawn-out strike, his own plan to do whatever it was to make himself serious money would go under with it. And Jan must be in league with him too. She lived with him, worked at Rose's. Cait wondered what they were plotting together. Robbing the place somehow, it had got to be. The stock was valuable. So was the machinery. Oh, but then what if Glen was planning to do the same thing he had tried the last time, and which had only failed because he'd made a blunder by parking the vehicle where it could seen by the general public? All he had to do this time was find a more isolated place to offload it.

He'd obviously got a job with Rose's so he could legitimately check the place over, see if changes had been made, in particular if the abandoned outhouses were still there and still vacant.

She needed to go to the police with all this information and get them to investigate Trainer, find out if he was up to no good and put a stop to it. But then she realised she could be pointing the finger of suspicion at a completely innocent man. First she needed to find out, one way or the other, if Glen Trainer was the man who had committed those crimes or if that was a different man entirely. There was only one way she could do so and that was to ask him to his face. Completely forgetting her arrangement with Belinda, she decided she would do that straight after work tonight by paying him a surprise visit.

Cait suddenly jerked up her head, realising that Mr Bowden was speaking to her. 'Oh, I'm sorry, Mr Bowden, I was thinking of something I have to do tonight that I'd forgotten about.' She then lowered her voice and continued, 'Look, what we were talking about earlier. Would you please not mention anything about it to anyone here? I mean you could be wrong, and our Mr Trainer might be completely honest and above board. But I am going to make enquiries about him and find out one way or the other, and if he does turn out to be the criminal Trainer I shall go straight to the police, put the matter in their hands.'

He looked at her, impressed. 'I won't say another word about it. Drink?' he said, handing her a glass of wine.

CHAPTER TWENTY-NINE

Cait lingered behind a little longer at work after everyone had left, to allow time for Glen and Jan to arrive home before she got there. Her nerves were jangling. On one hand her actions could be responsible for catching a criminal in the act; on the other she could be about to cause bad feeling between herself and two people she had come to regard as friends.

As she left work, though, and was making her way towards the steps leading up to the main road by the canal bridge, she stopped short on seeing the shadowy figure of a man loitering at the top. He seemed to her to be acting suspiciously. The night was a dark one and she was too far away to make out any of his features. Immediately she worried he was sizing her up before robbing her. It was too late to go back to the factory and make her way out of the front entrance instead as the night watchman had locked the door behind her and would have the gates closed by now. She had no choice but to continue the way she was going. Tightly clutching her handbag, her only defence from a possible attack, she continued up the steps. As she drew nearer, although it was still too dark for her to see his features clearly, the man seemed familiar to her. It was the way he was standing, with his hands thrust in his pockets, his head tilted to one side. Neil used to stand in just that way when waiting for her to arrive. Then Cait's heart leaped inside her chest as she realised it was Neil.

As soon as he saw the woman approaching him was Cait, he bounded down the steps to join her then stood looking at her awkwardly.

'Oh, it was me you were looking for. I'd no idea you knew I worked here.' Or that you could possibly want to see me, she thought to herself.

'I ... er ... didn't until I bumped into a mutual friend of ours, who mentioned that they saw you heading into Rose's as they were taking a short cut down by the canal. Said you looked very smart ... and, I have to say, you do, Cait.'

She smiled in appreciation of his comment. 'Thank you. Did you come looking for me for any particular reason?'

'Well, as a matter of fact I did. You see ... well, er ... that night we bumped into each other at the cab office ... well ... the Cait I knew wouldn't have apologised for her behaviour like you did, and I rather liked the new Cait and would like a chance to get to know her better. So I was wondering whether ... er ... you know, you'd like to go out with me one night and see how it goes?'

Cait couldn't believe she was being given another chance with Neil. She just looked at him for several long moments, wondering if she was dreaming this or not. In fact, she actually put out

361

her hand to confirm he was real. She smiled happily at him. 'I would like that very much.'

He grinned. 'Oh, good. What about next Saturday night?'

'That would be lovely. So tell me what time you'd like to meet me and where, and then we can decide together where we would like to go.'

He thought, Wow, Cait really has changed. The old Cait would have dictated the time they met as well as where they would go. He told her, 'Saturday at eight, outside British Home Stores.'

Cait suddenly remembered tonight's pressing engagement. 'I'll be there. Now if you will excuse me, Neil, I have to be somewhere.'

His face fell. 'Oh, not ... er ... meeting a boyfriend?'

She was pleased to see that he hadn't liked the thought of that. 'No. This is to do with work.'

'Oh, good. I mean ... right you are. I'd better hurry home too or my dinner will be cold. See you Saturday then,' he said as he turned away.

'Yes, see you,' she called after him.

Cait was so happy that she almost skipped all the way to Glen's and Jan's flat, but as she approached it the reason why she was visiting them hit her full force again and swept aside all thoughts of Neil. On the tiny landing outside the flat she paused just long enough to draw a deep breath then rapped her knuckles purposefully against it.

Glen had just lit the fire and was washing his hands at the kitchen sink. Jan had made a pot of tea and was about to pour them both a cup before she made a start on their dinner. The knocking resounded against the door.

Drying his wet hands on a shabby towel, Glen told Jan, 'I'll go.'

He opened the door and Cait barged past him and into the living area, to stand with her back to the fire. A confused Glen shut the door and hurried after her, wondering what on earth was going on. That she was deeply upset about something was very apparent to him.

From her position at the kitchen table, Jan heard the sound of outdoor shoes pounding the linoleum and knew the visitor wasn't their landlord as he always wore slippers when he was indoors. Coming out to investigate, she saw Cait, smiled and went to welcome her and offer her a cup of tea, but was stopped when Cait held up one hand warningly. A perplexed Glen came to stand by Jan's side, both of them puzzled by Cait's odd behaviour. She addressed Glen. 'I need to ask you a question, and I would like an honest answer from you.'

He looked taken aback. 'Well, I wouldn't answer you in any other way, Cait. What is it you want to ask?'

She took a breath, tilted back her head and demanded, 'Are you the Glen Trainer who used to own Rose's years ago and was sent to prison for viciously attacking a man and hijacking his lorry?'

The unexpected question had rendered Jan speechless.

Glen didn't hesitate to answer, 'Yes, I am.' Then he asked, 'How did you find out?'

Cait took a moment to answer, deeply distressed to have been told what she hadn't wanted to hear: that the two people before her were not the friends she had believed them to be. Finally she managed, 'Our visitor today was sure he recognised you. That's why I came, to find out if he was right or not.'

'Well, you now know he is. But I can only ask you to believe that I was totally innocent of the accusations made against me, Cait.'

Her initial shock was replaced by anger over what she suspected this pair of criminals were planning to do. Clearly they had used her, befriended her in order to get the information they needed from her. She laughed harshly. 'All guilty men profess that, don't they? I don't believe you any more than the jury who found you guilty. You'll be trying to make me believe you were framed next.'

Jan found her voice. 'That was what happened, Cait.'

She retaliated, 'Oh, you've both missed your calling. You should have been on the stage.' Eyeing them both in disgust, she continued, 'Since you were recognised by our visitor today, I've been trying to rack my brains for a plausible reason why you would return to the scene of your crime. The only ones I can think of are that you are either planning to rob the place or else repeat your former crime – taking more care this time not to be observed. You obviously thought it best to have a legitimate reason to be on the premises while you perfected your plans, just in case anyone saw you having a nose around and reported you to the police. Poor Mr Swinton was under the impression he was helping you make a fresh start by giving you a job, and all the time...'

Glen exclaimed, 'Cait! Please, stop. You have this all wrong. I wasn't planning to do anything like you're suggesting.'

She sneered, 'Well, I'd prefer the police to be the judge of that. I'm going there next, to report my suspicions of you.'

Jan was looking horrified. 'If Cait goes to the police, Glen, and they start showing an interest in you because of your background, you could end up losing your new job – and then you might never get another and land up back where I found you. I can't let that happen to you. You have to tell Cait the truth about why you got a job back at Rose's.' Then, terrified of Glen refusing and running the risk of a police enquiry, Jan couldn't stop herself from blurting out to Cait, 'There was nothing sinister about Glen deciding to get a job at Rose's. It was because it was the only way we could come up with for him to get the information he needed.'

Cait looked baffled. 'What information?'

Jan blurted again, 'About his daughter.'

Cait looked even more baffled. 'But why would you need to work at Rose's to find that out?'

'Because it's the only way he could get to speak to the person who has that information, that's why.'

'Jan, that's enough,' Glen ordered her. He then said to Cait, 'I think it's in your best interest to leave now. Do what you feel you have to.'

Jan spun round to face him, alarmed. 'Glen, don't do this! Think of the consequences for you.

365

Do you really want to end up back where I found you?'

He shook his head. 'No, I don't.'

'Then tell Cait the truth. Please, Glen, please,' she implored.

'The truth about what?' Cait demanded.

He shook his head and said with conviction, 'I can't. You know why, Jan. I can't do it to her.'

'Well, I can if you can't,' Jan responded fervently. 'You're a good man, Glen, a decent man, and you've suffered enough after what that woman did to you. I can't stand by and see you suffer any more, not just to save Cait's feelings I can't.'

'My feelings?' she said, bewildered. 'What have my feelings got to do with this?'

Jan blurted out, 'Because...'

Glen grabbed her arm. 'All right, Jan, you win. I'll tell her.'

She sagged with relief. 'Thank goodness.'

He then said to an utterly bewildered Cait, 'I think you'd better sit down. This story I have to tell you is going to come as a great shock and perhaps cause you distress.'

Cait began to feel afraid. She stepped over to the armchair Jan usually sat in and sank down into it, looking at Glen expectantly and waiting for him to explain.

Jan was sitting on the sofa, anxiously wringing her hands, ready to give comfort to the girl, which she knew she was going to need very shortly.

Leaning forward, hands tightly clasped, face grave, Glen began, 'I had recently lost my wife and been left with a young baby to care for when

I met your mother...'

Astonished by this, Cait declared, 'My mother! You know her?'

He nodded. 'I do, Cait. I was married to her.'

Astounded she cried out, 'What! My mother was married before she met my father? And to you?'

'I don't know whether it was before she married your father and was committing bigamy when she married me, or if she married him after she divorced me. If that is the case then as you were about a year old at the time, it could mean the man you think of as your father may not be at all.'

She snapped, 'Of course he's my father. His name is on my birth certificate.' Her face clouded in confusion. 'But then, if I was about a year old when my mother married you ... well, that means you were my father too for the time you were married? But I don't remember you.'

'You wouldn't, Cait. The first I knew of your existence was when I met you that morning in the office and realised you weren't who I thought you were.'

'Who did you think I was?'

'My daughter.'

'Oh! But where was I then while my mother was married to you?'

'I have no idea, Cait. Living with your father, I presume.'

This was getting all too much for her to take in and make sense of. She just stared at Glen speechless as he continued.

'As I said, I had recently lost my wife when I met Nerys. She was serving behind the bar of a hotel.

She was young and very attractive, vivacious, funny, with such a warm and caring nature, and ... well, she just bowled me over. I was ... and still am ... an ordinary-looking man, and I couldn't believe that a woman like her was showing any interest in me. But she was, wanting to know all about me, and before I left she had got me to agree to take her out on her next night off.'

Cait found her voice then. 'That woman you have just described is definitely not my mother. She is a very good-looking woman, true, but definitely hasn't got the personality you have just described. You're mixing her up with someone else.'

He told her gently, 'I'm not, Cait. Your mother and the woman I married are definitely one and the same. I couldn't fault Nerys for the way she cared for me and my daughter, looked after the house, always made herself look nice for me, was the perfect hostess to our guests. I had loved my first wife, too. Julia was a wonderful woman, soft and gentle, and made me feel safe when I was with her. But Nerys made me feel ... alive. I was constantly pinching myself, to check that I wasn't in a dream. I was to find out, though, that she wasn't really interested in me at all. It was an act she put on to fool me. What she was interested in was getting her hands on all I owned. My business, house, and what money I then had in the bank.

'Just over three months after we married, I found myself in prison serving a fifteen-year sentence for a crime I hadn't committed, but with no evidence to prove otherwise. Nerys had become he legal owner of all my worldly goods before I realised she was the only one who could have plotted and carried out the plan to frame me. By then there was nothing I could do about it. I'd signed everything over to her. The only thing that kept me going was the fact that she had promised to raise my daughter by my first wife as her own, and as she had always seemed to dote on her, treating Lucy just like she was her baby, despite the lies she'd told me, I believed she was sincere about that. But I now know she was lying and have no idea where my daughter is or where to start looking for her. The only person who could give me this information is Nerys herself, but for a long time I had no idea where she lived or even what she was calling herself now.

'It was Jan's...' he paused and smiled warmly at her before continuing '...idea for me to get a job at Rose's. I have such a lot to thank this kind lady for. When I met her, I was in a sorry state. I'd been living rough for years because I couldn't get a decent job with my criminal record. Jan took pity on me and gave me the opportunity to get myself cleaned up, put a roof over my head ... everything I needed, in fact, to start building a better life for myself than the hard one I'd been living. Her idea seemed the best way for me to find out where Nerys lived, so that I could go there and be reunited with my daughter again.

'As Nerys was the owner of the business, there had to be times she would visit it, to check that all was well and deal with important issues. My intention was to keep my ears open, find out when she was on the premises then go and confront her, demand that she let me see my daughter again. Jan took a job with Rose's too as we thought two people working together, trying to get the information I needed, had more chance of succeeding than just one.

'Then, of course, the first day we started working at Rose's we discovered Mr Swinton had died, and rumour had it that Mrs Thomas was abroad and her daughter was going to be deputising for her until she came back. I was sorry about Reg Swinton's death, but I cannot tell you what hearing the other news meant to me. My daughter was going to be in the same building as I was, and all I could think of was trying to find an excuse to be up on the second floor, waiting to catch a glimpse of her face. Jan and I thought it best to plan carefully how I was going to approach her with the news that I was her father. At that time I did not have any idea whether Nerys had married again or was just calling herself Mrs Thomas. But the opportunity for me to visit the second floor never came until I saw my chance during the union meeting, while the vote on taking industrial action was being counted.'

Cait spoke up then, her voice thick with emotion. 'I can't imagine how disappointed you must have been to find it wasn't your daughter after all, only me. Or before that, believing I was her and seeing the way I was behaving.'

Neither Glen nor Jan responded.

Cait got up and walked silently across to the window to tweak the shabby curtain aside and stare out into the grim, gas-lit street. She was lost in her thoughts. After a moment, she let the curtain fall back into place, turned around and asked, 'This isn't just a story you're telling to fob me off, is it? You've not made it up to put me off the scent when really you are planning...'

Glen interjected, 'Oh, Cait, I'd have to be a very cruel man indeed to tell you such elaborate lies just to provide myself with a cover story. No, every word I have told you is the truth.'

Deep down Cait had known it, but it was all too shocking for her to take in immediately. She silently resumed her seat and stared sorrowfully at him. 'I can't believe that my own mother could be so selfish and cruel as to live happily on what she stole from you, knowing you were rotting away in prison for something you hadn't done. Or that she was in fact responsible for a poor man being half killed when he tried to stop his van being hijacked.

'I asked my mother when I was younger how we lived as neither she nor my father worked, and she told me ... she actually told me that it was none of my business, but that the money came from a sizeable inheritance she'd had left her.

'I feel so guilty now I know the truth about where that money really came from! I've been living on your money too, Glen. It paid for the house I lived in, the food I ate, the clothes I wore everything, in fact, until I started to contribute just a little towards my keep once I was working. She's my mother and I feel in some way responsible for what she did to you. I feel I should try and make it up to you somehow, but I don't even know how to start.'

Jan reassured her, 'Whatever your mother did, there's no need for you to feel either responsible or guilty.'

'Jan's right,' Glen confirmed.

'But it's not fair that you've been forced to live so harshly while my mother and father want for nothing. There must be a way you can get her to restore what's rightly yours?'

'It isn't rightly mine any more, Cait. I signed it all over to your mother, without being compelled to. I've already come to terms with that. I'm just grateful that I finally have a roof over my head, Jan's good food in my stomach, and a job so I can pay my way. All I want back from Nerys is my daughter.'

Jan was looking at Cait closely. By now she would have expected the girl to be sobbing her heart out on finding out that her beloved mother wasn't at all the woman she had believed her to be. Instead, any emotions she was feeling were being kept to herself. That didn't seem right to Jan.

Cait was silent for a moment, deep in thought, before she fixed grief-stricken eyes on Glen and Jan. The emotional pain she was feeling was etched on her face as she told them, 'The woman you described ... the warm, caring, vivacious, funny woman ... I've never seen her at all. Well, yes, I have – but only when she's with my father. She dotes on him, fusses over him like he's a little boy she has to protect, will drop anything she is doing if he needs her for the slightest thing. She's never been like that with me. She won't allow me to get close to her ... never allows anyone else but im to get close to her. Should anyone even try to be friendly with her, she puts them firmly in their place and lets them know they are wasting their time. I know she doesn't love me. My father doesn't either. I've tried to rack my brains and understand why, but all I can come up with is the belief that they love only each other and don't have any left over for me. Like you have, Glen, I've come to terms with the fact that she doesn't have any feelings for me.'

Now Jan understood. Cait had never been shown any love by her parents, wasn't used to receiving it so didn't expect it automatically to be given her by others. It was Jan's guess that if she'd ever had a boyfriend and he'd shown her affection, then she would have wanted it to be shown constantly in an attempt to make up for what she didn't receive elsewhere. There were not many men who could stand to be with an emotionally needy woman for very long. This was why her fiancé had called off their wedding. She now understood why Cait had behaved the way she had, until Glen had put the fear of God in her and she had changed her habits. She had seen the way her mother treated others and consequently believed that was how she should behave too. Jan could never understand why some women couldn't love their children, but she had seen examples of it before. She'd had a neighbour once who'd had five children she openly adored, except for her middle child. When she had been born, she'd been such an attractive baby, very content, never causing her mother a sleepless night, but for no particular reason her neighbour's motherly feelings had never materialised. She supposed thi state of affairs was what had happened with Nerys and Cait.

The girl had lapsed into silence again and Jan thought she'd go and make them all a cup of tea, something she could do now as she had bought another two cups and saucers on receiving her first full pay packet on Christmas Eve. She could most certainly do with a cup herself after all this, but before she could get up Cait was saying, 'There is something I can do to try and make up for what my mother did to you. I can't get your business back for you, or the house she took, or any money ... but I could try and help you find your daughter. Lucy, that's her name, isn't it? I realise now why you called me that in my office when you found me there. It's a lovely name, pretty. But I've been thinking that if my mother had her adopted or put in an orphanage, she would have had to sign a legal document or something, wouldn't she?'

Glen's mind was racing. 'Yes, she would have.'

Jan excitedly piped up, 'And hopefully Nerys would have kept a copy. If we can find that it might give us a lead to follow.'

'That's what I was thinking,' said Cait. Then she mused, 'But I never found anything like that, any personal papers at all, when I had a rummage around in her bedroom ... not even in the safe. I would have thought that's where she would keep such private things.'

She then felt a need to explain why she had been searching through her parents' personal belongings. 'You see, they never talk about their past at all ... only told me they were both orphaned. I was intrigued to find out where I came from and thought that maybe there would be some old photographs of my grandparents, so I could at least see what they looked like. That's why I was having a good look around but, as I said, I found nothing. Well, except for my own birth certificate on a shelf in the safe and a small box with some mementoes that my mother had kept from when I was a tiny baby. Or perhaps they'd belonged to her, considering how she felt about me.' She decided not to mention the money she had helped herself to. She had just accused innocent people of being thieves and now she was realising that she herself was. 'So where the likes of my parents' marriage certificate and other personal documents are kept, I have no idea. Have you?' she asked them both.

'Most women I know, including myself, keep all our personal stuff in a box or handbag in the wardrobe. Your mother obviously isn't like the rest of us as you never found anything like that when you had a search around,' Jan mused.

When Cait had talked about the safe she had discovered, locked in a cupboard in her mother's bedroom, Glen had immediately known that this had to be the one he had inherited from his father in which he had kept his personal papers. Glen had followed suit. He said to Cait, 'And there was definitely nothing else in the safe besides what you found on the shelf? There was nothing in the drawer, for instance?'

She looked at him, frowning. 'What drawer?'

'The one in the safe.'

'I never saw a drawer in the safe. In the bottom half it was just a block of metal. My birth certificate and the box of baby things were on top of that.'

Glen's eyes lit up. 'So you didn't check the drawer then?'

'I told you, there isn't a drawer in that safe.'

'Yes, there is, Cait. That solid block of metal you described, well, that's the drawer. You push the front and it springs out.'

She exclaimed, 'Oh! In that case, I could still find some photographs or information about my ancestors. And, more importantly, information that could lead you to your daughter. Hopefully my mother did keep the adoption paperwork!' She jumped up from her chair. 'Come on,' she urged them both. 'Let's go and find out. There's a taxi office on the main road. Hopefully they'll have a car available and we can be looking in that safe in half an hour. Then tomorrow, all being well, you'll be on the way to being reunited with your daughter.'

CHAPTER THIRTY

Glen and Jan were anxiously waiting while Cait searched the safe drawer.

She had gone through the procedures of getting both the key to the cupboard and the safe key itself from where her mother had hidden them, nd then opened them both. From where she was kneeling on the floor she took a moment to flash a look over at Glen and Jan as if to say, well, here goes, then pushed her hand against the front of what she had thought to be a solid metal base. A metal drawer shot out to reveal its contents.

Glen and Jan meanwhile had been holding their breath, praying that the drawer contained what they had come for. From their position neither of them could see anything. Unable to contain herself, Jan blurted out, 'Does it hold anything, Cait, or is it empty after all?' Her mind was screaming, Please, please, say there is something. No more than Glen's was, though.

Cait put them out of their agony by nodding and telling them, 'Yes, there is a pile of papers here. Let's just hope that amongst them is something to do with Lucy.' She put her hand into the drawer and lifted out a sheaf of papers and began to search through them. On top of the pile was a thick document, the official lettering on the front page informing Cait it was the one Glen had signed, mistakenly believing it to be a power of attorney. Cait replaced that in the safe drawer. She then found the deeds to the house in the names of Samuel and Nerys Thomas, and put them back in the drawer too. The document below, that concerned the car. Now there were only three pieces of paper left. She scanned the top one and her face screwed up in utter bewilderment.

'Oh!' she exclaimed.

Both Glen and Jan urgently asked, 'What have you found, Cait?'

She shook her head. 'But it doesn't mak[
sense... It's a death certificate.'

Jan clasped her hand to her mouth in shock.

Glen froze as a vice-like pain squeezed his
heart. He uttered, 'My daughter is dead? Oh, no,
please don't let that be...'

Cait shook her head. 'No, Glen, she isn't.'

They both gasped in relief to hear this. 'So who
is the death certificate for then, Cait?'

She looked across at them both in utter confusion. 'Me,' she told them.

They looked back at her in surprise. It wasn't
possible for her to be holding a death certificate
in her own name when she was still very much
alive!

Before any of them could fathom how this state
of affairs had come about there was the sound of
the bedroom door opening and, to their horror,
they saw Nerys walk in.

At the shock of seeing her, Cait let out a gasp
of fright.

In the process of taking off her stylish coat to
hang it in the wardrobe, Nerys swung round to
see Cait down on her haunches by the open
cupboard, the door of the safe wide open too.

Throwing her coat on to the bed, Nerys furi-
ously exclaimed, 'What are you doing in here?
You're not even supposed to be living here any
more and you know this room is forbidden to you
without my permission.' She then noticed the
sheets of paper Cait was holding and her look of
anger turned to one of panic. She demanded,
'Give me those. Now! NOW!' she screamed
frenziedly as she started to head towards the

cowering girl. Then she froze in her tracks when a male voice told her in commanding tones, 'Leave her be, Nerys. She's helping me.'

She swung round in surprise to see two strangers standing across the other side of the room. 'And just who the hell are you?' she demanded. 'And what is Caitlyn helping you with?'

Glen took several steps forward so she could see him better and said, 'You don't recognise the man you married and then framed for a crime he didn't commit?'

Nerys frowned, studying his face, before mouthing, 'Glen!'

He said sardonically, 'At least you remember my name.'

'Why are you here? What is it you want?' Then she thought she knew, and smirked. 'Oh, if you think...'

Glen finished for her. 'That you'll hand me back what you took from me?' He gave a sardonic laugh. 'You went to a lot of trouble to take if off me and make sure there was nothing I could do about it, so I'm not stupid enough to believe you'll surrender a penny. I have to take my hat off to you. It was a clever plan you came up with, to give yourself a comfortable life without having to work for it ... with no thought whatsoever for the others you destroyed in the process.'

'So why are you here?' she snapped nastily.

'To find out what you have done with my daughter. Show me you have at least a shred of decency, Nerys, and tell me where I can find her, so I can get her back with me, where she belongs.'

She vehemently insisted, 'If *she* gives me those papers back, right now, then I will tell you.' She looked over at Cait, eyes fixed on the pieces of paper she had not as yet inspected.

A puzzled Cait couldn't understand why her mother was so desperate to get her hands on them. Her brain whirled into action. They had to hold information that Nerys was terrified of anyone finding out.

She made to look at them but was stopped by a frenzied cry from her mother. 'Don't you dare read those! They are my private papers. Give them to me NOW.'

Just then a voice was heard calling weakly from downstairs, 'Nerys... Nerys, I need you, darling.'

At her husband's summons she pushed Glen out of the way so she could call back down the stairs. The voice that only moments ago had been harsh and nasty had become tender and caring. 'I won't be long, darling. I'm just ... seeing to something. Make yourself comfortable by the fire and I'll be down in a minute.' Then she spun back again and told her audience, 'My husband needs me. Now get out, all of you, before I have the police called. And you,' she wagged a warning finger at Cait, 'give me those papers back before you leave.' She marched across, hand outstretched to snatch them from the girl.

But Cait wasn't about to let her until she had discovered just what it was her mother was so desperate to keep secret. Quick as a flash, she jumped up and dashed over to the bed, throwing herself bodily across it. She meant to twist over to the other side and position herself behind Glen and

Jan for protection while she discovered what her mother was trying to hide. She'd bargained without Nerys's determination to stop her. Lunging after Cait, she grabbed her legs, digging her nails deep into her flesh and pulling her back towards her so that she could grab the papers out of her hand. Both Glen and Jan dived immediately to Cait's aid. Jan threw herself at Nerys, trying to pull her away from her daughter, while Glen fought to wrench her hands off the girl's legs. In the confusion no one noticed that the offending papers had slipped out of Cait's hand when she had flung herself down on the bed, before they had fluttered to the floor on the other side ... all but Glen, that was. Finally he managed to ease Nerys's grip on Cait's legs, and Nerys and Jan toppled over and landed on the floor. As soon as Glen had pulled Cait safely out of reach of Nerys, he dashed across to retrieve the papers from where he'd seen them land.

Nerys meanwhile had scrambled up from the floor. Seeing Jan was nearly back on her feet too, she gave her a heavy shove and toppled her back down again. She looked round wildly for Cait and saw she was no longer on the bed but standing on the other side of it, with no papers in her hand. Nerys started frantically searching the floor. Meanwhile Jan was up on her feet and had dashed over to Cait to put a comforting arm around her, pulling her close.

It was Glen who stopped Nerys from searching for something she wasn't going to find.

'Looking for these?' he asked, holding the papers out towards her.

She froze rigid. Her face seemed to pale alarmingly, her eyes to fill with abject terror. It was apparent to her that he had read the information the papers contained.

Looking back at her with disgust and loathing, he said harshly, 'You know what I can do to you and your precious husband with this information I have on you both. I'll strike a bargain with you instead. Tell me what you did with my daughter so that I can get her back with me where she belongs. Give me back my house and my business. You can keep what money you have in your bank. Then both of you can pack your bags and make sure you get far enough away that you never risk bumping into me again. Either you agree to my terms or you know what the consequences will be. Oh, and one more thing. You agree to leave Caitlyn with us. You've obviously never loved your daughter...'

Nerys gave a shrill laugh. 'That's because she's *not* my daughter. My daughter is dead! When you lose a child you dearly loved, the pain and heartache of that loss never goes away. Then I saw a chance to put a stop to the never-ending torment through the arrival of another child in my life. I would make this child mine, change her name to my child's, and then she would become her and it would be like we'd never lost her.

'I tried and tried but I just couldn't love her, and neither could Samuel. Our love for our own child, our flesh and blood, was too great to share with another. I began to hate the sight of the other child, resent her for being alive when my own daughter was dead, but by that time it was too late for me to get rid of her so I had no choice but to put up with her until she was old enough to fend for herself. So have your precious daughter back with my blessing. Go on, take her now. Get her out of my sight!'

Glen froze at the significance of what Nerys had just told him. He spun his head to look over at Cait, huddled next to Jan who was holding her protectively. Jan was looking back at him, her face wreathed in shock. He couldn't see the look on the face of the girl he now knew wasn't Caitlyn Thomas at all but his own beloved daughter Lucy. She had her head buried in Jan's shoulder and he could see she was quietly sobbing. He desperately wanted to rush to her now, gather her in his arms, declare his undying love for her, but their reunion would have to wait as first he needed to deal with this selfish wicked woman before him, get her out of his and his daughter's life for good.

He gave Jan a look that asked her to stay here with Lucy and look after her while he saw to what he needed to do. Then he took hold of Nerys's arm tightly and, with her screaming at him to let her go, dragged her out of the bedroom and down the stairs, into the lounge where the other selfish, wicked individual, oblivious to what had been going on above his head, was waiting for her to attend to him. Pushing Nerys inside the room, Glen turned and shut the door firmly behind him.

CHAPTER THIRTY-ONE

It was gone eleven o'clock when an exhausted Jan sank down in an armchair opposite Glen to look worriedly at him. He was seemingly staring into space, looking absolutely shattered, though that wasn't surprising with all that had gone on earlier and what he was having to deal with now. She desperately wanted to go over to him and put her arms around him and offer him comfort, but not as a friend which she knew was all she was to him.

Sensing Jan had returned, Glen looked over at her and flashed a wan smile. 'Is she all right?' he asked, though in truth he knew it was a hollow question as it would take Lucy far longer than a few hours to accept and come to terms with the truth of her birth.

Jan nodded. 'She's finally fallen asleep. Poor lamb was absolutely exhausted. She'll need a bit of time but she will be fine you know, Glen. How could she not be with you as her father? You'll make sure she is, won't you?'

He nodded. 'If it's the last thing I do, I will.'

Jan then looked at him for a moment before asking tentatively, 'Are you ready to tell me what it was Nerys didn't want anyone to find out? I witnessed her signature on that paper you made her write out, giving you back legal possession of your business and the house, but I've no idea ow you got her to do that.'

He said to her, 'I'm sorry not to have explained before but I don't want Lucy ever to find out what I'm about to tell you. She's enough to cope with already, getting used to her new name, the fact that she's actually a year younger than she thought she was, plus learning just what monsters her supposed mother and father were. I can't believe she lived with them all those years, being treated so appallingly, when they realised they could not replace their own daughter.'

'Monsters!' Jan exclaimed. 'But what secret were Nerys and her husband hiding, Glen?'

'Oh, that man she lived with wasn't her husband. He never could be, not in the eyes of the law anyway. He was her brother. But it's worse than that. He's her twin brother.'

Jan gasped with shock. 'Oh, my God!' It took a moment for it to sink in before she said, 'No wonder she didn't allow people to get close to her, she was afraid someone might guess their secret.'

'Even after I had promised I wouldn't take any further action so long as she agreed to do what I said, she still insisted on telling me their story in an effort to make me feel sorry for them! She was terrified I might break my word and go to the police, have them arrested and put in jail.'

'So what is their story, Glen?' Jan urged him, desperate to know what had driven Nerys to act as wickedly as she had.

'She told me that right from when they were born Samuel and she shared an unbreakable bond. If their mother tried to part them, they would both scream hysterically until they were put back side by side. Samuel was born with a weak chest and heart, and Nerys always protected him. They needed no one else in their lives but each other. While they were growing up in Wales they were looked on as oddities because they were never seen out without each other and went everywhere hand in hand.

'When they were about fourteen they knew that their love for one another was far stronger than that of normal siblings. They made a plan that when they were twenty-one and no longer under their parents' jurisdiction they would run away together, go somewhere far away where no one knew them, and then they would live as man and wife.

'Then Nerys discovered she was pregnant. They were nearly sixteen at the time. They were overjoyed and couldn't wait to be parents to their baby, but they knew they'd never be allowed to keep it or raise it together once the truth got out.

'They had no choice but to bring their plan forward and run away together. With what little money they had managed to save and what they took from their parents, they packed up their belongings and stole away in the middle of the night and eventually arrived in Leicester. They stayed in a cheap lodging house for a few days while they got themselves jobs and two rooms upstairs in someone's house. For a short while they were blissfully happy, looking forward to the arrival of their baby.

'But very soon Samuel lost his job because of poor health, and it fell to Nerys to support them the small wage she was earning as a sock turner in a factory. Once the rent had been paid and a few shillings put aside for gas, there wasn't much left over to buy food or anything else they needed. Samuel fell ill with a bad cold which turned to pneumonia. He had to be hospitalised. The doctors managed to save his life but the worry sent Nerys into early labour and the baby was born a month early. The child was small, with a weak heart and lungs. Samuel and Nerys were told that she wouldn't live for more than a few days as there was nothing that could be done for her. She lived for three and they never left her cot side as their daughter gradually lost her fight for life.

'Grief-stricken for her dead baby, and in the knowledge that if she didn't do something drastic she would lose Samuel too, which to her was unthinkable as without him her life would be totally meaningless, Nerys vowed that she didn't care what it took, she would give him the kind of life the doctor had told her he needed to keep him alive and by her side. She knew her best asset was her looks. Told me she had nothing against me personally, in fact she quite liked me, but unfortunately I was the first man she came across who was an ideal candidate for her plan.

'In a local pub she found the type of tough she knew would carry out the hijack. After charming him into believing they had a future together, she told him of a way she knew of to make a lot of money. The morning after the hijack she went to visit him, pretending to be in a panic. She'd seen the police swarming all over Rose's, she said, and

had found out from a young PC that someor
had reported seeing the stolen goods being trans
ported into an outhouse at the back of the factory.
He'd given the police a very exact description.
With his criminal background it wouldn't be long
before the police came looking for the hijacker, so
it was best he take himself somewhere far away
until the heat died down. Nerys said 'she'd let him
know when it was safe for him to come back,
which of course she never did. The man walking
the dog who alerted the police to his suspicions
was, of course, Samuel – and there was no dog.
The rest you know already, Jan.'

Glen paused for a moment, heaved a deep sigh
and said tiredly, 'I'm just glad that Nerys is
finally out of my life for good. And Lucy's too.'

Jan sat silent for a moment as she digested this
horrendous story. What Nerys had done to Glen
had been selfish and wicked, but she felt a glim-
mer of pity for the suffering she had endured in
losing her only child. Nevertheless she was
overjoyed that Glen had finally got his daughter
back as well as what rightly belonged to him. His
and Lucy's futures were now secure. But their
good fortune would separate them from her. Glen
would now be back in the circles he truly belonged in, far removed from the one she occupied, and Jan knew she would have to prepare
herself to say goodbye to the man she had come
to care for very deeply. His absence from her life
would leave a big hole.

She asked him, 'Do you think you'll move into
the Thomases' house or sell it and buy another?'

'Oh, I haven't given anything like that a thought

et, Jan. I still keep pinching myself that I've got my daughter back that she's lying in your bed now fast asleep, and that come Monday I'll have a business to run. I suppose I should give our living accommodation some urgent thought, though, as it's not fair on either you or Lucy to be sharing a bed for long. I'll see about putting the house on the market and getting us another one as soon as possible. In the meantime, we could always rent a bigger place while we look around for a new house to suit us. Oh, goodness me, to think that only weeks ago I never dreamed I would live in a house again, let alone be thinking of buying one.'

Jan felt selfish for dreading the end of their time together. It could even be tomorrow they parted company if he found a house that suited him and it was available. She realised Glen was looking at her searchingly and asked, 'What are you looking at me like that for?'

'Well, it's just that now I'm a man of means, I can do something I've wanted to do for a while, and I was wondering how best to put it to you.'

'Put what to me?' Jan asked, puzzled as to what it could be.

'I wondered if you would consider letting me take you for a proper night out – as more than just friends, Jan?'

She was so astounded by his unexpected proposal, she stared at him speechless.

He took this to mean he had insulted her and added apologetically, 'Look, I'm sorry if I've offended you. We haven't known each other long, but I've wanted to ask you if it was possible you could look on me as more than a friend for a while now, but I had nothing to offer you. couldn't even pay for a night out for us. Why should you look twice at me?'

She was shaking her head at him. 'Oh, you silly man. I've felt the same way about you for probably as long. I didn't care that you hadn't two ha'pennies to rub together. It's you I love, not your money.'

He gawped at her. 'Did you say *"love"*?'

She flushed in embarrassment and said awkwardly, 'Did I?'

'Well, there's nothing wrong with my hearing and I'd swear blind you did.'

'Oh, in that case, I must have, mustn't I?'

'Oh, I see. Well, that makes all the difference.'

Her face fell. She was mortally disappointed that her declaration had put the fear of God in him and now he was backing off. 'I'm sorry I frightened you by coming on too heavy. Can we forget what I said and still go out together as friends?'

Glen responded with conviction, 'No, I'm sorry, I can't.' Then he looked at her earnestly and added, 'Because now I feel free to tell you that I love you too. Let's just cut out all the courting bit and get married, Jan.'

He received her answer to his suggestion when she jumped up in sheer delight and dashed over to him, throwing herself into his arms and hugging him tightly. It was apparent to him that she never wanted to let him go.

CHAPTER THIRTY-TWO

It was three months later when Glen poked his head around Jane Trucker's door and asked her, 'Would you mind if I borrowed Lucy for a couple of minutes, only I have something I want to show her? But only if you can spare her.'

Jane blushed as she did whenever she came face to face with Glen. She had really enjoyed working with Reg Swinton and never would have thought she could find a better boss, but she had been wrong. Glen surpassed him by a large margin. He was such a pleasure to work for, valued all his staff's opinions, always knew what was going on in the factory before the gossips got wind, thought nothing of rolling his sleeves up and getting stuck in when times called for it, and always sat in a spare chair at a worker's table at mealtimes, after first making sure he wasn't intruding, and chatting amicably away with them while they ate, when he could have sat in solitary state on the boss's table. His office door was never closed to anyone. Jane nursed a secret crush on him and was a little miffed to hear he was getting married very soon so her feelings for him would for ever go unrequited.

She smiled warmly at him and told him, 'Lucy's not working with me today, Mr Trainer. Mr Owens is showing her all that goes on in the stores so she's primed up a bit for when she starts her three-month stint down there on Monday. I can get a message to her to come and see you?'

In his excitement at what he had to show her, Glen had forgotten that Lucy was beginning her training, doing several months in every department so that she knew how they all operated, just like his father had set him to do when he'd first started with the company. Glen told Jane, 'Don't worry, it's not as if you haven't got enough to do, Miss Trucker. I'll pop down to the stores myself and find her.'

A short while later, standing at the front entrance to the works by the gates, Glen instructed Lucy to turn around and tell him what she could see.

She did so and looked in front of her, all around, then said to her father, bemused, 'What am I supposed to be looking for?'

He laughed. 'If I told you that it wouldn't be a surprise! I'll give you a clue. Look straight forward and up.'

So she did, and when she saw what her father wanted her to see, she gasped in delight. 'Oh, Dad,' she uttered emotionally.

He put his arm around her and hugged her to him fiercely.

'Does this mean I'm now officially entitled to throw my weight around?' she asked, tongue-in-cheek. 'Well, the sign does read "Trainer and *Daughter*, Quality Bespoke Shoes and Leather Goods", doesn't it?'

He answered in a serious manner, 'Yes, by all means, but don't expect me to come to your rescue this time.'

I hope I never give you any reason to have to speak to me like that again, Dad.'

He looked down at her, nestled by his side, love for her brimming in his eyes. 'I have no doubt whatsoever that you never will again.' His eyes lingered on her for a moment. Anyone who didn't know would never realise that the pair of them had been through such a long separation. The closeness they now shared was normally only achieved by a parent and a child who had never been parted. He knew she was still getting used to being part of a family, having parents – and he included Jan in that equation as she was proving to be as good a mother to Lucy as he knew her birth mother would have been – who openly showed their feelings for her. They enjoyed her company or just being around her, encouraged her to bring her friends home, but were not afraid to show their disapproval when she had said or done something with which they didn't agree.

Glen said to her, 'So you're happy then with the change of company name?'

Before Lucy could answer, out of the corner of his eye Glen noticed a ragged old man shuffling his way towards a short cut that led down the side of the works towards the canal tow path. He was carrying a sack Glen knew would contain his worldly belongings. Excusing himself to Lucy, he dashed out of the entrance gates and after the man. Catching up with him, Glen took out his wallet and removed a pound note, which he pressed into the old man's filthy hands. 'Buy yourself a hot meal,' Glen told him.

The man looked at the money in astonishme...
then up at Glen. In a cracked voice he said, 'A.
whole pound! You're giving me a whole pound,
guv? The type-a place I eats at nowadays, yer
lordship, this 'ud buy me four hot meals and I'd
have change. Bless yer heart, guv. You're a gent,
so you are.'

'Well, I know what it's like to be hungry.'

The tramp looked him up and down, noted the
good cut of his suit and the handmade shoes he
wore. He shook his head of matted grey hair. 'I
doubt it, sir. Maybe missed a meal, but not
several days' worth at a time.'

Glen watched the man as he shuffled off. I can
assure you I do know, he thought.

Lucy had watched what he had done, the same
as she had on many occasions now. She knew
that until the day he died her father would never
be able to pass by a needy-looking soul without
giving them something to help them on their
way. His compassion was only one of the count-
less good traits he possessed and she felt it was a
privilege to be his daughter.

When he rejoined her, he said, 'Now, where
were we? Oh, yes, I asked you if you were happy
with the company's change of name?'

She shook her head and to his dismay said,
'Sorry, Dad, no, I'm not.' Then she gave a laugh
at his worried expression and changed his frown
to a broad smile when she added, 'I'm ecstatic.'

He smiled in delight. 'Good, I'm glad. Of
course, you'll be at liberty to change it to what
you like when it all becomes yours, but for now
I'm glad you approve. Right, young lady, we'd

est get back to it before the workers all go on strike, thinking the bosses are slacking while they do all the work.' He leaned over and kissed her cheek. 'I'll see you tonight at dinner, love. I hope Agnes has made us one of her delicious steak and kidney puddings.'

'She won't have because she's got the afternoon off. And you won't be seeing me at dinner tonight for two reasons. The first is that I'm going straight from work to Belinda's as we're off to the flicks together. We're going to grab some fish and chips on the way.'

'You're out again tonight? I can't remember the last time we all sat down and ate our evening meal together,' he said, pretending to sulk.

'Oh, Dad, stop exaggerating. I admit, I just grabbed a snack last night as I didn't want to be late for meeting Neil, and of course I wanted to look beautiful for him, but the night before that I ate with you and Jan.'

'Oh, yes, you did. I suppose an old dad should be grateful for small mercies. How is that young man of yours? When are we finally going to meet him?'

'Well, as I said, we're just taking it slowly. You know what our history is, Dad, and the last thing I want is to appear to be pushing Neil into any-thing, but the way things are going, I'd say it won't be long. Anyway, the second reason you wouldn't have seen me at dinner, even if I weren't going out, is that you won't be eating dinner at home tonight yourself. You're meeting Jan, remember? To have dinner at the place you are thinking of for the wedding reception, to make sure the food is to

your liking. You're meeting her there at sr
o'clock.'

'Oh, thanks for reminding me. I'd forgotten.'

Lucy scolded him, 'Oh, you liar, Dad. You never
forget anything to do with Jan. You love that
woman more than anyone and can't wait to
marry her.'

'Very true I can't wait to marry her, but it's not
true I love her more than you.'

Lucy laughed. 'Well, equally then.'

'Okay, I'll agree to that, but don't tell Jan because she thinks I love you most and her second,
and then she might get above herself.' He took
his arm from around Lucy and gave her bottom
a playful slap. 'Now come on, I've got a business
to run.'

She slapped his bottom back. 'And I have one
to learn.'

Arms linked, laughing and joking as they did
so, they hurried back inside the factory.

The publishers hope that this book has given you enjoyable reading. Large Print Books are especially designed to be as easy to see and hold as possible. If you wish a complete list of our books please ask at your local library or write directly to:

Magna Large Print Books
Magna House, Long Preston,
Skipton, North Yorkshire.
BD23 4ND

This Large Print Book for the partially sighted, who cannot read normal print, is published under the auspices of

THE ULVERSCROFT FOUNDATION

Pan